TANNER'S GLEN

DAN CHEUVRONT

Cover Art by Lillian Rose Asterios

Edits and Formatting by Nia Shay

Created with Vellum

THE PIT OF HELL

"Godless sons-a-bitches."

Sheriff Austin Rawls slammed the Ford F-150's transmission into park and stared through the windshield. The long gravel drive had given him time to process what lay before him. But as he looked at the mismatched circus of emergency vehicles and the motley crew that swarmed the property, anger welled inside him. That, at least, felt better than the shock and despair that had hit him when he'd first seen the house, or what was left of it.

All that remained of the Weismann place was a charred ribcage and a section of rotted front porch, which lay to the side like a severed head. The magnificent old maple that once overshadowed it was half burned away, twisted limbs recoiling as if from something unclean.

He climbed out of the truck, slammed the door, and recoiled at the assault on his senses. The blare of generators pummeled his ears. An acrid smoke haze burned his eyes. The stink of diesel and charred insulation covered an undertone of rot that made his guts roll.

Rawls slapped his hat onto his skull and went to find an ass to kick.

A late-model Ford Expedition with a lightbar was parked under the utility pole. No markings, nothing to indicate the institution it belonged to. Two men in coal-black uniforms hefted a plastic tote into the rear compartment. The tote was stamped with a biohazard symbol.

"Where can I find Allen Curtze?" Rawls used the voice reserved for kids he caught smoking behind the grocery store freezer in Dixville Notch. The men scarcely looked at him. The older of the two nodded at the destruction's epicenter before going back to work.

"Arrogant prick," Rawls muttered, stepping past a large trailer with the letters FEMA emblazoned on the side, into full view of the house. He tried not to notice the empty beer bottle perched upright under the porch swing, which hung askew from a single chain. He hoped the man who'd left it there was huddled in a blanket somewhere sipping bad coffee or, by the grace of God, a cold beer.

A tall, heavyset man in a gray blazer and black tie stood near the root cellar, barking orders at a fellow who was wrestling himself into a blue plastic body suit. In the tall man's shadow was a youngish, sandy-haired man in a tan blazer a size too big for him, who was jotting something in a notebook.

The rot smell got worse, taking overtones of dead fish. It wasn't coming from the house and it sure as hell wasn't coming from that Johnny-On-The-Spot by the slag remains of the propane tank. Rawls ran a hand over his mouth.

As the blue-suit trudged off to other duties, the heavy man noticed Rawls and looked him over, tits to toes, evidently not happy with what he saw.

"Allen Curtze?" Rawls asked.

"Do I look like Allen Curtze to you?" The man turned to Junior Varsity and said, "Chief, I'm going to use the head. Can you take care of this?" He jerked a thumb at Rawls and stormed away, leaving him with the sandy-haired kid who was still glued to his notebook, a cigarette dangling from his lips.

When the man closed the book and turned his gaze on Rawls, all impression of youth vanished. "Hello, Sheriff Rawls." Allen Curtze plucked out the cigarette and smiled pleasantly, deepening the lines around slate grey eyes. His grip was ice cold, but firm. "Sorry about my partner. Gene can be an ass when he's tired. It's been a long forty-eight hours." He dropped the butt and crushed it under a heel. "What can I do for you, Sheriff?"

Rawls smoothed his shirt. "I see you guys had a busy night. Want to tell me what happened here?" Breathing was getting hard. If that smell got any worse, breakfast might just come up for air. He'd never experienced anything quite like it, and had no category in which to place it.

Curtze offered no explanation; he didn't even seem to notice it. "The fire started late. Sometime around two a.m., I'm guessing. By the time we arrived the house had already mostly burned. There wasn't much we could do."

More blue-suits in heavy boots drifted among the debris and ash, prodding at piles with long pikes and shovels. "Why wasn't I notified?" Rawls asked.

"We're still officially under quarantine, so this is federal jurisdiction. I'm actually surprised you got through the checkpoint."

Rawls grunted. "They weren't going to let me. When I promised to be back in an hour with Amanda Reynolds and the Channel Six News van, they got helpful real fast." He nodded at the house. "Where is Noah Weismann, Mister Curtze?"

The sandy-haired man regarded him soberly. "Did you know him?"

Rawls burned as much heat as he could back into Curtze's cool gaze. "Of course, I know him. Have since he was tiny."

"I'm sorry."

Rawls gritted his teeth and looked out over the flood ravaged valley, the once beautiful meadow, now a desert of baked mud littered with the half-buried corpses of trees, stripped bare and left to stiffen and decay under the merciless sun. "You have a body?"

Curtze stepped past him and made his way to the remains of the house. Rawls followed. There was a canvas tarp in the yard several feet from the pit, a white backdrop for something dark and organic. His stomach knotted when the impression of burned driftwood disintegrated and the copper convex of a skull took shape, followed by the dull sheen of teeth and the crescents of clawed fingers.

"Christ Almighty." He stripped off his hat and turned away. In his twenty-two years as a civil servant of Coos County, he'd seen plenty of bodies. Even a few fire victims. But this. After everything else. If he let himself, he could look at that porch and imagine the face of an eight-year-old boy who'd been locked in that house for three days, having borne witness to something no child should ever see.

Then there was two years ago. The boy had become a man. But Noah Weismann had worn that same haunted look as he stood on the porch and watched them take his mother's corpse away. If anything should have been the proverbial blood on the doorpost, the sacrificial lamb that let God's angel of death pass over this place, that should have been it.

Since Rawls had nothing worthy of the moment to say and Cutze stood silently with his hands in his pockets, he turned to the hollowed-out crawlspace whose foundation stones were bleached white by intense heat. It looked like the marbled fat of a gutted animal. From the piles of ash, he recognized the coils of a mattress and the opaque eye of a television peering back at him. There was even a leather-bound Bible covered in soot, the impressed letters barely legible.

"It's a goddamned shame," Rawls said, turning the hat in his hands. "Nobody should have to die that way." He forced himself to look at the remains of the last Weismann to escape this godforsaken place, taking comfort in the fact that this time it wouldn't be him hauling away the corpse.

"I am sorry, Sheriff," Curzte said.

Rawls jabbed his hat at the gutted house. "How does something like that happen, huh? A healthy kid, not even thirty years old? The place just burns down around him?"

Curtze didn't answer.

Rawls faced the smaller man. "Who the hell are you people?"

"Like I said, there's not much I can give you right now. But I can tell you, young or old, accidents happen. The power out. Fall asleep with a candle or lantern burning. An old house like this would go up pretty fast. I'm sure you've seen it happen."

"Bullshit." Rawls said it mostly to himself. He settled his gaze on a muscular Case excavator tied to a flatbed trailer. "What the hell do you need a backhoe for, anyway?"

The heavy man had returned, now flanked by a pair of black uniforms with sidearms. They had "all business" written across their faces.

"You people don't have enough fire equipment here to put out a grass fire." Rawls said. "But enough men to storm Normandy. You aren't here to help people. You're here to bury something."

Curtze reached into his blazer pocket and handed him a card. It was plain white with *T. Allen Curtze*, a phone number and *Parousia Inc.* emblazoned in blood red letters. "I'll know more by Wednesday. You call me first thing, eight a.m., and I'll answer every question I can. Until then, Sheriff, I really must insist you leave us to our jobs. We have a lot of work yet to do."

The man had done this before, knew how to handle questions from pain-in-the-ass people. Rawls considered using the Channel Six angle again, or getting in his truck and calling the governor, but what would be the point? With the flood, the outbreak, and a cleanup that would go on for months, nobody cared. They wouldn't raise a ruckus over one dead kid in the ass crack of nowhere. Certainly not *this* kid.

The gorilla in the suit took a step forward, nothing threatening, just suggestive. Rawls pocketed the card. "Fine." He turned his back on all of them. "I will be in touch, Mister Curtze."

"I'll look forward to it."

Rawls cut between the Asshole King and his jesters and trudged heavily back to the truck, not bothering to see if he was followed. He wanted to be as far from here as possible, and had no intention of setting foot on the place again. He drove away without looking back.

The two Parousia men watched the F-150 disappear into the trees. As the wind carried away the dust, the bigger man said, "Your phone's going to be ringing off the hook tomorrow morning. You going to answer?"

"Sure." Curtze pulled a pack of Newports from his pocket and lit up.

"And tell him what?"

Curtze offered the pack to his partner who shook his head. "The truth, Gene. At least as much of it as my superiors will allow. By then they'll have come up with something plausible."

They turned to the cellar as the backhoe roared to life. Having thrown off its chains, it dragged itself off the trailer like a freed dragon.

"As to truth," the big man said, "I'd like to know that myself."

"About Noah Weismann? Or about what killed him?"

Gene Morgan's face tightened as they made their way toward the mouth of the cellar and the fetid air grew thicker. "You painted a lovely picture for the sheriff back there, Chief, I'll give you that. But your story doesn't square." Morgan met Curtze's gaze. "Your white whale isn't here."

Curtze raised an eyebrow. "You don't think that odor is coming from the rose bushes."

The maw of the cellar stood open, its doors peeled back. An odd material dangled from the stone lip. It looked almost like Spanish moss, but was too light and diaphanous. When the backhoe clanked to a stop and set its teeth on the earthen mound, the material rose gently as if the cellar had released a breath.

Morgan toed a fossilized footprint in the sunbaked earth with the tip of a polished shoe. The heel, crescent arch, and toes were crisp and distinct, as if they were recently laid. But they were not fresh. The flood had passed weeks ago.

"All I know is that we tracked this thing to hell and back and lost sixteen men for our trouble. We never so much as glimpsed it. Now it just up and dies right here, plants a big white flag telling us just where to find it? And the host." Gene nodded at the ash heap. "Already neatly disposed of for us. Weird, don't you think?"

"Sure." Curtze blew smoke. "Everything about this organism is unusual."

"Which is why I don't think we're going to find her in there. And I'll tell you something else." Morgan waited for Curtze to meet his eyes. "That corpse is not Noah Weismann."

"Really?" Curtze glanced pointedly at the body bag, which still lay open near the gutted house. "Now this I've got to hear."

"I'm no pathologist," Gene said, "but that skull does not belong to a man under fifty. You took a real risk letting Rawls near it."

Curtze drew on the cigarette and shrugged. "Maybe. You'd need dental records to be sure. Know anybody around here who is going ask for that? Weismann has no known next of kin. And there are the twenty-one others from this valley who are still missing, who you and I both know will never be seen again."

"That's not the point, Allen." Morgan stepped around to face his boss. "I want to know what the hell happened here. I want to know what happened to the man we saw ten days ago."

Curtze dropped his cigarette and stamped it out. "Well, so do I, soldier. But that's not going to happen until we see what's in that cellar."

1

TANNER'S GLEN

- Noah -

Someday, the world would end in fire. At least, that's what Scripture said. Romans, Revelation, one of those old joy killers. Ma could have quoted him chapter and verse. But like so many things that woman had preached, this too was probably bullshit.

Even so, as Noah Weismann watched the little flame dance at the end of his lighter, he thought – not for the first time – about helping Judgment Day along. Maybe not the whole world. He'd start with the house. The rotted porch boards under his feet would go up like kindling. No gasoline required. He would set alight the barn next, the vehicles too. Then the woodshed and the outbuildings, every last blade of grass on this wretched place.

Christ the Lord, Noah. Listen to yourself. His sister Jessie's voice, as close and real as if she were sitting beside him. She would have given him no end of shit if she could hear his thoughts now. Perhaps she could. Maybe there really was an afterlife.

Instead of fulfilling prophesy, Noah breathed life into a fresh cigarette. He snapped the lighter shut, letting night slip in again, and sat back against the rough planks of the porch swing.

There it was. He could see it now. Beyond the sagging eaves and vacant yard, draped in soft moonlight, was Tanner's Glen. Fireflies drifted in sparse constellations across the acres of prairie grass that surrounded the pear orchard. From the porch, the old trees looked like knobby giants huddled on an island, the image made more vivid by a pale mist gathering at their feet.

This scene had once been a source of pleasure to him. After a day's work, chores finished - such as they were - and a beer or two in his belly, he liked to sit here in the swing, smoke a cigarette, and just be. This was the closest he ever came to worship, the Glen the closest place to a church.

Nights like this, listening to the eerie trill of the treefrogs, watching the valley settle into darkness would calm his mind, make him empty as the bottles at his feet. No longer. Something was wrong with the Glen, a taint in the air he couldn't put his finger on.

He'd noticed it a few days before as a restlessness in his animals. Later it was in the calls of night birds, a cautious hesitancy, as if they were afraid of waking something up. Even the crickets whispered now. And were there fewer fireflies? Yes. He was sure of it. As he listened to the gentle rush of the distant river and breathed in the odors of this baked, late-summer evening, he felt it too. The place had turned sour.

Though he wouldn't have admitted it aloud, this new sickness lent power in the old stories Daddy used to tell about Tanner Weismann's disappearance a generation ago. Right here in the meadow that bore his name.

A flash rippled across the horizon, beyond the serrated line of the forest. Seconds later, a low rumble shook the valley.

"Here it comes," he muttered before taking a deep drag on the cigarette.

As much as he fantasized about seeing this place burn, he might not need to bother. Channel Six News said it would be here before midnight. Remnants of Hurricane Angeline had made her way up the coast and was climbing the spine of the White Mountains to have it out with another system sweeping out of the north. Supposed to be a real bitch, too, though that wasn't how the weatherman had put it. "A rare and potentially dangerous meteorological phenomenon," if memory served. Biggest thing to hit the valley in fifty years. The end of the world might not come in the form of fire. Perhaps for Noah, it would come in the form of a flood.

Let it wash this place clean. Good riddance to all and praise Jesus.

Motion caught his eye. A black shadow detached itself from the corner of the house and slid toward him like ink spilling across the floorboards.

"Hello, Samson."

The little creature brushed his leg. He reached down to stroke a tattered ear before a lanky cat hopped into his lap.

"Where the hell have you been?" Samson arched against Noah's palm. "You come back to beat up on Riley again? Or did all your gals finally run you off?"

They both raised their heads as another flash cut the darkness, turning the horizon yellow-white.

"We really looking at the end of the world here, old man?" Noah looked at Samson. "Maybe the weatherman was just full of hot air."

The cat ignored him. It chewed at something stuck between the pads of a paw. Noah raised the cigarette to find it burnt to the filter. He tossed it and lit another.

A sudden change in the air stopped him mid-ritual, first slowing his lips, then shutting them down completely. The crickets fell silent. The treefrogs followed suit. He raised his head, startled by a heavy silence. He flicked the lighter closed and listened hard as smoke leaked from his nostrils.

The fireflies winked out, starting from the pear orchard and spreading across the meadow in a wave. It was like watching a city blackout from space. Life died. Soon the Glen was a dark void.

Noah sat very still, hardly breathing. Only the distant lightning testified of time's continued march. And now, with the hush deep enough to feel, he felt the nearness of the storm.

"Well, that's different," he said, his voice loud even in a whisper. He looked at the cat to see what he thought about it, but Samson was gone. Noah was alone.

He finally took a lungful of air and drew on his cigarette, feeling exposed. The trees reaching over the roof were too close, the tips of their branches like claws. He shifted his feet and nearly screamed when a bottle toppled beneath him and fell into its empty brethren.

Tanner's Glen was gone, the chapel closed. Whatever had been stirring in its sleep the last few days had just woken up.

He got up and picked up his bottles with deliberate slowness, pretending he didn't feel unfriendly shadows gathering beyond the porch. But as he stepped off the last stair and his boots hit gravel, he was all too aware of how quickly his steps carried him to the barn.

The weatherman had called it right. The storm hit just before midnight. A huge crack of thunder woke Noah from a dead sleep and brought him bolt upright. He blinked as lightning cut vertical slashes of atomic white through the barn slats and left pillars of fire on his pupils. The rabbits scuttled in their hutch. The hens cackled in their coop.

The lightning bolt must have torn a hole in the roof of heaven because it started gushing a second later. Noah scrambled out of the cot and jerked the skylight shut - it was nothing but a flap in the roof to let in fresh air. Now all he could hear was the roar of Armageddon outside. Lightning flashed and deep rumbles shook the loft.

He caught a look at the clock. 11:39.

A second later the power went out. The drone of the fan went still and the ancient freezer downstairs shuddered and died. The air soon grew thick and he was alone with the storm.

2

DELUGE

- Noah -

He woke to the noise of driving rain. It started as a distant murmur, but swelled to a roar that tore him out of sleep and left him gasping in a knot of damp sheets.

He sat up, groaned as pain pressed on his eyeballs, and fumbled for his cigarettes. The old six-pack payback, as Daddy used to call it, was starting to become a regular breakfast guest. He peered at the clock and saw the power was still out. And just to promise it would stay that way, a thunderclap shook the roof and damn near knocked him off the cot.

"Fuck!" He slapped ash off the canvas before it could burn another hole in his bedding. He'd slept poorly until the storm had finally given way late last night and let him slip away. Now the hiatus was over. It sounded like the roof was on fire.

He waited for the nicotine to dull his headache, then got up, pulled on jeans, and pawed through the chest for dad's old pocket watch. God bless Daddy and his fine tools; the thing still worked. How long since he'd last wound it? Probably Jessie's funeral.

7:19. Late. But it wasn't like anybody waited for him to show up to breakfast.

He slid down the ladder. Ground level was cooler, but the refrigerator was a stale void, with just a half-burned six pack and carton of milk.

No coffee this morning, praise Jesus. No steak and eggs either, not unless he wanted to boil water the old-fashioned way, but he would have no fire in Daddy's barn. He wasn't starting the genny either.

He sniffed at the milk carton, winced, and emptied it into Riley's bowl. "Hey Riley, get your lazy ass up."

Strange. His shout stirred the sparrows in the rafters, but failed to produce the fat grey cat who would ordinarily be underfoot begging for his breakfast. While Samson was never at hand for morning roll call, Riley was a pudding who seldom ventured past the yard.

He went to have a look outside.

The sky churned an angry green and the earth boiled like the base of Pike's Falls. Everywhere else was whitewashed. He could barely see the trees and couldn't see the Glen at all. A lake swelled in the yard between the house and the root cellar. His eyes lingered on the pale margins of the Glen where mist and heat swirled like angry phantasms.

No wonder Riley was hiding.

The aura from last night was still there too. He felt it gnawing at his nerve endings and thought about Daddy's old stories of monsters that slipped out of the river at night to steal the souls of children. Like Tanner Weismann. They didn't seem so silly just now.

His gaze drifted to the yard where it settled on the real nightmare of this place. However sinister the Glen, it held no stock over the menace of Ma's house. Wreathed in a curtain of rain, it looked like a beached and bloated corpse. It spoiled an otherwise decent piece of earth.

He was going to need a lot of buckets. And he'd better get his ass over there, or rotting floors and drafty windows would be the least of his problems come Christmas.

Noah went to the tack room to gather gear before slouching back to the door to consider a miserable hundred-yard-dash to the kitchen door. Overhead, a pretty little waterfall cascaded from the eaves of the barn. I should have taken Will's offer, he thought, then tucked buckets under each arm and ran.

He'd fallen into the river in early March once. He'd hit loose dirt and went ass over teakettle into the drink while Daddy laughed himself stupid. He felt that same slap-in-the-face shock as he sprinted across the yard, shouting and swearing. He hit an ankle-deep hole in the dooryard that finished him off, sluiced his undercarriage and soaked him to the shorts. By the time he reached the house he was shivering, pissed off, and having serious thoughts about leaving this whole damned enterprise.

But he was inside now, entombed in the relative silence and the familiar musk of mildew and decay. And it was dry. Mostly. He wrung out his shirt over the sink, pushing aside dishes that had been there since the last ice age. There were fresh droppings on the counter next to the coffee pot.

Goddamned rats. They got in no matter what you did and they shit on everything. Even in the gloom he could see where they'd been gnawing on the wooden handle of a pan.

He really needed to clean this place up. And he would, too. He made that promise to himself as he opened a drawer and gathered towels that smelled like a clogged drain. *As soon as this rain clears out. When it dries up a little.*

He checked the bathroom, pulling the shower curtain aside and seeing to his relief that nothing disgusting was crawling out of the drain. The toilet gurgled.

He went to the cellar door, peered into inky blackness and wasn't surprised to hear water trickling down there. He pulled a penlight from his pocket and aimed it down the staircase where an oily surface rippled as if alive. He guessed maybe six, seven inches already. The old sump pump was offline, if it even worked anymore. No way was he going down there. There was nothing but a few shelves and some of Ma's old canned goods he wouldn't touch if he were starving. And he could hear the muttering and shuffle of rats.

Ma's proverbial chickens come home to roost, and the chief reason he slept in the barn now. He shut the door and turned to face the rest of the house.

There was a puddle under the wood stove. He'd have to cap the flue, but that could wait. Jessie's old room had a leak under the window, which he fixed by blasting it with fast drying foam in a can. Other than that, things on the first floor were okay. But it wasn't the downstairs he was worried about.

He stood at the bottom of the narrow staircase, looking into a blackness too thick for the penlight to penetrate. Most of the windows up there were boarded. The master bedroom, which stood sentry over the hall, was invisible. He felt rather than saw the crude outline of Ma's door, where a sleeping spirit sensed his presence and stirred.

Come on up here, Noah. Come see what I have for you.

He could hear the creak and shift of something waking up, water running through the house like cold blood through veins. *Let's get this over with.*

The stairs groaned, the cracked face of the door materializing with each step. Heat wafted off the door as if it were radioactive and he averted his eyes as he turned down the hall. Rat trails zigzagged through the dust on the floorboards.

A thick curtain hung over the window at the end of the hall. He swept it aside and breathed easier, having a clear view of the dooryard and the barn. He should board this too. Because the idea of this house staring down at the barn made his hair stand on end.

There was just enough light now to make the hall less evil. His old bedroom stood to his left, just this side of Ma's room, where he found only one leak, but a good one. A large pool gleamed under the window. He stooped to mop it up and as he rung the water into a bucket, he became aware of the closet door. When he was a kid he liked knowing it was close to where Ma and Daddy laid their heads at night. What monster would come out of such a place? But that surety was long dead.

He finished quickly, tossed an empty bucket under the drip, sealed the boarded window with foam, and got the hell out.

Ma's sewing room was better. Its large, lightly curtained window looked over the Glen and let in a friendlier light. Ma had spent many an afternoon here in those early years, before her devotion to the Good Book and eventual madness had led her to other things. The old Singer sewing machine sat where it always had, thread still in the spindle, years untouched. Its works were strewn with cobwebs and dust. Patches of rust bloomed on its bed plate.

His gaze rose to the picture of the solemn, perfect face of the Christ inclined heavenward, awash in a beam of holiness, eyes transcendent.

"God bless this house," he said, put a bucket under a drip, and left.

Soon he stood at the master bedroom door, working up the guts to open it. He put his ear to the door and listened. At first hearing nothing, allowing him to hope he wouldn't have to go in. Then came soft, rhythmic tip-tapping from the guts of the room.

"Damn it!" He closed his eyes, counted to ten, and forced his hand to the knob. The off-balance patter told him there was more than one leak. He held his breath, turned the knob and the pushed open the door, which swung with a sigh. Old smells engulfed him: mildew, rot, and older, uglier things. Dim light from the hall stretched inside, but not far enough to reveal anything within easy reach. He stepped into the room, sweeping the beam across the rug, but carefully, passing quickly over a dark stain under the bed that wasn't from water. The faded, moth-eaten edges of the quilt hung raggedly off the mattress and the knobby legs of the dresser seemed to move as the light passed over. He dared not look at the black eye of the mirror.

There was a drip near the far wall, another near the closet door beside the bed. He slid along the wall and dropped a bucket without seeing what it would catch.

The other was on the bed itself. The muted tapping told him it was near the pillow where her head had once lain. He almost couldn't do it. It took some hard self-talk to get him to turn the light on that bed and look.

Do it, Noah. Or you'll be pulling that bed out of Jessie's room when the ceiling collapses.

He did, half expecting to see a corpse lying there. There wasn't. Just decades-old bedding stained by hard use and an assault by the elements. He placed a bucket and left without mopping up.

3

THE RIVER

- Noah -

"Come on, you old bitch!" Noah pumped the gas pedal hard. The sluggish engine cranked but wouldn't catch. Two solid days of shit weather had saturated the barn with a rich jungle humidity. The truck was pitching a real fit about it.

"Filthy whore!" He mashed the floorboard. The starter chugged, slowed. "You godless, spread-eagle...rain-fucked piece of shit. Wake up!"

The truck coughed, belched smoke, and guttered to life.

Noah breathed in the sweet smell of gas fumes and exhaust. "Oh, you're a good girl." He stroked the dashboard.

The weekend had brought plenty of other miseries along with rain. Everything he touched was damp. The power never came back on and the genny wouldn't start, so the barn was dark and stagnant as a dog's insides. With nothing to do but fret about the house and ruminate on family history, he should have gone mad with boredom.

Fear relieved that tedium. Whatever spirit had taken up residence here two nights ago was growing, tightening its grip on this place, squeezing off the oxygen. Something was wrong with the Glen.

He slid out of the pickup, not wanting to kill himself and his livestock with poison air, and heaved open the main doors to reveal a leaden sky and rain-beaten earth. He could see the forest and orchard now, since the heavens had taken a break from drowning the world. The pear trees wore dull shrouds over slumped shoulders. The grass bent low around them as if in supplication. Everything was still, frozen in a watery, windless death.

He hadn't seen a single creature move outside the barn since Friday. Even during a rain you'd see a sparrow flitting between trees or outbuildings, but now not so much as a cricket stirred. His cats hadn't returned either. For the third morning in a row they were absent for breakfast, their bowls untouched. There was hope for Sampson – he was roamer and tough as iron, but he didn't think he was going to see Riley again.

Time to get the hell out of here for a while, restock his supplies, and lay eyes on other living, breathing souls. Will Brennan would have coffee, by God.

He climbed back into the truck and eased out of the barn, getting a dumping of rainwater from the gable, which he slapped away with a salute from the wipers. He shut the main doors and at last turned up the drive and headed toward Benton, whistling a little tune as the farm faded in his rearview mirror.

~

The sight of the river sobered him up again.

He hadn't expected to see so much water so soon. Long before he reached the bridge, the headlamps caught movement in the trees. He gave up trying to tune the radio – all he could get was static – and peered through the greasy light where coils of motion gathered to a single rolling mass.

As he reached the curve, an angry rumble rose above the engine noise. Noah thought of an old story. If legions of demon-crazed swine were set loose in the forest, this is what he might witness.

The road veered as if fleeing, a futile move because the river soon cut east again, forcing a collision at the bridge. Its iron ribs resolved from the trees, parting a path like Moses and the Sea. He pulled to a stop and watched the struts tremble as the river raged past the pylons. He opened the door and the noise became bone-deep, like a mountain uprooting itself. A wave of vertigo had him reaching for something solid as he stepped onto the steel deck and felt the violence beneath his feet. The body of a large tree rolled over in the muddy current, its rust-colored roots reaching up before it was sucked down and seen no more.

He'd lived in the Glen twenty-eight years and had never seen anything like this. Nor had Daddy, he was sure, because if he had, he'd have told Noah stories that would have rivaled even those of Tanner Weismann's demise. This was not the clean, friendly river he knew, born high in the misty falls of the White Mountains. This was an abortion, swelled by the filth and pollution of crop fields and other low places. It already smelled like decay.

The water was rising fast, almost before his eyes. There would be a grace period once the river left its banks and spread out over the valley. It would rise more slowly then and, if he was lucky, he'd have another day, two at most, before river took the bridge and sealed off the farm from the rest of the world. On that happy note, he fled to the truck, crossed the bridge, and drove on.

~

Benton IGA was a madhouse. He almost turned around when he saw the cars lining the street, but the prospect of days without a smoke was more terrifying than a few backward glances from neighbors.

Inside he was greeted by a press of bodies, mostly mammas with grocery carts and kids with snow-day grins. Hood down and eyes on the floor, he grabbed a basket and headed for the far aisle, nearly running smack into Matt Drier. The kid must have been on assignment, because he had a bale of toilet paper under an arm and a scowl that could melt paint. Noah ducked past without making eye contact.

His mood fell from sour to pissed when he saw the back cooler.

Stripped clean. A couple cases of Coors Near Beer and Mickey's Hard Lemonade graced the racks, but that was it. That's what he got for screwing around yesterday and not beating the rest of the alcoholics to the punch. He stuck his head inside to make sure he hadn't missed any and saw Mel the Meat Man come around the corner with a cart full of his namesake. Since Mel doubled as Benton's local minister and had been the first person besides Sheriff Rawls to see Ma's corpse, he got the hell out of there.

He grabbed up a box of crackers, two loaves of bread, and a large jar of peanut butter, and found the back of the line where he tried to be invisible. He hoped by the good graces that they weren't out of smokes.

The line moved like molasses uphill. He saw the register and muttered a curse. The efficient Maggie Halbach was absent, replaced by Hurricane Irene, getting in at least fifteen words to every *boop* of the scanner.

By the time his turn had come, it was seven-forty and he was aching for a cigarette. Irene finished off another victim, turning to shout at a soaked, sandy-haired kid who had just stumbled through the electric doors. He hurried forward, red-faced and resigned, and took Mrs. Porter's bags.

"I swear that boy wouldn't know hustle if it slapped him in the backside and introduced itself." Irene looked up, once, twice, shook her head and scanned Noah's crackers.

"My nephew Adam. Good boy, but ain't got the sense God gave a turnip. Came up to help with the rush, but he's about to wear me ragged keeping him on task. How are you, Noah? You still up at that farm?"

He asked for two cartons of Newports which, bless America, she had.

"I expect the river's about to beat down your door, isn't it?"

Noah shook his head. "Not yet." He glanced back down the line.

She followed his gaze and said, "School's canceled. Everything's canceled. Store's closing at noon too. I guess you don't watch the news, do you?"

"Power's been out." He pushed the rest of his gear forward, hoping she'd take the hint.

"Another round supposed to hit this afternoon. Big one. They say it could break records going back fifty years. Maybe even the Flood of Thirty-Six. I sure hope Maggie keeps her wits on the road today."

Noah glanced at her. "Where's she headed?"

"You haven't heard?" She stuffed the cigarettes into the sack. "She's gone to North Carolina to be with her sister. Susie lost a son on Saturday."

"Jesus, what happened?"

"Drowned. His little brother's devastated. Bad enough they had all that damage from Angeline, you know. Then Trevor goes missing during the cleanup and turns up in the river on Saturday. Just awful." She handed him his bag. "You need any help with that?"

He shook his head.

"That's good, because Adam's taking his sweet time. Listen, you take care of yourself, Noah."

"Always do." He gave a small salute, put his head down, and got out of there.

The bell clanged as Noah pushed open the door to Benton County Seed's main office. As he shook out his parka, a pair of bespectacled eyes peered over the counter.

"What the hell are you doing here?" Will Brennan half-rose from his seat in front of a little television at the desk behind the register.

"Making sure you don't sit on your ass all day." Noah hung his parka on the peg. "Which I see you've got a good start on. Got any coffee?"

Will resettled, pointed. Noah a poured himself a cup.

"Thank you, Jesus," he said, taking in the first hot liquid he'd had since Friday. "Where is everybody?"

Will smiled and nodded at the TV, where a grey image of a Doppler churned counter-clockwise around the colon-shape of Lake

Michigan. "Thought I'd give them all a day off," he said. "Early Christmas present. Wasn't that kind?"

"Shame. I was going to have Rocky help me clean out bay seven this morning." Noah took a chair across from Will and pulled a fresh pack of cigarettes out of his shirt pocket. Will snorted and switched off the television.

"Now why would you pick him for a job like that? You'd throttle that little bastard inside of ten minutes just for getting in your way."

Noah blew smoke and sat back, "You misjudge me, Will. Me and that *little bastard* have been getting on pretty good lately, in case you haven't noticed."

"That so?"

"Seeing as you let him off to go play video games all day, our budding relationship is on hold and I'll have to clean out seven myself. Thanks for everything."

Will grunted. "Funny," he said, studying the bowl of his pipe. "Two months ago, you wouldn't have given that boy a cracked bucket and sent him out to bail creek water."

"Like I said. We're learning."

"Maybe," he said.

Noah scowled. "Maybe what?"

"Maybe nothing." Will shrugged. "Maybe just the prerogative of the old to speculate. And hope a little."

"Oh, Christ, give it a rest. I don't have ulterior motives."

Will rocked back in his seat. "A young man of your age. Rocky's older sister out of college now for, what, three months?"

Noah shook his head, "Forget it, old man. You're on the wrong train."

"Smart, real pretty. I think I'd be making friends with Little Brother too, even if the only thing rocky about that kid was his head." He chewed on the stem of his pipe. "Let's see, what's her name? Lilly? Leona?"

Noah stubbed out his cigarette and stood. "I'm going to go empty bay seven before it all turns to silage. You got any more fatherly words of wisdom before I go do something productive?'

Will's expression grew serious. "Actually, I do," he said. "I want you to forget about that for today and get your skinny butt home before things get bad. That crap's two years old anyway and isn't worth saving."

"I'm way out of the flood plain. Trust me, I'm fine."

"There's a lot of low country between here and there. Any more of this shit and you'll be swimming home. Or better yet, you ought to come stay with Helen and me until this blows over." Will narrowed his eyes. "In fact, that's a hell of an idea. Why don't you run on up, pack a bag, and come on home with me? It's only supposed to get worse from here."

Noah shook his head, "It'll hold another two days. I tell you what, I'll get the bay cleaned and see what the weather looks like then." Noah nodded at the TV. "You'll be watching your soaps all day anyway. You tell me if the weatherman says Hell's on its way."

Noah finished the last load just after eleven a.m. By then rain was pelting the roof and making it hard to hear. The noise was good. He got lost in the simple work of shoveling and stacking and forgetting that the rest of the world existed. For a short time, his mind was quiet and empty.

He didn't realize how late it was until Will came and told him. He saw the empty bay and whistled. "This floor hasn't seen daylight in a century."

"It's my own fault," Noah said. "Should have done it ages ago. No idea the roof was this bad."

"You save any?"

"Couple ton, maybe."

They looked at the puddles on the floor.

"I'll fix that roof as soon as the monsoon is over," Noah said. "Scout's honor."

Will waved a hand. "You're the last one who should feel guilty about overdue maintenance. This place was a dump two years ago, remember?"

Noah nodded. "Praise God for new management."

"Wasn't management who did the work."

Noah sat down on a grain sack and smoked. "How's the weather?" As if he needed to ask. It sounded as if the heavens were dumping nails on the roof.

"Shitty," Will said, "Which is what I've come to tell you. Helen called me and said she'd tan my hide if I didn't bring you home this afternoon. She told me to tell you she's making her famous peach cobbler."

Noah let out a breath. "I'm tempted. Hell, for her cobbler I'd even consider spooning up with you tonight. But..."

"But nothing," Will said. "I'm not doing it for you. I'm sparing my own ass."

"Sorry, Will. I can't."

"Why not?"

Noah stood and cranked the jack. "If that river does come up, it'll be days before I'm able to get out there. I've got the animals to feed and a leaky house to take care of."

"Well, I guess that means you haven't thought about my offer."

Noah tugged the jack into motion. "What offer's that, Will?"

The older man followed him out of the bay. "Selling me the farm."

"I told you, you don't want that dump. The house needs to be bulldozed."

"Like I said. I need a project. A new hobby on which to spend my golden years."

"That place will put you in the goddamned nursing home inside of a week," Noah said. "Besides, why would you want a patch of dirt that won't grow pigweed, let alone anything to make money? You don't have any money anyway."

"You'd be surprised what a fellow can save in over forty-two years of crap jobs. Besides, it's time Helen and I got away from town."

"Bullshit."

"More to the point," he continued, "it's time you got away from here and went someplace where you can get a decent future. You need to do something with your life while you have one, Noah."

Noah straightened, blood rising to his cheeks. "I am doing something with my life, Will. I'm holding that shit hole together. This one too, for that."

He stopped. He hadn't meant to say that. He'd meant to say "rebuilding". He was restoring the farm to what it had been before. Before all that crazy shit had cut the place down to a skeleton. The work was just taking a little longer than expected. But if he said it, Will would just give him a look and Noah didn't feel like arguing with him.

"That's no life for a young man. You need to get out into the world. Get some education and go do something you won't look back on in thirty, forty years when you're old and used up like me and kick yourself for not doing it."

Do something with your life. Get out of here. Just what Jessie had preached. Where had it taken her? Noah wanted to remind Will of that, but didn't. "Well, thanks, Will. It's good of you to be so concerned for my welfare and my future and all. But it takes money to do those things, and I haven't got it."

"You will if you sell me the place. Besides, you don't spend a damn thing. Surely you have a few bucks tucked away somewhere, don't you?"

Noah pulled the jack to a stop, grabbed a bag, and hoisted it onto a pile. "I'll meet you up front, Will. Thanks for the offer."

~

Noah and Will stared out the office window. The rain fell with biblical fury. Culverts and ditches overflowed and the streets were becoming rivers. Already Main Street was swelling to a lake. The sky was a murky green.

"Jesus, they need to sound the sirens. If I'd known it was this bad..." Noah trailed off as a gust of wind shook the roof.

"Nobody here to sound the sirens for," Will said. "The town's dead."

He was right. The grocery store was dark. So was the filling station. The street was empty of cars save those parked at curbs in front of houses, many of which were in water up to their fenders.

A small pickup rolled down the hill from Ditch Creek Road, wipers flailing. The truck slowed to a crawl as it passed the seed company and came to the first swell of river rolling down First Street, then stopped, tail lights going bright red.

The churning water raged on while the driver waited for a sign from God. Noah could see the guy in the cab craning over the steering wheel, trying to see the other side and actually thinking about making a run for it.

"Don't you do it, mister," Noah said.

The truck hesitated, the man's face turned skyward as he peered through the windshield, then leveled on the water. The truck lurched forward.

"You turkey," Will muttered.

Spray shot from the wheel wells. The truck's ass wobbled in the current but kept going, farther than Noah would have expected, almost reaching the half-way point before the tire-spray peaked and the vehicle lost contact with the road. The fountains died, the tail lights sank and the truck began to drift. The driver pounded the steering wheel.

A roar of thunder tore the sky as if it were laughing. Noah and Will both winced as hailstones hit the roof, sporadically at first. Then the water in the street began to boil and the world went white with ice chunks the size of a child's fist.

"Good God," Will shouted. "It's the damn end of the world."

The man in the truck was motionless now. All he could do was sit and hope for a better future. But that future might be a long time coming and a whole lot of bad could happen in the meantime. They all watched and waited and still the storm kept up. Hail pounded the truck and everything else it could reach. Trees reeled and branches flailed, shedding leaves and limbs by the bushel.

"Well, so much for all my sweet corn this year," Will said.

That the truck's windshield didn't shatter was a miracle. But the water kept climbing and the pickup slowly began to disappear. The man seemed to be stuck in some kind of eddy where the rivers came together and slowed just enough to keep the water from hauling him off. But his good fortune, if you could call it such, wouldn't last.

Noah turned and headed into the shop.

"Where are you going?" Will called.

"To pull the poor son of a bitch out before he drowns."

Will followed. He didn't argue as Noah stepped inside the machine bay and pushed the doors apart. He ducked away from wind and iron-hard rain. The storm screamed in as if it had been waiting for a way inside. Hailstones skittered across the concrete floor.

Noah mounted the Deere 544, an ancient front-end loader with a massive bucket and four-foot tires. He fired it up with a rumble that challenged the storm and rolled out into furious winds. Will closed the doors behind him.

He motored the loader through the rain and hail, which slapped the glass hard enough to make Noah squint as he rounded the elevator and rolled into the flooded street. Water poured past the big tires but the machine held its course. He raised the bucket and saw the dead truck, now in water up to the windows, several yards down the street, the water churning around it like cyclone.

Noah slowed and studied the water. He chose a path and maneuvered around the worst of the current, because even something this big could be carried away by water like this. He pulled in behind the pickup, lowered the bucket, and positioned it under the rear bumper while a young man scared seven shades of shitless stared back at him. Noah gestured, pointed up the street in a direction that would take them straight into the current rather than across. He made a motion for the man to put the vehicle in neutral and crank the wheel, which he did.

Noah gave the loader gas and the truck began to move. Soon they were cutting through the river in steady progress up the hill. At first water spilled over the truck's hood, but that lessened as the vehicle surfaced. A moment later they were on solid ground and the truck shed water from cracks and crevices, mostly from the cab itself, like a sunken ship pulled from the sea. Noah smiled at the thought of the kid being soaked to the ass.

"Serves you right, you crazy bastard." The man was lucky he'd be pulling off wet clothes instead of the mortician doing it for him.

He pushed the truck to the top of the hill and stopped, then pointed at the City Office and machine shed before heading toward it. A minute later the truck was under the canopy of the Benton City Maintenance building and out of the storm.

"I think I'm going to get out of here, Will," Noah said as he stepped off tractor minutes later.

Will looked at him. "Why don't you just stay with Helen and me till this blows over? Please?"

Noah shook his head. "Thanks, but I need to get back. I've got animals to take care of."

"A handful rabbits ain't worth a human life, son. Don't be foolish."

Will wouldn't understand even if he could explain. Hell, he didn't know if he understood himself. Staying put would have been the smart thing to do after what had just happened, but this wasn't about good sense.

He'd been shut out by weather once before. Two years ago, a mother of a snow storm had closed down the road after he'd been stupid enough to leave. A complete whiteout had kept him locked down for hours. When he could finally see to drive, he'd discovered the winds had buried the road in four feet of snow. He wouldn't have cared, except Ma had been sick then, and two days had passed before the plows got through.

Jessie had left home not long after, and who could blame her after what happened? Ma was in a real state by the time he got home. So was Jessie, damn near as crazy as Ma and sick with exhaustion. Ma's screaming had been the first thing he heard when he got out of the truck.

"Noah! Where's Noah! I want Noah! Don't you touch me, you whore!" She'd shit herself and wouldn't let Jessie near her. He'd finally had to give her sleeping pills to shut her up.

No, he wasn't staying away again. Not tonight. Not for this. He assured Will that if he left now, he'd be able to handle whatever he ran into between here and home, and if he couldn't he'd turn around and come back.

Will didn't buy it, but there was nothing he could say in the end. He told Noah to be careful and to call when he got home.

By the time he was on the road, the hail had stopped, but the rain was still full tilt. Twice he had to floor it to get through standing water, the very thing he promised Will he wouldn't do. Stupid. But he got through. By the time the road narrowed and the bridge came into view, tree limbs and debris littered road. He was amazed to see that the river had risen another eight or ten feet.

Once he crossed that bridge, there would be no coming back. Not for days. So much for optimism.

The plugged culvert was another problem. Water surged over it with barely a pause. Beyond that, a stretch that had been merely soft when he'd crossed that morning, was a swamp. He stopped and measured his chances, trying to guess how deep it was, watching the headlights drown in oily murk where the current slithered over the road.

He went for it.

The engine roared and Noah prayed as dry land turned to sea. The truck hit the water with an actual smack and went momentarily weightless as spray hit the sky. The truck fish-tailed and drifted toward a huge oak hugging the road, but the oak wasn't the problem. The ditch at the end of the culvert was deep enough to sink a Sherman tank and swirled like a black hole.

"Oh shit!" He cranked the wheel and gunned the throttle. The front fender slammed against the tree and bounced off. The bounce saved his ass, throwing the truck toward the center of the road where the front tires caught and yanked him past the vortex. He watched it slip harmlessly by and thanked God for big, sturdy trees.

But he wasn't out of the woods yet. A long stretch of lake lay before him and soon the tires were spinning. He bore down, throwing water and mud and curses, working the wheel to find something solid to bite into. The tires finally did their job and dug into the roadbed, carrying the truck through in a drunken line to dry land.

By the time he pulled the truck into the barn and killed the engine, his hands shook and he fought back a fit laughter, knowing that if it took hold, he wouldn't be able to stop. He'd never been so glad to have his feet on solid ground. He was almost happy to be home.

4

JESSIE

- Noah -

Cleaning the truck took hours. Afterward, he was coated face-to-ass with river grease and the barn smelled like a sewer. But the job was done, by God. The engine, now clean and squared away, would start if he needed it to.

He wouldn't. Sometime in the night, the river had swallowed the bridge. Noah was now officially a castaway, his sturdy old Chevy dry-docked until further notice. But as Daddy used to say, better to have it and not need it.

Looking at the godawful mess, Noah thought of the hours spent keeping the truck clean and tuned for Jessie while she'd been going to school. For the year or so before she left home, it had been her escape vessel, getting her off of the farm and out of range of Ma's poisonous tongue, which was always more acidic for her than for him. Several weekends and holidays she would come home only to tear out like a doused cat before the engine had even cooled. The truck was the only vehicle save the tractors that Noah had bothered keeping. He'd sold the rest, including Ma's Oldsmobile.

Jessie left for good not long after Ma had her last episode. And the irony of the whole thing was that Ma's venom wasn't what drove her away. She'd said she couldn't stand to watch Ma suffer like that, *so needlessly*. As if the whole fucking thing was his fault. She'd left angrier at him than at Ma.

Could he really blame Jessie for leaving? Had he really expected her to waste her life here, the way he had wasted his? Maybe if she'd stayed put, she would still be alive. God has a funny way of making you regret hurt feelings and injured pride. Noah hadn't said a word to her in six months when her future mother-in-law had called to tell him she was gone. Their last conversation hadn't been nice. *He* hadn't been nice. Now she was dead and there was no making things right.

His nightly porch session almost didn't happen that night. By the time he finished cleaning up - two minutes of ice-cold agony under the spigot with a bottle of dish soap, because he wasn't going in the house tonight - the light was almost gone and the Glen had a green, murky cast. Thin wisps of vapor rose and disappeared from the acres of grass, as if the earth were bleeding souls. The sight sent a shiver through him.

He sat down anyway, gasping as his butt hit the sodden slats of the swing. He watched for Samson, surprised by an intense longing for the stupid cat's company. An ache for a beer followed, want adding to want.

The rain had slowed at least. And the air was cooler. He closed his eyes and listened to the gentle hiss on the roof and the distant rumble of thunder, a reminder that the system was staying a while. He heard something else now too, just above the rain, an eerie rending felt in his chest. He couldn't quite see the river, but it was there, chewing through the forest and tearing it up by its roots, a bit at a time. Millions, maybe billions of gallons carrying boulders and trees and lord knew what else with it. Bodies, maybe. He thought of Maggie Halback's nephew, dragged to his death by a monster just like this. He thought of his uncle Tanner who'd met his end just there, beyond the tree-line a generation ago. More to come, he thought. Because this thing wasn't so much rising as growing. The river was alive; it was hungry and it was coming.

A shudder went through him as he realized he should have taken Will's offer. He'd be eating Helen's famous peach cobbler right about now. Too late. He'd made his choices; now he had to pay for them. All of them.

"Noah?"

The sound of her voice startled him. She was the last person he'd expected to call that night, and he didn't know whether it was fury or joy that hit him hardest. "Hey Jessie," he said.

A heartbeat's silence on the line.

"How are you?"

He didn't like the way she said it. "Just fine. Good, actually. You?"

She sighed. "Not bad. Making it, I guess."

The void dragged on and he was tempted to let her soak in it, because she deserved a little suffering after what she'd done. "So, how's school going?" he asked. "Midterms over?"

She huffed a laugh, "Yeah. Thank God. At least until my grades come in. Then we'll see if they don't throw me out for good."

"I know better than that. Didn't you make the President's list last semester?"

"Dean's list. Barely."

"Whatever," Noah said. "Scholarships don't grow on trees. You've done this, what, two years?"

"Yeah."

"And money's okay. Right? Do you need money?"

Dangerous waters. He knew better, but the words tumbled out. He wished he could *see* her, wished he could look her in the face instead of having to speak through the fucking dry static of a phone line. The stinging behind his eyes was starting to piss him off.

"No. Money's just fine, Noah."

"Right. You've got Billy's parents, don't you?"

The silence this time was laced with heat.

"Sorry," he said. "I didn't mean it to come out that way. I just wanted to know if you were okay."

He wanted to say a whole lot more, wanted to scream at her about how much her decision hurt, how selfish she was to leave him when he needed her most. She hadn't been interested in listening the first time and she sure as hell wasn't going to sit there and let him try again. For a moment he thought she'd hung up. He nearly screamed because this was *his* fault all over again.

She hadn't. "Of course I'm okay, Noah. I didn't call to talk about money." She hadn't even bothered correcting him on her fiancé's name.

"Why did you call?"

"To see how you were doing. You know, talk. Because it's been a while."

"Yeah. I guess it has," he said, wishing he could keep back the sarcasm. "And it's not your business anymore to worry about me."

"It's always my business," she said.

"Everything's fine here, Jess."

"You're not still sleeping in the barn, are you? Jesus, tell me you're sleeping in a bed like a real person?"

"It's cooler there in the summer," Noah said.

"Well, it's not summer. It's practically winter."

Noah didn't answer.

"Don't you ever get the creeps out there?" she asked. "I mean, being by yourself?"

"There's nothing to be afraid of out here. You lived here too. Remember?"

"All I know is that if it were just me, that place would scare the hell out of me. I don't know how you do it. You remember that old pear orchard, where we used to play?"

Noah grunted. "I don't recall *you* playing out there."

"The older I got, the less I liked it. Especially after Dad's stupid story. You remember that?" She made a sound of disgust. "God, I knew it wasn't true but still..."

"I remember," he said, finding Daddy's old lighter in his hand.

The vision of it cupped in his father's gnarled fingers was so vivid he was afraid that if he looked up he'd see him staring back at him from the kitchen table.

"You were never scared, though," Jessie said. "I never did get that. I figured it was some male, macho thing, right?"

A Noah thing. But she was right about the rest. When he was a boy he'd spent every minute he could down there. He spent hours exploring the Glen, looking for hidden caves or man-sized holes in the ground.

Often he would just sit and daydream, pretending that the orchard wasn't an orchard at all but a forest. And not like the forest on the other side of the river, but magical. Dark and beautiful, full of strange creatures that would watch him from their dens and might, with enough time, get used to his presence and come out to meet him. The fun part was not knowing whether these things were cruel or kind, whether they would tear him to pieces or become his best friend. Their nature changed from day to day, and often as not he imagined himself into such a scare, especially close to dark, that he would end up tearing back to the house without looking back until he was bent over and gasping at the front door. But no matter what, the creatures he imagined were always beautiful and captivating, worth even the risk of being eaten alive for a single glimpse.

"Kids' stories," Noah said. "Dad was drunk."

"I know," Jessie said, "but it's the idea. It sticks with you. Like when you have to keep a nightlight in the bedroom, even when you're a grownup. Or maybe I just watch too much TV, huh?"

"Maybe," Noah said. "Or maybe you're just a chicken."

"Yeah, and maybe you're a little crazy, Noah."

"Just like Ma," he said, the words coming before he could stop them and hitting dead center.

"That's not what I meant," she said.

Then what did you mean, you stupid bitch? "I know. Sorry."

"I just worry about you, Noah. I can't help it. I hate to think of you being out there alone."

"Then why don't you come back? Take your old room and move

back in." He hadn't caught that one, hadn't even been able to stop it midstream. He didn't even have the sense to regret it, despite the aftertaste.

"Noah," she said. "You know I can't. Even if I wanted to, Bobby..."

"Bring Bobby with you. Hell, I don't care. There's room. I won't even ask the asshole to pay rent. Just come back."

"Noah..."

"You never know. I might start liking him, given time."

"That's out of the question and you know it." There was shaky laughter in her voice but no humor.

"Why?"

What he was doing was pointless. Even if he were serious, and he was not entirely sure he wasn't, he knew she would never, ever set foot here again. Why would she? She'd been smart to get out in the first place.

"Don't be stupid, Noah. You know why."

"Do I? Tell me, then. Why can't you?"

"Because that place is a fucking black hole. I wouldn't go back there if I had no other place to go, Noah. And I sure as hell am not going to drag Bobby into that misery."

"You think it's a misery to live with me? If you're so worried about me..."

"Don't even try it. You know that's not what I'm talking about."

"What the hell are you talking about, then?" His fingers had tightened around the lighter, hard enough to hurt.

"I'm talking about *that place!*" she said. "It's a grave, and you need to get out of there before it buries you. I don't know what you think you owe Dad or anybody else by staying there, but you're not helping anyone. Get rid of that fucking death trap and get a real life."

"Don't you dare lecture me about family responsibility, do you hear me? You left me. With *her*, remember? I was changing that woman's diapers and watching her rip herself to pieces and you didn't even say goodbye! What the hell was I supposed to do, Jessica?"

"You could have called the doctor. Like I told you to in the first place. You could have gotten help."

"Bullshit! Who would have paid for it? You have any idea how much it would have cost?"

"Well, guess what? She's not there for you to take care of anymore, is she? She's dead. So leave!"

He couldn't answer. He strangled the receiver, surprised it didn't break in his hand. Maybe if he'd just hung up right then, the situation could have been salvaged. "So that's it," he said at last. "After all this time. You think I killed her."

"Don't be ridiculous. I didn't say that."

"You didn't have to say it, Jessie. It's practically leaking out of you. I've always known. And you know what? Fuck you! You wouldn't understand a single goddamned thing about commitment or loyalty or sticking to something you started. You abandoned me. You abandoned her. And I don't really give a shit what you believe or what you think I did to her. I did everything I could.

"So listen carefully to me, Jessie. I don't ever want you to call here again, do you understand? I never want to see you again, or speak to you. Stay the fuck out of my life."

Those were the last words he ever spoke to her. She'd honored his wishes and never called again. Six months later she was dead. One phone call from Bobby's mother, a few clipped words, and that was it for his big sister, Jessica Anne Weismann.

A crash brought him back to the present.

He gasped, finding himself in near perfect darkness, the air rippling with an electric charge. For a moment he floated on a cloud of terror, disoriented and unable to remember where he was.

His groping hands fell onto something clammy and smooth like the flesh of a corpse, which turned into nothing more than the porch beam, whose pale outline gave him time and place again. He was standing on the front porch. The abandoned swing wobbled unevenly. He must have fallen asleep.

His gaze settled on the front door of the house as his blood turned to ice. The noise that had woken him hadn't come from the sky. It hadn't come from the forest either, or from the barn or one of the sheds.

The house.

Something is in my house.

He stopped breathing and listened hard. For a moment he heard nothing. Then a muffled hiss snaked through the wall and wound around his heart.

"Ma," he called, "is that you?"

A crazy notion, a paranoid fantasy cooked up by a guilt-soaked brain. But no, that wasn't true. Did he really think his devils wouldn't return to exact retribution? Sure they would. Or rather *she* would.

He swallowed, reached for the door. Better now than later. Let it be over. The hiss resolved to a clatter, and with crystal clarity he understood. Not a ghost. Not a demon. The ceiling. Rain and rot had finally brought down a chunk of the house. The relief made him laugh out loud. Just Ma's fucking house coming down around her ears. He rested his head against the door, laughter shaking him like a sob. Tears rolled down his cheeks. There were rats in there, too. He could hear them shrieking as they scurried across the living room floor, their den torn open.

"You can have it," he said, turned around and abandoned the porch.

5

THE SCREAM

- Noah -

Closing himself in the barn that night was sweet relief. The familiar smell of old hay, engine grease, and animals covered him like a warm blanket. He was glad to hear signs of life from Mork and Mindy for a change. The two rabbits bounced around their cages like they were stir crazy.

Noah didn't blame them. His brief escape from this place yesterday had only made today worse. He used to be good at this, going days without seeing another soul with nothing to do but scrub Daddy's old tractor or fix fences or work odd jobs around the barn. But the sickness in the Glen was chewing through him like the rats in his mother's house.

A kerosene lantern hung on the peg beside the door. He lit it and sent skittish shadows fleeing to the corners of the barn as he made his way to the hutch to check his animals. As lantern light touched the hutch, the pinball rattle stopped. A beady black eye gleamed back at him for an instant before retreating.

"What's wrong, you guys?" He opened the latch and reached in to stroke Mindy, the little doe, but she wasn't having it. She bolted for the corner and buried her head in the straw, trembling.

Not cagey. Terrified.

Mork actually screamed when Noah reached for him, a piercing cry that made him jerk back. He closed the cage and backed away.

"That damned flood's not getting in here, guys. There's nothing to be scared of."

They didn't agree. Noah wasn't sure he did either. He turned and let the lantern push away silly notions of ghosts and fairytale goblins. The beetle eyes of the tractor glittered. The familiar corners and shapes of the barn seemed to tilt as if the walls were falling in – an illusion of light, he knew, but the effect on his nerves was just as strong. A shiver rolled up his spine as the panorama continued and he found himself looking at the large sliding doors of the barn that came together at a single black seam. This was all that closed him off from whatever foul thing now haunted the Glen.

That gap was too wide. The last person to come through had done a sloppy-ass job of closing up. He set the lantern down and stepped forward to pull the doors together, feeling the night stir as he grasped the pull handles and wrenched them closed. He considered putting a chain through handles, but with a few hard words talked himself out of it. *You're as bad as your sister. There's nothing out there!*

The rabbits said otherwise.

He fed and watered the two hens. They were both fine, settled in their roosts, oblivious and stupid. He didn't bother checking the cats, though. They weren't coming back. Riley had no doubt gotten his fool ass in the river and drowned. Samson was smart enough to have quit this place.

Finally, he climbed the ladder to the loft and undressed for bed. How he longed for the noise of the fan, or the radio, or something to challenge the noise of the river chewing its way through the Glen and the ugly silence in the barn. Tomorrow he'd call the power company and give them murder.

He thought sleep would prove as elusive as a spooked rabbit, but he was wrong. Despite his nerves and the uneasy silence, he fell asleep almost at once.

He woke some time later with a strangled scream and a racing heart. He sat up in bed staring at pitch black, trying to figure out what had brought him up. Probably a dream he couldn't remember. He usually remembered the dreams that woke him, but the only thing between his ears right now was the thud of his heart and the question of why his veins were full of electricity instead of blood.

He held his breath and listened. It was raining again. Hard.

Thunder, he thought. Was that what had woken him? Then came a low, distant rumble over the grinding river and he let out his breath. Just thunder. Another storm. That was all. Not exactly something to cheer, but nothing to get worked up over either. He flipped on the light, which of course didn't work.

"Damn it," he muttered.

So much for the hope of dry land. So much for peace, for getting off this fucking rock and seeing daylight again. Fine.

"Come on and get me then, you bastard." He groped for his cigarettes, felt the comfortable cool of the lighter. The metallic snap made a burst of sparks. The flame never caught.

A scream cut through the night, slicing through the deluge outside. Electric fear shot through the cracks in the walls, came up the ladder and slammed into him. Noah jerked as if hit by lightning. The lighter fell from his hand and clattered to the floor. He sat ramrod straight in darkness, skin hardening to goose flesh.

"Christ, what the hell was that?"

His mind had no reference for what he'd just heard. Nor was there any experience in the Glen or in the valley he could draw on to give it a name. It was dry and hard, like the rattle of a viper or the clatter of locust wings, but far too sharp and loud to have come from any insect or reptile.

Already his brain was changing it, struggling to fix it to something familiar and real, and losing the nature of it in the process. "What was it? What was it?" He whispered it over and over again, trying to hold on to it.

Whatever the thing was, it had been close enough to scare the bejeezus out of the rabbits and start the hens to cackling. They'd all gone mad in their cages. He strained to hear over their panicked racket.

Mountain lion! The idea struck and wedged into place.

Of course. People said that the cry of a mountain lion sounds like a woman's scream. And there were many who claimed to have seen them in the valley over the years, though Noah hadn't. Plenty of forest here for them to hide in and never be seen. He pictured the big cat in his mind and tried to hear it. The sound in his imagination wasn't right. It was definitely no woman's scream. *But what else could it have been?*

He sat in the frozen air for several minutes, sweating and shivering at the same time, waiting. The noise didn't repeat. No sound but the rain and the river. Nothing moved outside. Even the animals in their cages were still now. He marked time only by the rumble of the approaching storm. Several times his brain created the beginnings of half-sounds beyond the walls, but nothing that actually became real. Each time his breath caught, he discarded it as the work of an overactive imagination trying to strain every last sound out of the air.

He stayed up for a while before making himself lie back down, not knowing when he would be able to sleep again. Eventually he did, though, and nothing else disturbed him outside of his own nightmares.

6

THE VISITOR

- Noah -

Three days passed without incident.

No more ceilings collapsed, no shrieking devils crawled out of the Glen. The storm let up too, giving way to gentle rain, so he was no longer terrified of being struck by lightning every time he left the barn.

On the morning following the scream, he did a thorough check of the yard for animal tracks and found only a set of opossum prints across the drive. That a mountain lion had invaded the yard seemed less and less probable. He knew this place, knew the area and the kind of animals you could come across out here. Raccoons could get themselves into mischief, sometimes getting into the barn or into the attic and raising hell. A pair of old boar coons would get into a scrape in the trees near the house and make a racket that would scare the pants off a city slicker. One night a bobcat raided the chicken coop by tearing through the wire in the run outside. By the time Noah had climbed out of the loft, the beast was gone with a hen in its jaws. But the noise of the hungry cat ripping into a clutch of terrified chickens was enough to raise a corpse from the grave. There were black bears here too, but they tended to keep to the hills and never came near the house. By the end of that day he'd dismissed the noise as the product of a cooped-up mind and fevered dreams.

The house was done for. One peek through the living room window at the hill of soggy plaster on the floor was enough to convince him. He'd thought the rooms on the second floor were fine. He never considered what damage the rats were doing between the floors. God knew what they were doing in the other crevices and recesses.

The matter was settled. Noah would take their advice – all of them, both living and dead – and sell this place. Hell, Will Brennan could have it. As soon as that fucking river let him out of here, Noah Weismann was history. He had no idea where he would go after that, but with a torrent cutting through the orchard and over the road, he had plenty of time to think about it.

But making the decision settled his nerves. Noah fell into an easy routine, rising at first light, doing the chores and tending to the animals before setting himself to cleaning the barn and the machines. He considered the job a last memorial to Daddy – restore his barn and tools to the way he would have kept them if he were still living. The Holy Word of Braden Weismann made law once more: *Take care of your tools, Noah, and they'll outlive you.* Which was one bit of folk wisdom that had proven true.

He polished the tractor to a spit-shine, scrubbing out the corners with a toothbrush. The old Ford 8N hadn't looked this good in years. Hell, it would probably win a ribbon at the county fair this year if he entered it. And maybe old William B. would do just that.

The following day, everything changed. The morning started well; the rain stopped. It didn't slow, it didn't taper off. It just stopped, as if God had turned off a faucet. Noah kept his hopes in check, expecting another broken promise, but by afternoon the clouds had clearly gone into retirement. He watched a distant shaft of golden light trying to coax a rainbow out of the clouds.

"Well, son of a bitch." How many days since all this started? How long since hearing another voice besides his own? He had to think about that and decided it was time to start marking the days, just to stay human. No telling how many more nights would pass before he saw another face.

Zero, as it happened.

The first shock of the day came late that afternoon when he discovered his chickens were gone. A slammed door or a dropped wrench usually set them to cackling, but not today. The coop was silent. He figured they were outside patrolling their run. But on his way to dump a waste bucket in the corral he found the pen empty.

He studied the matter for several minutes, walking the screen along the run and checking the nest boxes inside, finding no tracks or signs of a predator, or even signs of a chicken. The latch hook was loose, though, which meant he'd forgotten to lock it that morning. But the tongue-lashing he gave himself for it didn't solve the mystery of his missing hens.

Chickens did not simply vanish. Even if they did manage to find themselves outside the coop, they didn't have the brains to up and flee the country. And bobcats and raccoons didn't slip into barns in the middle of the day to unlatch coops and sneak off with live animals under each arm like a cat burglar.

The barn was getting quieter by the day. Samson and Riley were gone. Now the hens. Even the sparrows and barn swallows had vacated, leaving the rafters like empty bleachers at the end of a season. Only the fidgeting rabbits assured him that the barn yet preserved life other than his own.

Two hours later he saw the child.

Evening had settled in, the day's work finished. He was giving himself a spit bath under the spigot when he spotted something out in the Glen. He froze, half-dressed, heart pitching up, unsure of what he was looking at, but certain it was alive. He thought of his chickens and took a step toward his shoes.

The thing was bone white, impossible to miss against the dark backdrop of the orchard. His eyes struggled to sort out the shape, but eventually they did and his breath caught.

A young child stood absolutely still in the middle of the Glen. At first his mind wouldn't accept the idea because the figure was so out of place. Everything about the scene was wrong. A child so close to that terrible river should have thrown him into full rescue mode, but the way it just stood there, looking at him, held him to the spot.

"Hello!" he shouted.

The child didn't move.

The sex was hard to tell at this distance, but he could see the child was naked, at least from the waist up, and the absence of shape suggested some years from adulthood.

He slipped into his boots and made his way across the sodden yard, wondering why the kid showed no sign of understanding him. *Scared out of her mind, that's why.* He didn't blame her. The impression of a she grew as he got closer.

Where the hell did you come from?

Scanning the Glen from timber to road, searching for some plausible answer, he found none. No one could have gotten out here, not by car, nor on foot. The closest passable road would be up near Judd McPherson's place, which was eight miles over the pass.

A thought struck him.

She fell into the river. Washed up here.

A ridiculous idea. No living thing that fell into that monster would ever be seen again.

"Are you okay?" he shouted. Still no movement. He'd decided she was a girl because of her hair, which was a tangled mess.

He waded into knee-deep grass, soaking his jeans. It occurred to him that even though she'd escaped the river, she could easily catch sick. One way or another, she was in bad trouble. How in the name of Jake was he going to get her out of there? He kept walking and the child remained as still as the pear trees.

"Are you hurt?" he asked, when he was close enough to not shout. He stopped. The huge black eyes were locked on him, sending a warning tickle to the back of his neck. They were so black they seemed to swallow up emotion, making her look wild, especially with her body set like that, as if ready to bolt, or maybe charge. It was one of the most eerie things Noah had ever seen.

"Hey. You okay?"

He raised a hand and took a step closer. The child shifted, moving for the first time, head turning to follow Noah like stone coming to life.

He stopped.

Definitely a girl. She wore not a stitch of clothing, in weeds to her hips, shoulders tight, legs like coiled springs, fingers splayed. *Careful now.* He couldn't tell her age for sure, but thought she might be around ten.

"Honey, where are your folks?" He studied her from where he stood, coming no closer. He extended his hand, hoping she'd come forward, fearing she wouldn't. "Hey, sweetheart."

She gasped, oval face coming to life as she sank into the grass, an act that both surprised and relieved him. She was no longer a wild animal in a human body but a frightened child. How long had she been out here, he wondered?

"Take it easy. I'm not going to hurt you." He took a small step forward. "Let me help you." Then he paused, seeing if she'd relax. She didn't. "It's okay." Hand held out, another cautious step.

She ran. A burst of motion, a blur of white. She flew like a startled grouse.

He lunged at her and missed, swore and stumbled after. She made for the orchard, outstripping him easily as he struggled through the tangle. *So fast.* The girl shot through the grass like a torpedo and disappeared into the pear trees.

"Stop!" He plunged through water-laden branches, switches lashing his face. He brought up his hands and pushed blindly through, ready to grab her. But when he breached the barrier and fell into a gap between the trees, the girl was gone.

A flash of movement, a hiss of leaves. *There.*

He ducked under the orchard's outstretched arms, slapped away cloying hands, and ran. The river lay mere feet away, unseen and on the hunt. He heard the gurgle of its little fingers slithering through the orchard just ahead. He prayed he wouldn't have to hear her scream as the monster took her.

He broke through to the next gap and there she was.

"Wait!"

The girl paused, turning to gaze at him with those alien eyes, all trace of fear gone.

"Don't move!"

She did. She turned, slipped into the underbrush, and disappeared.

"Damn it!" He trudged after her, running on until a muddy churn swelled around his feet. He screamed and grabbed a nearby branch, managing to scrabble back out before the current took him. But it was only a shallow backwater. It swirled in a murky eddy at his feet, chuckling at him like the whole valley was having a joke.

"Fuck you." He turned around to look for her trail.

He made a circle around the orchard and found nothing, no furrow through the grass but his own. She'd just disappeared.

He pushed south toward the road, following the edge of the river, calling out as he hunted, not wanting to believe what he already knew. He reached the edge of the Glen and stared out at nothing. The river swept on through a large section of the meadow until the trees turned west and faded into the horizon. No movement, no pale form in the distance, just a drowned valley.

He turned a desperate, useless circle, panning fields, forest, and meadow. Ma's old house looked almost pretty huddled against the dusky trees, warm and Rockwellesque.

What the hell was she doing clear out here anyway? And where were her parents? Who let their children run wild when God was in the middle of ending the world? Whoever they were, they deserved a good kick in the ass. But so did he. She'd been right there and he'd let her slip through his fingers, never imagining that years of heavy smoking and treating his body like shit might cost someone else's life. Others had died because of his bad choices, hadn't they?

He made his way back to the orchard, dragging his guts with him and trying to keep his eyes from stinging. He paused at a mud slick that stretched a good fifty yards across the Glen. It was surrounded by mats of beaten grass like crude crop circles. The evidence that the flood had receded a little made him feel no better. The bridge wouldn't be open for days and the closest place he could go for a ride up to town was miles beyond the mountain ridge.

The only thing he could think to do was call the sheriff's department. Maybe they could get a crew out here to help search for a body. If he couldn't find her today. He marched back to the house and opened the kitchen door for the first time in days, swallowing a lump of terror because there were more important things right now than his superstitions and fear of rats. He blinded himself to the shadows and shapes huddled in the corners, deafened himself to the murmur in the walls and headed straight to the phone. He picked it up and screamed in outrage.

"What is this shit?"

The line was dead.

Noah pounded the hook like Morse code, got more silence for his trouble, and threw the handset against the wall. It smacked the floor and dangled from its cord. So much for the goddamned twenty-first century. First the power, now the phone company. In the age of drones, cell phones, and free internet porn, was it too much to expect that most basic human services actually worked when you needed them to?

He pulled out his pocket knife and slit the yellowed wallpaper, running the blade down a seam in the wood paneling. *Rats. It was those fucking rats...*

He tore the paneling from ancient studs, popping out tiny brown nails that spun across the floor. He followed the line up the wall to where it disappeared through dust-thin insulation. Everything was fine. No frayed ends. No sign of chewing.

He kicked the door aside and stormed out of the house to the junction box. Nothing he could do if the line was damaged from there. He gazed up at the transformer and the yard light, followed the electric line as it bobbed merrily from pole to pole down the driveway and out of sight. He hurled obscenities at the power company, the phone company, the U.S. government, the principalities and powers for abandoning him out here, and at himself for his stupidity in allowing it.

Only one thing to do now. It was getting dark and he didn't have much time. The girl was either huddled up somewhere close or she was dead, devoured by the river. If there was even a chance of the former, he had to pursue it. He wouldn't leave her out here to stumble to a frightened oblivion without trying.

7

MAN HUNT

- Noah -

Tanner's Glen slipped deeper into darkness as Noah took up the search for the little girl. He started at the end of the drive, then worked his way north along the river toward the forest before descending into the bowl of the Glen. He scanned the grass for trails or prints in the silt that stretched across the meadow in long, foul-smelling bands.

He wanted to call out but didn't. An instinct older than language kept him mute, eyes darting at shadows and dark hollows under clusters of loosestrife.

Nothing out here to be scared of, Jack.

It was true. Nothing stirred. No sign of the kid. Not even a breath of wind.

The forest rose out of the meadow like the bars of a cage. Legions of ancient hardwoods stood in ranks miles-deep from ridge to river, walling off the Glen and signaling the end of Noah's search. If he didn't find her trail by the time he reached the tree-line, where prairie gave way to the tangle of underbrush, they'd both be out of luck.

But there was no underbrush. Reaching the corner of the Glen where forest and river met, he found the trees buried to their ankles in filth. The torrent had stripped the earth bare, devouring every sapling and shrub, every blade of grass. What remained was a waste of grey mud five acres wide.

He wrinkled his nose, catching the stench of decay, and scanned the flat. It was smooth and slick as oil, its surface unblemished save for the scattered bones of driftwood.

Maybe his search wouldn't end after all. The desolation extended far into the forest. A track would be easy to find in there, as long as there was river to vomit up mud, as long as he had the guts to go in and look.

You got no light and it's almost dark. But his traitorous fingers had found the hard edge of the lighter in his back pocket. *No way. Dumb idea.*

Would he really leave her out here to die? She was dead already. Could he sleep without knowing? The fading light wasn't waiting around for his conscience and fear to slug it out.

A fly landed on his cheek. He slapped at it irritably, then noticed the subtle drone coloring the silence.

The buzz of insects became a haze over the sludge several paces away. He took a step forward, ignoring the squelching mud and worsening odor. His skin prickled as a shape resolved itself beneath the shifting cloud.

Not a corpse. Something worse. A depression ringed by a mound of earth, as if something had pushed its way out of the ground, like a crawfish.

If a crawfish were the size of a man.

"No," he whispered. "Not possible." It was just a story, *just a goddamned ghost story to scare kids.* Except it wasn't. Daddy's homemade nightmare carved right here in the earth was as real as the river.

Boots tugged free and sank in again, carrying him on a slow march toward the black eye of a pit. He was unable to stop, because some things you had to see to believe.

But it wasn't a hole leading to hell. The Glen had played a trick on him, screwed with his worked-up mind. Noah stared at the body of a cat, so ruined by the elements that it was nearly indistinguishable from the silt.

"Goddammit." He stooped next to the remains of one of his missing animals. Of his two cats, Riley was always the most likely to do something stupid like falling into the river.

He reached out to touch the matted coat, ignoring the smell. *Poor little shit.* Used to never leave Jessie's lap, so long as she was sitting down. Riley had howled and followed Noah through the barn for days after her death. As if the cat knew. Well, they were together now, weren't they?

Noah grabbed the tail and pulled the corpse out of the mud, checking for signs of injury or something that might explain how a relatively healthy animal might have fallen in the drink. No signs of a predator. The body was clean except for a small wound at the nape of the neck.

A quarter-sized patch of pale skin surrounded an opening in the flesh, like a bullet hole but smaller. It was swollen and festering with maggots. Noah swore and dropped the body.

Had someone shot his cat? Maybe Riley had ranged too far and had gotten himself shot before falling into the river and being washed up here.

Bullshit. This was no bullet wound. It didn't look right. Maybe a bite that had gotten infected then? Regardless, he wouldn't leave Riley out here to feed the buzzards.

Mist was already pooling in low places across the Glen. He'd be lucky to make it back to the barn before full dark. Better to bury the cat at the house than trek all the way back here with a shovel.

"You're like a scared little girl," he muttered, as a gust of wind rustled the grass beyond the mud flat.

The distant orchard was nothing but a black hump rising up out of the meadow now. Maybe he'd bury Riley there in the morning. Nothing had bothered the body yet, probably nothing would. The valley seemed so empty of life anyway. It was a wonder the flies had found him. This chore would keep until morning. He turned to leave.

Another breeze played along the grass.

His footsteps faltered. Something was not right. One look at the trees told him what it was. They were dead still, their leaves hanging heavy and listless. There was no wind here. Not a bit.

Icy fingers raked his spine and sent his heart bolting. Vision brightened the world to hard edges and sharp points as Noah scanned for a way across the field. The trees were too close; they were a wall threatening to fall on him. His gaze snapped to a patch of tall loosestrife not twenty feet away, shaken to life by a breathy hiss. Grass moved in a smooth ripple, stalks enlivening as something cut toward him in a lazy arc.

"Why didn't I bring the damned gun?" His feet carried him backward, nearly tripping him as his boots sank into mud and anchored him to the spot. The grass went still.

A burst of memory, unwelcome and sudden. The ragged scream that had come out of the Glen two nights earlier.

Well, shit. The house was miles away now. In the dying light, the purple tips of loosestrife looked like bloody spears.

If he could just get his feet out of this soup. Muck sucked greedily at his boots. The stalks rattled, close, steps away.

"Shit!" He threw himself forward, tearing free with a mighty heave fueled by pure terror, and bolted across the Glen. Had Tanner's own devil come out of the ground after him, he couldn't have mustered more speed.

He never saw what followed, but his ears testified of something at his heels, rattling through the meadow like a chain manacled to his ankle. The barn drew closer. The edge of the yard loomed just ahead. Almost home. *Run!*

Expectation, hot on his neck. Certain knowledge that some monster would bring him down. Any moment. He'd be done. Join Tanner, Ma, Jessie. His fucking cat.

Nothing touched him.

He'd made it.

Feet slowed, eyes chanced a glance back. Nothing but the cut V of his own trail. And darkness pouring in behind it.

Something grabbed his foot. He screamed and went down in a tangle of legs, splashing face-first in the yard, sputtering, turning, fists bared, ready to fight to the death.

Where is it?

There! A flash of movement. A fallen branch half buried in the grass rocked gently, sending ripples through the foamy lake in which he lay.

He let out a sigh and collapsed back into the water, fighting for breath and soon fighting back laughter. "Idiot." He coughed, still shaking. "Chicken shit. Yellow-assed son of a bitch!" After all these years, a silly story could still make him piss himself. He was too soaked to know if he had. Daddy would be tickled pink.

Stay out of the Glen, his father always said. The Glen was no place to be at night. You can look but don't you dare go in.

So let it be, he thought and pulled his hands out of the mud, looking down at his soaked clothes, at his one bare foot, at the single pink toe pushing through his sock. He wiped his hands on his shirt and laughed some more.

The scream shot out of the Glen and shook the wall of grass at his feet.

The sound was immediate and unfixable, breaking all thought. It was the voice of shattered glass, the dry crack of broken timbers and the angry snarl of a forest fire mingled into a single, drawn-out howl.

Fear held him fixed for only a moment as the sound fused to his brain.

The branch jerked to life again. A mass shifted behind the veil of weeds.

Noah stumbled in a backwards scramble, feet peddling in the icy water until they found purchase. He sprinted for the barn.

Another shriek hit his back halfway home. Then again as his hand reached the door latch. Had he been willing to chance a glance over his shoulder, he was sure he would have seen it. His body had other ideas.

He hurled himself into the barn and threw the door shut,

swinging the block into place and backing away. He fell against the tractor and the scream that came this time was from his own lips.

"Oh Jesus." *That was no mountain lion. No goddamn way was that any animal that belonged here.* Not a cougar, not a raccoon or a bear or a moose or any animal he had ever seen or heard of. He waited for the creature to sound again but it didn't. Only silence outside.

Then the clink of the lighter and a plume of yellow light sent shadows fleeing at his feet. Barely aware of the cigarette in his mouth until the first tang of smoke filled his lungs, he exhaled and waited. The cigarette burned down, followed by another. Three butts littered the floor before he detached himself from the tractor and went in search of the lantern. Pitch black now. Wobbly legs carried him to the tack room, where he found the light. He lit it and checked the other doors, making sure they were shut tight.

The rabbits.

They were there. His two remaining companions were huddled and shaking in a corner of their hutch.

8

GHOST STORIES

- Noah -

Noah was seven when Daddy first told him the story of Tanner Weismann's disappearance.

The earliest version came with no details or embellishments, a simple object lesson meant to keep adventurous little boys out of the Glen after dark. That Tanner had drowned was a detail Ma had supplied, and only after Daddy refused to say it.

"That's a matter of speculation," Daddy said. "Nobody ever found a body."

Ma's fury at her husband's pigheadedness only goaded him into telling more colorful versions of the story, especially when he'd been drinking. But as much as he enjoyed getting under Ma's skin, he was serious about the Glen.

Daddy had few rules. Ma's devotion to iron discipline, as much as his father's general apathy, gave him little reason to get after Noah and Jessie about matters of cleanliness and ordered behavior. But the one rule he was willing to cut a switch for was this: You stay out of the Glen after supper. Period. If Noah asked why, Daddy would say, "So the devil don't eat you. Do as I say."

Noah caught the idea of Tanner's disappearance like a cold. He spent whole afternoons wandering the pear orchard or searching the riverbank for man-sized holes in the ground. He obeyed his father's sacred rule, though. After Daddy finally spilled the full story of Tanner and the river, Noah never had to be called home again. Sunsets often found him trembling but safe on the porch steps, heart thundering from a mad sprint out of the grass. There, he would watch the Glen sink into shadow, his imagination lighting up like a thunderhead.

One night, Daddy was drunk and he and Ma were fighting. Really only Ma was mad. Daddy goaded her while she waged her own slow campaign of hen-pecking. Noah sat at the dining room table and was supposed to be doing his homework, but was too busy watching Daddy's eyes dance. His father would occasionally catch Noah's eye and wink, as if the two of them were sharing a private joke on Ma, who stood at the sink washing dishes. Daddy was always more fun when he was drunk, at least to a six-year-old boy. He was happy, at least, and Noah knew not all men were like that when they drank.

"Why can't I play in the Glen, Daddy?" he asked when Ma had paused in her preaching.

Daddy looked at him, then at Ma's back as she brutalized a skillet. "I ever tell you about your Uncle Tanner?"

Of course he had. Everybody knew about Tanner. He fell into the river when he was fifteen and drowned. It had happened down in the Glen, not far from where the orchard was now, but a long time ago. Before even Daddy was born. Noah remembered because Tanner was a boy too, like him, but older.

Noah nodded.

"Well, I'm going to tell you something you don't know about Tanner," he said.

Ma's shoulders squared.

"You want to hear what really happened?" Daddy leaned close. "Everybody thinks he fell in the Piscatoqua and drowned but he didn't. You know what happened to him?"

Noah watched Daddy without saying a word. Ma heaved a sigh.

"Devil ate him!"

Noah laughed and Daddy poked him under the ribs.

Ma spoke without turning around. "Braden Weismann, you're going to find yourself answering for your idle fairytales someday. You mark my words. You're going to give that boy ideas."

Daddy ignored her, his eyes locked on Noah's, settling in for a good story. "I'm serious," he whispered.

"Did not," Noah said.

"You know how I know? Because we saw the hole he came out of. Devil came right up out of the ground and grabbed him. Then he pulled poor Tanner down under and gobbled him up."

"You saw no such thing, Braden," Ma said. "You weren't even born then. That was just a fool story your daddy told you and now you're going and putting it in that boy's head."

Daddy looked up and raised an eyebrow. "Well, I wasn't there. Technically that's true." He looked shrewdly at Noah. "But my pa never lied to me about nothing, by God. He saw that hole with his own eyes. Looked like a big crawdad hole. Mud all bunched up around it like a beaver dam. Except it was man-sized. And it was deep and black. Couldn't see the bottom. You want to know why the Devil ate your Uncle Tanner, Boy?"

Noah dared not move, terrified Daddy would suddenly sober up, or Ma would swoop in and drag him off to bed.

"Because he wouldn't stay out of the Glen, that's why." Daddy said. "Your Grandpa told me about it. Said he loved to play down there, just like you do. And then one time there was a big flood. Rained for days and days and the river came all the way up into the Glen. When it went down again, Tanner went right back to playing. He'd just stay there all day long. And wouldn't come back for supper. Nobody knew why and he wouldn't tell nobody what he was doing, even though Daddy warned him, told him it still wasn't safe. Tanner wouldn't listen.

"Then one night he didn't come back. Everybody looked for him but they didn't find him. They said he drowned. But my daddy knew better. Want to know why?"

He didn't wait for Noah to answer.

"Because he found something down there. He found that hole in the mud and you know what else he found? He found Tanner's boots not ten feet from where he found that hole. They were just sitting together like he'd taken them off and set them down. I guess the devil doesn't like the taste of boot leather."

Noah grinned but didn't laugh.

"Nobody ever found his body. That's how else Pa knew. Tanner ought to have washed up somewhere. But he didn't."

Ma had had enough. She rounded on them both, spatula in hand, soap bubbles trailing. "Now you quit telling him foolish nonsense and let him go to bed before his soul shrivels. Noah, off you go!"

After Ma had kissed Noah and silenced his protests, she sent him upstairs to bed.

Daddy never said a word about the story after that. Noah asked, but when he was sober, Daddy would say, "He drowned in the river. You stay out of the Glen."

When he wasn't so sober he'd say, "I told you, boy. Devil ate him."

9

MISSION

- Noah -

Bird song greeted Noah as he woke the following morning. He lay awhile, listening to a sound he hadn't heard in days. It should have been a comfort, but the warble of a single robin atop the gable brought home how empty the world had become.

He sat up and kicked over the lantern, swore and picked it up, but the flame was long dead, the tank empty. A stupid waste of kerosene. Last night, the prospect of turning out the lights after the boogieman chase had been less appealing than a skinny-dip in the river, so he'd let it burn.

The thought of monsters and the flash-bang of memories that followed got him moving.

He stripped out of the filthy jeans he'd slept in, threw on a less-filthy pair and pulled a shirt over his head. Sometime over the last several days, face stubble had become a patchy beard. Tomorrow or the day after, he'd take a razor to it, and take a proper bath too. And stop living like such an animal.

Right now, he had a job to do and precious few hours in which to do it. Somewhere in the flood-ravaged wilderness was a lost child, and if she wasn't dead already, she was alone, terrified and in real danger.

Judd McPherson's farm lay some eight miles to the west over the ridge, and was the closest place you could walk to without crossing the river. There, Noah could make a call to the Coos County Sheriff's office and get a search party out here. *Who knows? They might even send a chopper from Burlington or a team with dogs to track her down.* If all went well today, they'd have her found by nightfall. After that, Noah would be free to leave this place for good.

He grabbed spare clothes, stuffing them into a pack. Boots too, since his current pair was a man down, one of them buried in the mud somewhere by the river.

Images of the girl kept stirring in his head. Maybe because he'd dreamed of her last night, and in the dream, she had claws and teeth. Apparently his subconscious had found a face to personify the ravenous flood. And the silence. And the loneliness. And the thing that stalked the Glen, whatever the hell it was.

A sick animal. Had to be. Disease could do terrible things to critters, make them act wrong. The girl faced this danger too, and unlike Noah, she had no place to hide at night. The thought of it gave him a chill. Come what may, he wouldn't leave her to die out here alone.

In the tack room he gathered the rest of his gear: knife, flashlight, spare batteries. He grabbed the machete too, running a thumb lightly over the blade to test its edge, hoping he'd not need it. Too much bushwhacking and he might not be out of the woods by dark. That would be a very bad thing.

He decided to check the phone one last time. If by some chance the service was back on, this whole trip wouldn't be necessary.

On his way out of the tack room he caught sight of the rabbit hutch and stopped dead. How many times had he marched past without noticing it, too focused on his mission to see that one of the doors hung wide open?

He made his way to it and peered inside. The cell stood empty; the little doe was gone, like his two hens the day before.

"Goddammit!" He slammed the door, latched it like he should

have in the first place and worked the flashlight out of the pack to go look for her.

"You're losing it, Noah." *Forgetting the easy things. That's how it starts. Just like it did with Ma.*

He shone the light into the cage to make sure the buck was still there. He was. The single pearl of an eye peered back at him from the corner. Noah turned to make a search, but hadn't taken more than a step when he saw the slash of light crawling across the floor.

"That's not right either."

Somewhere above thinning clouds, a pale sun was rising, illuminating all kinds of missed details. The hair on the back of his neck rose as he tried to make sense of the gap in the main doors. He distinctly remembered closing them last night. But what stole the breath out of him, had him dropping his pack and stumbling forward, was what lay outside.

On wooden legs, Noah made his way to the entrance and looked down, not daring to touch it. Still caked with mud, but erect and resolute, like a lone soldier returned from a war, was his missing boot.

"Hello!"

Noah shouted into vacant air, scanning the Glen. Nothing moved. No voice answered. Shudders racked him like a sickness.

"Pull it together, man," he told himself. "It's just a damn kid."

The only explanation that made any sense was that the girl had found the boot and brought it back. Then she'd opened the doors but was too frightened to come inside.

He shouted once more and pulled the doors shut. They did not move easily. Could a small child pull them apart?

Maybe. Probably. Fear can do that to a person, give them strength they shouldn't otherwise have, which he knew by experience. The more important matter was that she was still alive, which made this mission all the more urgent.

He went to the gun safe, found the 30-30 and loaded it, then took up his pack and set off for the house to try the phone one last time. He wasn't surprised when he put the receiver to his ear and heard fuck-all.

"Assholes!" He slammed it down. There would be hell to pay when this was all over, he'd make sure of that. Sprint could shove next month's bill straight up its south end.

With fresh outrage fueling his steps, he got out of there and set off for the timber. He didn't intend to set eyes on this place for a very long time.

His starch didn't last long. At the north end of the property, beyond the old root cellar, was an access road that would take him out of the valley and up to the McPherson farm. Daddy had cut the path decades ago to get to a gravel bar on the river, which he used to keep the drive maintained. Noah hadn't touched it in two years, but it was relatively clear of underbrush, leaving him a clear channel through the next half mile of forest.

The moment he set foot on the path, he felt it. The stillness, the deadness in the air, the *presence.* Thick trees closed in on him and the air became heavy and jungle-like. He never saw it or heard it, but he knew it was there. Twice he looked over his shoulder, sure he would see something standing in the path.

"I know you're there," he told it, which seemed crazy and stupid. But Noah had lived in these woods too many years not to trust his instincts. He kept the rifle at the ready and continued on.

The access road gave way to a vast meadow, bordered by the river to the north and the ridge to the west. Through a hazy mist stood the distant tree-line where the logging roads threaded their way deep into the hills, steadily zigzagging up the mountain side.

He skirted the meadow, finger resting on the trigger guard, feeling the *presence* behind him the whole time. The shadows shifted, drawing his eyes. Every dark hollow of underbrush hid some unseen menace. These he gave a wide berth.

At last he reached the base of the hill and the mouth of the first logging road that would take him up the mountain to Judd's place. The road was overgrown. Saplings grew in the furrows between the ruts, reducing the trail to a narrow slash and visibility to no more than twenty yards. But it was passable, so he made his way inside.

According to Daddy, these roads were so old you could still find the ruts of mule-drawn carts used before the days of gas-powered chainsaws and heavy trucks. The timber from these hills had kept the old paper mill in Benton running well into Daddy's lifetime, though now most of the roads were abandoned, and the mill had been closed for forty years.

The forest rangers maintained a few roads and horse trails for hunting. In November you'd sometimes run across a party on horseback. The Weismann boys had done their share of hunting here too before Daddy's accident. Noah had loved running these hills for deer and turkey and fishing the creeks for brookies. Not so much once Daddy was dead, when money got tight and hunting, in or out of season, had become a necessity.

Only when Noah reached the first major switchback did he notice the tension in the air had eased. He stopped to make sure his senses were telling him the truth. The sky above the canopy had brightened a little and a few birds sang. There, on the trunks of those hickory trees, came the burry chatter of nuthatches. His shoulders settled; his chest loosened. Whatever had been following him was gone.

The day improved as he continued climbing and the valley fell farther and farther away. The hum of insects colored the air, further lightening his mood. Though deadfalls blocked his path and rhododendrons often choked the trail, he crawled over or hacked through without losing much time. The rifle was now slung over a shoulder.

I might actually get out of here alive.

Optimism took a hit when, late in the morning, he found the steep horse trail that would take him over the ridge. While the road continued on, winding easily across the hillside, the trail corkscrewed up the mountain at a miserable angle. Another two miles of narrow, rock-strewn switchbacks, steep grades, and deep crevices lay before him.

This is where it gets hard. He took a pull from his nearly empty canteen and got climbing. He moved steadily at first, enduring his burning thighs and aching lungs with the resilience of a soldier on the eve of victory. But a solid decade of self-abuse had taken a toll. Soon he was hacking and wheezing like a hag, pulling himself up by saplings or leaning on stone crags.

"Up you go, Hoss." He reminded himself of what waited in the dark, that things worse than pain may find him on this hill come nightfall. Up he went, battling on, until at last his lungs shut down and he collapsed in a coughing fit that brought up phlegm thick as tar.

Jesus, it never used to be this hard. He scowled up at the hill, hating it, cursing it for standing between himself and escape when he was so damned close.

He sat on a rock and smoked until his chest and muscles quieted down. Then he finished off the water and pressed on, resting every few feet. He nearly cried for joy when the trail broke over the crest to a familiar road that led to Judd's farm. He'd made it. Another two hundred yards at most. The walk would be easy.

But no sooner had he stepped onto the road when his feet faltered and he found himself tugging at the rifle strap. The silence swelled again like a bad infection, smothering all sound as it went. The birds shut up. The last few cicadas fell silent.

Just timing? Maybe it was just him, too exhausted now to prevent a keyed-up imagination from telling stories again. But with each step down the path he grew more certain it was not just in his head. Scanning the thinning undergrowth, heart pounding, he told himself that Judd's farm was right around the corner and any moment now, the man's dog would start barking.

The trail curved and disappeared behind a stand of birch trees, their white trunks like skeletons. As Noah moved through them, the canopy thinned and let in more light to cast shadows. Then he saw it.

He froze, tightening his grip on the rifle, stopping short of taking aim. The thing in the road didn't move. Fifty yards ahead, black under the shadow of a lone oak, it crouched low and tight to the ground, waiting.

He took a tentative step forward and when it still didn't move, he made his way toward it. An animal all right. But dead. He could see the flies.

The large coyote stared up with glassy eyes, the corpse no more than a day old. Noah kneeled, grimacing as his knees cracked. The animal looked healthy, besides the obvious – coat thick and shiny, no sign of mange or rabies, and no visible injuries. Young, too, no grey in the muzzle.

He reached out and stroked it, seeing Riley all over again, probing the legs, the hips and joints. All fine. Some fast-acting disease at work here, something so quick and lethal you were dead before you even looked sick.

That might explain the thing in the Glen. Its voice shattered by some virus or water-borne bacteria.

Noah brushed the hair at the nape of the neck. It fell away in clumps, leaving a circle of white flesh the size of his palm. In the center of the bare skin was a small wound, red and inflamed, like a large insect bite. The same thing that had killed his cat had also killed this coyote. And was probably killing everything else too. An insect, a mosquito maybe, was a carrier for some new infection.

Plague.

The word hit him like a wave of nausea. He thought of the girl, her strange behavior and her odd appearance. She was infected, he realized. If she wasn't dead already, she soon would be.

He stood, unable to endure the silence any longer, and made his way quickly to Judd McPherson's farm.

Noah stood at the edge of the property, gazing at the house. Everything was wrong. Mollie, Judd's border collie, should have come bounding up the trail half a mile ago, wagging her tail and barking her head off. There were no chickens in the yard. No rooster crowed. Even the sparrows that usually swarmed this place were absent. The farm was a tomb.

"Judd?" he called, his voice echoing across the empty lot. He moved forward, gripping the rifle, leaving the shelter of the trees and feeling as though he were stepping into a still picture. The house was dark, no light or movement from the windows. Not a single sign of life.

"Judd!"

No answer.

This wasn't unexpected. Judd McPherson was well into his nineties and near stone deaf. The TV should have been blaring. He reached the screen door and peered into an empty kitchen. A few dishes cluttered the sink. A half-finished sandwich and an abandoned coffee cup sat on the table. He glanced at the garage and utility sheds and saw Judd's pickup was parked there.

Not good.

"Hello, Judd? Anybody home?" Noah opened the screen door and stuck his head inside. No sound. No lights anywhere. He sniffed the air. No smell of rot, at least. If Judd had died, he'd done it recently. There were the stairs leading to the old man's bedroom.

Noah shuddered. No way. Not yet.

He stepped out and checked the sheds. The garage was a wreck, tools and engine parts scattered everywhere, oil staining the dirt floor. Battery chargers, defunct welding boxes, and other crap were stacked crookedly in every corner. A chipper-shredder and garden tiller were abandoned in the yard next to a rusting Ford pickup that hadn't turned over in a decade. The place would have made Daddy scream.

A pair of spectacles lay on the work bench. He picked them up and looked at them. Bifocals. He swore, put them back down and moved on, wanting to get the hell out of there. He thought about taking Judd's truck and driving to town. This side of the pass, he wouldn't have to cross the river. But he wouldn't do that until he made sure the old man wasn't lying dead out here somewhere.

But as his search continued, he grew more certain that simply finding a body would be a blessing. Something had happened here. The chicken coop was empty. No sign of the army of cats the man fed at the barn, or the half a billion sparrows. Noah couldn't think of a single scenario that would explain what he was seeing.

Except one. The dead coyote, Riley. The girl in the Glen.

An outbreak was spreading through the valley, though whether it had started here and was working its way out, or the reverse, he didn't know. Probably the flood had brought it, and some biting insect had spread it.

Reluctantly he turned back to the house. Time to make a phone call. Send for the police and get the hell out of here. Noah hoped to God he himself wasn't sick. But he hadn't been bitten yet, had he?

Something moved.

He turned so fast he almost missed it, rifle up, finger on the hammer in time to see the shadow slip behind the house.

"Judd?" He crept forward, rifle leading, and slipped along the wall. There. A soft scraping sound, like metal on metal, just around the corner. Or the rasp of insect wings. A very large insect. His back against the wall, he peered around the corner.

A wheelbarrow stood in the empty yard. Nothing else. Nothing moved. Except something lay in the wheelbarrow, black and shiny, like the carapace of a huge beetle.

A crunch of grass, a breathy hiss. Behind him.

Noah turned, eyes wide, stepping back, shouldering the gun, finger on the trigger, as the scream hit him in the face.

10

JUDD MCPHERSON

- Noah -

Time stopped. For a frozen instant, two lives teetered on a scale, a rifle barrel feet from its target. For days after he would remember fine details in the tiny window of his vision and wonder what kept him from pulling the trigger. Soon enough he realized that the scream was his own and that the creature in front of him was a human being.

"Jesus Christ!" Noah lowered the rifle and sagged against the house. "Judd, goddamn it. I nearly killed you."

Judd McPherson leaned on a shovel, his craggy, bearded face serene, as if having a rifle pointed at his head was a common greeting. Not serene, Noah would later decide. *Indifferent.*

"Well, I'm real glad you didn't, son," the old man said. "Would have made a bad day for both of us, I think."

Judd raised the shovel and hobbled past him, making his way around the corner without a word or a backward glance. Noah stared after him, slung the rifle over his shoulder, and followed until Judd reached the wheelbarrow.

"Judd?"

The man set the shovel inside the bucket, hoisted the load with a grunt and wheeled it toward a narrow finger of grass that stretched into the trees. The black object in the wheelbarrow was a trash bag, its red ties dangling over the bucket.

"Where's Mollie?" Noah stepped in beside him, knowing the answer, catching he faint whiff of death even through the plastic.

The older man nodded at the bag.

"What happened?"

Judd shook his head. "Don't exactly know. Found her this morning. Down there just off the timber line." He gestured in the direction Noah had come from minutes ago.

"She didn't come home two nights ago, so I started looking for her. Finally found her yonder."

Noah nodded. "I'm sorry."

They continued on another twenty yards to a cove surrounded by forest where a large locust tree spread its branches over the lawn. A patch of bare earth lay between two gnarled roots, at the edge of which was a stump turned on its end and carved into a crude bench. Next to the stump was a ring of grey ash in the soil. Judd put down his burden and stared at the ground, pulling a pipe from his breast pocket.

"Do you have any idea what happened?" Noah pressed, leaning the gun against the tree.

The old man didn't answer, tottering unsteadily as he worried the pipe between his teeth. Noah studied Judd's bent frame and saw there wasn't much left of him beneath the tattered overalls and shaggy, tobacco-stained beard. He'd lost weight, and was filthier than usual, a strong, terminal odor wafting off him like heat. Old Judd was never particular about hygiene, but this looked like something more.

At last Judd spoke. "Something got to her, that's all I know."

"She get sick?"

The older man's face hardened, irritated by the question. He shrugged. "Maybe. She was old like me. Her time, I guess."

"Well, I'm real sorry, Judd."

"So am I," he said, and moved to pick up the shovel.

Noah got to it first.

"You didn't come all the way up here just to bury my damn dog." Judd reached out for the shovel but Noah pulled away.

"I'm not going to stand here and watch you do it yourself either," Noah said. "Now where do you want her buried?"

Judd shuffled over to a spot several paces from the tree but within sight of the makeshift bench. "Here will do."

Noah stepped in and shoved the blade into the rain-softened earth, praying he wouldn't be chopping through roots for the next two hours.

Judd eyed Noah hard as he worked, chewing the stem of his pipe.

"Look, you can shift me in a bit if you want," Noah said.

At last the old man went to the stump and lowered himself with a groan. A swollen knee and length of shin poked through a long tear in his pant leg, the flesh white as exposed bone.

After some minutes Judd asked, "What brings you up here? You walk all this way?"

Noah wiped the sweat out of his eyes. "Came to use your telephone, actually. I spotted a little girl wandering around the meadow last night. No idea where she came from. I tried to talk to her, but she took off like a shot cat and now I can't find her. My phone's out and the bridge is under water so you're my only option."

Judd grunted. Noah paused to read the man's expression, but couldn't. Judd wasn't acting like Judd at all. Normally he was so happy for company you couldn't shut him up. His face would be split in a grin, all gums and few gnarled teeth, talking to his dog as much as to you. But today dragging a sentence out of him was like pumping water out of bedrock.

The man smacked the back of his pipe and sent ash spilling into the grey ring beside the stump. He reached into a pocket for a bag of tobacco, packed the pipe, then patted his pockets.

Noah slipped the lighter from his own pocket and handed it to him.

"Thanks," Judd said. With shaking hands, he snapped the cap

and held the flame to the bowl. When done, he studied the lighter, thumbing the three letters, B.E.W, embossed in the casing.

"This your pa's, huh?" Judd said, handing it back. Noah lit his own cigarette and took up the shovel again. "How long's he been gone now?"

Noah hacked at a small root in the bottom of the growing hole. "A long time." He could have told him the years, months, and days.

Judd gazed thoughtfully through a haze of smoke. "God, but time gets away from you. Not for you so much, I expect."

Noah dug harder, ignoring the bitching in his shoulders and back.

"He was a good man, your pa. Shame what happened."

Noah shrugged. "Like I said, it was a long time ago. So, about that girl? You suppose I could use your phone?"

"Nope," the old man said, smoke leaking from his mouth and nostrils. "Afraid you can't."

Noah turned, starting to get annoyed himself.

Judd gave him a flat smile. "My phone's out too," he said. "Power, phone, whole shooting match."

Noah looked at the man as if waiting for him to finish a joke. When the punchline didn't come he said, "Well then, can I trouble you for a ride to town?"

"You can trouble me all you want. But I'm stuck here same as you."

Noah jammed the shovel into the mud. "Why?" He was tired, his legs barking at him for the forced march to this godforsaken hovel, and now Judd was playing games with him. He had no time for this.

Before Noah could get really good and pissed, Judd said, "I'll show you." The older man put his hands on his knees and rose. "Come on." He motioned for Noah to follow.

Noah glanced at the sack in the wheelbarrow.

"She ain't going nowhere, son. Come on with me. You need to see this."

Judd made his way toward the house. Noah matched his pace, keeping a lid on the questions, afraid the man might go into some kind of fit. He reminded Noah of one of those pictures of concentration camp victims. Not the body so much as the eyes. The shell-shocked hopelessness in them. Judd McPherson had gone downhill in the weeks since Noah had last seen him.

They passed the house and ended up at the pickup outside the garage. Judd opened the driver's side door, popped the hood, and came around to the front. He felt for the lever and lifted it with an effort. Noah moved in to help.

He nearly dropped the hood when he saw the engine.

"Holy shit," he murmured, the hood hovering halfway up. Judd relieved him of the burden, propped the hood with the rod, and stepped back to give Noah room to stare at the engine well.

"What the hell is this?" he said, only vaguely aware of the older man standing over his shoulder, not hearing his reply. He reached into the cavity where the engine should have been to finger the substance that covered it.

Judd caught his wrist. "I wouldn't."

"What is it?"

The old man shrugged. "I don't know," he said. "But I sure as hell wouldn't touch it."

It looked vaguely like spider silk: clear, fibrous, and gleaming, as if still wet. But the similarity to anything arachnid ended there. Rope-like cords stretched out of a white mass over the engine block, splitting into multiple branches and tying into the firewall like nerve cords. Surrounding everything were millions of tiny strands shooting off the block. They merged into a thick, fibrous membrane that cocooned the engine. Of the entire motor well, only the upper portion of the radiator was still visible. Everything else, including the manifold and air filter, was completely encased. A few iridescent cords clung to the hood, despite stretching several feet. There was a strong odor of acetone and rotten fruit.

Noah stooped and looked under the truck. The underside looked like it had sprung white roots and tethered itself to the ground. He grabbed a stick and poked at it. There was a crackle as the threads pulled apart but the main mass grabbed the stick and held on, the membrane solid as concrete.

"Mother of Christ," he said.

Judd grunted. "Tried to start it two days ago. Wouldn't even click. Opened the hood and saw this. It was a whole lot harder to pry open the first time."

"I'll bet," Noah muttered. "You think this was some kind of insect?

Judd shook his head. Noah pulled on the stick and was amazed by how much force it took to get it out. He stared at the wad of silver-white, like a crude cotton swab, and tossed it away.

"This ain't no damn bug, boy," Judd said.

Noah turned to Judd. "How do you know that?"

"Found the same thing in the tractor. Battery is just covered with it. Got the ATV too. Even got the goddamned lawn tractor."

He paused, seeming to watch Noah to make sure he understood, and added, "When you get home today, Noah, do me a favor. Check your phone box on the house."

"Why?" he said, feeling a twist in his guts.

"Because that stuff's why my phone don't work." Judd headed back toward his dog and the half-dug grave, leaving Noah to stare at the engine well as if it might start talking and give him the answers Judd couldn't. Or wouldn't. He slammed the hood shut and followed.

"Judd, what's going on here?"

The man didn't look at him. "You need to get on home, boy." he said. "Long trip back to your place."

Noah shook his head. "I can't do that. I told you, there's a missing girl out there. One way or another, I got to help her. I'll walk to town if I have to."

The man pulled the pipe out of his mouth and spat. "You forget about that girl and look out for yourself." He pointed the stem at him. "Stay the hell away from her, you understand? Now get home and get yourself safe."

"Safe from what, Judd? What the hell's gotten into you?"

Judd waved a hand. "Forget it," he said. "Forget it and go home."

Noah caught the man's shoulder.

"Look," the old man said, "If you're set on getting to town, you go now. But it's a fifteen-mile trip from here and there ain't but one house on the way. So you best be leaving if you're going to get there by dark."

A distant rumble of thunder turned their two faces upward and shook lose a spatter of rain from the darkening sky.

"Goddamn this weather," Noah said. "We're all going to drown if this shit doesn't quit."

"Well you better get moving," Judd said, "Before it decides to go again."

"Flood will come whether or not I help you bury your dog," Noah said. "Now come on and quit arguing with me."

Drizzle hissed through the trees. Noah hurried to finish. When the hole was dug, Judd helped him maneuver the bag into it.

"You know what I think?" Noah said as he started filling in the grave. "I think it's some sort of sickness. A virus or something."

Judd didn't say anything.

"It killed my cat. I found a coyote on the way up here. Now Mollie. Last night something chased me out of the Glen."

Judd looked up, eyes hard. "Did you see it?"

Noah shook his head. "It was in the grass so I never did get a look at it. Scared the hell out of me though. Made some kind of noise. Nothing you'd hear out of healthy animal, I know that."

Judd watched him, chewing sullenly on his pipe.

"Police need to know about that too," Noah added. "If they don't already. I just hope to God it isn't spreading to people." He used the flat of the shovel to pat down the grave. "I tell you what, Judd. If it makes you feel better, why don't I just stay here tonight? Set off early tomorrow morning."

The old man shook his head. "No, you don't want to stay here. You need to get on home. Forget town and go before it gets dark on you."

Noah set the shovel against the tree. "Why? What the hell do you know that I don't? Have you seen something?"

The man glared at Noah as if he were too thick to see simple common sense. He took the pipe from his mouth as if he were about to say something, but simply lowered his gaze and mumbled something Noah couldn't catch.

Another rumble of thunder, more insistent than before.

Noah's patience broke. "Judd, I swear to God." He let the shovel fall and rounded on him. "If you had any idea what I've been through in the last six days you wouldn't be sitting there talking to me like I'm some kind of idiot. Now you'd better open your gob and start talking, because if you don't, I'm going to open up that damn hole and throw you in it too, you understand? You know something. What the hell is it?"

Judd's eyes were hot with outrage, his spine stiff. If the man had teeth he'd have broken his pipe. For a moment Noah thought he would call his bluff and storm off, but at last the man's shoulders slumped. He barked a laugh and for an instant the old Judd returned.

"Stubborn little bastard," he said. "As bad as your pa ever was. You'll think I'm crazy."

"Little too late for that."

He really did laugh then. His shoulders shook. But after a few revolutions his face twisted into something more like a sob. "Killed my goddamn dog." He looked up, eyes red and leaking, pleading. "Why'd they have to go and kill my dog?"

"Who killed your dog?" Noah said.

Judd pulled out a filthy handkerchief and mopped at his eyes. "Same thing killed your cat. Same thing'll kill both of us before the end. You should have been gone from here an hour ago. Should have got out of the valley when you had the chance."

"What, Judd? What the hell are you afraid of?"

"Killed your Uncle Tanner, too," he said. "You know that?"

Noah stared, words caught in his throat, suddenly unable to breathe. He stepped closer, trying to gauge just how insane the man really was, if anything he said could be believed.

"Your pa surely told you."

"He drowned in the river. A long time ago. Dad wasn't even there."

"Who do you think told him the story?"

Noah's turn to laugh. He couldn't help it; it rattled out of him like a scream. "That's ridiculous. How can you possibly--?"

"Because I was there, goddammit!" Face hard again, eyes like live coals, no longer tired or crazy. "That flood came in '38, same as this. And those screams you hear? They came soon after. Animals disappeared. Then people. It's happening all over again."

Noah took a knee and leveled with him. "Have you seen it?"

Judd's eyes fell. "No, I never seen it. I just seen what it does to people."

"Which is?"

"Go home, boy." It came out in a growl, like the beginnings of a cough. He did cough, clearing his throat and spitting. "It's going to get dark early," he said and then put his hands on his knees and stood. "You get on home. Then you get inside and keep the door locked at night. Keep that gun close. You got it?"

"What about you? You're not safe either."

Another angry smile. "Oh, I'm safe enough. I can get indoors and batten down before sundown. Besides, I'm an old man. I don't have anything to worry about."

Noah frowned. "What does that mean?"

Judd grimaced, coughing again, long and deep and ugly. "Never mind. Just take your rifle and go."

11

THE INVADER

- Noah -

The sky rumbled as Noah made his way down the mountain. The air thickened to a murky grey, shrouding the forest in early twilight. He tried to move quickly, picking his way down the steep trail with no pause for rest. But the descent proved treacherous, forcing him to slow his pace.

"Damnit!" His foot slipped on a mud-coated stone in the path. He grabbed a tree to keep from going ass over toes and almost dropped the rifle.

Time had gotten away from him and it was Judd's fault.

When Noah had left that morning, he hadn't counted on having to bury the man's dog. Nor on getting the tour of the McPherson version of Ripley's Believe It or Not. He wouldn't have minded any of this had Judd not turned soft in the head.

Instead of hoofing it on to town like he should have, Noah had stuck around trying to get answers out of the old rip only to find that his mind was gone. The man had even glommed onto Daddy's old Tanner Weismann story, for Christ's sake.

But that cob-webbed engine was no product of dementia. Neither were the dead animals or the sick thing in the Glen. There was some truth to what Judd said. Mixed up though he might have been, the man was right about one thing. Something rotten festered in these hills; something unnatural. Dangerous. And despite what Noah told himself, Judd's words had worked themselves into him like a thorn in the flesh.

Occasional fits of rain and drizzle kept him damp and caused his thighs to chafe. But the storm held off. No presence hounded him this time, no aura of resistance. It was as if the forest wanted him back. He kept the rifle at the ready every step.

By the time Noah reached the farm, the Glen was already settling into dusk. He stood at the end of the access road, listening to the eerie silence that smothered the place, studying the vicious edge of meadow slicing across the yard. The house, the cellar, even the barn were still and lifeless corpses, as if they too had caught the disease and were rotting away. Never in his life had home felt so unwelcoming.

He forced himself toward the house. The utility pole loomed over the kitchen. The dead eye of the yard light stared blindly down at the junction box around the corner.

Check your phone box, Judd had said. The words didn't sound so ridiculous now. The rifle needed oiling, the receiver and barrel rain-spotted, which would soon turn to rust. But that would wait.

Setting the gun aside, he kneeled next to the junction box and pulled the flashlight from his pack. Deep breath. Shaking hands reached out, slid around the housing. Fingers found the catches and pulled, straining to pry them loose. They didn't budge.

"Shit." The clips were corroded.

No time for this. Noah stood, considered giving up on the whole stupid enterprise. What if Judd's crazy had infected him too? He headed for the barn to get a screwdriver.

Instant relief inside, the familiar smells gave him the first normal moment since leaving that morning. Moving through the darkness here was second nature. Feeling past the machines and vehicles, he made his way to the work bench before bothering with the flashlight.

He snapped it on. Something moved behind him, like a whispered breath across the back of his neck. He spun and strafed the floorboards with the flashlight. Shadows fled.

Nothing else moved. No sound but his own ragged breathing.

A form detached itself from the blackness, vanishing again in a blur of motion. He slammed the rifle to his shoulder and swung after it, flashlight clamped to the stock. A skitter of claws across the floorboards, too fast to catch. A humped back slipped around the corner and disappeared into the tack room. There was a thump. A clash of enlivened metal. Then silence.

Noah pierced the doorway with light, face pressed to the rifle stock, but the angle was too sharp to see inside. Slow steps, pressing his back against the truck, sliding closer, bringing more of the room into view. A row of wrenches hung motionless. But as the light slid farther inside, they woke up, first trembling, then swaying, then swinging.

Clink - clink - clink.

The room shrank. Shadows slid away. No place left to hide now. His hands shook as he thumbed the hammer back, ready to blow a hole into hell. The last refuge of the room vanished.

The room exploded.

A shriek blasted Noah's face and sent steel flying like shrapnel. The creature tore across the bench and slammed into the wall, sending more objects clattering to the floor. Noah bore down and caught it in his sights. Two luminous eyes shone like green moons as a hiss spilled from sharp, glistening teeth.

Noah sighed and lowered the gun. "Samson, you scared the shit out of me!"

Laugher threatened to bubble into hysteria. He raised the light and studied the small cat coiled in the corner. "Hey," he said, voice soft, taking a slow step forward. "Hey, buddy. It's me."

Samson growled, ears flattened.

"Shhh. Easy." Noah extended a cautious hand. "It's just me. Samson?"

The animal relaxed, a slight loosening of the spine.

"Damn, I'm glad to see you, fella. I thought you were a goner. You okay?"

A thought stopped him short. *What if he's sick?* He looked the cat over, peering at the eyes, the little black nose, mouth and coat. No sign of disease. Other than being scared witless. Noah reached out, palm down. The cat's ears went flat again.

"Hey," Noah said. "Relax."

Samson struck like lightning, ripping trails of fire through his flesh and wrenching a scream out of him. He snatched his hand back as the cat shot out of the tack room, claws scrabbling across the floor.

Noah pried the cover off the junction box, jamming the screwdriver into the housing and wrenching it loose without caring if it broke. The cover crackled like Velcro as it separated from the base. His mouth went dry when the insides came into view, or at least what should have been insides. Thousands of silver fibers clung to everything, anchoring to a thick mass where the wire junction used to be. Noah stared at a miniature version of the bug shit orgy he'd seen under the hood of Judd's truck.

Rain fell in icy sheets, soaking him through and chilling him to the bone as he stabbed at the mess in the junction box. Lightning flashed and thunder rumbled like distant bombshells.

Noah wiped at his face to keep his eyes clear. The first layer was soft as cotton candy and peeled away easily. But the deeper he dug, the harder the substance became. It held to its host like cancer in the brain. His surgery had removed most of it, which now lay in a sticky ball at his feet. The rest held tenaciously to the crevices, covering the essential parts, forcing him to chip and scrape at it with the screwdriver.

Despite his efforts not to touch it, tiny splinters flecked his hands. Invisible fibers crawled up his wrists and arms. Judd's warning had been a good one because his skin tingled and burned.

Nearly dark now. He needed the flashlight, which, of course, he'd left in the barn. No time for that now. Just a few more minutes. Nervous glances over his shoulder, rifle in easy reach. At last the wires appeared, the goo peeling away like flakes of dead skin. Fear turned to panic when he saw that the cables were melted, the circuits blackened and burned through.

"Shit, oh shit!" The words were lost in the roar of rain. Nothing to see but murky shapes and gloom.

What now, Noah?

He needed to get out of here. Now. The river had gone down a lot since yesterday, surely. Maybe the bridge was open. Maybe he could just drive out of here. Just maybe, for once, God would actually take pity on him instead of grinding him down.

You owe me this, you son of a bitch. After all you've put me through.

Noah grabbed the gun and marched through darkness and stinging rain, toward the barn where the truck waited, anger chasing back fear. For a moment he felt strong again, in control of his own destiny, ready to overcome whatever heaven threw at him. After all the failures today, he was still breathing, still upright, still willing to try. Unlike Judd who seemed ready to roll over and die.

Not me. I will not sit here on my ass and --

It burst out of the grass. Bone-white and low-slung, bigger than any cat. It tore a hole through the meadow and streaked across his peripheral vision like lightning. An electric scream followed like a shockwave, throwing his legs into motion before eyes could turn to look.

He ran, crossed the distance to the barn, kicked open the side door and threw himself inside. The scream smacked the door behind him as he shoved the bolt into place, backing up and raising the rifle.

The creature screamed again, just beyond the door, close enough to hear its breath hit the wall. Dark motion slid across the slats and it took every ounce of self-control not to shoot through the wall. The shadow crawled along the barn's flank, grazing the boards. Toward the main doors. They were open.

Noah got there first, grabbing the braces and yanking them shut. *Think!* A chain lay on the floor outside the tack room. He grabbed it, rattled it across the boards and through the handles, wedging it tight just as the hiss reached the seam. He fell back, took aim.

"Sick coyote my ass."

A throaty death-rattle issued from a large chest cavity beyond the door. And there was that sick-sweet smell of alcohol and fruit again, enveloping him like noxious gas.

It can't get in here. It can't. He said it over and over again like a prayer, pressing the butt of the 30-30 to his shoulder and trying to talk his finger into easing up.

The doors shifted. The chain rattled against the brackets as it went taut, cracking a fissure of pale light between the doors.

BOOM!

A plume of fire seared his vision. The explosion was huge in the closed space. But he had no trouble hearing the outraged shriek as it rose and faded, its owner fleeing into the night. Acrid gunpowder replaced the stink of rot. The scream rose once more, far out in the Glen, protracted, angry.

"Oh..." He expelled pent-up air and lowered the rifle, relieving muscles he didn't realize were cramping. "Holy shit. What the hell are you?"'

That pale monster had come straight for him. It had chased him to the barn and then tried to open the doors. Sick animals don't do that. Sick animals don't spray cobwebs into trucks and phone boxes. The smell removed all doubt that this was same abortion responsible for Judd's truck.

Truck.

"My God!" The revelation struck with actual force and for a moment Noah couldn't breathe. The truck hadn't been started in days. He turned and groped for the hood, finding it, worked his way to the cab and popped the latch.

The thing had already been inside the barn already. *There's your missing chickens, Noah. Rabbit too.* The dead animals? Riley? Mollie? What could it do to him?

Desperate fingers sought the catch under the hood, expecting at any moment to feel the tickle of acid and fibers on his fingers. The hood rose with a groan until the spring caught and held. No resistance. No fresh burning of his skin. Bent over the engine, palms outstretched, he felt only metal, the hollow disk of the filter cover, the solid cool of the manifold.

"Thank you, sweet Christ." The engine was clean. Noah slumped against the truck's grill and fought a wave of nausea, talking himself out of vomiting. *Still okay. Still alive. It's okay.* The barn was locked up tight. The creature was gone, with an object lesson in the risks of fucking with a fully armed member of the planet's dominant species, hopefully bleeding out from a hole in its guts. Tomorrow he could get out of here. *Tomorrow.* In the daylight.

He closed the hood and made his way to the loft, exhaustion heavy enough to buckle his knees. As a precaution, he pulled the board out of the sky light and let it slam shut, plunging himself into darkness. He fell onto his cot, ignoring the wet, and was asleep almost instantly.

12

SECURITY BREACH

- Noah -

He dreamed of bad spirits with quiet hunger watching him from the shadows, of spiders creeping out of holes and leaving slime trails on their way into the barn. He dreamed of pale monsters with swollen bellies that came to drag him into the earth and devour him. Of dead little girls with black eyes crawling from the bloated river.

He saw the emaciated corpse of his mother as she screamed his name and thrashed in the bed at the top of the stairs, the smell of decay oozing from beneath the sheet that covered her.

"Noah, help me!" Her cracked voice reached across the years to strangle his heart.

"I see him! Noah, I can *see* him! He's here, he's here. Noooaaaah!" Screams rising to gale force, then collapsing to a broken moan. "Let me out! Let me out of here! Please! Let me out!"

Noah woke to cold air and flecks of rain on his face. The pale eye of the skylight peered down at him as the ghosts of dreams slid away. But his heart hammered; his insides churned as if the nightmare wasn't over.

He lay very still, not breathing, trying to understand why everything felt so wrong. The open flap letting in the night was trying to tell him something, but his sleep-drugged head was slow to catch it.

I didn't leave that open.

Something moved in the darkness below the loft. A creak of wood, the soft hiss of flesh sliding across the floor. This was no cat.

He reached for the cold steel of the rifle at his side and found only the empty canvas of his cot. His blood turned to ice; frantic hands groped in vain. The rifle was gone.

The door of the rabbit hutch rattled. A sharp squeal from the animal inside as Noah blindly swept his hands across the floor boards beneath the cot.

Gone. The rifle, the flashlight, gone.

Another muffled cry from Mork, his last rabbit, as if it were being stuffed into a heavy sack before the sound was cut short with a crunch.

Jesus! He plunged a shaking hand into the pocket of his jeans for the lighter. Clumsy fingers flipped the cap with a burst of sparks before a wobbly light filled the loft platform.

Everything went quiet.

He saw it. A dull gleam against the wall. Noah scrambled out of the cot, snatched up the flashlight and turned it on with a clink that sounded like a gunshot. Light hit the rafters, enlivening a swirl of dust motes and hard shadows. He strafed the corners of the loft.

Where was the goddamned rifle?

There was an angry hiss from beneath the loft. It spun him like a turnstile. He stabbed the light downward, at the maw of the hay room, but before the beam touched the opening, a scream filed the barn.

It was a fire set loose. A dry crackle of timbers and a shriek of warping metal tore through his senses and nearly shook the light from his hands.

A blur of white shot across the floor, the rapid patter of clawed feet marking its progress between the truck and the wall. He sent the beam slicing after, but it was too fast. No sooner would he corner the creature when it would bolt, shrieking and sending tools clattering.

A kerosene lamp shattered on the floor. The main doors boomed as if struck by a battering ram, chain rattling. Then it careened off the truck and came right for him, scrabbling toward the loft and disappearing under his feet. There, it went silent.

Noah aimed the light between the cracks of the boards, straining to see movement on the ground.

"Where are you, you son of a bitch?"

He edged to the lip of the platform and peered over, angling the beam under the loft, but found only blank floor. A stack of pallets sat against the wall next to the freezer. It must be crouching there. Noah leaned, but the light couldn't reach without him spilling off the loft.

Skylight. He could reach it. Maybe he could get out through there.

What then, Geronimo? Swan dive into the river and swim away?

Without the gun he was a sitting duck. A caged rabbit.

"Shit." He got down on his belly and scooted over the edge, arm extended, until the light touched the foot of the nearest pallet, his free hand hooked between the planks to keep him from falling.

Stupid. This is a bad idea.

The thought grew louder as the last shadow disappeared, revealing empty pallets and a rusty ice box.

The creature was gone.

A telltale scrape of wood under claws, not on the floor. God no, not below him. Above him.

His terror gave way to a calm certainty that he was going to die. No way could he get off the floor in time.

The thing was climbing the wall.

His light slid up the rafters, moving of its own volition. Noah pulled himself into a crouch, legs like coiled springs.

A dark shadow loomed over him. A scream exploded and Noah dove. Too late. A block of iron slammed into him, driving the wind out of him and sending him tumbling toward the edge. He caught himself, fingers digging in just in time as the thing hurdled over the top of him and crashed to the floor with an angry howl.

He pulled himself up, groping for the light which spun just beyond his fingertips.

A splintering crack and the screech of hinges shook the loft as the creature hit the side door. A final scream raked the outside wall and shrank into the night, leaving Noah prone and gasping, spread-eagle on the floor. The barn fell silent again, save for a mournful groan of the shattered door. The thing was gone.

Noah glanced at the spot where the door used to be, just to make sure it was empty before limping to the truck, ignoring the pain in his hip.

He threw open the door, climbed in and held his breath as he turned the key. After a brief struggle the engine roared to life and headlights flooded the main doors. With cry of jubilation, he leapt out and unwound the chain, tossed it aside and heaved the panels apart, not watching the light crawl into the murky drive.

Back in the truck he revved the engine, lurched out of the barn, and slalomed across the mud-slick drive to the road that led to the river. *Please, God, let the bridge be open.*

He pushed the truck through a warzone of debris on instinct and luck. The road was as unfamiliar as the surface of Mars, and when it turned south toward the bridge, he barely recognized where he was.

Moving water crept into the truck's beams.

"No..."

How could the flood be so high? After all this time? This was crazy. A waste of time and gas. But no way was he spending another night in that place.

Headlamps slashed through darkness and hit the wreckage of the flood's fury. Debris grew denser and several times he swerved to miss chunks of driftwood. At last the rusty gleam of the bridge appeared, followed by the river itself. The livid surface crawled through crisscross bands of iron, its massive body stretched wide, swallowing up road beyond each end of the bridge.

Noah slammed on the brakes. The truck skidded to a sideways stop mere feet from the torrent's edge.

He pounded the steering wheel and screamed, staring at the distant bridge in a mix of rage and despair, hating the water, hating the rain and the Glen and God and all things that had conspired against him so cruelly. This single, useless little man at the ass-end of the universe. What possible reason could there be for this?

But he knew the answer.

Reckoning.

The chaos roared even over the growl of the engine. The bridge beams shook with it. The bridge wouldn't be open for days, maybe even a week. And it might as well be forever.

"The fuck I'm not." He jammed the transmission into reverse and spun the tires.

There was one thing to do, come first light. He couldn't drive out, so he'd walk out, by God. Hike back out to Judd's - and piss on that old man - then take the road fifteen miles to town.

Getting through the night might not be so simple. Couldn't stay in the barn. No, the bug from hell was alive and kicking and not even a thirty-caliber bazooka blast to the face had talked it into leaving the country. Twice it had breached the barn now. No, more than that. It had taken the chickens too.

Stay in the truck? Not a bad idea. Lock the doors. Probably wake up in the night to find that pale fucker staring in at him. No way in hell. It was probably smart enough to bust through the window with a hammer. It had taken the rifle, plucked it right out from beside him where it lay on the cot.

The thought was like the river churning over the bridge. How could it be that smart, smart enough to know what a gun was, and smart enough to find a way inside?

Why hadn't it killed him then and there? After it had just chased him into the barn?

Maybe this thing was taking its time. Maybe Noah was one more rabbit in a cage and his number hadn't come up yet. Rationing its food source.

There was one place left for him to go that might be safe. The idea wasn't pleasant, but it was the only place he could make secure quickly enough.

Just for tonight. Tomorrow, he was out of here.

The root cellar was a place he wouldn't even want his corpse buried, let alone pass a night. But it had one entrance that with a few nails and a board would be tighter than Fort Knox.

He stopped at the barn long enough to grab scrap lumber and tools. By the light of truck's headlamps, he glimpsed the rabbit hutch hanging open and empty. He made a point not to look at it. Same for the shattered side door, which hung by a scrap of metal. After loading the truck and throwing a spare lantern and matches into the cab, he went back to close the doors when something caught his eye.

A dark glint flashed at the edge of the headlights, in the rafters. He knew what it was even before backing up to get a proper look. It swayed a few feet below the center beam like a dry leaf in a breeze. It was just too damn perfect. More proof that he'd fallen into his own personal purgatory. Noah laughed.

The beam of the flashlight caught the rifle rotating in thin air, held aloft by fine, silvery cords that glittered prettily in the small light. It hung muzzle down, butt wreathed in a cocoon of silk.

He drove through a swamp that used to be the front yard. The lights swept over the moldering house, through the ranks of trees standing over the mound of earth that would mark his final resting place. He halted the truck a few feet from the entrance and lit the lantern, turning the gas to full volume before killing the engine and stepping out with his gear. He should have taken two trips, but he got it in one. At the cellar door, he dropped everything but the lantern, threw the panel and grimaced at the smell. He lowered the lantern, gazing at the sheen of black water.

Better than the alternative, kid.

He turned and pulled the lumber and tools inside before pulling the panel shut and closing himself in dense silence.

Two short two-by-sixes served as crossbeams, which he hammered to the door with a fistful of sixteen-penny nails, imagining the bristling spikes sticking through the other side. *Claw over that, asshole.*

He minced into shin-deep water as the foul surface rocked to life. The bloated body of a rat bobbed beneath a shelf. Dust and cobwebs clung to everything - normal cobwebs, thank God. He swept the jars off the middle shelf, sending them splashing into the murky water, then crawled onto to the narrow platform, wondering if would hold his weight as it groaned in protest. It did.

He lay on rough plywood, forearm as a pillow, the crowbar cradled to his chest – his only weapon now, as well as his exit key first thing tomorrow.

So, this is what it's like to be buried alive. Staring at the next platform just inches from the tip of his nose, he laughed again. If only Jessie could see him now. And she'd thought him crazy for sleeping in the barn. That made him laugh more and in that close space he really did sound like a man who'd lost his mind.

At last he turned off the lantern and darkness closed in around him.

13

THE HOST

- Noah -

Noah huddled over the twelve gauge, its muzzle on a makeshift tripod and pointed at a fist-sized hole in the side door of the barn. A cigarette wedged in his mouth, he poured smoky curses on the empty yard, waiting for the creature to return.

"Where the hell are you?"

Three nights he'd sat in ambush for a chance to blow the monster to hell, this creature that had wrecked his life, and his barn. The insults had reached critical mass, the last of which had been the destruction of his father's rifle.

He'd almost killed himself getting it out of the rafters. Standing on the ends of his toes on a rickety extension ladder, he used a hay hook to grapple the rifle and pull it within reach. The alien cord that tethered it was tough as a bale string, and when it finally snapped he'd gotten an object lesson in physics, nearly slingshotting himself off the ladder.

Spitting curses and jitterbugging down the rungs, he reached the floor intact, but the same couldn't be said for the gun. His pestilent little friend had done a real number on it. The magazine and firing chamber were clogged with that cobweb shit, and as he took apart the action it shed flecks of rust. The components were frozen and corroded beyond repair.

"Son of a bitch!"

He hurled a wrench at the wall. It crashed into ranks of tools and brought them down in a noisy hailstorm. He kicked a tin pail that ricocheted off the bench and eventually came to rest amidst the other metal objects scattered on the floor, rocking weakly as if in pain. Here was another piece of his old life torn away from him, one more piece of his father, an artifact with good memories of which there were fewer and fewer by the day.

"I've got to get out of here." His voice was rough from lack of use. "Before I go crazy. Soon I'll start talking to myself." Then he would have to strap himself to the bed to keep himself from tearing off his own face the way Ma had.

He left the tack room and the mess to consider his options. No way was he traipsing into the wilderness again without a decent gun. Not after seeing what that thing could do.

His only other gun was the single-shot twelve gauge; a substantial weapon for sure, but only at close range. And unless the beastie was willing to stand still long enough to make the one shot count, it wasn't going to be of much use.

Maybe escape wasn't the best idea. Why risk thirteen miles of his ass exposed when the creature seemed perfectly willing to come to him?

So, with hammer and nails and most of a day, he'd turned the barn into a fortress. By evening, the wrecked door was a wall of two-by-sixes that would stop a Sherman Tank. The main doors sported hefty new braces with a catch and crossbar so they couldn't be opened from the outside. The skylight was sealed shut with four-inch nails that stuck straight through the roof. It would probably leak next rain, but he didn't care.

As the sun settled beyond the grey horizon on the third night after seeing Judd, Noah stationed himself at a shooting hole in the north door. With Dad's old goose-gun propped on a knee, he watched the yard while scraping clean a can of beans with a plastic spoon. His supplies were getting low. And the beans and motherfuckers, as Daddy used to call them, tasted as bad as the name suggested. But it was better than another round of crackers and peanut butter.

He could wait all night. Let darkness come. All he needed was for the fucker to try the door again or to poke its face into that hole. At point blank range, a blast of size-four, copper-plated shot would take out Godzilla. Given recent history, he wouldn't have to wait long. The pale bastard would be dead by dawn.

But three dawns had come and gone without so much as a sound from the creature. The enterprise devolved into a theater of his own progressive madness. The first night, Castle Weismann was quiet as a cemetery. Several times he lost his nerve and turned the flashlight on the hole only to see empty yard.

He knew it was out there, biding its time. The thing was smart, probably knew exactly what Noah was up to and was simply waiting for him to drop his guard, which wasn't going to happen. If that little beast decided to come play with him again, it would find Noah Weismann ready and waiting, with ears pricked and nose up. And one hell of a bite.

Dawn number two found him unconscious and sprawled against the tractor tire, the shotgun lying on the floor. He woke in a panic, arms flailing, expecting to be wreathed in cobwebs.

The bastard is messing with our heads, isn't he, precious?

Night number three, he might have made it to seven p.m. before he threw in the towel.

He couldn't make himself leave the barn anymore, not even in daylight. Just opening the door was enough to loosen his bladder and make his skin itch. He did it long enough to listen to the distant rumble of the river, which grew fainter by the day.

Tomorrow. I'll drive across that bridge and not even God will stop me. Surely it would be clear by then.

But when it came time to take up the gun that evening, his eyelids were drooping within minutes. To stay awake, he chain smoked until his last pack was down to one lone soldier.

He swore and stood, gazing at his nest of insanity, the gun-rest made of scrap lumber, the discarded cans of his last several meals and the litter of butts and ash all over Daddy's floor.

"Fuck this." One more night and that creature wouldn't have to do a thing because he really would end up babbling and lying naked in the yard. He would cross that dammed bridge if it killed him, climb over the trusses if necessary.

He grabbed an ax and a handsaw from the tack room and threw them in the back of the truck. He tossed the flashlight and ammo into the cab and started the engine before dragging open the front doors to a muggy, gray evening. He backed to the truck, gun at the fore, climbed in, and drove away.

Moving felt better. The rough shake of the cab and grumble of the engine evened out his breathing and eased days of tension.

The barn and the Glen disappeared in the rearview mirror. He shouldn't have looked back; was lucky not to have turned into a pillar of salt.

~

"Thank you, God." Noah leaned over the wheel, staring at the deck of the bridge, tears of relief brimming. "Thank you, sweet Jesus!"

The bridge was an ugly sight. But it was open. The river oozed sluggishly-several feet beneath the girders. The trusses wore rags of cast-off forest woven into laterals like thatch. The deck was sluiced in mud that lay in actual drifts. The far end of the bridge was clogged with a dam of driftwood. It would have to be cleared before the truck could pass through. But he was prepared for that.

He got out and breathed the first free air he'd tasted in days. That air stank of rot and river, but he didn't care. Grabbing tools and the shotgun, he waded through the muck to the log jam, pausing long enough to kick aside chunks of driftwood and toss bigger limbs over the side. A mangled car fender lay against the railing. This too went over the side, just for the pleasure of paying the river a final insult. The water swallowed it with barely a ripple.

He spent the next several minutes hacking at the waterlogged tree with the conviction of a man who has rediscovered hope, ignoring the pain of cramped muscles from days of sitting on his ass.

Only once did he pause to catch his breath. The forest lay in ruins on either side of the river. The trees were sick things, their leaves yellowed and limp. Many were stripped of bark up to the shoulders. Some had their roots exposed. Others leaned over the river, ready to fall. The disgorged bones of their brethren lay in heaps at the riverbend.

When the bridge was clear, he didn't linger to admire his work, but made his way back at a sliding trot, knowing that this was the moment in scary movies when the victims let down their guard and got their asses handed to them.

He reached the truck alive, tossed in his gear and practically ripped off the door getting in. Only with his butt in the seat, the door locked, and the engine running did he allow himself to celebrate.

"Holy shit." He sat back and stared at the open road. "Motherfucker, I did it!"

He whooped and struck the roof with a fist, then lit his last cigarette and enjoyed it more than he'd ever enjoyed a cigarette in his life. Catching a look at the mirror, he did not recognize the wild-eyed vagrant staring back at him, the beard and the hollow cheeks. He stuck out his tongue and laughed a dry cackle that reminded him of the creature.

"Hi Daddy. Good to see you. Miss me? We made it."

But when he looked back at the road his smile faded, his lips parted and the cigarette fell from his mouth.

"What...the...almighty fuck?"

She stood in the road in front of the bridge, just between the trusses, blinking at him with those strange black eyes. He'd been sure she was dead, caught up in the river and drowned or devoured by that white monster. Wrong again. The girl from the Glen was right there, alive and well, no more than twenty yards away.

Except it was not her. It couldn't be. She had the same tangled hair and wild, alien eyes. But this was not the same person who had outrun him in the pear orchard days ago. She was too old. The curve of hip and swell beneath her gown put her a decade beyond the child who had eluded him. So did the angles of her face, the sharp chin and cheekbones.

Nor did she crouch like a spooked coyote cub, but stood at full height, eyes defiant, as if daring him to run over her.

She was dressed too, though barely. A gown or slip as pale as her skin hung from thin straps over her shoulders. It was stained and tattered, frayed at the hem. She was barefoot.

They stared at each other while Noah thought about what to do, afraid she'd run if he got out or tried to talk to her. She had that look. It said crazy as a shithouse rat.

Without so much as a change in expression, she turned and ran into the forest.

"Oh, for Christ's sake." He was out of the truck and after her without a second thought, leaving the door swinging and the engine running. Only when he reached the ditch and waded into mud up to his knees did he realize the seriousness of his mistake.

Just let her go, you idiot!

"Stop!" He skirted the river, right on her heels, slogging through the muck, gaining no ground but not losing her either. His lungs burning, sucking wind, coughing and cursing, he trudged on while the rumble of the truck faded and fell silent behind a wall of forest.

The young woman stumbled, but kept her feet, somehow staying on top of the mud rather than sinking in like he did. Once she tripped and fell, turned to look at him with terrified eyes.

"I'm not going to hurt you!"

But she got up and staggered on with stained knees. A surge of pity pulled at him as she clambered over a fallen oak, tottered at its apex, and fell over the other side.

Boots churning, he reached the tree seconds later, hauling himself up and over, scraping his belly raw as he slid down the other side. He came down in boot-deep mud and found the space empty. She was nowhere in sight.

"Dammit!" He scanned the forest, finally spotting her in a thicket a few yards away, watching him.

His hands rose in a gesture of meekness. "It's okay." Mud gave back his boots grudgingly. "I want to help you!"

She didn't bother to run this time, but watched his slow progress with a cold curiosity, wild as anything he'd seen yet. He blinked, alarm bells going off.

She turned with placid indifference and melted into the trees like mist.

All he could do was watch her go, dumbfounded and a little relieved. Then he was alone again, darkness thickening around him. The weight of his predicament fell on him like a bucket of ice-water.

It's just this kind of crazy shit that's going to get you killed, Weismann. He began to retrace his steps, fear putting the fight back in him, giving him the strength to scramble back over the oak and power through the mud. He hadn't made it twenty feet when the scream tore through the forest, halting him mid-stride.

"That's bullshit!" There was no mistaking it. That dry-rattle shriek he'd recognize with his head buried in the sand and his ears full of cotton.

He held his breath, praying he'd just had the most vivid hallucination of his life. The fantasy collapsed when the cry came again, sharp and close, the distance halved, from the direction of the truck, of course. His little pale friend had found him. And this time there would be no hasty escapes to the barn.

He tore himself out of the swamp, finding strength and speed born of animal fear.

When the creature sounded again, not fifty yards away, he knew with certainty that this was the moment it had been waiting for. It could have come for him at the barn, while he lay unconscious on the floor, but why risk it? Just wait for him to make a mistake and boy, hadn't he made one now?

Noah scanned the ground for a weapon and found only a rotted log. As he snatched it up, a hiss came from directly behind him. He spun to face it. There was nothing to see. No movement, no shadow or shape. Just trees.

"What are you waiting for?" Shouting felt good. Better than whimpering and begging like a coward. "Yeah, go fuck yourself. You hear me?"

The thing answered with a long shriek as brittle as chipped ice, triumph in its voice. A branch snapped somewhere behind him. The thing was circling him.

He raised the club, cocking it like a bat, ready to send its ugly head flying over the river, when another scream came from his left, farther down river.

Christ, you got to be kidding me. Higher pitched and sharper than the first, the cry of a second demon melted whatever steel he'd managed to summon.

It shouldn't have mattered. One could do him just fine on its own. But the idea of multiple pale-skinned aliens fighting over his corpse turned his guts to liquid. What if there were hundreds of these things crawling over the valley? The forest teeming with them, breeding and spreading up and down the river while spitting their cobwebs into every last phone box from here to the ocean? He could have died fine without having that happy thought in his head.

The first monster answered, practically in his ear. *Come on over,* it said. *Plenty for both, planted up to his ass and ripe with fear.*

He reached into his pocket and dug out the lighter, lit it with a burst of sparks that sent the trees to dancing in a sickly yellow light. Two silver orbs shone like harvest moons before melting away with a wet hiss. He thrust his puny torch forward, trying to catch it. No use. The light wavered in his shaking hand and revealed nothing.

Everything went quiet.

This is it, he thought. That moment of calm just before the hurricane blows you to pieces. Ears straining, scarcely breathing, Noah waited. Something snuffled beyond the range of the lighter. The little flame quivered in a traitorous breeze. He cupped his hand over it, watched in horror as the light fluttered and died.

"Shit!" Desperately he clawed at the flint wheel. Hot metal seared his flesh as he tried in vain to make the lighter work and got only a few sparks.

Something slammed into him like a runaway truck, knocking the wind out of him and sending him face first into the mud. Pain ripped through his knees and hamstrings as he was uprooted from his boots. Hot breath fell on the back of his neck as a scream filled his ears, splitting his skull with an insect's rattle and pouring that alcohol-fruit smell over him. He was vaguely aware of an answer from a few yards away, angry and frustrated. Whatever was on top of him seemed to raise its head and snarl. *Mine. Find your own.*

Noah thrashed uselessly as steel vices tightened around his arms. The other creature drew closer, filling the air with its own reverberating cries. They sounded like scavengers at a kill.

He squeezed his eyes shut and waited for teeth to sink into him, hoping his death would be quick.

But when the blow came, it wasn't what he expected. There was a flash of searing pain in the small of his back, a bolt of electricity, as if he'd just been hit with a taser. Liquid fire exploded in from his middle and spread through his entire body. Arms and legs went rigid. He couldn't breathe for all the pain, couldn't move, as if his body were being filled with concrete. It seemed to last for hours. An agony he could never have imagined ruled his body until softening into something worse. A heavy cold that dragged him toward sleep.

Well, fuck... In his last moments of consciousness, he realized a new horror. Riley, the coyote, now him, victims of a huge blood-sucking insect armed not with teeth but an acid stinger. The picture of a lantern-eyed spider, all joints and pincered fangs fastening onto him and draining his bodily fluids was the last image in his mind before the poison reached his brain and turned out the lights.

14

MARKED

- Noah -

If this was death, it wasn't so bad. Nothing like what he deserved. This was comfortable, warm, like his old pillow mattress nestled under a stack of quilts that smelled of cedar chips. This was soft sunlight filtered through the bedroom curtain, the thump and murmur of familiar souls drifting through the floorboards. The smell of sausage and the pitched laughter of his older sister. He could almost believe that Ma was sound and in her right mind, chatting with Daddy, who was sober and whose eyes burned only for her. Jessie right in the middle, a firecracker who ruled the place like the young dictator she was.

But this was life as it should have been, never as it was. Not even in the best years before Ma joined that faith-healing cult and his father died the kind of death you only read about in horror novels.

Warmth faded. Real memories swept aside the peace of dreams like an overplayed promise. He wasn't dead.

Forcing his eyes open, he saw a world that made a lot more sense. The junction of earth and sky. His was a bed of filth under a blanket of grey murk and cold. His face pressed into the mud. Not so comfortable either. Numb with cold, his whole body tingled like an arm that had been slept on all night. His ears rang and his head felt like it was full of water instead of brains. The worst hangover of all time.

A moan escaped him as he lifted his head and looked upon spindly trees that surrounded him like mourners at a funeral. He pushed himself to hands and knees, pulling free with a squelch, and sat back on his heels. Palms pressed to his eyes, he tried to remember what the hell he was doing out here. His memory was no good, a broken radio catching mostly static, music coming through in dark snatches.

A shiver that had nothing to do with cold raised gooseflesh on his arms. He wasn't alone. That shape above him was too pale and still to be natural.

She was perched on the fallen oak, squatting on her heels not ten feet away. The girl was silent as marble, easy to miss, studying him with those strange eyes.

"Hey." His voice was harsh and cracked, rough enough to frighten a child. She didn't move.

He struggled to his feet, which was harder than it should have been. His head spun and a wave of nausea hit him hard enough to send him right back down. *What the hell did that thing do to me?*

Fear cleared his vision and exhumed memories that should have stayed buried. He tentatively reached for the dull pain in the small of his back.

"Ow! Son of a bitch." Just above his belt. A raised bump that sent a jet of electricity through him at the brush of a fingertip. He inspected his hand and swore at the smear of blood, then eased himself against a tree and leaned back to wait for his head to clear. He tried swallowing, which was a mistake. His throat burned as if he'd swallowed a gallon of sand, and his mouth tasted like copper.

"Where'd you come from, huh?" He didn't expect an answer and got none. When he opened his eyes, she was gone. He sat up, turned, and found her crouching at his shoulder.

"Jesus!" He spun to face her, then sagged against the tree. "You're as bad as those things out there. You know that?"

Searching his pockets for his cigarettes, finding nothing, he sighed and tried to get to his feet again.

"Sorry." He grunted. "No offense." He leaned forward, braced his knees and heaved himself up, managing to not vomit or pass out. *Bonus.*

She jumped up and ducked behind a tree, hands braced against the trunk as if ready to spring into flight but her face remained neutral, as if running away were simply in the script.

"Trust me. I'm in no shape to chase you." Another round of pocket patting, searching for something else, though he couldn't remember what. The imprint of his body in the earth reminded him of a chalk outline at a crime scene. There were no prints but his own. And those of the young woman behind the tree, who seemed to have relaxed.

She looked up at the slate-colored sky, squinting as if divining some message from the clouds. He wondered how long she'd been out here, stumbling around in that filthy slip. How had she managed to escape the mayhem that had befallen him last night? She cocked her head, turning an ear to the sky. Maybe she hadn't. *Maybe this is what happens to you. They bite you and you go mad.*

Her eyes fell back to him, as if sensing his scrutiny, and regarded him with an expression he couldn't read. Then she looked over her shoulder, pushed off from the tree and ran.

"Wait." It was half-hearted, barely a croak. She darted, cat-quick, through the trees and was out of sight in a heartbeat, her white form fading like mist. He stared after her until there was nothing to see, unable to make sense of her, unwilling to try.

A rose hue had crept into the eastern sky. Distantly, a robin sang. The night had given way to an ugly new dawn. He turned and began the laborious slog back to the truck.

How long it took him to reach the road he didn't know. His head was a balloon tethered to a string, drifting several feet above his body. The pain in his head and joints disappeared quickly, but was replaced by a detached sense of vertigo. He felt nothing when the truck came into view, neither relief nor anxiety over the state it might be in.

The door hung open. The engine was dead, the lights dark. He climbed in, turned the key, and wasn't surprised when nothing happened. Nor was he surprised when his palm began to burn. Already the details of the cab were resolving themselves.

He pulled his hand from the wheel and tiny silvery threads came with it. The wheel was wreathed in silk, glittering like a Christmas ornament. Wiping his hand on a pant leg, he noticed the passenger side and began to laugh. The shotgun, or what used to be the shotgun, as well as the box of shells were wrapped in beautiful crystalline cocoons. Maybe in time they would become butterflies.

He didn't stick around to find out, didn't bother checking the engine, which he knew would never run again. He slid out of the seat and trudged back to the farm like a man walking asleep. At no point did he consider following through with his original plan to leave. Benton was now open to him. But it never occurred to him to step across the bridge.

He didn't die the slow, agonizing death he thought would come as the day wore on. The joint pain and nausea were gone by the time he reached the house. The bone-deep chill faded. By late that afternoon he felt pretty good. Better than good. It should have scared the shit out of him that some vile, mystery venom was inside of him, working voodoo on his head and making him not care whether he lived or died.

There were other side effects, too, that were not so pleasant. The itch at the base of his spine gnawed at him. He couldn't see the wound, but could sure as hell feel it. To the fingers it was just a raised bump on the skin. But all around it was like a thousand tiny insects burrowing into him, eating their way to the bone. He dug at it until it bled and had to force himself to stop before he made himself septic.

But this was the least of his symptoms, the most natural anyway, as natural as something like this could be. The tingling in his body he'd felt upon waking settled into his bones and became a detached numbness that muted pain and blunted emotion.

He saw the world through a pane of glass, a filter of euphoria that made fear into something far less rational. For days he'd suffered an itchy nervousness bordering on terror that had him looking over his shoulder and jumping at every noise. Now he couldn't manufacture even mild alarm.

He still felt that thing watching, but couldn't manage to care.

The most disturbing change, though - disturbing had his head been right - was that he was starting to see things. They weren't big things, no lights in the sky, no flying cows or visions of Elvis walking on water, but they were weird enough and maybe symbolic enough to assure him things weren't right in the old attic.

He came out of the barn to take a piss after spending three straight hours scrubbing the tractor and saw the light on in Ma's old bedroom. He caught it out of the corner of his eye, a bright yellow stain in the forehead of the house that stopped him midstream.

He blinked and it was gone, dark as always, the house a dead husk. The joke made him laugh. *Was it a good joke?* Someone was having fun at his expense because the power was out, and there hadn't been a live bulb in the fixture of that room for almost two years.

Later, while scouring the kitchen drawers for a spare pack of cigarettes – sometimes miracles happen - he heard a thump upstairs. That it came only once, just that single bump, didn't matter. He'd heard that goddamned noise so many times, crammed into a period of two weeks, ceaseless, night and day, day in and day out, he would have recognized it his sleep.

He stared at the ceiling, drawer junk clutched in his hands, waited to hear it again, because it never came only once. *Never.* There should be a storm of it.

In the silence that followed, irritation swelled to a sick kind of fury that had him snatching up the lantern and pounding up the staircase to Ma's room. He opened the bedroom door and had no trouble walking right into the dank air, lantern casting a halo over the mold-stained room.

The bed was green with age and rot, but empty. Rat tracks and water stains streaked the warped floorboards. The room was otherwise lifeless. And there was the leg of the corner bedpost hovering a quarter-inch off the floor, cocked like a fist over a dime-sized divot in the bare wood. But of course, that hadn't moved either, not in over two years. When he saw what he expected to see, which was absolutely nothing, he turned and closed the door.

He found a pack of GPCs in his old bedroom of all places, and a box of matches in the kitchen – he'd lost his lighter in his scrape with the monsters. The smokes were under a loose floorboard where he'd hidden them all those years ago, back when Ma would have skinned him alive if she'd caught him smoking, and before he had enough cash for anything but these cheap shit sticks.

They tasted like they smelled. He grimaced when they touched his lips. But beggars can't be choosers, so he smoked them anyway.

Maybe it was numbness that had him sitting on the porch swing instead of locked up in the barn where he sure as Sherlock's shirt should have been. It wasn't to enjoy the Glen, which wasn't a nice place anymore, not since its mutation wrought by the flood.

If he'd been willing to think about it, the idea of waiting there for the thing to come out and find him would have seemed like suicide. Maybe this was like when a shark marks its victim by taking a bite out of it, then waits for it to bleed out before coming to finish it off.

Let it come. If it kills me, what have I lost?

He waited there, as still as the dead house, watching the Glen fade while the forest held its breath. He didn't actually think it would come, because it was too clever for the direct approach. But come it did.

He was staring at the grass, which trembled under a breath of wind too soft to hear, when something shifted at the edge of his vision. A tiny movement, subtle as wood smoke, but enough.

Maybe I'll get a good look at you this time.

The creature stood absolutely still. The ripple that had drawn his attention was gone, but it was already halfway across the porch. How long had it been there? And why had it let him know it was there? He knew it had. The thing could have pounced on him before he'd even realized something was wrong. But that wasn't how this creature operated. It liked to play games with him.

So, play back.

Fear fluttered at the edges of his consciousness, light as moth wings, unable to cross this strange new barrier in his brain. His heart quickened from chemicals the creature's appearance set loose, but his mind remained calm.

Slowly he turned his head.

The pale young woman blinked back at him, unperturbed, as if she'd simply been waiting for him to notice her.

15

VISITATION

- Noah -

So it wasn't a monster come to drag him back to the river and devour him. Just a barefoot girl in a tattered slip. Harmless.

Even so, the little moths of fear fluttered against the glass pane of his consciousness. Was it fear? He was no longer sure. He was a stranger to his emotions, no longer able to sort out the signals of his own body.

For something to do besides staring at a half-dressed woman, he reached for his cigarettes and slipped one between his lips. "You shouldn't sneak up on people like that." He struck a match. The flare under his cupped hand temporarily blinded him. "Folks out here tend to be crazy. Shoot-first types, if you know what I mean. Those of us who still have guns."

He glanced at her. She'd moved, just a step or two, but closer. The porch boards should have warned him, but they remained in mute conspiracy.

He coughed, sudden and involuntary, and scowled at the cigarette between his fingertips. The old GPC tasted like it'd been soaked in formaldehyde and rat piss.

He dropped it and stamped it out. "Do you talk?" He looked sidelong at her, not wanting to meet her strange eyes. "What's your name?"

Crazy as a beetle in a hen house. He was sure of that. She looked healthy enough, though in need of a bath. Her hair was windblown, flecked with bits of leaves. Dirt smudged one pale cheek and her feet were a mess. She must be cold. The air had turned chill since last night and that slip of hers was thin as tissue. Beneath her brow, those coal-black eyes were fixed on him.

"Hey. Are you hungry?" He finally met her gaze, willing her to understand. "Hungry?" he repeated, putting his fingers to his lips and raising his brows in question. *The poor girl's simple.* That was the word you were supposed to use now. *Retarded* wasn't politically correct.

Her expression changed, as if she could read his thoughts. Not a smile exactly, but something darker. With slow steps she made her way across the porch boards, as if approaching a wild animal she didn't want to scare away.

Curiosity overruled his alarm and he remained still, expecting her to stop before she was close enough to touch him. She breached that barrier and kept coming. He found himself sliding backward until he ran aground on the arm of the bench. The swing creaked ominously, jarring the silence.

She paused, gazing at him with that not-quite smile, more in the eyes than on her lips. Then she reached for him, penetrating his space in a motion too swift to escape.

As her fingers brushed his cheek, he caught her scent and went rigid. Strange, very different. Unexpected. So was his reaction. As she leaned into him and her breath tickled his ear, he was both embarrassed and frightened by his body's sudden awakening - no numbness there - and hoped to God she couldn't see it.

The smell of flowers and earth wrapped him up like a cocoon and for a moment he couldn't move. The pane of glass in his head shattered; brain and body slammed back together like a car wreck. Her hand cupped the back of his neck as she drew a long breath, evidently taking in his own smell, which couldn't have been nice. At last he wrestled back the controls of his mutinous body and jerked away, coming off the bench.

He couldn't make sense of what had just happened. Her change in behavior, the sudden return of his emotions, the sheer weirdness of everything was too much to process.

She seemed unperturbed by his retreat, studying him as if taking his measure. No, she definitely wasn't slow, or simple. Completely crazy, yes. But not simple.

She rose and slowly extended a hand. Her fingers were closed around a small object he couldn't make out.

When he didn't move to take it, she placed it on the bench where it settled with a light clunk. Then she backed away, turned to the porch steps and ran, glancing back once before disappearing into the Glen. Her pale form was quickly swallowed by the night. Only when she was out of sight did he turn to look at what she had left him. It was his father's lighter.

Noah dreamed that night. They were poison dreams filled more with the aura of fear than shapes or faces he could remember. At first, he flitted between the simple darkness of his closed lids and snatches of the past that were too quick and broken to catch. They left a tang of bitterness that lingered and accumulated like rust.

Then they began to build inside him, squeezing up and out from mounting pressure until he was ready to scream. But when he would have given anything to open his mouth, vent himself and be empty again, he couldn't. Nor could he wake up. Getting away should have been as easy as opening his eyes; he was just inches under, but the surface of consciousness was made of glass.

White fear strangled him as a dry cackle that sounded like a swarm of insects spoke his name. "It's here, Noah," it whispered in his ear, past his ear. Inside him. "It's finally come for you. You're doomed."

He screamed himself dry, screamed until there was nothing else in the world but scream. The ghosts vanished. The air cleared. The surface of consciousness returned, almost. Close enough to catch the smell of straw, engine oil and old lumber. Something else too, pleasant, like flowers and rain chased away the last reek of nightmare and he dreamed of soft whispers in his ear, cool skin on his face, someone warm beside him.

He stirred, wanting to see who it was, struggling with everything he had to open his eyes. But then came a brilliant flash of pain. A lightning stroke, sudden and intense, in the small of his back. Then soft warmth spread like bath water over his whole body and drowned him into a deep, dreamless nothing.

~

When he awoke, she was there. He opened his eyes to semi-darkness and found her perched a few feet away. Squeezing his eyes shut and opening them again, he rolled into a sitting position.

He felt no real surprise at seeing her, though God knew he should have. His screwed-up head was doing a number on him again.

When a rational thought did hit him, it wasn't with much force. While he worked the ache out of his joints, he wondered how she'd gotten in. He'd made a fortress out of this place and yet here she was. Then he remembered. He hadn't bothered latching the main doors last night. The catch still lay on the workbench where it would do fuck-all for keeping out monsters.

Only thing missing was the damned welcome mat.

Lucky for him, the first to test his shitty security system had been a human being. She was squatting on the balls of her feet next to the cot, like this was exactly where she was supposed to be.

She was also staring at him like he was the most interesting thing on the planet, close enough he could smell her, and the sudden awareness of it jerked him fully awake. The feeling that lit up his insides caused him to shift out of range, scooting to the end of his cot and sitting bolt upright. He looked at her, then looked away.

She watched him with that odd curiosity he'd seen last night. She sure wasn't afraid anymore.

"You are a strange girl," he said, and looked down at his jeans, which lay in a pile on the floor a few feet away. He pulled the blanket over his lap and felt suddenly like a prisoner in his own home.

A terrible itch caught fire in the small of his back. He scratched at it and moaned when it finally started to cool. *Goddamned bloodsuckers.*

He slid his pants over with a foot, then bent down and pulled his cigarettes and lighter from the pocket, shook one free and grimaced the second it touched his lips. He stared at it as if it had bitten him, then stuffed it back into the pack.

He looked at the lighter and held it up.

"Thanks for this," he said, glancing at her and then tossing both the lighter and the cigarettes onto the cot before bending over to grab for his wadded-up jeans.

"Do you have a name?" he asked, trying to pull on his jeans without exposing himself any more than he already had. He waited for an answer, and when he didn't get one said, "I'm Noah."

Still no reply. She watched his lips as if surprised that sound was coming out of them.

He sighed, not sure what to do next.

"Can't you talk?" He looked at her more fully now, suddenly struck with the thought that after trying like hell to catch her the other night, and failing, here she was. Sitting in his bedroom. And he had no idea what to do with her. Until now he'd assumed she'd tell him where she lived, how she'd gotten lost, and would...act like a human.

He almost laughed at himself out loud. *God help her.* Because his experience in taking care of insane women hadn't turned out so well.

Nor could he put his finger on what bothered him about the way she was looking at him. Something very childlike and innocent about her face, the funny way she stared at him, like small kids did at strangers and weren't embarrassed for being rude. But it was more than that, though maybe it was part of why she'd looked so young at first. Maybe.

He was finally able to pull the jeans under the blanket and slide them up his legs, though he didn't know why he'd bothered to strip them off last night, after all that had happened. He really had lost his mind. Before he could get them buckled, she moved.

He snapped upright, pulling the bedding tighter into his lap, and yelped when she slid onto the cot with him.

"What are you doing?"

She ignored him, or rather ignored his question, and slid closer until he was nearly off the end of the cot.

She kept coming, eyes locked to his, washing him in her strange scent. Too shocked to move, he did nothing as she touched his face for the second time in eight hours. At his flinch she withdrew, but only for a moment. She leaned forward, putting her face in his hair and breathing in, the fingers of both hands knotted in his hair. She lowered herself, seeking him with her lips and then pressed them against his own.

He pulled away, hands on her wrists. "Wait a minute, honey. Let's just slow down here." He wasn't sure who he was really talking to. Holding up a hand as if to ward her off, he scooted off the cot and tried to get to his feet. She followed, kicking the cot aside with a flimsy clatter and stalking him across the loft floor, then fell on him like a hawk on a snake. She shoved him down, yanked away the blanket with surprising strength.

He fought for control, searching for every scare tactic and scripture he'd ever heard about fornication and the damnation and disease and all that came with it. But his body had lost interest in good judgment. Sanity and virtue both packed their bags and left him alone. With her. He wrapped his arms around her waist and his mouth no longer resisted her.

It happened quickly, in a blur of clutching hands and strewn clothes that left them both breathless and trembling. When he tried to lift his head minutes later, spent but somehow still inside her, she pushed him back down and buried her face in his neck, stroking his breastbone, tracing the ridges of his neckline. Her caresses were more like those of someone comforting a frightened puppy than someone stroking a lover, and the oddity nearly made him laugh.

He wanted to say something. God knew what, but his brain was still out to lunch and he couldn't seem to pull a thought together, though somewhere in there was a vague knowledge that this was one mistake he would be sorely regretting later. She spoke first.

Not in words. She smiled at him with that not-smile, then lifted her gaze, as if aware for the first time of her surroundings. Without further warning she sprang off of him and grabbed up her tattered gown. He yelped at the sudden separation and watched, stupefied, as she slipped into her garment and over the side of the loft platform in a single motion.

"Hey!"

By the time the word was out of his mouth, the only thing left of her was the soft padding of her feet across the floorboards. He scuttled to the edge of the loft, reaching it just in time for her to look back at him, then slip through the gap in the doors and vanish.

He stared slack-jawed at the fresh void for several minutes before shaking himself awake. He sat back and tried to process what had just happened and couldn't find it in himself to feel shame over what he'd done.

And Ma called Jessie the whore.

In truth he didn't have the energy to think much about anything. Exhaustion flowed over him, like he'd been chased all night by nightmares. He righted the cot, grabbed his blanket, and lay back down, intending only a few minutes sleep before getting on with the day.

Why bother? It's not like there's any real work to do around here. He fell into a sleep from which he didn't wake until early that afternoon.

16

THE LAST HOUR OF JUDD MCPHERSON

- Judd McPherson -

Judd McPherson sat at the kitchen table, smoking his pipe and watching the last light bleed out of the window. The house was nearly dark now, settling into a profound, end-of-the-world silence.

He'd parked himself there an hour ago, intending to have a proper supper before retiring to the recliner where he ended up most nights. Instead he'd sat and watched daylight die while his corned beef sat on a plate in front of him, untouched.

His appetite wasn't so good these days, which he knew wasn't a good sign. But fretting over that now would be like fretting over termites when your house was on fire.

Tomorrow, he thought. *Maybe tomorrow.*

Though the thought of venturing out in the dark wasn't any worse than the prospect of spending another night alone in this godforsaken place. The house was a dead thing, as lifeless as the forest that surrounded it, just one soul short of a grave.

Judd sometimes woke from dreams of better days to this unholy silence and the weight of loneliness would crush the breath out of him. Mollie was gone now and no place offered refuge from her absence. Hell, with the power out, he couldn't even turn on the radio. And he would dance a jig to hear Paul Harvey's voice just now.

That wasn't quite true. He wasn't completely alone. One of those monsters was still out there, prowling outside his door. Though his little guest had been quiet of late. His own wood-devil.

Something had happened to it. Or drawn it away. He pretended not to know where the thing had gone, but he knew.

Maybe young Noah had listened to him, did exactly as Judd had told him and gotten the hell out of the valley, or locked himself inside that root cellar and not so much as sniffed at the door. But he didn't believe that either, and knew it wouldn't make any difference if he had. Noah Weismann was a doomed man.

When this whole thing had started, there were more of them. Three, maybe four, screaming, fighting and raising Cain like coons squabbling over an ear of corn. But that passed within a few days. They seemed to prefer the valley over the hills. He supposed that was where they'd gone.

All except one. A single wood-devil kept coming back to lurk at the edge of the property, just out of sight. Watching. He knew when the thing was there just by the feel of the air. Once, on his way to the shop, he'd caught a glimpse of it, flitting between the trees like a hunting fox. That sent him high-stepping back to the house for the shotgun. But by the time he'd returned with both barrels cocked, it was gone.

He didn't know why it stuck around; that much was truth. What could it possibly want with a used-up husk of a man with barely four breaths left in him? Maybe to make sure he stayed put and didn't run off to tell somebody that it was happening all over again. Which was funny, because he sure as hell wasn't going anywhere.

Judd shivered in the chilling air, noticing for the first time that the summer heat was draining with the light. The thought of his blanket and the relative comfort of his easy chair in the next room stirred his complacent body. He took a slow drag on the pipe, which cast warm light over the table, then slid the chair back and stood.

Or tried. A bolt of pain, bright white and hot enough to tear a cry out of him, shot through his groin and put him right back down. The damned trick hip was pissed at him for sitting too long. He sat with his eyes and jaw squeezed tight until the bitching stopped.

Slow and easy now, Gus. Slow and easy.

He tried again, slow and easy now. With cracking knees and a groan of floorboards he gained his feet, found his balance, and hobbled to the living room where his recliner and the quilt waited. Instead of sitting, he stood with his hand resting on the back of the chair, looking at the front door.

"You ought to at least warn him, you old bastard."

And what was he going to do? Grab a walking stick and hike down that hill like a kid? In the dark? With his bad knees and hips? All he could do was hope his warning had been enough.

But it wouldn't be, by Saint Peter's grave. No, it wouldn't. Judd had lived through this himself and knew well that Noah had one chance; the same chance Judd had seventy-five years ago, the same chance as any man of age who hadn't gotten the hell out of the valley when they should have. Noah's only prayer was that the thing wouldn't want him, that it had found something wrong with him, something down deep, that it didn't like. Maybe all those cigarettes would give him a few extra years if he'd done enough damage to himself.

Judd had been sick when his number came up. Rheumatic fever, which had both nearly killed him and saved his life. Tanner Weismann had received no such pass. He'd been healthy, and so disappeared with the rest. Many had. Drowned, everyone said, because not even the few who'd survived wanted to believe what had really happened. Those who'd evacuated and returned certainly didn't believe. Nobody had tried to stop it, because they didn't know and because they couldn't make themselves know.

Tomorrow, he thought as he gazed at the worn cushion in his chair. *I'll go tomorrow.*

No sleep would come to him tonight. Didn't much these days anyway. Wouldn't until he drew his last breath, probably right there in that chair. Perhaps by spilling his pipe on the blanket and setting himself on fire.

What difference did it make whether he gave up the ghost sitting here hoping he wouldn't burn in hell for eternity, or died falling down a mountain and breaking his useless neck? At least that way would be quick. He would go with a clean conscience.

He took in a lungful of air, which stirred the phlegmatic humours again. Pressing the handkerchief to his lips to suppress a coughing fit, he thought maybe he'd just take a little walk after all.

Might be just what the doctor ordered. Fresh air, exercise to cure what ails you. The moon might come out tonight. Could be the prettiest evening in weeks. He'd been doing foolish things up here by himself for thirty years now, and everybody knew that living alone would kill him in the end.

By the time he set off, walking stick in hand, miner's lamp fixed to his cap and a ten-gauge slung over his shoulder, the night was black as tar and the moon was a no show, smothered by a blanket of clouds. But the forest let him through, opening up her arms and receiving him like a lover. *Welcome back,* she said. *I've been waiting for you.*

The journey, should he finish it, would take him most of the night, and he would likely find the Weismann farm empty. And if it wasn't, well, then maybe he'd get a chance to save the boy. *Who knows?* If he could still shoot straight, he might just rid the world of one of those little monsters.

The way over Jake's Saddle and around hill they used to call Goblin's Bald was easy walking, even for a man with such rusty joints. He took it slow and stayed clear of the horse trails. They were straight down and would kill him faster than a heart attack. He made his way to the treeless hilltop where a logging road would take him down smooth and easy.

It was not smooth and easy. The trail was not as gentle as he remembered. When he finally reached the valley floor in the final hour before dawn, he was leaning heavily on his stick, wheezing and feeling every fiery grain of sand that chewed away his joints. He didn't dare sit, knowing there would be no getting up again. He wouldn't make it another half-mile, either.

The clouds had thinned, revealing a moon that hung heavy just over the tree-line. Pale light pooled in the old hay meadow bordering the Weismann property. Judd McPherson was close, by Jesus, and there hadn't been a word from the wood-devil.

He switched off his headlamp, thankful the batteries had held, and let his eyes adjust enough to see the path. Step by slow step he continued on, relieved to see a world beyond what could be squeezed into a narrow cone of the lamp.

There was a solid wedge jutting from the jagged line of forest that he hoped was a barn instead of another giant spruce. He thought he saw an owl scud over the treetops, a dark ghost crossing the moon for an instant before vanishing. His eyes weren't what they used to be either, but even a hint of life here raised his hopes. *Maybe*, he thought.

Had Judd McPherson looked back at that moment, he might have seen the first orange glow of the inferno that would reduce his home to ash. Had he lived just a few minutes longer, he could have watched the whole thing, an eruption of heat so intense that for a few minutes it could be seen in Benton. But Judd was spared that agony. He would die in ignorance of the forces and authorities that would attempt to wipe away all evidence of his existence.

When he reached the access road that lead to Noah's farm, his wood-devil finally found him. As at other times, he knew it was there without hearing or seeing it. The hair rose on the back of his neck. He froze mid-step, tightening his grip on the walking stick, and scanned the tree-line, not expecting to see anything but the pale trees that barred the forest. He focused on breathing, certainty giving him a strange calm as he let the walking stick fall and unslung the shotgun.

At that moment he wished most keenly that Mollie was with him now. She couldn't have helped him, but she sure would have made him feel better. She'd be all bristle and snarl right now.

Slowly, almost casually, he brought the gun around and cocked both hammers, first one, then the other. Even his dull ears heard them fasten into place.

He waited, knowing he might never see it coming, hoping he wouldn't.

For maybe twenty breaths nothing moved. The leaves didn't stir, the moon cowered behind a cloud, and all there was in the world was his shuffling heartbeat. Then a shadow passed, quick and silent as a night bird. He slid his finger onto the first trigger and slowly turned, hoping to die with as much dignity as an old man could.

At first there was nothing. Just a bare patch in the path, the moonlight playing tricks. But then there it was, standing in the road not ten feet away, white, solid and still as marble, watching him. If it had any fear of the gun, Judd didn't see it. All he saw was moonlight reflected in two silver eyes.

He wanted to blow its head off. But he couldn't move, suddenly frozen by an unexpected stir of memory that stripped away seventy-five years and made him fifteen again. For all he knew he could have been standing at the outhouse door under angry skies, staring at the trees, shaking with fever, with fear and with feelings no kid as sick as he should be able to feel.

"What the hell took you so long?" he asked, trying to feel brave though having barely enough strength to hold the gun. Even so, he managed to raise the barrel, calling on every bit of courage he had.

For Noah, he thought.

It made no sound when it came.

17

THE GREAT LEAP

- T. Allen Curtze -

Beneath a low branch of a locust tree, illuminated by a pale shaft of moonlight, was a mound of freshly turned earth. At its head was a crude wooden cross, with a single word carefully carved into the lateral.

The man kneeling at this humble grave was turned slightly away as if in respect. He gently ran a finger over the letters, which spelled the name *Mollie*.

His dress didn't fit the setting. Polished leather shoes, slacks the color of bone, and a tie that in the ambient light of the swollen moon was the color of old blood. His narrow shoulders and sandy blond hair gave him the appearance of youth. But the deep creases in his face, the cigarette between his lips, and the holster beneath his arm dispelled the illusion.

He ignored the rumble of engines behind him, the sporadic clatter of metal and the burst of raised voices, keeping his back to the harsh light that bleached the face of an elderly, two-story house several meters up the hill.

He shifted his gaze to a weathered stump standing upright in the earth. Upon its bench-smooth surface was a tobacco pipe. Whether it had been left there on purpose as token of respect or on accident was unknowable.

The creased-faced man reached out as if to take it, then hesitated as a soft buzz emanated from a breast pocket. He pulled out a cell phone, peered at the screen, and answered. "Good morning, Gene. You're up before the enemy."

"Yeah. Where are you?" The voice was rough, as if just emerging from sleep or suffering a hangover.

"Still finishing up the McPherson place."

"Jesus, it's three a.m. I take it you didn't find him."

The weathered man wedged the phone between shoulder and cheek, pulled a mint tin from his pocket. "You would be correct. From the look of it he just up and walked off the place. The bed's still warm but the place is empty."

"Well shit." Gene muttered. "We could have used some good news. The natives here are sick and tired of hearing bupkis about their missing hombres."

He cupped a hand over the phone to filter distant shouts. "That makes two of us. But we knew the chances of finding him were slim. All we can do is wait until the sectors are clear so we can conduct a more thorough search."

"McPherson has a niece up in Pittsburg," Gene said. "We'll follow up with her, but I doubt this old bastard just slipped past our checkpoints to hobo halfway across the country by himself."

"Yeah, I doubt it too."

A rustle of movement on the other end of the line suggested the switching of ears. "Any sign of you-know-who? The one your boys are calling The Walker?"

Curtze peered at something in the dirt near the grave. He plucked a small object and held it up to the faint moonlight. "Now where the hell did you hear that?"

He studied the cigarette butt, turning it in his fingers before glancing over his shoulder.

"Word gets 'round, Chief. That's all I'm going to tell you. Now out with it. Did you find your super morph or not?"

"It's funny you mention that." Curtze dropped the butt into the mint tin, pulled a flashlight from a coat pocket, and swept a beam over the ground. "This whole place is dirty. We found resin on everything. Not just the things that produce radio waves or electrical fields. It looks like a nest site, except McPherson isn't a suitable host. You want to know the truth? I could use your eyes up here."

"So, after three days without a word from our favorite Martian, you just happen to stumble across her calling card. Eight klicks off the grid in some hellhole not even God knows about. You want to explain that?"

"I got lucky."

"Bullshit. It's never about luck with you."

Slow steps carried Curtze in a widening circle around the grave, the light drifting over hard-baked earth and faded boot prints. "In this case, I'm afraid it is. Now what did you call to talk to me about, Gene?"

Morgan huffed an irritated laugh. "Fine. Be that way, you cagey bastard. Maybe I'll let Amos fill you in how I just made your life easier and you won't have to explain the continued security breach to the E.D."

"You caught them?"

"Sure as hell did. Our little party of bootleggers have slipped under the wire for the last time. My team just cornered them in a farmhouse south of Mill Pond. I'm on my way up there now. Ringleader's a fellow by the name of William Brennan."

"Brennan." Curtze mouthed the word as if it was distantly familiar. "Are you expecting trouble?"

"Nope. They're just out looking for kith and kin. They don't want hassle any more than we do. I am going to put the fear of God into them, though. And I may just toss Brennan in the brig for a few days."

The flashlight beam fell on a point beyond the tip of Curtze's expensive shoes. He bent and plucked another cigarette stub out of the grass before making it disappear. "Do what you think's best. Just be careful."

"Always."

"One more thing."

A moment's silence passed. Somewhere in the forest, a night bird screamed. From the dome of light surrounding the house, a figure emerged, casting a long shadow as it made its way down the hill toward the locust tree. Curtze quickly killed the flashlight and tucked away the tin.

"What's that?"

"Get some sleep. You looked like a dead man this morning."

Gene Morgan grunted. "Well, thanks a lot, sweetheart. Maybe you should practice what you preach. I might actually listen to you. I'll see you tomorrow, all right?"

The call ended. Curtze pocketed the phone and turned to face a compact man in a black uniform.

"Did you confirm the samples?" Curtze gazed over the man's head at the broken-down house.

"We're running the material against Twelve's sequence now. We won't have results for another hour, but it fits her pattern."

The two of them made their way up the hill toward the roar of truck engines. Lights strafed the windows from inside the house, throwing shadows of the hard-angled figures who scoured each room like scavengers. There was a crash, followed by a storm of angry shouts.

"How soon can you be done here, Sam? If you can finish the analysis at the lab, I'd appreciate it."

"I have something you might want to see first."

Curtze shielded his eyes as he stepped into the harsh glare of floodlights. A black Ford Expedition sat next to a utility truck with a boom and cherry picker, and the words Mobile Power and Light on its doors.

"I have a flight to catch first thing in the morning for a debriefing with the E.D." Curtze raised his voice to be heard over the noise. "Can this wait?"

His black-clad companion paused at the head of a broken walkway leading to the house, forcing Curtze to turn. "Oh, I think you'll find this worth your while. Jacqueline will understand. We won't need long."

Allen Curtze followed the stocky man up the porch step into a cramped room that stank of tobacco, mildew, and body odor. There was a small television on the corpse of a console radio. A moth-eaten gingham quilt stained by years of hard use was draped over an ancient recliner.

On an end table was a framed picture of a middle-aged woman in large spectacles and a permanent wave that had gone out of style in the seventies. It lay on its back. A pair of smudged reading glasses sat next to a glass, half full of cloudy water.

"Tight quarters," Sam said, nodding at a broad-shouldered man muscling a bulky black case toward the door. He reached the foot of a narrow staircase and gestured for Curtze to take the lead. "Please."

He started up, warped steps shrieking under his weight. He ran a hand over the rail, then blew dust from his palm. At the banister he paused before a trio of framed pictures, his creased face slackening as he focused on the one in the center.

The photo was a rustic black-and-white of a man with hard features in a thick wool suit and the expression of a lifetime of deprivation. Curtze studied it, washed of emotion, a flat blank, as if he'd stripped himself of feeling. His chest rose and fell once before following his companion to a narrow loft door.

The room beyond was a mausoleum of piled boxes and dust. Walls of rotted cardboard fortified by old lamps, wooden chairs and a few bundles of picture frames wired together filled the room. Curtze wrinkled his nose as if reacting to a bad smell, following a narrow channel carved through the clutter, the wooden floor clean of dust, as if only recently cleared.

"You bring me here just to see an old man's hoarding problem?" His voice lacked conviction, as if uttering a hope he knew would soon be crushed. Without prompting, Curtze pushed through lacy filigrees of dust-covered cobweb, slid between the heaped walls of cardboard and ancient bundles of National Geographic magazines, some old enough to be valuable had they not been chewed by rodents and rot.

A breeze lifted his hair. Moonlight streaked his weathered face, giving him a harlequin mask of black and white as he approached the open gable window, which proved to be the source of both the night wind and the pale light. The window was propped open by a book, cocked at an odd angle. But this wasn't where Curtze's gaze came to rest.

His face hardened as he stared at the small alcove set into the window. The alcove was an outpost of an eerie order. The waist-high platform had been swept clean of the familial refuse that dominated the room, and used by someone, or something, for other purposes.

The platform glittered with artifacts of metal, plastic, and glass, all arranged in neat columns. A matchbox and its two-dozen or so matches were lined up in a row, along with a Bic lighter that had been painstakingly disassembled, its flint wheel, striker, plastic button, and reservoir arranged in lines of schematic precision.

"Notice how they are organized." Sam brushed against Curtze as he peered past his shoulder.

Curtze touched a cracked Coke bottle, which collapsed into pieces on contact. It lay in a sort of commentary to the shattered hand mirror whose pieces had also been carefully reassembled.

"You'd almost say it's the work of a child, if not for the care by which they're arranged. Perhaps an autistic child."

The remains of a transistor radio occupied a large space in the center nearest the window. Semiconductors and wires and tiny components were set according to size, shape, and color, darks fading to lights, larger to smaller, including several frayed lengths of wire. Six D batteries occupied their own space.

"Except of course there were no children here. Autistic or otherwise. And there are, of course, these."

The corners of the alcove glittered with fine, gossamer fibers, which also glazed the floor at their feet and the surfaces of a few nearby boxes. Sam plucked one from the window sill, raising it up to catch the light. It was stiff, roughly six inches long and resembled a translucent porcupine quill.

"Now we know why there are so few other morphs in this area." Sam rotated the fiber, which was tipped in a black knob that resembled dried flesh. "She's doing our job for us," he said. "Killing her competitors. And collecting trophies. This one still has its venom sack." He dropped the fiber to the floor.

"Hush, Sam," Curtze said. "Please." He straightened, face set in concentration. The room was littered with them, making the corners shimmer like strange frost. "For God's sake let me think."

He ran a hand through his hair, eyes on the floor, seeing nothing but his own thoughts. The only sound was the shuffle of hard leather soles and the creak of old wood.

"How many of your men have seen this?"

Sam cocked his head. "Deacon and Kovalevsky. They're the ones who found it."

"They came straight to you?"

Sam nodded slowly.

"Good."

"The board will want to hear about this."

Curtze shot the man a look. "Out of the question."

"I'd think you'd be happy, Allen. It validates everything you've said for the last twenty years. I believe you had a name for this evolutionary event horizon, did you not?"

Curtze faced Sam, face hard. "This is a rogue. Pure and simple."

"She's learning, Allen. She's tapping into the latent memories from her sire, or very likely, studying members of her prey species. Which is why she's kept this elderly man alive. She was studying him. Observing. Learning from him. This is your great leap. The board will listen to you now."

"No."

Sam closed his mouth. His brow furrowed.

"Mason, you put all your resources into finding Twelve. You understand? All other concerns are secondary. Find her!"

Curtze stepped past Sam Mason and made his way to the door.

"May I ask why?" Mason said.

Curtze paused at the threshold. "I want you to burn this, Sam. All of it. Every building, every lean-to, every vehicle. It's all ash, do you hear me? Leave nothing."

18

RATS IN THE ATTIC

- Noah -

Sleep left as it had come. Suddenly and brutally, like a blow.

Noah jerked his head up and found himself crumpled in the north doorway. The jamb dug painfully into his back. One knee was crushed to his chest and a leg was splayed drunkenly in the yard. But at least that damned house was quiet.

He groaned, levered himself up, straightening his bent leg with a crack.

Daylight had abandoned him, leaving him in an eerie silence. The memory of a nightmare pulled his gaze to the second-floor window above the kitchen. Nothing. Ma's room was dark, the house a dead husk. Like it was supposed to be.

This should have been a relief.

For most of that evening he'd listened to the bedpost punch the floorboards of Ma's bedroom, a constant racket he could not escape, not even by clamping his hands over his ears. It started early that afternoon, after he'd crawled out of bed in a dry-mouthed haze, with the infernal itch at the base of his spine. Those miseries were soon eclipsed by the "thump", "thump", "thump" beneath his temples that grew and grew until it took on actual force and direction.

By the time he realized where the noise was coming from, the light was on upstairs. He stood in the yard, opening and closing his eyes, rubbing at them, trying to get them to work right. But the light stayed on.

He resigned himself. Instead of hiding, he sat down to watch, thinking maybe she'd just pull aside those curtains and show her face. She never did, of course. She couldn't. She was tied down to the bed up there. The ropes were tight, the knots secure. He'd made damned sure of that.

Something worse than fear and isolation was chewing up the wiring in his skull. And here was something else, a little bonus that put a few extra new nails in his cross. The thing doing the chewing might be the same nasty rat that had burrowed into Ma's attic. A parting gift, maybe; a genetic heirloom passed from mother to son, listed in the fine print of Ma's last will and testament. *Do not open until Christmas.*

But Ma was quiet now, her spirit still, her pound of flesh exacted. Something else had yanked him out of sleep, and it wasn't the terrible itch or the pain in his joints. His heart hammered like Ma's bed post.

Why?

The answer came an instant later.

The shriek came as a long, single-syllable curse that started sharp and serrated, widened to a full pitch with notes of red, before terminating in a decisive crack, like the blade of an ax in a tree.

The relief was enough to make him laugh; his heart actually slowed. So, his little friend had returned. Good. He was ready for another round, by God. He dragged himself to his feet, idly scratching at his back.

The main doors of the barn stood wide open. Like a Gatlinburg hotel flashing a vacancy sign at the roadside. No mystery why. Had Ma not stopped by for a visit he'd have waited for *her* all night. The thought of the girl gave his guts a little tug. Would she be here now, if he weren't surrounded by all these ghosts and monsters? Probably. *The bastards.*

The scream came again, firing across the Glen like a gunshot, slamming against the tree-line and bouncing back. Somewhere behind the house, maybe around the root cellar, he thought. It hadn't come any closer.

"You trying to scare me?" He could practically see it perched on the stone face of the cellar like a gargoyle, maybe calling for its friends or perhaps for him.

What do you look like?

The moon was a soft corona behind the broken clouds, shining sliver-white. Nice to see a friendly face, or near enough. She gave just enough light to see pale creatures hiding in corners.

Not such a crazy idea actually, to face the thing that fucked you over and turned you into a zombie. *Why not? If that's what you want.*

The machete lay on the workbench. Its blade gleamed dully in the pretty light. Not a great weapon. Close quarters combat only, but better than a wet stick.

Rrraaattt! came the cry. A clear invitation if there ever was one.

Maybe I'll just do that. He stepped out of the barn and strode across the yard toward the root cellar.

~

The shriek came close and hard, just around the corner.

Noah pressed his back against the house, marveling at this strange new super power, the glass pane between himself and the world, with that Glen goblin close enough to tighten his skin like a kettle drum. He was almost giddy, drawing shuddering breaths like a teenager about to lose his virginity. *And isn't it just like that? That death and sex are such close siblings?*

The cellar was twenty yards away. All he had to do was step away from the house and he would see it. He might even get lucky and spot the creature before it spotted him. A stupid thought. Getting the jump on the thing wouldn't do him a lick of good without a gun. And why he hadn't he grabbed the machete? That was an interesting question. He hadn't brought a flashlight, or a crowbar, or even a pocket knife. He suppressed another urge to laugh, clamping his teeth to stop it bubbling out of him.

Oh, you are so screwed, Weismann!

At least there was no one here to tie him to the bed and force feed him applesauce through a tube. Then again, who would end his suffering once the rot in his brain had eaten away his sanity? Who would hold the pillow over his face until he went quiet and still? Who would finally put him to sleep?

He took a breath, stepped around the corner, easy as a dream.

There was the root cellar hunched like a sleeping goblin, bathed in a shaft of moonlight. All around it the beech trees joined hands and formed a ring, with the great maple tree in the midst hovering over all like a doting mother. Picturesque, really. Scatter some fireflies and sprites into the scene and you'd have a fantasist's perfect Midsummer Night's Dream.

Except there was no monster on the cellar. No pale boogieman scurrying into the night. No devil with red claws and hungry maw.

"Little shit stood me up." He examined the shadows while pretending to smoke a cigarette, even flipping his lighter open, spilling murky light over the cellar's ancient face. He pretend-smoked another, waiting for something to happen. Nothing did.

A flutter of movement caught his eye, but it was just a dead leaf drifting from Mother Maple to the sagging corner of the front porch.

The tension in his chest settled to a dull ache. He shambled to the porch, the itch in his back the only fire in him now. He peered over the railing, hoping to find something, anything – *or someone* - sitting in the rotted swing. It rocked softly, as if by some invisible hand. But the porch was empty.

He hauled himself up. The railing groaned and wobbled precariously, but held as he stepped over. He put a hand on the swing to still it before making his way to the front window where the yellowed curtains hung in tatters. There was just enough light to see the ruin inside.

Nothing had changed since the night the ceiling had collapsed; the rest of the upstairs hadn't fallen in. That was too bad. Maybe if the whole house had collapsed and there was nothing here but a shell...

The thought ended abruptly as his skin prickled. No mistaking the movement this time. It made no attempt to hide, though it made not a sound. A solid shape slid into his periphery, descending from the porch eave like a spider on a thread, folding up on the railing.

But this was no spider. The *wrongness* of it all came together at once. The thing was pale white, with long, angular limbs that stretched, shifted, and settled on the rickety board that had no business holding its weight. Then the smell of hyacinths and rain flowed over him, went into him, and turned rotten. "Jesus..." As his gaze settled on it, the thing began to moan, low and guttural and liquid, not unlike Ma when she'd breathed her last. It raised the hair on his arms, sent his heart skittering back into motion, and taught him that he was still very capable of natural fear.

The creature was eyeless and faceless; a distortion of nature. Those spindly claws circling the rail were too long to be fingers; the blunt end of that limb was almost a foot. A small, misshapen head hung limply beneath the rail, tethered by a neck that was far too long. He didn't realize it was a head until it rose, the neck bowing unnaturally as the unearthly moan hardened to a growl *and there were the eyes*. They were gleaming daggers through wispy clumps of hair.

"Aren't you a sight?" he murmured.

It slid off the railing and hit the floor with a thump. The joints began to piston and bend like some infernal machine as it crawled across the porch, its acid, moon-silver eyes fixed on him.

"Okay, I take it back." His legs carried him backward. "I don't want to see it."

The thing hissed and came faster as he seized the front door handle. The decaying frame cracked in protest - it hadn't been opened in years. He threw his shoulder into it once, twice.

The creature screamed and lunged. The door gave.

Noah fell inside and slammed the door. But before the latch

caught, the creature struck, knocking him on his ass into a pile of rat shit and broken ceiling.

He sprang up and fell against the door. The creature screamed. A limb flopped at his feet before slithering out of sight, letting the door bounce shut. He turned the bolt and leapt back as the creature made another assault, battering the door with enough force to rain dust and plaster from the ceiling. It struck again and again until Noah was drowning in white powder; choking on airborne death.

Nights ago, that thing had shredded the barn door like paper. Maybe it had weakened since then. Maybe not. The door wouldn't last much longer.

He wheeled to the kitchen and the back door. A shadow drew his eye to the window and he realized too late what was about to happen.

Shit! He had just enough time to shield his face as the window exploded.

A deafening howl filled the room as a white mass careened into the pile of debris on the floor.

He hurled himself toward the kitchen. *I hope you sliced out your own guts.*

He shoved the table, spilling it against the entry, and sent the two chairs after it for good measure. He tore at the back door. Wood splintered. A table leg sailed past his ear and hit the wall. He shoved through the door and fell onto the lawn. The kitchen erupted into chaos.

The barn was miles away. Too far; he'd never make it. He angled right and sprinted around the corner of the house toward the cellar. From inside the kitchen came the amplified fury of claws ripping through the door.

Go. Just go! He flew past the cellar, dodged through the dancing legs of the beech trees, and plunged through a barricade of underbrush. Branches raked his face; vines and brambles tangled his feet. His shirt snagged and tore. The forest turned on him like a hungry animal and tried to chew him to pieces.

Did it matter? This thing was playing for keeps now. Twice it had him and let him go. Now it was hungry, pissed off. If it caught him, it would gut him like a fish and devour his insides. The thought of its pallid flesh on his filled him with revulsion beyond reason or fear.

He stumbled out of the underbrush into open ground, recognizing the tractor path. A narrow slash through the forest lay before him, leading nowhere but giving him space to run and a way to put distance between himself and the house.

He paused, panting, listening, hoping. Silence. No more shrieks. No snapping of underbrush.

Maybe.

A dark profile materialized at the end of the path near the house. The shrunken head rose, swiveled, spotted him, and screamed.

"Damn!" He ran, though he didn't expect to escape. He heard it coming, ripping past the wall of underbrush, huffing like a charging boar. *Here's to the virtues of futile struggle*, he thought. *I hope you choke on my bones.*

His own scream rose in answer to the shriek of triumph at his heels. He braced for impact, gritting his teeth just so he wouldn't bite off his tongue, and put everything he had in his last second of freedom.

The impact never came.

Instead, the underbrush at his shoulder exploded with another ear-splitting cry. He dove on instinct, covering himself, sure the monster had flanked him. But as a rush of wind blew past his ear, followed by a meaty crack of bodies amidst a cyclone of screams, he knew this was not so.

The other one.

A disharmony of not one, but two voices rose behind him. A mayhem of tearing trees and feral snarls — the cries of demons, as if hell itself had broken open. The sound of it would make an archangel piss himself.

Noah didn't look back. Even when the noise faded and the only sound was his ragged breath and desperate feet, he kept running.

In the end, it was no demon that brought him down, but cruel mother earth. The pale glow of the meadow lay before him when his foot hit a depression and his ankle rolled. He heard the pop before the pain hit, before he even hit the ground. A bolt of lightning tore through his leg, slammed through his balls, and crashed into his ribcage. The earth rose up to meet him and knocked the wind out of him, leaving him in a heap of agony.

He would have cursed had he the breath. Instead he lay, open mouthed and bug-eyed, wondering how he'd ended up on his back feeling like he'd been hit by a truck. When he could breathe again, he rolled onto hands and knees and retched.

The seizure passed. The dregs of adrenaline evaporated and the pain retreated to his ankle, where it concentrated with real heat. He dragged himself to the edge of the path and inspected his ankle, rolling up his pant leg. It was already swelling, his boot tight around the flesh. He didn't dare touch it.

He was alive, but in a world of shit. He hauled himself up with a low branch, balancing on his good foot. One hobbling step crumpled him like a broken marionette.

More swearing and tears. What was he supposed to do now, crawl over the mountain? He'd do that before he gave up and let these things feast on his still-living flesh.

The scene on the porch replayed. He squeezed his eyes shut, shuddering with an effort to drive it away. Because he'd seen some god-awful shit in his life, but never anything like that. And the worst of it was not what he'd seen. Not even what he'd smelled the instant before the air turned sour. It was what he'd felt.

Some places the mind shouldn't go. The sensations and memories of *her,* of her hands on him and her scent inside him and him inside her, and the *thing* on his porch. He couldn't. His sanity was already on the brink of collapse.

You'd better get moving, mister, or it'll be sooner rather than later.

The meadow shone through the gap in the trees, flooded by moonlight. He never wanted to lay eyes on that nightmare again or hear its voice. It might be worth dying on the mountainside.

He crawled hand over hand, dragging his bad leg to the light, groaning with every jolt. *One step at a time*. He knew he wouldn't make it ten.

He did, though, and another ten after that, and then another. He made sixty and reached the meadow before anything happened.

His pursuer came silently this time, announcing itself as cool skin gliding against his own.

He would have screamed himself empty had a hand not covered his mouth. Then the sweet smell of earth poured over him like warm water. This time it was the right smell, *her* smell, uncorrupted and pure. Soil, flowers, and spring rain. Relief and joy filled him and turned his body to wax in her arms.

19

WITCH DOCTOR

- Noah -

She'd found him.

Good Christ, he'd thought he was a dead man. Now, wrapped in her scent and the heat of her body, he felt invulnerable. All traces of fear fled like a bad dream.

She withdrew enough to let him look at her. Her face was an oval moon in the darkness, pale skin made more so by large black eyes that swallowed all other light but their own.

"Honey, am I glad to see you." He touched her cheek to make sure she was real, that he wasn't hallucinating.

She turned into his touch, then rested her hands on his shoulders and gave him a dark look.

"I know," he said. "We're in trouble. We..."

Her thumb came to his lips, quick and firm. She shook her head once, glanced over her shoulder, then turned back to him to see if he understood.

He nodded. And wanted very badly to kiss her, monster be damned.

Instead he focused on the pain in his ankle and thought about what to do next. Was it broken or just sprained? Could he walk with her help? He doubted it. The barn was a long way off. So was everywhere else. She looked strong enough, small though she was with her delicate wrists and narrow shoulders.

His gaze settled on her slender neck, on that smooth, little hollow above her breast bone. God help him, he wanted to do more than kiss her. He wanted to bury his face in her and savor her wonderful smell. He wanted to slide his hands beneath that slip and find her breasts, which were full and erect and right there. He wanted to tear it off. Take her right here in the ferns and the dirt under the light of the moon.

She watched his thoughts play out like a picture on an IMAX movie screen, the corners of her eyes playing with that not-quite smile.

He dropped his gaze.

When her thumb lingered and slipped between his lips, he looked up. Her eyes were fixed on the place where their bodies met, as if his mouth was altogether new to her. When her gaze rose, the spell broke, her expression sharpened and she stood, pulling him but by the hands.

Crazy. Not stupid.

He tried to get his weight under him, swallowed a cry when his ankle said hell no, and shook his head. "I think it's broken. I can't."

She hauled him up anyway, slipping under his arm and encircling his waist in a smooth, practiced motion. She looked up at him as if to say, "Are you just going to stand there looking stupid, or are you going to get moving?"

He snorted a laugh. It echoed in the dead air, making him wince. "Right." When she nudged him toward the house, he squeezed her shoulder to draw her gaze. "Are you sure? What about...?" He nodded at the forest.

She shook her head, pointed east toward the river.

"How do you know?"

She didn't answer, but her eyes held his until he shrugged.

"Okay. Let's get the hell out of here."

And they did. Only once did she slow or show a sign of distress or some emotion that might fit the circumstances besides her eerie calm. Even then it wasn't right. A few yards up the path, her gaze strayed to the underbrush and her body tensed. He followed her gaze and saw the pale flesh of broken saplings, caught the spicy scent of crushed ferns. A narrow, barely noticeable notch was cut into the wall of underbrush. But her expression was not what it should have been. Not fear. More like disgust.

Not stupid. But crazy.

He suppressed more laughter as they made their way past the house and the open wound of the shattered front window. He wasn't afraid of it now. He wasn't afraid of anything. She could have led him straight into Hell and he'd have let her.

By the time they reached the barn, his ankle was screaming and he was streaming sweat. His foot felt as if it was being squeezed in a vice, and he imagined the flesh ready to burst the laces of his boot.

She maneuvered them inside, closed the door behind them, and led him to a wooden tool box where she eased him down. He gasped in a mix of relief and renewed agony, reaching for his boot. But when she padded off, he straightened. He had no breath to call after her. All he could do was watch her become a silhouette against the moonlit gap between the two main door panels. His stomach plunged. But instead of slipping out and disappearing, she grabbed the braces and hauled them shut. The doors slid together with a heavy rumble and a boom.

Light disappeared. He sat in near-perfect darkness listening to her quick footsteps between the truck and the tack room. They slid to a stop beneath the ladder, before hands and feet played a scale on the rungs. How the hell she moved like that in the dark was a wonder.

A thought hit him like cold water. *She's been here before. Yes, of course she has. But how many times?* A memory flared, unbidden and unwelcome, of standing before the doors as something or someone pried them open from the outside. The boom of the shotgun and the blistering, red flash, and...

No. He slammed the doors on that writhing limb of crazy before it breeched his skull and joined the chewing rats.

The distinctive pop and hiss of a match brought him up. The flare above the balcony soon settled to a mellow orange glow. It set her shadow to dancing on the pitched ceiling. The lantern, he realized, just before her face appeared over the ladder with the item in question held over the loft. She slid wicked slick down the ladder and returned to him, a blanket tucked under her arm.

She looked at his ruined ankle, then back up at him. Her expression was strangely innocent, as if her pet kitten had just been run over by a car and she could not understand why it wasn't getting back up. She cocked her head, then pulled up a torn corner of her gown and wiped it across his brow. He was too surprised to react, but the sight of her bare body made him go rigid as the satin passed over his forehead.

She knelt and gently put her hands under his injured leg. He let her do it, but his intake of breath made her pause. She raised her knee, and settled his calf on her thigh, studying the boot laces. She picked at one of the loops and tugged. He winced.

"That's okay." He tried to pull back, but she gave his calf a squeeze and shot him a warning look. After a bit of experimenting she had the knot loose and was soon pulling the lace free of the grommets. The seam widened and the boot released its death grip on his ankle. He could have cried with the relief. There was a spasm of pain as she tugged the boot off. Then she gently rolled off his sock and they were both staring at his bare foot.

It wouldn't have been pretty under the best of circumstances. But the sight of his blackened toes and ankle swollen to twice its normal size, not to mention his ragged toenails, would have made a mortician turn his head.

"Christ on a bike," he muttered as she probed the tight flesh with delicate fingers. "Broken. Yep. Definitely broken." But the pain of her soft hands was nothing like the brutality of tight lace and leather. She met his eyes, her expression serious.

"What?" he asked with a prick of nervousness.

She squeezed her eyes shut, then opened them again and looked at him expectantly. He frowned and shook his head. She held him firmly, pointed at him and repeated.

"Nothing you can do, honey. All we can do is bandage it." He didn't want to do even that.

He wasn't sure what she had in mind. Whatever it was clearly involved him closing his eyes, which meant something no sane doctor would recommend. Again he tried to pull away, but with no more success than before. Another severe look, eyes wide and scolding, like she would sit there all night until he by god did what he was told.

He'd be safer having brain surgery in a slaughterhouse. This pleasant warmth, this calm, this idiotic desire to trust her. Not good at all.

He shrugged. "What the hell." Not understanding, but not needing to, he closed his eyes.

His lids fluttered when she lifted her slip and placed the sole of his foot against the smooth warmth of her belly. She squeezed his calf, painfully this time.

"All right, all right. Sorry." He fought more mad laughter.

Her hands fastened around the swelling, which made him grit his teeth, ready for something a lot worse. He felt subtle movement in her skin beneath the sole, followed by a strange wetness, like a kiss. No time to interpret what it meant. White-hot fire shot through the sole of his foot and up his leg. He screamed. His eyes flew open, not so much from the pain but the surprise. So unlike what he'd expected. Sharp and electric, the sensation softened to a gentle heat that spread through his whole body, starting at his ankle and working its way north.

He gasped, looking at his still swollen foot, now an outline beneath her gown and saw she was looking at him with that not-smile, expectant. Satisfied.

He shook his head, staring, tongue frozen. When he was finally able to get something out it was something lame like, "How?"

Robbed of greater eloquence, he relaxed, letting the odd sensation settle into his groin and belly, going deep into him like a shot of whiskey. Damn, did it feel good.

"Holy shit." He raised his foot, which she released at last. "Holy, holy, holy, shhh." He brought it into his lap and wiggled his toes, poking at the tight purple skin that even now looked less angry. No pain. None at all.

"Lady, you are you something else."

He put his foot on the floor and tried to stand but she was on him instantly, pushing him back down and giving him a face that said, "Are you crazy?"

Now he did laugh. It swallowed him whole and wouldn't let him stop. She studied him with cocked eyebrows. *We're both fucking crazy,* he thought, and laughed some more. If Ma's ghost was in this place, she was in good company.

His laughter faded as the very memory of pain disappeared and something else took its place. It rose from his core and spread. An awareness of not just her, but of *her.* The moment he'd first seen her on the path tonight and that sudden flare of desire. That was pale and transparent next to this. A match to a bonfire. Her smooth skin, the swell of her breasts, the nipples hardening before his eyes, the goose-flesh on her bare thighs, her parted lips. Her rich, unbelievable smell that even now grew stronger.

He would have moved first if she had not. She came to her knees and took his face in her hands and kissed him, deep and slow and hard. The feel of her, the taste of her, the brush of her tongue overwhelmed his circuits. He had been kissed before. But this was no kiss. This had no context. This was being set on fire and hoping it would never stop.

She broke the connection, drew in a long breath, exhaled a shuddered sigh. Her smile was gone, replaced by something hungry and furious. She bared her teeth, which may have been sharp points, but he hardly cared. She kissed him again. His arms encircled her, crushing her to him, his own mouth turning sharp and predatory.

She broke long enough to glance over her shoulder and kick aside a tool box that must have weighted seventy pounds. It toppled and rolled with a clash of metal, coming to rest somewhere out of sight. She yanked him off the box and onto the floor.

The wave of pain as his heel struck the floor did nothing to the desperation that now fully consumed him. She shoved him down and pulled off her slip before attacking his shirt. He gave her help she didn't need. It tore.

She straddled him and pressed her mouth to his chest and as her tongue and lips and teeth played up his body to his neck and he forgot all about his ankle, all about the monster in the darkness, about the ghost in the house. He forgot himself, forgot how to feel pain or anything but this hunger that was more intense than anything he'd felt in his life. As she stripped off his jeans, his very life ceased to matter. The departure of her body from his as she pulled away his clothes was a small eternity.

But then she was on top of him again, took him inside her and his vision blurred. She began to draw him out, pushing him down, pulling him in deeper, grinding her hips into his. It felt as if his very soul were being pulled down, concentrated in his loins to flow out of him and into her. As he finished and died inside her, solid ground gave way beneath him and he was floating on a cloud. "Stay with me," he whispered in a half-dream as sleep pulled him swiftly and inexorably away from her. He felt it coming the instant she rolled off of him, the sensation heavy and chemical. She lay behind him now, her belly pressed to his back where he could feel a strange but not unpleasant pressure just above his tailbone. A gentle, pulsating heat, a drawing, like a deep kiss, but more. He had no idea whether it was real or just the stirring of a brain holding to the last dregs of consciousness, the feeling of her pulling at him. But her breath in his ear, her smell in his nostrils, that was real enough. And he wanted it to stay.

He fought to stay awake, if not to talk to her, then just to be conscious of her. But he was so tired. He tried to sit up, to turn and face her, but she held him still, stroked his face, and he knew he couldn't hold on any longer.

"Stay," he repeated, "Please."

His eyelids fell. Her only answer was her hand on his face and her lips pressed to the back of his neck. It was the last thing he felt before black waters closed around him and drowned him in a gentle abyss.

20

THE SCARLET WHORE

- Noah -

The girl stayed.

He opened his eyes and found himself tangled in a blanket on the barn floor. But he wasn't alone. Her warm scent covered him like bathwater. The rustle of another body in the room with him, the solid presence of her short-circuited a surge of panic.

Good thing. Had he charged off to go look for her just then, he'd have fallen on his ass. He sat up to a typhoon of dizziness and nausea. He cradled his head in his hands while tears stung his eyes and fire burned in his throat. *Jesus.* This was like waking up in the river mud all over again.

He forced his head up and found her sitting on the hood of the truck, her pale body just visible in the weak predawn light trickling through the barn slats.

She was absorbed with a dark, cylindrical object that she gripped in both hands. The sharp clicking told him what it was. She peered into the lens as if she'd never seen a flashlight before, turning it at angles, then shaking it. She found the switch again and clicked it repeatedly, eyes intense.

He'd last seen it in the cab of his pickup the night the creature had attacked him. He shuddered, envisioning her crawling through those cobwebs to get to it, wondering what had possessed her. When had she done it? Last night?

Brave little thing. Completely crazy. Then again, she'd spent days out there on her own and was more or less fine. Better than him.

"Batteries are dead." His throat was crushed gravel.

She looked at him as if only just remembering he was there, then hopped down and padded over to him, clutching the flashlight. She pointed at his injured leg. It was still wrapped up in the blanket.

He shucked off the cover and exposed his ankle. The flesh was an angry purple fading to violet, bordered by the yellow of an old bruise. He rotated his foot. There was little pain. The swelling was almost gone.

He got to his knees and stood, careful not to put any weight on it until he was upright. He nearly toppled over, would have had the girl not been there to steady him. The problem wasn't his ankle but his head, which felt as if it had kept on rising, floating into the rafters. His vision danced with tiny pinpricks of white, narrowed to a point, and almost vanished altogether.

She held him upright until his eyes and legs got their act together.

"Sorry," he said.

She let go of him. He took a few tentative steps, wincing at a stale bolt of pain.

"Jesus." He was limping a little, but so what? Last night he figured he wouldn't walk for a month. Now he barely felt anything.

"It's not even swollen." He looked down at himself, saw he was still naked and couldn't even blush about it. They were well past modesty now. But it was funny he'd only just noticed. And how had he become so thin? His rib cage looked like the rungs of a ladder.

"How did you do it?" He threw her a quizzical look.

She didn't answer, but seemed as rapt at the sight of him walking as he was. There was something about the way the bones grated in his ankle with each step that he didn't like, that didn't seem quite natural.

Another wave of dizziness forced him to lean against the wall.

"What are those things out there?" The words were out before he knew they were coming. It was a question she could never answer. He wasn't sure he wanted her to.

"You've seen them. Haven't you?"

She held his gaze, her eyes sharp and intent. Clearly she'd understood. Then her eyes fell to the flashlight. She worked the switch again, slowly pressing and releasing.

A flash memory of that creature's silver eyes, the lank hair, ugly angles and spidery limbs, horrifyingly human.

He felt a wave of pity for her, wondering what it must have been like for her, how terrified she must have been, hiding, running. Had it done to her what it did to him? The burning itch in his back gnawed distantly at his spine even now. Did she too have such a wound? How close had she come to death out there?

As to what they were, he was willing to bet both his eyes that they were unknown to science. Maybe even from outer space, though he would never say that aloud, not even to her. But it wasn't that bad of an idea. Ma would have called it pagan nonsense. God only knew what she would have made of all this. God's judgment on all these wicked sinners here in the valley maybe? It made the idea of an alien invasion seem less ridiculous.

Unless it was all just for Noah. Wouldn't that would be ironic? Ma's personal theology put to a real dilemma. Jessie? Hell yes. In Ma's book Jessie had it coming. But she had already gotten hers. Not Noah, not Ma's precious, sinless, favored child.

For all he knew it was the whole damned planet, a War of the Worlds scenario of which he was just one victim among millions. He hadn't talked to another soul in days. Before the girl, the last person to utter a word to him was Judd McPherson. Now what would he say to this alien theory? According to Judd, this had all happened before. Just here, in the valley. And it had taken Tanner Weismann. Judd thought that it would eventually take them all.

She sat down on floor where they'd slept, crossed her legs Indian-style, and twisted the cap off the flashlight.

"What the hell do they want?" The question was more to himself. But she looked up at him anyway and held his gaze. Her expression was strange, haunted, almost sad. He was about to ask what was the matter but then she pointed at him.

He frowned. "You mean 'us'. They're after people."

She shook her head once. She laid aside what was left of the flashlight, now in pieces. The four D-cell batteries were stacked in a neat little row next to the metal cap and spring. She had also taken the head apart and the little bulb lay next to the lens. It reminded him of a schematic laid out in 3-D. She'd done it with incredible speed. One second the Maglite had been whole and intact; the next it was in a dozen pieces and arranged like a little shrine on the hood of the truck.

The flashlight conquered, she rose and came to him, took his hand, turned it over and ran a thumb over the wound Samson had given him. It had had scabbed over and healed in a matter of a few days. She met his eyes and shook her head. She pointed at him.

"*Me?* Why? I'm not the only one in the valley."

Her huge black eyes bored into him as she held his hand, gently stroking the knuckles. His own gaze drifted as he tried to pull together the picture that she saw, but he obviously didn't.

"That thing had me down there at the river that night."

She let his hand go as he paced.

"It stung me, or bit me or something. Probably would have killed me, except..." The machete lay on the workbench where he'd left it the previous night. He idly fingered the edge. "You were there. You drove it off, didn't you? How?"

He felt foolish for saying it; part of him wished he hadn't. Now that it was out he watched to see what she would do with it. What other explanation could there be? If she hadn't saved him, what had? Her expression said enough. It was slight, soft, and then gone, but it was enough.

He lifted her chin. "Why? You could have been killed."

She put a finger to his chest, then laid a palm over his heart. The touch lingered. Her black eyes drifted, lost in some private memory perhaps. Of what horrors, he could only imagine. Then she touched her own chest, shook her head and looked at him as if asking if he understood.

He wasn't sure he did, other than that she seemed to think she was safe and he wasn't.

"What makes you so special?" He stroked her cheek. "Who are you?" he asked, wishing she could tell him.

Her expression flattened and she pulled away, but he held onto her.

"Well, I'm glad you came. Whoever you are." She probably didn't understand. She didn't have to. That almost-smile returned and she leaned into him, slipping her arms around his waist and laying her head on his shoulder, then nuzzling his neck.

"I'm glad you chose me," he whispered, breathing in her smell.

In time she pulled away, her expression serious and suddenly distant.

"What is it?"

She shook her head, making her way to the main doors. The light streaming into the barn was stronger now, the awful morning sun about to peer over the horizon. He understood.

"Don't," he said, his voice more urgent and pleading than he meant. "Stay here." He reached for her again, despair wrapping its fingers around his throat. She stepped out of reach, gestured at the doors, and seized the brace bar.

"Please," he said, desperate panic tearing his dignity away. *Hold on! Let me give you something to wear, some shoes, something to eat! You have to be hungry. Just stay.* All the things he should have said earlier. Now they were in his head, but he couldn't say them. She set the beam down and shoved the doors aside.

And if she doesn't come back?

The very notion of it made him want to scream, made him want to grab her and hold her down, force her to stay. The idea of her leaving him – never mind the fact that he didn't even know her name, hadn't even known she existed until a few days ago – seemed unbearable.

She looked back once, her body silhouetted in the gray light, then vanished.

He would have felt good and sorry for himself had he not been so exhausted. The moment she was out of sight, an incredible weariness fell on him, as if someone had jerked a plug and let the strength drain out of him. He went to the blanket, still wadded on the floor, and lay down.

Just a few minutes. He held the blanket to his face, breathing in the faint traces of her, and fell asleep.

~

As far as Noah could remember, Ma had only ever hit him once. She'd gotten pretty violent near the end of her life, after her mind had burnt to a nub when all she could see was Daddy in the room with her. But he couldn't hold her responsible for that. Except for her very last moment, she barely knew when Noah was in the room.

He'd received only one beating in his life, but it had been a good one. The funny thing was, it was Ma's certainty of Noah's natural purity that had earned it for him. As usual, Jessie had caught the worst of her fire that night, though it wasn't physical. It would have been better if it had been.

None of it was Jessie's fault. But seldom did Ma's parental discipline have much to do with rationality. Daddy might have actually intervened that night had he been alive to do it.

Noah had had a nightmare. He'd tiptoed down to Jessie's room like he was little, though he was almost nine then, years past sleeping with his big sister. But this one had been bad. Daddy's accident was fresh. Doc Anderson had taken him away only a week ago and the house still smelled of blood and disinfectant.

"Noah?" She was still mostly asleep, her voice cracking. She squinted at the dull light from the hallway.

Noah listened for Ma, but he'd been very careful not to make a sound. He knew every bad-tempered board and where to step without setting them to howling.

"What are you doing?" she asked.

"Sorry," he said. "I...I can't..."

"What?" A note of impatience entered her voice, sleep falling away.

"I saw..." He couldn't finish. She'd think he was crazy. Noah shifted from foot to foot, knowing he should just go back to bed. He couldn't. Nor could he ask her for what he wanted either. He shook all over.

She sat up. "Noah? Are you okay?" Her question was spiked with worry. She was fully awake now.

"I had a bad dream," he managed.

He thought she was going to get mad at him. But the frown softened, and when she spoke she wasn't mad. Her gaze rose to the ceiling as if she too knew that waking Ma would be a real bad thing.

She pulled back the covers. "Come on."

He padded over, crawled in, and turned over on his side. He was glad when she put her arm around him. He tried to hold the tears back, but they came anyway.

He didn't know how long he'd been asleep when Ma found them. He must have been under deep. The door banged and harsh light hurt his eyelids. Ma's voice hit him like a thunderclap.

"What do you think you're doing!"

Noah screamed, unable to remember where he was or recognize this woman who stood over him. She was a scarecrow, thin and drab in a shapeless nightgown, face hard and haggard and eyes bloodshot. Her hands shook.

"I'm sorry!" Noah squealed, not sure what he was sorry for. But Ma wasn't looking at him. She was looking at Jessie.

"What?" Jessie said. "What's the matter with you?"

Jessie had always stood up to Ma. She'd never been scared of their mother the way he was, and though he couldn't take his eyes off this woman, he could feel Jessie's anger by the way she held him.

Ma's voice was a growl. "You get away from him, you little trollop!"

She spat out the last word like it tasted bad. Ma never swore, but this was far worse than anything Daddy ever said. It wasn't the first time she'd called Jessie that, but it was the worst.

"Get away from him, do you hear me?" She lunged for them.

Jessie flinched like she was expecting a slap. Noah expected it too. He wasn't prepared when Ma fastened a hand on his arm and squeezed. It hurt.

"Stop it!" Jessie didn't let go of him. She wrapped herself around him. "Let him go!"

Ma shoved Jessie hard and dragged Noah off the bed and across the floor.

He tried not to cry, but he'd never seen his mother look like this. And she was hurting him. His arm was going to break. He said "I'm sorry" over and over again, but no one seemed to hear. Jessie stormed after them.

"Leave him alone! He was scared. He just had a bad dream."

"Don't you dare speak to me about my son, you filthy little slut!" Ma's fingers dug into him. "You think I don't know what men do? What they think about? And you let him in your bed."

"He's nine, for Christ's sake!"

Noah stared at Ma, pain forgotten. Ma's eyes went wide. Her face looked as if it would split open.

"Don't...you...*dare!*" Tiny flecks of spittle hit Jessie's face. "Speak that way in my house. Do you hear me? You will not take the name of our Lord in vain so long as you live under my roof. Now you shut up and get back into your filthy bed, you scarlet whore!"

Ma's finger twisted in the air, like she wanted to dig it into Jessie and make it come out the other side. His big sister stood in her bedroom looking suddenly younger than himself. She looked small, like a breeze could blow her away. Noah tried not to see but couldn't help it. There were tears in her eyes, tears of rage as well as hurt. And fear. Jessie looked at Ma as if their mother had grown horns and a tail.

Ma hauled Noah out of the room and up the stairs.

"Where are you going?" Jessie followed, but the fight had gone out of her. "Mom, what are you doing?"

She reached for her, but Ma shoved her back.

"He wasn't doing anything, okay? Mom!"

Ma didn't listen.

She hauled him into her room, slammed the door, and locked it. "I'll teach you, boy," she muttered. Noah stood very still, watching his mother and growing more terrified at every word.

"I'll teach it out of you now. Never again. I swear, you won't be like *him*, I promise you."

She came out of the closet with a coat hanger. "I won't let you. I won't let it happen. Not to you, Noah!"

"Momma?"

"Come here," she said. He didn't move, so she came to him.

"I'll teach it out of you before it burns your soul black." She grabbed his arm and brought the coat hanger down hard on the backs of his legs. She hit him again and again until he was crying so hard he couldn't see.

"Mom, stop it!" Jessie's voice, high-pitched and watery. "For God's sake, you know what he's just been through. Momma, please!"

He didn't hear anymore, couldn't make out the words. Jessie kept screaming and Ma kept hitting. She talked while she did it, muttering words he couldn't understand. About Daddy and about sin. She kept hitting even after he'd wet his pajamas and couldn't stand anymore.

21

SWEET DREAMS

- Noah -

He was working on the generator when she returned that night. Or he was trying. He'd started the project not because he cared about having power again but because he needed something to keep his hands occupied. He was constantly fishing in his pocket for cigarettes, which he could no longer smoke, or flipping Daddy's lighter open and closed, turning it over and over like a talisman until he thought the embossing would wear off. Toothpicks weren't helping. He'd chewed so many that the back of his throat burned with a gritty acid.

Worse was that fucking sore in his back. God, it itched. The torment should have eased by now, but it was driving him mad. He was constantly digging at it. His fingernails were now bloodstained. If the wound wasn't infected already, it soon would be.

Even with the generator in pieces and the reasons for its refusal to fire a puzzle worth his full attention, he couldn't keep his hands on task.

Jesus, what the hell is wrong with me? He felt like an addict in need of a fix. His whole body was charged with need. This was beyond a craving for nicotine, or alcohol, or Oxy, or any other chemical he'd tried. Never had he felt anything like this. The reason was no mystery.

It was well after dark, the lantern having burned for perhaps an hour, when the air pressure shifted. He looked up from the muddle of engine parts to see her step into the lantern light, bringing with her that wonderful smell. Spring rain, sun-warmed skin, and ripe fruit.

It was like a latch clicking, a bolt sliding into place and fitting just where it was supposed to. Relief and need warmed his insides like strong alcohol, sinking into his belly and spreading. For a moment he simply soaked her up, reveling in her presence.

"Hey," he said.

She reached up and stroked his hair. Her touch set off a hunger that consumed him like a forest fire, sucking the oxygen out of him. His face flushed. He dropped his gaze, ashamed that such lust had taken him so completely, that he was so helpless to it.

He was better than this.

She took his face in her hands and kissed him hard, filling him up with her, and God help him, her lips were sweeter than he remembered. She pulled away, leaving him trembling and gasping like a landed fish. She was looking at him in a way he'd never seen before, in a way he didn't like. It was more than desire. It was the look Jessie used to give him when she'd trounced him in a game of checkers or won an argument. Or got Ma good and pissed off.

A spike of anger turned his shame and lust into a powerful kind of greed he hadn't even known existed.

He grabbed her, ignoring her intake of breath, and pulled her into him. He pressed his mouth over hers and tried for all the world to suck his wind back, feeling the bones in her shoulders shift and her body writhe in his arms. He didn't stop. Shocked and horrified as he was, he pinned her to the floor, unbuckled his jeans and yanked up her gown. As he entered her, she gasped and tightened her own arms around him and wrapped her legs around his waist. Her hands twisted in his hair and he was swept away in a tide.

When he opened his eyes, it was dark and he was alone again. He reached across the blanket and found only space.

"Fuck." He sat up slow this time, anticipating the wave of dizziness. Even so, when he got to his feet, the vertigo spun his head like a top. He slumped against the tractor, seeing stars, cradling his head.

This wasn't nicotine withdrawal. Something vital had been taken from him. A recompense for his vile act, no doubt. That she had stolen his essence and then abandoned him was no less than he deserved.

When vertigo passed and he could stand up straight without wanting to vomit, he made his way toward the front doors, feeling his way along the flank of the truck.

"Hello?" His voice was muffled, as if he'd spoken in a padded room.

He remembered stirring from heavy sleep during the night, blinking at the edge of consciousness, having the impression of her arm over him, her head on his chest. He'd felt her kiss, her hand on his face, and had gone back to sleep. She was definitely gone now.

He moved on shaky legs, wincing with each step, his ankle hurting like hell. The thin light of a distant moon streamed through the slash in the doors and told him that dawn was still some hours away. It did little to help him navigate the clutter and tight quarters around the workbench.

Tools and generator parts rattled as he groped for the lantern. That was easy enough to find. But the matches were a different story. After lots of swearing, knocking over a can of nails, and generally making a mess of things, he heard the familiar clatter of the little box at his fingertips. He lit the lantern and a small circle of the world swam back into view.

The only sign she had been there was the flashlight, its components arranged in precise order on the hood of the truck. He stared at it while fighting back an irritating prickle at the corner of his eyes.

He drifted aimlessly through the barn, eventually finding himself back at the workbench, staring at the disarray and uselessness of his own work. His tongue stuck to the roof of his mouth and tasted like ash. He was thirsty enough to drink a pond dry. His stomach growled, but it wasn't food or water he wanted.

He picked up a jar of screws and threw it against the wall. It shattered and sent metal and glass flying. The shards glittered prettily in the orange lantern light.

"Damn it," he muttered, gazing at his bare feet and the shambled mess of what used to be an oasis of order, cleanliness, and pride. *You really let yourself go to shit, Noah.* Daddy's voice echoed in his skull.

He trudged to the tack room, found a broom and dust pan, and made a half-assed effort to sweep up, chucking glass, screws, dirt and all into a waste can that hadn't been emptied in weeks. Naked, lantern in hand, he limped outside to the spigot to quench his raw throat. He saw the house and froze.

"Jesus Christ." The lantern grew heavy in his hand, sank and dangled at his knee.

While the rest of the world was frozen in colorless death, the house was dancing a jig. That cursed rat nest blinked and flickered like a bad TV picture. It flashed with bolts of color like psychedelic lightning. The Glen should have been alive and breathing, humming with the insects and night creatures. Instead it was a husk, while Ma's vampiric house pulsed with stolen life force.

He ran a hand over his face as if to wipe the scene away. When that didn't work, he closed his eyes and counted backwards from ten. This wasn't real. None of this was real. *Go the fuck away, bitch.*

He opened his eyes again. The house was still, nothing but a rotted corpse. Good and dead like it was supposed to be. Tears burned his cheeks as silence swelled back in and he was the only living thing on the planet.

The bedroom light came on.

"Shit!" He stumbled, turned away, and lurched to the barn as fast as his bad ankle would allow.

This was really happening. He was going out just like his mother. His brain was going to boil in his skull until he was a screaming, bed-shitting idiot. If only one of those aliens would come back and finish the job. He'd welcome them like princes.

He slammed the door and fell against it. There had to be a way out of this. There was always a way. Besides offering himself to the boogieman. Or taking himself to the top of Pikes Falls and throwing himself off. But what?

The answer was obvious. He had one hope. And no matter how crazy it might seem, he couldn't drive it off. The idea was as right and as necessary as rain on parched earth.

He raised the lantern, praying he would see her perched on the tractor. But the barn was empty. He wanted to scream. He might have done just that had he not seen something very odd on the floor near the tractor.

Why hadn't he seen it earlier? It was a pyramid of plastic-wrappers and little cardboard boxes, like an offering to the gods of junk food. Little Debbies, a crumpled packet of chocolate doughnuts, Snickers bars, flattened peanut butter cups, and a smashed Twinkie made up the bulk of the structure, but a scattering of hard candies and two dented soda cans gave it an artistic flare that put a grin on his face.

As if pulled by gravity, he shuffled over, set the lantern on the hood, and grabbed a soda can. He cracked it open and slugged it in messy gulps that left him gasping. A wet belch echoed off the walls.

He dropped the empty can, smile spreading, and picked up the Twinkie. He laughed. *You little thief,* he thought as he tore off the wrapper and shoved the whole thing into his mouth. That was one mystery solved. How she'd survived out there all this time and looked none the worse for the wear while he looked like a cast member of Schindler's List.

But a diet of this? Unlikely. A week of this shit and your teeth would rot out of your skull. Right now, the prospect of death by sugar sounded pretty damned good. He ate every last bit of it, right down to the red and white mints, crunched them up like ice chips.

He was sucking the last few drops from the second soda can when he saw movement near the front doors. He swallowed and raised the lantern to find a familiar, luminous shape that made him forget all about his appetite. She sat cross legged on the work table, studying the pad of her right foot.

Where the hell have you been? He wanted to say it but didn't. Something in the way she held her foot reminded him of his wounded ankle.

He lowered the light and studied her. She was beautiful, so still and so perfect, like an exotic bird too rare to risk scaring away. Had it not been for her pale skin and that oval face, which glowed like a winter moon, he might never have noticed her. She looked up.

"What's wrong?" he said, once he could speak.

She went back to her foot, biting a lip in concentration, picking at a sticker or a thorn. He went to her. With a wince, she plucked something from her heel and held it up to the light.

"Oh, honey." Noah closed the distance and wrapped his hands around her fingers, which held a little sickle of glass. "This is my fault."

He plucked the shard from her and laid it aside before bending to examine her foot. She tensed, but relaxed as he cradled her ankle the way she had done for him two nights ago. He straightened her leg and began to massage the arch, carefully avoiding the tiny wound, which didn't bleed, except for a droplet of clear liquid.

"You got tough little feet, you know that?" He held her gently in both hands, prodding the flesh with his thumbs, surprised at how soft it was. The skin was dirt-black, so unlike the milky white of the rest of her.

"You're going to get an infection if we don't clean this up."

He told her to stay put and went to find the first aid kit, which was buried somewhere in the tack room. After several minutes of rifling, he found a cracked and dusty plastic box that contained bandages, aluminum packets of alcohol wipes, and antibiotic ointment.

He told her it might sting a bit and began to clean the area around the wound with a wipe, making the white underneath show, watching her face for signs of pain. She winced but otherwise didn't move.

"I need to find you some shoes." He shook his head, angry at himself for not thinking of it sooner. *I guess you've had your mind on other things, haven't you, champ*? "And clothes." The frayed edge of her slip rode up her thighs in stringy tatters.

As he spoke, her gaze alternated between his lips and his hands, which gently worked the muscles of her foot. Soon her own lips parted in apparent pleasure.

"Feel good?" He smiled.

Her eyes rolled sleepily, her body softening as she sank against the wall.

"Where do you go out there, huh?" He marveled at the delicate bones and soft skin of her instep, wondered how such a fragile thing could be such a survivor.

"I had cat named Samson," he said. "Clever son of a bitch. Tough as iron. He'd take on cats twice his size. Win, too."

His thumbs made slow circles in the ball of her foot, working the tissue below each toe, then moving the toes themselves. She twitched, her calf knotting as if he'd tickled her.

"Sorry," he said. "Anyway, Samson pretty much ran this place, you know? Wouldn't let another tom cat within ten miles of the house, except for Riley." He shook his head. "I don't know why he put up with that little shit. Except Riley was fixed, so" – he shrugged – "no competition, I guess."

She listened silently, dreamily, showing no sign of understanding. That didn't matter. He was happy just to have some reason to talk.

"Anyway, you remind me of him, a bit. Of Samson, I mean. I would have thought he'd survive judgment day. But then those things out there." He nodded at the doors. "They came, and I haven't seen him since."

He saw the faint lines of the mostly healed scars, white across the back of his hand. His gaze drifted, settled on the empty rabbit hutch.

"Maybe he's okay." He thought of poor Judd McPherson, wondered if the old fool was still alive. "If anything could survive this, he could. Probably fifty miles from here, with luck."

His hands started again. She smiled with her eyes. He didn't know if that meant she understood or if she was just happy he was back on the job.

They'd had an entire conversation the night before and she seemed to take in every word. Now she acted as if he was speaking a different language. Or not speaking at all, simply making noise like the grownups in a Charlie Brown cartoon.

"Are you hungry?" he asked. "Hungry?" He put a hand to his mouth, then felt ridiculous when she shook her head.

"Thirsty?"

She shook her head.

"I don't get it." He put her foot down and reached for the other, which she eagerly presented to him. "You never eat. You can't have made it out there all this time on junk food and table scraps."

As he massaged, her breathing slowed. She made a strange clicking sound deep in her throat that made him look up. Her eyes were closed now, head tipped against the wall. A sound of pleasure perhaps, which he wouldn't have been able to tell without looking at her. The noise was...odd, as if coming through damaged vocal cords.

She'd obviously been stealing for herself too. But that she'd gotten it all here intact was a marvel. The river stood between here and the nearest farm, and the next closest place was more than eight miles over the mountain. She sure as hell hadn't found that stuff at Judd's.

He thought of his neighbors. Of Elaine and Richard Galloway, just over the river. They still had kids at home. Rick Junior, who everybody called Rocky. He was what, sixteen? Seventeen. Noah gave an involuntary shudder. Surely they'd gotten the hell out. The Galloways didn't have a river between themselves and civilization. Nor were they stubborn and senile like old Judd McPherson. Or stubborn and insane, like Noah Weismann.

Her feet were cleaner now, but still a mess. Little pebbles of dirt gathered under his thumbs as he rubbed the soles. Her hair needed a wash. She hadn't bathed in God knew how long, though he sure as hell wasn't going ask. Even he knew that you never told a woman, even a crazy one, that she needed a bath.

"Hey, I've got something for you." He lowered her foot. She opened her eyes and raised her head, looking for all the world like a cat after its owner stopped stroking. Her put-out expression made him laugh.

"Come on." He tugged at her hand. "You'll like this. I promise." She hopped down and followed.

"How's your foot?" he asked, pointing.

She then did something that surprised him. She balled her fist and stuck up her thumb, like a hitchhiker.

He raised the lantern and together they made their way across the yard to the now silent house. Only when Noah reached the kitchen door did he stop to consider what he was doing. The giddy joy of her return had jettisoned his good sense.

What the hell was he thinking, bringing her here? She may have faced those creatures out there, but something a hell of a lot worse lived in *here*.

He was about turn around, take her back to the barn, when she surprised him again. She stepped past him, crossed the threshold, and tugged him along after.

Once inside, he was fine. There was no shrieking upstairs, no phantom lights or pounding of bedposts. The bedroom upstairs was silent.

Maybe Ma's afraid of her. More crazy from the rats in the attic. *There's nothing there. She's in your head, you stupid fuck.*

The girl was watching him again, a question mark on her face, waiting for him to do something. He wished he knew her name. Wished she could tell him. Maybe he should give her one.

He took a deep breath, made his way to the sink, and rummaged through the cupboards until he found the big canning pot. It took a lot of clattering and cursing to get it out. Once done, he shoved everything back under the sink and stood with his new prize. She was working on one of the knobs on the stove.

"Oh, no, no, no!" He grabbed her hand and pulled it away, then pointed at a burner. "See that?"

Her black eyes narrowed as she bent to look.

"Watch." He nudged her aside, turned the knob, struck a match to the burner. There was a *flump* of blue flame. She hissed. The sound of it set him back on his heels. Hauntingly familiar – coming from her lips, it made his hair stand. She didn't notice him staring because she was fixated on the ribbon of blue-yellow flame.

"It's all right, see?" He waved his hand over the burner. She stepped closer, peering at the fire before extending her own hand.

"Careful."

While she was occupied, he jostled the pot under the faucet and turned the tap, watching her walk a half circle around the stove, dipping and inspecting each burner. She tugged open the oven door and looked inside.

He hefted the pot to the stove and set it over the burner, turning the knob until he had strong blue flame.

"Ok," he said, taking her hand again. "While that's heating, let's find you some clothes."

He led her through the living room, sent shadows scurrying like rats for the corners, leaving behind the carrion of moldy furniture. Beyond the couch was the heap of collapsed ceiling and the glittering shards of the shattered front window. A tattered ribbon of curtain drifted languidly in an unseen draft. He shuddered at the memory of the spider-limbed freak coming through the glass.

Meanwhile his companion gazed at every object the light illuminated, taking in everything, more fascinated by the bookshelf and the long-dead potted plants than the evidence of alien invasion.

They stepped over a swollen hump in the floor, where the boards had festered near the stair well.

"Watch your step," he said. "I'm afraid I haven't been taking very good care of the place lately."

He didn't dare look up the staircase as he led her through the archway and past the hall closet to Jessie's bedroom.

Light expanded into the mostly empty room. There was an old dresser in the corner with a frame that once held a mirror, but little else. The hiss of their feet over the dusty floor whispered off the walls in an amplified echo. Noah released her hand, made his way to the closet, and shoved aside a curtain of moth eaten dresses hanging from a bowing rod. A coffin-sized cedar chest lay on the floor at his feet.

He bent, grabbed the rope handle, and hauled it into the middle of the room. When he opened the chest, the smell of cedar and history filled his head and sent his heart into a spasm. Here were his sister's old things: her clothes, her diaries, some of them anyway. The ones she'd left behind when she moved out, along with a few old copies of YM magazine from before she was fourteen.

The girl loomed over his shoulder, a few strands of her raven hair tickling his cheek, her scent pushing dark emotions back into the past where they belonged.

"Okay," He got his act together and sorted through the clothing for something that might fit her.

"You'll need jeans." He found some buried under the stack of diaries and magazines. "Some shirts." There were a lot of those, T-shirts and hippie blouses Jessie had seemed to love once she'd hit thirteen, and wore despite Ma's calling her a tramp, and then promptly lost interest in once she'd hit ninth grade. He also found a pair of sneakers, worn but usable. Certainly better than the nothing she had now.

A pale hand shot past him and snatched up an old photograph. She clasped it in both hands, eyeing it carefully before scrutinizing Noah.

"Jessie and me," he said, pointing at a teenage girl and the small boy in the center.

"That's my father and...that's Ma."

It was one of the few family photographs they'd ever taken. Once Ma had found Jesus, she couldn't abide cameras. "Devil's foolishness," she'd called it, "Living in the past to the forsaking of the present."

This one had been taken at the county fair twenty years ago. Daddy was sometimes sober back then, and happy. Ma was still human, not so hardened by holiness, her mind years from the mania that would later eat up her brain. Jessie had an arm draped over

Noah's shoulder. They'd just ridden some nightmare called The Corn Sheller, and it had scared the shit out him. Not that he would tell his big sister that. She'd known, of course, and hadn't teased him about it. Hadn't said a word that he'd screamed like a girl before catching himself and bearing the rest of the ride in terrified silence.

The picture was of the four of them right after they'd stepped off – after he, Jessie and Daddy had stepped off – taken by some poor fellow with a Polaroid camera trying to sell photos to everyone coming off the ride for fifty cents. Noah's face was white even in the grainy picture. Daddy had felt sorry for the guy and gave him two bucks for it, not knowing he was buying the last good memory Noah would have of them as an actual family. Ma found her faith not long after, Daddy drank himself straight to his "accident" a year later, and that was pretty much it for Weismann family happiness.

The girl shifted her gaze from him and back to the picture, fingering the face of the little boy.

"Long time ago," he said. "Though it doesn't seem that way. God, I still remember that damned ride. Jessie had no idea how close I came to puking in her lap." The steel rib cage of the thing was visible in the picture's background.

Her expression was strange and unreadable. He wondered if she had any idea what she was looking at, if she made the connection between the figure in the picture and himself.

"There's a better picture in the barn," he said, tugging the photo from her fingers and setting it carefully back in the box on top of one of Jessie's journals.

"The one of just Jessie and me. You've probably seen it. We're older in that picture. I look more like me."

To his surprise, she nodded slowly, as if deciding this was the best way to respond to someone talking about the voices in their head. She reached up and laid a finger to his cheek, almost as she had done the photograph.

She leaned in and placed her lips on his, soft and lingering. He shuddered, let out a breath as his face flushed and his treacherous body woke up. He stepped back.

"Hey," he said, taking her hands. "Let's try on some of these clothes."

He didn't have any underclothes for her and felt no shame for not being sorry about it. He helped her slide into a pair of jeans, a process more tricky and intimate then it should have been, but after some initial confusion and overbalancing, managed to pull them over her hips and fasten the button. They were a little long and a bit loose, but fit surprisingly well. He'd thought he might have to find her a belt, but they snugged against her hips very nicely.

He remembered Jessie being bigger. Strange how time distorted your memories. He lifted the slip over her head. She raised her arms obediently, getting the idea quickly about how T-shirts worked. She soon had her arms through the sleeves.

"Better," he said. She looked down at herself, as if realizing that her form had changed. She pulled at the clothes, ran her hands over the coarse denim and took careful steps as if she were in knee deep mud.

"It's all right," he said. "You look great."

She frowned at him before turning her attention back to this strange new skin.

"Here. Try these on." He took her hand and pulled her to the floor. He straightened her leg, taking her foot, amused at a glint of eagerness in her eyes.

"Not this time," he said, giving her toes a squeeze. "Shoes."

He held up the left sneaker and slid it onto her foot before tying the laces. He did the same with the right, then pulled her up.

She let out a little huff and goose-stepped in a circle around the room, scowling as if she'd stepped in something really bad. Finally, she sat down, tugged them off and gave him a screwed-up face, shaking her head.

He raised his eyebrows. "That bad? But what about your poor feet?"

Her face relaxed, but held on to that little shadow. Again she shook her head.

He laughed. "Fine. We'll talk about it later," he said. "Baby steps."

He went through the rest of the cedar chest, looking for a jacket or a heavier shirt that might keep her warm on cool nights, not that there were many of those now. Since the rain had gone, the nights were warming up again, air heavy and thick. But it didn't hurt to have an extra layer if she needed it. Jessie certainly wasn't going to miss them.

He went through each, holding them up one at a time, asking what she thought. But she was more interested in the laces of the rejected shoes.

Why are you doing this? he asked himself. *Are you planning on keeping her?*

She soon grew bored of the sneakers and returned to the cedar chest. There was a flutter of pages as she flipped through one of Jessie's diaries. He watched from his pile of clothes as she held the notebook open, peering at the tight letters as if she'd never seen writing before. She found a ballpoint pen and turned it over, discovering the button and the business end. She left a mark on her hand and stopped to gaze at it, frowned, then looked curiously at the notebook. She drew a slash across the page. He winced, but what the hell. It wasn't like he was going to read them. He'd tried once. Never again. Still he had to fight the urge to snatch the pen out of her hand.

She seemed to read his body language, because when she glanced at him, she pulled the pen away and put it down. There it was again, her odd mix of innocence and cunning. In her own way, she was as alien as those things out there. Whatever they were, whatever she was, they'd all come for a reason and they were connected somehow. What that connection was he didn't know, but was sure that if the aliens were here to harm, she was here to help. She'd already saved him twice.

What if there were more out there like her? That gave him a start. The idea of multiple versions of her was as disturbing as the thought of legions of humanoid spiders crawling across New England. He wanted her to be unique, his own personal guardian, sent just for him. He wanted to know that she was his alone, and he was hers. That seemed right. Natural, even. As natural as any of this could be.

Another unwelcome thought. If she were here because of the creatures, then her presence here was just as temporary. The notion that those creatures out there were an infestation that would run its course like the common cold and then be gone felt true to his bones. Judd McPherson had said as much. They couldn't stay forever. They would disappear as quickly as they had come, once they'd finished whatever business they'd come to do.

That meant that she would go too, his angel, who had not only saved his life, but had also ended two long years of loneliness and despair and might have saved him from his own rotting brain. A lump swelled in his throat, squeezing off his airway. He dropped the article of clothing he'd been handling.

God, what if I lose her too?

He'd be worse off than before. And he would rather be stranded here with her in a world of darkness, silence, and in constant threat of monsters than to try to be normal without her.He couldn't go back to his old life. There was no old life to go back to. He was happier than he'd been since...well, since that picture in the chest.

Was he happy? Who knew what the hell happiness really was? What he did know was this. If she left, he'd find a way to go with her. If he couldn't do that, then he might just take that trip up to the top of Pike's Falls.

She was watching him again. The weight of those black eyes made him feel exposed, as if he'd voiced his thoughts aloud. He went back to his work.

The pile of clothes that might yet be useful had dwindled to a handful of shirts and a pair of sweatpants he wanted her to try on. They might be more comfortable than the stiff denim jeans. He plucked up an oversized tie-dyed shirt, a psychedelic horror with the words "Make Love" in pink velvet letters on the front and a peace sign like a big bull's eye on the back. He remembered the weird, but mercifully short craze his sister had gone through when she'd been fifteen, just after the Iraq War ended. He made to toss it at the discard pile, but a hand shot out and snatched it up before it could hit the floor. With an intake of breath, she unfurled the thing, which fell open like a tent. She held it to her face, breathed it in, even nibbled at the collar, as if expecting it to taste as wild as it looked.

"You got to be kidding me."

Her expression said that she wasn't.

With a sigh, he got up to help her put it on. But she was already peeling out of the old and wriggling into the new. He groaned as her body disappeared. The horrible garment fell over her shoulders and hung to her knees.

"God in heaven," he muttered as she turned front and back. A surprisingly familiar motion, as if the instinct to pirouette in a new outfit was simply written into a woman's DNA. Soon she squirmed out of the jeans and left them in a heap on the floor, next to the abandoned shoes.

"Well, it's an improvement over the slip. Sort of." He took her hand. "Come on. I got something better for you. You'll like it. I promise."

She let him to tow her back to the kitchen, still captivated by the shirt, fingering the letters. The water was at a solid boil now. He turned off the burner.

"Think you can entertain yourself a minute?"

She barely seemed to hear. He hefted the pot, staggered to the entryway, paused. "Listen, don't touch the burner, okay? It's hot." Another pause. "And stay away from the knives."

She nodded carefully, as if afraid he might go into some kind of fit.

"All right, make yourself at home." He hobbled across the uneven floor, wincing with every step, his ankle bitching at him, until he set the still-steaming pot on the bathroom floor. After catching his breath, he returned to the kitchen, found a box of candles in the junk drawer, which he pocketed, all except for one. This he lit and made his way back into the hall.

The girl, meanwhile, had found her way to living room and was now studying the bookshelf with its dusty figurines and the huge copy of the King James Bible Ma had made Noah and Jessie read every night before dinner.

In the bathroom, he set the candles around the base of the sink and on the back of the toilet, lit them all and stepped back to admire the effect. Hardly romantic. But there was light enough to see. He turned on the taps over the ancient clawfoot bathtub and went to the closet for soap and shampoo. It was all old, but he didn't think stuff like that had an expiration date.

A shadow crawled up the wall beside him, making him jump.

"Hey!" He turned to find her standing in the doorway, staring at the screaming faucet as it gushed into the tub.

"You're not supposed to be here." He glanced at the noisy tub, which he guessed had brought her in the first place. "Yeah, it's hard on the ears, I know. Now out you go."

He shooed her away, closed the door and turned off the tap. Then he upended a bottle of bubble bath and scented oil into the bath. After this, he poured in hot water, a bit too fast. Steam erupted like a geyser from the tub, enveloping him in hot vapor.

"Damn!" His arms and face began to burn as he emptied the pot and staggered back. Bubbles blossomed and flowed over the side, pattered to the floor. The empty pot fell with a clang as he reached for the door.

His hand had no sooner touched the knob than it flew out of his reach. A rattling cry sent Noah's heart thundering in fresh terror. He would have fallen into the tub had hands not grabbed him and hauled him off his feet. He was dragged, spluttering and kicking, out of the bathroom and tossed onto the hallway floor. He held out his hands to ward off this new attacker, but she slapped them aside and fell on him, making a strange keening noise as she pinned him down, ran her hands over his face, chest, and arms, her black eyes huge.

"Hey! What's the matter?" Now he understood. "It's all right!" He grabbed her wrists. She slowed her frantic pat-down, though not by his efforts to restrain her. She met his eyes and, seeing no pain, relaxed. Her odd moaning stopped, thank God.

"No burns," he said. "See? I'm fine." He spread his arms, tried to smile.

She scrutinized him as if searching for a lie or a trick. Finding none, her face furrowed in confusion before hardening to anger. She cast a glance over her shoulder at the thinning mist in the bathroom, then pushed him down, pinning his wrists, staring at him through narrowed eyes.

"I didn't mean to scare you." He laughed. "Relax!" He worked an arm free. "I was just making you a bath."

He wiggled out from under her and she let him. "Come on." He grunted and stood clumsily, his ankle smarting. "Let me show you."

He led her to the bathroom. She grimaced and pulled back, nearly yanking him off his feet again, but he put a hand on her arm and beckoned her forward.

At the door, she hesitated, shook her head, then let him pull her inside. She lifted her feet at the water on the floor, eyes widening, and stared at the mound of foam cresting the tub.

"Look." He put his hand into the water. He did it slow, testing it, before plunging it in.

"Perfect. Come try it."

He had a time coaxing her to him and getting her to put her own hand in the water. She seemed to have made up her mind that the room had almost killed him and she wasn't giving up on her prejudices easily. So she had a stubborn streak. The thought made him laugh out loud, which made her scowl at him again. He laughed harder.

Eventually, her curiosity got the better of her and she brushed her fingers over the bubbles. They hissed softly in the wake of her touch. That did it. Her contempt dissolved and she thrust her hand in up to the elbow. This time his laughter gave no offense.

Coaxing her out of her shirt was easier this time, though she wouldn't let it out of her sight and waited until he placed it reverently over the towel rack where she could see it before letting him guide her into the tub.

He noticed something he'd seen earlier while they were in Jessie's room – a mark on her body. He hadn't been certain what it was before, but now he had a better look at it. A small scar on her belly, just below the navel, a two-inch pink line that didn't look healed. It was stark on her white skin, and he wondered how he'd never noticed before, even in the dark. She saw him looking at it and turned away. He flushed, embarrassed and a little irritated for suddenly feeling like he'd invaded her privacy, but she was smiling at him.

He took her hand and lowered her into the water, soap bubbles billowing around her body like storm clouds. She gazed at him with wide eyes, then down at the little mountains of foam as if they were some kind of new life form. She let out a breath as the heat crept over her body, and then she settled against the back of the tub. Finally, she closed her eyes and ducked her head under the water, re-emerging a second later with bubbles in her hair. She made strange clicking noises in the back of her throat. He wondered if something was wrong with her, and then realized it was laughter. It was like laughter without flesh, like the bare bones of it. It sounded eerie.

She kicked her feet and splashed, then she stuck out her tongue and made a face, spitting out a mouthful of the bitter water.

"Yeah, you don't want to get that in your mouth," he said. "Or your eyes." He dabbed at her face with a washrag and cleared the soap from her brow.

"It smells a lot better than it tastes, doesn't it?"

She turned to him with a look of pure happiness, then scooped up bubbles and plopped them onto his cheek, chittering in that odd laugh.

"Yeah, you're a kidder, all right." He brushed it off and took up a bottle of shampoo. She saw it and stopped splashing. Water and foam were flowing over the tub and soaking the floor, but who cared. It wasn't like the place wasn't already ruined. He opened it and held it up, letting her sniff the perfume smell of it. To his surprise, she didn't really react. She took in the new smell and then looked at him as if waiting for him to decide whether it was good or not.

He poured some of it into his palm and then began working it into her hair. Already it looked better. The snarls might not be so bad after all. The thought struck him that she might smell different after he was finished, and he almost regretted what he'd just done. He gently scrubbed her scalp and foam began to swell through the dark waves of her hair.

There was a knot under her skin near the hairline, a lump the size of his thumb that made her flinch when he touched it.

"Ooh. Sorry, honey."

He looked at her but she didn't open her eyes, didn't seem to give it another thought. He paused and parted the hair, revealing an oddly purple welt that he didn't like the look of.

"Did something hit you?" he said.

She caught his hand and pulled it away, giving him that strange smile. Then she placed his hand farther back on her scalp, telling him to keep going. He did, careful to avoid the tender place, enjoying the sound of her deep breathing. She let him work for several minutes until her hair was a haystack of white. He rinsed and used the conditioner too, working his hands through her hair until there wasn't a tangle to be found.

The act of pouring water over her head stirred a memory of his mother lying in the same tub as he rinsed her stringy, graying hair, her mouth agape not in pleasure but in a stupor, drugged to the gills. He'd just stripped Ma's fouled bedding and clothes, pumped her full of alcohol, stuffed the laundry in the wash, and then carried her down the stairs to the bathroom. She'd been so light and wasted by then he'd had no trouble. He had her clean and strapped down by the time she came to. The sudden, unwelcome vision made him shudder.

"All clean," he said, putting on a smile. He gazed at her, wishing suddenly that she had a name. Should he offer a guess? Or offer a new one? Instead he said, "How about something to eat? You've got to be hungry."

He stood and was about to tell her to stay put so he could heat up a bowl of soup when she grabbed his wrist, expression not so much questioning as demanding. Stay, it said.

"You need something in you besides Moon Pies and candy bars, okay? Let me make you some proper food."

She shook her head and gently pulled. He put his free hand on hers. "I'll be right back."

Then the pull wasn't so gentle and he had to brace himself on the lip of the tub.

"Hey..."

But the look on her face wiped away his smile. She rose and put her lips to his, then came down with both hands locked on him. He pitched forward and fell on top of her with a muffled splash and a cry of surprise. She wrenched his hand free of the tub and pulled him the rest of the way in, pressing herself against him, hips, breasts, and mouth melding into him, arms encircling him before he could recover himself. She turned him over and pinned him, pulling at the fly of his jeans under the water's pitching surface.

By the time they were finished, most of the bath was on the floor. They lay together in three inches of tepid water. Noah wondered as he lay beneath her, sliding into unconsciousness, if this was normal for two people in love.

In love? Was that what this was?

One thing he was sure of, their moments together weren't softening. They were getting worse.

Worse. That was a strange word to use. They sure as hell weren't making love because everything human about the girl, and about himself, ran screaming every time it happened. There was no mind or even choice involved in any of it. Just instinct. It all felt more like...

Yeah, there was a word for it all right, but not even *that* felt like the right one.

And it wasn't like it didn't feel good. God, no. Even the exhaustion that hit him like a wrecking ball afterwards was soaked in a kind of drugged ecstasy. But that was it. There was something really not natural about it, which he guessed answered his question about the whole two-people-in-love thing.

This wasn't normal for anybody. This, whatever it was, was not love.

He tried to stay awake, to take something decent out of the whole thing, look at her, talk to her, show her some respect, but his body wasn't interested. She wasn't interested in helping either.

His eyes fluttered, but he felt her hand on his face, stroking, strange voice shushing, then her palm pressed over his eyelids, forcing them closed again. As he slipped away he felt the strange, not-exactly-painful press on his lower back, as if she were pulling something out of him, draining him to a husk.

22

ANGELINE

- Noah -

Ma was screaming again. Her voice tore through a veil of dreamless sleep, a knife to his skull. Reality poured in like pitiless sunlight.

"Christ, Ma." He groaned. "Can't you give me one goddamned hour?"

Hadn't he just put that woman to sleep? Hadn't he poured enough alcohol down her throat to put her out for a week?

I'll have to get something stronger. Maybe he could buy some OxyContin from Rudy Miller in town.

He got up, or tried. His head did a summersault and his vision narrowed, sending him back onto his ass. Staring at his toes, he wondered why he wasn't wearing any clothes. And why he was sleeping on the floor. In the goddamned barn, no less.

He remembered, then. Right. Ma was dead. Planted two years ago, next to Daddy. Noah was alone, stranded here by a flood. *But you're not alone, are you?*

Not quite.

The screaming outside was getting worse, insistent. *You'd better get up here, Noah. Or you'll have a real mess to clean up when I'm done.*

As if there wasn't already. As if she hadn't shit herself and wasn't squirming in it right now, spreading it over the sheets. There may already be blood.

"All right, goddamn it!"

He hauled himself up, climbed the lugs of the tractor tire until he was on his feet.

"I'm coming, you man-hating bitch."

How much longer could she last? Two days? Three? She was sucking booze through a straw, and ate practically nothing, spit up most of what he fed her. Practically bones.

But he'd been telling himself that for weeks.

God, he couldn't bear the thought of spooning more Jell-O or instant mashed potatoes into her greedy infant's mouth. It made him sick just thinking about it. It was more obscene than wiping up her blood and shit.

A ragged howl penetrated the walls of the barn. He put his hands to his ears but it did no good. The woman's cry pierced his skull like a spear. He couldn't shut her out, couldn't even dampen the sound of his own name. He stalked to the door, threw it open.

"Shut up...shut up...shut up, you filthy cunt!" He threw a rock. It hit the side of the house, well short of the window. A rotted plank broke loose and fluttered to the ground where it shattered. Ma went on, unfazed.

He collapsed, falling to his bruised knees and dissolved into choking sobs.

Angeline.

He dared not utter the name aloud. Not here. The name he'd given to *her*. The girl the flood had brought to him. To do so would be to murder her, to give that demon in the house power over her. Ma was scared of her now, disappeared whenever *Angeline* came home. Always. But if his mother knew her name...

No, he would not do it. But how he wished she would come to him now.

This was his dark, his moonless night. This was drowning, held under until every member screamed for air, for *her.* His whole body was agony. He screamed until his lungs collapsed and his throat burned to ash. His bladder let go. Warmth spread over his legs.

Well Christ, Noah, ain't you a piece of work.

His voice died. The only sound was the wind through the Glen and his own ragged breath.

The demon was gone.

When he opened his eyes, she was standing in front of him, between himself and the house, silent and still as stone, beautiful, naked, her eyes black windows he wanted very much to fall into.

He made a noise somewhere between a sob and a laugh, raised a hand.

"You see?" he said, pointing at the window, now dark. "I told you she was afraid of you. Didn't I tell you?"

How could he explain to her that two people had been murdered up there? Or how that room wasn't done yet, how whatever evil had settled up there wouldn't be sated until it had the last one, the worst one, the overflow for the whole family's accumulated evil, the scapegoat upon whose head it all fell.

The best, most colorful end was surely to come. The way it had all happened, the way it was still happening, starting with Ma's conversion and ending up with Hurricane Angeline bringing the creatures to the valley and Ma coming back from the dead. It was one reason why he still believed in God.

But there was no judgment in her eyes, no disgust or pity or even concern. Only hunger.

His craven body responded in kind. *Jesus, was this all it ever came down to?*

She came to him. He rose to his knees, arms encircling her waist. She let him press his face to that strange little scar on her belly, which was already hot, moist, and acrid-tasting. It reminded him of other secret places he wanted to explore. He buried his face in the lovely hollow between her thighs as she stroked his hair. But she did not let him linger. She pulled him to his feet, took his hand, and led him to the barn.

~

It was different this time.

When he lay, spent and panting on top of her, waiting for what came next, she surprised him. She slid out from under him, and instead of performing her ritual, the peculiar act that was both feeding his craving and killing him, she rose and held out her hand.

He stared at her. She stared back. When he didn't move, she took his arm pulled him to his feet like a child.

"What is it?" he asked.

She pointed.

He shook his head, panic welling like blood from a wound. "You're not leaving now." His voice cracked. "You just got here."

She pushed him gently but firmly, not to the door, but to the workbench where the generator lay in pieces. He stared without comprehending. She grabbed something and thrust it at him.

He blinked at it. It may as well have been an abacus for all it meant to him. His eyes swam. A wave of vertigo made him sway on his feet, but it was not the kind of vertigo he wanted.

She was depriving him of something essential, something he'd earned.

"This? Now? Are you serious?"

Her answer was to take his hand and close his fingers around the object he now recognized as a screwdriver. A laugh fell out of him, though this wasn't a bit funny. She had broken the ritual, betrayed a trust. Only nights ago, he had understood what she was doing and what it all meant. The night he'd named her.

As they'd struggled together in the bathtub, as the water pitched over the side and flooded the house, he thought of the hurricane that had started all this. They named hurricanes, didn't they? This one had a name too. As she strained to push him under, straddling him, hips grinding mercilessly, he couldn't remember what it was.

When at last he'd collapsed under her, exhausted and used up, her face flushed and triumphant, the name came to him.

Angeline.

Her dark eyes lit as if she'd heard it in his thoughts. *Yes!* She'd claimed it, donning it like a laurel, the prize of a conqueror. But he wouldn't let her have it. He would not speak it.

She'd punished him for it. She'd crawled off him and turned him over, holding him face down to finish him off in the bathwater. But the tub was empty so she drained him instead, pressing against him, her belly tight against the small of his back. That place below her navel grew warm, spread like an open mouth, like a kiss. Then a burst of white-hot pain. There was always pain, a nail through the flesh. But it didn't last.

An instant later, pleasure spread through him like warm sunshine in March, starting at their point of contact, flowing through his core, through his limbs before flooding his head. While she did whatever it was she did, he would float on a tide of bliss and soft joy. Sleep came shortly thereafter, taking him slowly, gently away.

Always while he was under this spell, she would leave him, to return only hours later. He would wake, numb and unable to feel pain or fear or grief at her absence. He would rise and wander through the barn like a corpse in a graveyard. He never knew how long this trance lasted, having lost the sense of time. Even the notion of night and day was gone. He stayed shut up in the barn when she wasn't with him, so he was always in darkness.

But inevitably, sensation would return. His feet would go raw, his joints would grow hot and rusty, his throat burned with thirst that would not be quenched no matter how much he drank. In those moments, he would hate her. For what she was doing to him, for draining him dry, making him addicted to her. And then for leaving.

Soon he was trembling like a rabid animal, terrified he would never see her again.

Oddly, as Noah tried to make sense of the machine on the work bench, he felt cheated, deprived, her denial bordering on cruel. He had waited, suffered in her absence, enduring the extra insult of the monster upstairs, and now this. He *needed* that ritual.

He wanted to throw the screwdriver and scream until she gave him what he wanted. An hour before he would have, but at that moment he couldn't muster enough outrage. There was only a curious impulse to obey, which scared him.

With a sense of loss, he gazed at the jumble of parts, the grisly work of a butcher surgeon. She nudged him again, gently but insistently, lighting the lantern and making a pool of wavering light.

"All right, all right. Jesus, woman." He ran a hand over his face. "Keep your shirt on, will you?"

She didn't get the joke.

He stared at the mess until, slowly, it all began to make sense again. He remembered what a generator did, why it was in pieces, why a carburetor was important and why he'd decided this one needed to come off of the motor. The damned thing was fouled, or something. A jet plugged? A valve not seated properly? God knew.

He'd started this project days ago, back when he could still concentrate. Focus wasn't so easy now, especially alone with that ghost drilling holes in his skull with the bedpost.

He raised the screwdriver and saw that it was a slotted, and about the right size. Did she know, or had she just gotten lucky? He glanced at his companion who watched him quietly, black eyes fixed on him as if to say, *Well? Are you going to stand there with your thumb up your ass?*

Hands shaking, he managed to turn the screws that held the carburetor to the motor. It wasn't easy. He had a flashback of his father working on the Ford tractor. Even drunk, the man had sure hands. It was only when he'd been sober that he'd struggled.

Noah's hands got steadier and the carburetor was soon on the workbench, bleeding black fluid like a rusty heart.

He took everything apart. Float, gaskets, valve, every piece, inspected and cleaned. A can of compressed air blew the jets and inlet. She tensed at the blast of aerosol but seemed used to it now.

By the time the carburetor was clean and sewn back onto the

generator, he was exhausted and his vision was blurring. Several times she'd stopped him to push the water jug at him. Once she'd brought him a bag of Doritos and a plastic jug of orange juice, which was piss-warm and turning south with fermentation. He'd drained it without taking a breath.

"Okay. Let's give this thing a try, huh?"

Together they maneuvered it onto the floor. Then he pulled the cord. The engine choked, sputtered and died. He tried again. And again, and again.

"Shit."

He put his hands on his knees, wheezing, barely able to stand. "Goddamned thing." He shook his head, seeing stars again. "Too much gas."

Angeline watched him impassively, patiently.

"First it wouldn't get enough gas. Now it's getting too much. It's a piece of shit." He threw a rag at it. The generator took no offense.

She stepped over to him, took his face in her hands and studied him. Was that worry in her eyes, or was she just hungry? He frowned. Something was definitely different about her. He could see it clearly now. She was paler than before, so pale her skin seemed to glow from within. It gave her a blue, transparent cast. And what was this? Was she taller? Yes, he now thought he had to look up slightly to meet her eyes.

"I need some air," he said. He grabbed another rag and wiped his brow as he stepped toward the door, then into the hard-baked clay of his ruined yard. For all the other functions that were failing, his night vision seemed to be getting better. He could see the house, the rustling grass in the Glen, the spiked heads of the purple loosestrife and the sawblade outline of the pine forest beyond the oaks. Yes, he thought. Dawn was on its way. She would be leaving again soon. But not before she fed.

A scream echoed off the trees beyond the Glen. Not Ma this time.

"I'll be damned," he muttered. "You're still kicking around out there after all." So the little beastie wasn't dead.

The insect rattle came again, well past the river and deep in the forest. Last he'd heard that sound, the creature had been trying to tear through his front door. It would have killed him that night had the other one not come along to kick its ass.

He put his back against the barn and sat, pulling his knees to his chest. Angeline joined him. Together they listened to the broken cries of a creature that was not what it had been only days ago. Something had changed. Its voice had gone brittle, weak.

"It's dying, isn't it?" Noah asked. He looked at the girl who watched the forest with dark calm. For a moment she remained still, like she was turning something over in her mind. Then she nodded.

"Bloodsuckers," he said. "They've up and run themselves out of prey." This made sense. All this silence. Whatever the things hadn't killed, they'd run out, virtually emptying the place of life. Everything but Noah. And the girl.

"Good," he said. "I hope it rots."

A stab of pain hit him as he realized what that meant. She was watching him again, eyes soft, appraising. As if waiting for him to come to the realization.

He reached out and took her hand. She squeezed and didn't look away.

"You're leaving, aren't you? For good, I mean."

He didn't want to look at her then. Didn't want to see the answer in her face. But he already knew the truth. Their time together was ending and he would soon lose her. He smiled to himself. He wasn't going to last much longer anyway, at this rate.

She touched his face, turning him toward her. She kissed him tenderly and it was answer enough. He tried to pull away, but she kept his hand, kept her gaze on him.

After a while she stood, tugging him up with her. When he was upright, she gestured to the barn. It was time. What the hell. He might as well enjoy this while he still could. Because this time, she would not deny him – or spare him – everything he wanted.

23

BLOOD SACRIFICE

- Noah -

He awoke sometime later to an empty barn and a terrible certainty that that she was gone forever. Whether a dream or a cruel instinct had planted that seed, he didn't know. But it sprouted, put down roots, and grew big enough to resurrect him from a death-like sleep.

The haze cleared quickly, thanks to distant clatter filtering through the walls. He blinked, dragged himself to his feet, and staggered to the door, a cold terror setting teeth into his heart as the sound intensified.

"Bitch, why can't you leave me be?"

Ma was really outdoing herself. Every window pulsed with watery light, and the walls shook with a roar that said Satan was tearing his way out of Hell. It was so real and raw, Noah could smell tang of sulfur in the air.

Odd. It wasn't sulfur and brimstone. And the noise was strangely familiar.

Noah shambled across the yard. The bedroom window, the very eye of Ma's stronghold, was as dark as a dead man's asshole. The light and noise came from the living room window.

Was he dreaming? Or was the power back on?

By the time he reached the shattered kitchen door he understood. The generator. This wasn't Ma or the devil. Or the power company. It was the broken-down generator, somehow restored to life.

Gas fumes burned his eyes as he stepped into the kitchen. The floorboards shook under his feet, the clamor loud enough to rattle his teeth and make his head throb. He slipped around the corner into the living room and the mystery was revealed.

Angeline sat stock still and straight as a board in front of the television. The murky screen showed a woman in tight pants doing yoga on some tropical beach. The picture was terrible, staticky, and bleeding oily color. Neither this, nor the apocalyptic noise of the genny clattering a few feet away seemed to bother her. Angeline sat Indian-style, inches from the screen, way too close.

The reason she wasn't dead of carbon monoxide poisoning was because there was a box fan pointing out the front door, which was propped open, leaning on its damaged hinges. The shattered front window helped too.

Broken plaster bit into his feet. He barely noticed. He stepped up behind her, staring at the whole setup. Christ Jesus, she'd actually done it. Somehow she'd got that fucking generator to run. After dragging it across the yard and into the living room. The heavy old beast weighted more than she did.

Then somehow, she'd figured out how to use an extension cord and join the battered old television to the generator's outlet. He had no idea where she'd found the fan.

You cunning little monster.

Without taking her eyes off the screen, somehow knowing he was there, she held out her hand, beckoning with her fingers like a child.

When he didn't move, she glanced over her shoulder. A shadow passed over her face, whether in understanding or in judgment of his cowardice, he neither knew nor cared. She turned back to the contortionist on the bath towel, who bent over backwards with her arms thrust over her head. Angeline reached out to touch the screen as a sailboat slipped into the background, but jerked her hand away from the crackle at her fingertip. Her shoulders quivered. He could just hear that odd clicking in her throat. Her face twisted in an expression he now recognized as laughter.

She tried again, stabbing at the little craft as if it were a biting insect. Getting bolder, she covered it her index finger as it drifted off screen. When it was gone, she laid a palm over Yoga Girl and looked back at him, eyes full of questions.

He didn't bother explaining, couldn't make himself heard if he'd wanted to. Besides, he had questions of his own. *How the fuck did you do it? How did you figure this out? What the hell are you?*

He'd hadn't realized the television still even worked, though "worked" was an overstatement. It hadn't been turned on in months.

Angeline grasped the knob and turned the channel. Yoga Girl disappeared, replaced by a man in a suit standing before a backdrop of a ruined city street. There were military vehicles and men with rifles. There were triage tents. Blurry red letters scrolled across the bottom of the screen, most of which he couldn't read. He was just able to make out the words State of Emergency and Quarantine before she turned the knob again. She spent the next several minutes clicking back and forth between the news man and Yoga Girl, laughing with each metamorphosis. Maybe she liked the sense of power, watching the man die and disappear over and over again.

He ought to stop her and find out what the hell was going on out there, but decided he didn't want to know. Whatever was happening in the world didn't affect him. He was no longer part of it.

Dust rained from the ceiling. He looked up and held up a hand, caught grit in his palm and rubbed it between his fingers. Too goddamned loud to hear, but he could feel the resonant thud of the bedpost on the floor upstairs.

Nice work, Ma. Pretty good for a hallucination.

Angeline had moved on. The screen showed the stony face of Gary Cooper in black and white, pistol in hand. She leaned forward as men in cowboy hats fired smoke clouds at each other and a barn burned around them. Ma might be right here in the house with them, but by God she wasn't going to let Angeline know. Noah was afraid too, he realized.

She just might be the end of both of us, Ma. That wouldn't be so bad. At least Noah wouldn't give Ma the satisfaction of having done it herself.

24

INVASION

- Noah -

The solution to the problem upstairs came the following day. Like a revelation from God, it was so obvious and clear he couldn't understand why he hadn't thought it up days ago.

He was taking a piss by the woodshed, listening to the screams from the second-floor window. His urine was dark yellow and smelled like sick, like Ma's room in those last weeks before she died.

Every day as Noah got weaker, the demon upstairs got stronger, angrier. She no longer begged or wailed about seeing Daddy in the room with her. More and more, she was able to tear out of her restraints and drag herself off the bed and claw at the window overlooking the yard. Sometimes he could see her skeletal face leering at him from the shadows. Occasionally he could make out her words.

"He's going to kill you, Noah! For what you did to me! He's coming for you!"

He couldn't decide whether she was talking about God or Daddy, though he supposed it didn't matter. The woman was crazy. Daddy had come for her, not for him.

Then he understood. He realized what he was doing wrong, that he wasn't powerless, nor did he need Angeline to solve this problem. Hadn't she been trying to tell him? That Ma's curse, this slow destruction of his mind was punishment not for what he had done, but for what he was *doing?*

The more he thought about it, the more it made sense. He'd killed her, all right. By neglect. The same way she'd killed Daddy. Now that she was dead, he was *still* killing her. By neglect of what was hers. The barn was in perfect order, healthy and whole. Daddy's shrine, lived in and cared for. The other he'd left to rot all these years, letting the rats take over. The worse it got, the more that woman's anger grew.

He could fix this. She would leave for good. Noah wouldn't go insane. He and Angeline could live here together, in peace.

Noah turned his back on the woodshed and faced the house, the leaning porch, the shattered front door and the flaking roof. Yes, he'd start with the roof because it made no sense to fix the inside if the outside wouldn't keep the weather out. There were shingles and underlayment packed away in the hayloft, from over four years ago. Ma had been giving him hassle about it even then, until he'd gotten tired of her bitching and bought the material. He'd meant to get around to it, but there were always other chores to do. When Ma lost her marbles, the issue became moot. As did every other useless domestic chore, like washing dishes and mowing the grass.

Christ, there was a lot of work to do. And he could barely walk straight.

One log at a time, son. His father's advice for splitting a whole winter's worth of wood. It would serve here too.

He spent that afternoon rounding up tools, a ladder, hammer, flat bar, nail belt. Moving was hard at first. His head swam and his throat burned with constant thirst. How in God's name was he going to climb a ladder, let alone haul up a bundle of shingles?

As the day wore on, his joints loosened and his head cleared. He felt better. Lethargy faded. He should have done this days ago. By evening he was on the roof tearing off the old shingles, having lost the fear that the exertion would kill him. It confirmed that his thinking was right about what needed doing.

And praise Jesus, the screaming had stopped, along with the pounding on the bedroom floor. That affirmation did as much to ease the pain as anything else.

He climbed down that night, exhausted but elated, and stumbled drunkenly to the barn like Daddy on his last day as an ambulatory creature. Noah was alive. Ma was quiet as a lamb. Angeline was waiting for him.

The next day he did the same, rising earlier, working longer. He went slow, resting a lot, drinking more. By evening, the west side of the roof was stripped. Tomorrow he could lay paper and maybe start on the east side. Maybe take a look at the porch, if it was still safe to walk on.

He staggered down the ladder before collapsing under the old maple where he fell asleep. Which was where Angeline found him that night.

He wondered later, as he lay beneath her, face down in the grass and drained all over again, that if she kept this up, he would never finish this project and Ma would be piss out of luck. Too bad for her. If Angeline noticed what was happening to him, she sure didn't change her demands on him. He supposed only death would change things now, but he was wrong about that.

He'd been on the roof three days when the strangers came and ruined everything. It was early afternoon. Noah was trying – mostly failing, thanks to the fucking wind – to lay tarpaper on the west side of the roof. He heard them coming before he saw the dust cloud bloom over the Glen. He listened, hammer stalled mid-swing, trying to decide if he was having another mental episode. But the noise was too ordinary, and it wasn't coming from the house.

He peered over the roof ridge to see a dust storm swelling over distant trees.

He should have been happy to see that there were other living humans out there, and that at least one of them hadn't forgotten about him. He wasn't. His first impulse was to scurry down the ladder and hide in the bushes like a scared rabbit. Then he thought of Angeline and fear turned to acid rage.

The dust billowed, hit sunlight, and turned pink-orange before spitting out a black SUV. Sleek and expensive with windows dark as shark eyes, it hurtled down the drive like somebody was late for their own funeral. A moment later, a second truck appeared.

Noah gripped the hammer like a club. Nobody around here drove shit like that. Certainly not the freaking power company, who needed their asses kicked for not coming sooner. These people, whoever they were, needed their asses kicked for trespassing.

He slid off the roof and down the ladder faster than he should have. As he rounded the corner of the house, the two land yachts slid to a stop, one behind the other in front of the barn.

The trucks idled while dust drifted, their occupants hidden behind tinted windows. The rumble of engines died, one after the other. Doors swung open and closed in synchronized clunks that reminded Noah of those cop shows, the ones where they swoop in on some boarded-up shithole, screaming and pointing their guns before dragging off a meth head who's so tweaked he can't remember his own name.

Let them try.

The two men who climbed out of the lead car laid to rest any notion that Regional Power and Light had its act together. Their blank faces were masked by reflective sunglasses. They wore coal-dark uniforms with a red insignia on the shoulder that Noah couldn't make out. They both wore sidearms and radios on their hips.

The driver strode around the vehicle to join his partner where they both stood like robots waiting for someone to give them orders, showing no interest in their surroundings, including Noah, who stood under the pole light clutching a hammer and staring bullets at them. They waited expectantly on the second car. Noah did too.

The driver's side opened first. A large, dark head rose above the cab, followed by thick shoulders vacuum sealed in a fancy grey suit. He wore no sunglasses. His naked gaze strafed the barn and then the house.

The passenger door opened next. The man who stepped out could not have been more different from the driver. He was fair-haired and wore a tan blazer and the kind of wrap-around sunglasses worn by old people who hate the sun and other people in equal measure. He stared at the Glen as his meaty companion stepped around the truck.

They looked like real-estate prospectors trying to decide where to drop a shopping mall. Big Dark looked at the barn as if it would be the first to come down if he had anything to say about it. Noah hated him on sight.

Tan Man said something over his shoulder, which caused the driver of vehicle number one to pull out his radio and talk into it. Tan Man nodded when Dark tapped him on the shoulder, turned away from the Glen and stepped in beside his partner. They made their way across the yard, pretending not to see Noah. Only when they reached the shadow of the house did Big Dark straighten his tie and lock eyes with him. The other followed a half-step behind, head down.

"Noah Weismann?" Big Dark's voice matched his face: thick, low, and stupid. The smile was put on and half-assed. It pissed Noah off more. He wanted to rearrange the man's teeth with the hammer.

Neither of them seemed to notice that he was armed, though they'd stopped just out of swinging range.

"Are you Noah Weismann?" the man repeated.

Noah glanced at the two statues by Truck One. Radio Rick had put the walkie away. Both now stood before their mounts like bouncers at a nightclub.

"Who wants to know?"

Dark glanced at his partner, who remained a blank behind the glasses. Noah felt a tickle along his spine when he looked at this one, like he was somebody Noah had seen somewhere before, even with the face mask.

"We've been a little worried about you, Mister Weismann," Big Dark said, causing Noah's blood pressure to rise. "Your friend, a Mister William Brennan. He seemed to think something had happened to you."

Maybe not start with his teeth after all. Maybe sink the hammer into his skull, claw first. Dig out his brains. "Who the hell are you people and why are you on my property?"

Tan Man shifted, immediately drawing Noah's attention. He took off the glasses. "We're with FEMA, Noah. Federal Emergency Management Agency. This area has been hard hit by flooding in the wake of hurricane Angeline. We're looking for survivors, assisting local residents in recovering. I'm Agent Curtze; this is Agent Morgan. Can you spare us some time?"

Noah stared, hammer loosening in his grip. Hadn't he seen something on TV about a quarantine? He couldn't remember.

Dark Man reach into his coat, produced a badge, and held it up. Noah ignored it.

"Do I know you?" Noah said to Tan Man, knowing good and well he didn't, but wondering what it was about him that made him say it.

Big Dark flashed a holster as he tucked away the badge.

"No. I don't think so." Tan Man's gaze drifted to Noah's hammer, causing Noah to look too. He almost hid it behind his back.

"Are you alone here? Do you have any relatives?" When Noah didn't answer, Morgan leaned forward like he was going to touch him. "Son?"

The hammer rose a degree. Morgan backed up. His partner touched his shoulder.

"Look, we're not here to cause you any trouble. But we have a situation on our hands and lots of people are still missing. We're just trying to make sure everyone's safe, including yourself." Tan Man shifted, leveling his gaze. "Your friend, William Brennan. He's missing too. Did you know that?"

Noah shook his head. "No."

"He went missing about three days ago. We were hoping maybe you'd seen him. That he'd come to see you."

"I haven't seen anybody."

Tan Man nodded at the house. "You're alone here? No one else is here, is that right?"

Noah chewed his lip. It was cracked and bleeding. "Yeah."

Tan Man and Big Dark exchanged glances, which Noah couldn't read. Dark pointed. "What happened to your window?"

"Tree branch hit it. Wind."

Dark Man's eyes narrowed. Noah was about to tell him where he could go stick that pistol and badge of his when Tan Man reached into his pocket and produced a photograph.

"Have you seen this woman?"

Noah's blood froze. Tan Man held out the photo like he wanted him to take it, but Noah couldn't move. The image was clear enough from where he stood. It was black and white and grainy, but there was no mistaking the profile.

Tan Man raised his eyebrows. Noah's paralysis broke. He took the picture, hoping they'd attribute his shaking hands to the heat. It had been taken after dark with some sort of fancy night vision. She was turned away so it wasn't all that clear. But it was her. Angeline's features, unmistakable. He made a show of studying it, shook his head, and handed it back.

"I haven't seen her. I haven't seen anyone. Haven't you been listening?" Noah nodded at the forest. "The bridge has been out."

Big Dark glanced over his shoulder as if seeing for himself, then back at Noah. "The flood's been gone for over a week, son," he said. "Didn't you know that?"

Noah wanted to run, to head for the barn and bury himself in the hay, or better yet seal himself in the cellar. Cracking Big Dark's skull no longer seemed as important as getting away from Tan Man's pale eyes, which saw right through him, right to the girl, to Ma, to *him.* What he'd said about not knowing him was a lie. He *did.* Somehow this man knew Noah inside and out, which was more scary and dangerous than those alien monsters had ever been. He could ruin everything. All he wanted right now, more than anything, was for this man to be gone and out of his life and to leave him and the girl alone.

"Look," said Tan Man. "I can see you're busy and need to get back to your work."

Noah didn't want to look back into those cold eyes, but he did.

"We're going to leave now, okay? But before we do, I need you to do something for me." Tan Man held out a cell phone. "If you see this woman or Mister Brennan, would you please contact me? All you need to do is turn it on and hit the icon on the screen. It will patch you right to me. I'm afraid you can't use it for anything else, but you can get to me, day or night. Even if I don't answer, someone will be here in twenty minutes. Understand?"

Noah took it because it was the best way to get the man to go away.

"You also need to know that we are offering assistance to you in any way you might have need. Medical aid, food, clothing..."

Noah shook his head. "I'm fine. I have everything I need."

"How are you on water? Gasoline for your generator?" Tan Man asked.

"Fine," Noah said.

The two men were silent for a moment. They looked at each other, came to some unspoken agreement, and Tan Man nodded. "Thank you for your time. If you change your mind, call."

~

Then they turned and left. The two statues became men again and climbed into their truck. A second later, so did Big Dark and Tan Man. The engines came to life and the SUVs were moving, one behind the other, circling the drive and then disappearing the way they'd come, leaving another trail of thick dust.

When the last car disappeared into the forest, Noah dropped the hammer and stumbled to the barn.

25

MOVEMENT PATTERN

- T. Allen Curtze -

"Jesus." Gene Morgan ran a hand over his face, leaving the wheel precariously at half-staff as the Ford Expedition rocketed down the pitted road. "Just the smell of that kid." A shake of the head. "What the hell was that back there, Chief?"

Morgan's partner searched his pockets, apparently not for the pack of Newports, which was already in his hand. A fresh cigarette smoldered in his mouth.

"How old is that?" Allen Curtze nodded at a paper coffee cup in the console, the orifice of the lid silt-stained dark with crystalline residue. Without waiting for an answer, he plucked it up, popped off the lid and sniffed.

"Tell me you're not."

Curtze tipped a small silver flask over the cup. The smell of alcohol mingled with the funk of cigarette smoke and old fast food from the empty cardboard boxes littering the floor.

"Here. Take your medicine. You look like shit." Curtze pushed the augmented cup at Gene, who scowled and warded it off.

"Suit yourself." Curtze shrugged, sipped, and sighed with apparent satisfaction.

"All right, come out with it. Tell me how you knew?"

The grey-eyed man in the tan blazer with the cold, boozed up coffee raised an eyebrow. "Knew what?"

"That kid back there! He's so infected he's practically bleeding morph venom. He should be buried in a hole at this stage. Instead he's standing outside like he's waiting for the fucking rapture and turns on us like a rabid dog the moment we ask how he's doing. Where the hell was the morph?"

"Good question," Curtze frowned into the cup, fished inside it with a finger. "Very strange, isn't it? Hey, have you had breakfast? What do you say we slip away for the afternoon, hit that diner up in Belford? You know the one I mean?"

Gene jerked the wheel, throwing the truck around a deep crater, flirting with the ravine at the edge of the road before whipping it back to true.

"They've got the best deep-fried catfish and onions I've tasted north of the Panhandle. Vidalias sweet as apples. Slices like hubcaps. Jesus, Gerald!"

The engine roared as Gene hit the throttle and sliced around the sharp turn leading to the bridge, both hands tight on the wheel. Curtze clamped a hand over the cup.

"Will you relax? There's no reason to risk premature death for onion rings. They're open till eleven p.m."

"Will you be serious? For fuck's sake, Allen, I'm trying to have a conversation with you."

Curtze glanced over his shoulder through the back window. The view was empty save for cirrus clouds of dust drifting over the forest road. "You gave the impression you were trying to break land speed records. Or the axles."

"I want to find this thing before it slips away again. If it hasn't already. God only knows what horrors these folks are in for if Twelve manages to lay her eggs. I don't want to have to explain to the board how we let the most evolved morph Parousia's ever seen just walk off into the sunset, do you?" Gene glanced at Curtze. "I mean, this *is* Twelve, right?"

Curtze rolled down the window and pitched the cup, which hit the wind and sailed out of sight, leaving a spatter on the rear passenger window. "I think so." The window came up again. "But remember. It's no different than the any of the others, in the end. Same goals. Same needs. Same weaknesses. She'll follow the same patterns. We have time, Gene."

"Yeah? I sure as hell don't see a pattern. Factoring in the McPherson place, this thing now has an effective territory of twenty-six kilometers. Not to mention the range is asymmetrical, which makes it damned near impossible to pinpoint a nest site. But you apparently found it. How?"

Curtze gazed at the side window, eyes distant, face serious. "Because there's always a pattern. You just have to know how to look for it."

The buttresses of the bridge rose up before them, followed by the defunct Chevy pickup. Gene hit the brake and swore as the red and blue lights of a wrecker switched on. He cut around the large flatbed as it reversed, flashing the operator a dirty look before gunning past and rocketing over the bridge.

"Well professor, I think you're going to have to school me right about now, because I'm clueless."

"It's gravitating to people, not just to an area. When we get back to the lab, I want you to try something. Go to the map and remove every pin within two klicks of our camps, including the labs. I think you'll see something more typical of a territory. It's big, but it's still a pattern. The Weismann farm is ground zero."

Gene glanced at Curtze. "You telling me that this thing has been following my crew around like Jane Goodall trailing a troop of monkeys?"

"Chimps, you mean." Curtze lit another cigarette as they passed another abandoned farm, a small single-story stained to the hips from the receded river. An ancient International pickup and a slightly newer Ford Fairlane huddled near the remains of the barn like frightened animals, their cruising days long behind them.

"Don't be a dick."

Curtze released a smoky breath. "Your analogy isn't so far off." His face creased into a humorless smile, his grey gaze distant. "Twelve's not avoiding our camps; she's following them."

"Why?"

Shrug. "Like you said. She's studying us. Learning."

Gene Morgan went silent, chewed the back of his knuckle. The desecrated farm fell from sight, along with the meadow, swallowed up by forest as they ascended the steep road into Whitman's Pass.

"That's not what these things do." Gene said softly. "They eat, they breed, they die. They don't go on safari. They wouldn't waste the calories." Gene noticed his colleague's gaze on him and shot him a glance. "What?"

"That's not quite accurate." Curtze drew on his cigarette and earned a narrowed gaze from Gene. "Not with all of them."

"That they don't go on safari? Or don't die?"

"They don't all die after nesting. We think some individuals undergo a fourth life stage. Certain chemical triggers cause a few of them, some of them, to behave differently. To learn faster. When they nest, after they've consumed the host and laid their eggs, they undergo a final metamorphosis."

"So, of these pestilent little cockroaches we don't manage to kill, some of them rise up and become what? Day traders? Real Estate brokers?"

Curtze grunted. "Something like that. We think they defend the nests. The incubating larva. They're called Guardians."

"We've never seen anything like that. Have we? Why have I not heard this?"

"It's not something we broadcast. Only a few members of the board know."

"And you've seen these things? These resurrected, enhanced versions? Jesus." Gene's pressure on the throttle had relaxed. The truck rolled forward at a comparatively sedate speed.

"A few." Curtze waved a hand, scattering cigarette smoke. "Now let's pick up the pace here, my friend. We want to be home by dark."

Gene stomped the pedal, throwing Curtze back in the seat. "So how the fuck do we kill it?" Gene said. "Before it spawns the next generation of super demons?"

Curtze brushed ash off his pant leg. "You may have already fired the opening salvo." He turned to Gene and smiled. "If we play this right, I think Twelve will come to us."

26

HURRICANE ANGELINE

- Noah -

Noah's rest was short-lived. He was shaken into confused consciousness by a deep rumble that rattled the loft. It seemed to come from everywhere. He fell out of bed and stumbled to the ladder as the noise grew, like a Harrier jet landing in the front yard.

Rage rekindled. He threw his hands to his ears and screamed. Those trespassing, lying assholes were back. This time he would make sure Big Dark and his little tan friend never returned. He grabbed the machete off the workbench and shoved open the doors.

A hot blast of dusty wind and sunlight hit face. He raised a protective hand as a huge white truck barreled past, momentarily blocking the sun, and lurched to a stop with a howl of air brakes. The apocalyptic noise gave way to the rattle of a large engine. A rain of dust settled on the truck's massive flanks.

Noah slid back under the shadow of the gable. For several breaths, his burned-out brain couldn't parse the meaning of the watermark emblazoned on the side. The words were foreign. Slowly they began to register, along with the dull shock over how bad his condition must be. American Red Cross, it read in blood-red letters.

The man who climbed out of the cab wore clean blue jeans, a white apron, and a crisp, new cap with the same red markings. He ignored Noah as made his way to the back of the rig where he was joined by a carbon copy of himself, right down to the same black Stanley steel-toes. Clone A opened the back door with a rattle of heavy rollers. Clone B leapt up and disappeared inside.

"You got it?" Clone A said. A shout of affirmation followed. The man accepted a large cardboard box, tottered, turned, and dropped it in the gravel with a thump before reaching for another.

The same sequence followed. More boxes. The pile grew. Most were plain cardboard. Some were cellophane-wrapped cartons of bottled water. There were red gasoline cans too, along with the sleek black frame of a generator, which Clone A handled with little care.

"Heavy fucker." He grunted and let it bang on the ground.

A shout from inside the truck. "That's a two-thousand-dollar unit, man."

"Yeah, well feel free to trade places with me any time." Clone A caught a bundle of toilet paper hurled at high speed and tossed it at the stack of boxes. It bounced off and rolled to the side.

"Asshole." He gave the back of the truck a stiff, Coos County Road Salute before slapping dust off his trousers and heading for the cab. Clone B leapt off the platform and followed.

Doors slammed. The truck chugged into motion, bent stiffly around the loop, and roared down the drive. leaving the cardboard offering in a forlorn heap.

The whole affair hadn't taken five minutes. Noah felt as if he'd just survived a war. Stunned and shaking, blade limp in his hand, he stumbled across the yard and stared at the heap of supplies he neither wanted nor had asked for. He used the blade to slice through the tape of the topmost box.

Assorted canned goods: soup, creamed corn, green beans, and condensed milk. Corned beef too, all name brand stuff. Another box held cartons of Little Debbies, the kind they'd stopped making a few years ago. There was instant potatoes and ramen noodles, five-pound bags of rice, black beans, and a container of salt. Spam too. Honey roast ham flavor he wouldn't feed to a starving dog. Toiletries, razors, shaving cream and even blankets, dull green and coarse as sandpaper.

Christ, he could last till judgement day with this. Just how long did they think he'd be trapped here? Hadn't Dark Man said he wasn't trapped anymore? The three five-gallon gas cans and the generator looked brand new.

Noah tried to process what all this meant, why it gave him such creeping unease. Maybe it really was the end of the world out there. And he was safer here at the ass-end of nowhere. Jesus, if they only knew.

.It took an hour to pack everything to the barn. The job knocked the piss out of him, too. The generator was a heavy bitch. Certainly would be quieter and more efficient than his own, if those two cyborgs hadn't busted it when they'd thrown it out of the truck. He didn't recognize the make, couldn't even pronounce the name because the words were all in German. He would have fired it up had he the energy.

Noah was about to leave off and go back to bed when he saw something that stopped him cold. From beneath a loose flap of one of the boxes, he caught a flash of familiar color. Reflexively he tore it open and gazed in stunned rapture at the first carton of cigarettes he'd seen in weeks.

And praise Peter and the saints, they were Newports. His very own brand. The box was full of them. Noah Weismann would not want for nicotine for the next ninety years. He opened a carton and held a pack to his nose, breathing deeply.

Fucking ambrosia.

He pulled out his lighter, saw a single box of Blue Devil matches, and frowned. He upended the whole box, spilling everything to the floor. Cartons thumped. The little box landed with a soft rattle. Just one box. Was this somebody's idea of a sick joke? What kind of sadistic asshole packs a man a whole gross of his own brand of cigarettes and leaves him one goddamned box of matches?

He tucked a cigarette between his lips, popped the lighter, and shook his head. "Government dipshits." Smoke hit the back of this throat. He blew the cigarette out of his mouth and vomited.

Liquid agony spread from his sinuses to his gut, turning him practically inside out. He dry-heaved on hands and knees until his vision darkened and stars danced on the inside of his skull. When it was over, his lips still tingled where the filter had touched him.

As he cleaned up the mess, Noah thought of Big Dark again and wished he'd killed the man when he'd had the chance. He found a bottle of Excedrin, swallowed four tablets, and went back to bed.

"What do I do now, Daddy?" Sometime later, Noah sat on the cot, shivering and staring at the cell phone. The little screen displayed the same emblem he'd seen on the caps of those black-clad guards earlier today, a pair of flaming birds joined in the center and the name Parousia Inc. A cartoonish silhouette of a man's head sat front and center, under which was the name T.A. Curtze.

The screen went dark again. He hit the button, made the little swipe of the finger to bring the screen back, a trick that took him twenty minutes to figure out. The firebirds returned.

"I hate you," he muttered, though he wasn't sure who he meant. Those Red Cross people who'd left him with sustenance and nothing else? Big Dark, for coming here? Himself for not going with them?

Angeline.

It was nearly dark and she hadn't returned. He knew why. He might never see her again, might be consigned to a slow death with nobody to bear witness but Ma and his own rotting mind.

He doubled his fist, ready to smash the phone to pieces. Maybe he should push the button, tell Big Dark to get his ass up here just so Noah could have the pleasure of carving him to meat scraps with the machete. Or maybe he'd go with the man, let them level this hellhole. They could send him a picture of the new shopping mall.

That would show Ma and Angeline both, for coming here and giving him hope, then slowly killing him before leaving. *Vampiric bitch...*

There was a crash.

For the third time that day, his shattered nerves took a hit. He dropped the phone as a hearty boom mingled with the bell-like clatter of cans.

Jesus B. Christ, what now?

A familiar scream froze the words in his mouth.

He got to his feet, gripping the machete like a bat, making for the edge of the loft as nonperishables rained on the floor below. He hadn't heard that sound in days, had thought the thing was gone for good. Now here it was here in the barn again and the sun hadn't even set.

Then why was it *her* smell that filled his senses?

"Oh." He lowered the blade, stood at the edge of the loft. Angeline stared back at him.

Something was wrong with her. Rage poured off her like rain off a roof. She stared accusingly at him with hard, black eyes. Her chest rose and fell as if she'd run a marathon.

"What's the matter?"

She turned her gaze to the boxes, what was left of them. Most were done for, just shredded bits of cardboard, their guts scattered across the floor in lurid labels and scraps of paper. She grabbed one of the survivors and hurled it against the wall, her face twisting into a snarl.

"Hey!" He scrambled down the ladder as she snatched up a carton of cigarettes and tore it in two. She took up one of the army blankets, sniffed it, and held it away from herself as if it was infected with smallpox.

She screamed that awful scream again. He tripped over a can of Folgers Coffee, nearly went to his ass, but caught himself. God, he wished she wouldn't do that again.

A box of tissues sailed over his head, smacked the ladder, and fell like a shot bird. Cans flew and skittered across the floor. Life Cereal burst on the air and fell like confetti from a piñata. Finally she picked up a can and threw it at the tractor, smashing the left headlight.

"Hey, goddamn it!" He stepped in front of her. "What the hell's wrong with you?"

Not wise. She might throw him next. Or wouldn't that be an irony if she brought down the barn and left Ma's rat-infested house standing?

She grabbed the blanket and thrust it in his face, stomped her foot hard enough to shake the floor.

"Just take it easy!"

She slapped his hand away and shoved him hard enough to make him stumble.

"Jesus! It's just food." He held up a box of Minute Rice. "See? It's not rat poison. It's just folks from town trying to help. And they're gone. Now will you relax?"

He wasn't sure how gone they were. Nor did he know if it was safe for them here anymore. But he wasn't going to tell her that, and he sure as hell wasn't going to tell her that Dark and his pasty-faced friends were looking for her. He just wanted her to stop looking at him like that.

"They're gone," he repeated, softer. "It's okay..."

Her expression slackened, the anger draining away. But he wasn't comforted. This new expression was worse.

She turned, eyes flat.

"Hey." He followed, not daring to touch her. She dropped the blanket, stepped over the toilet paper and torn boxes, and made her way to the front doors.

"Angeline, don't. Please."

Now he was really scared. Terrified. This was it. The moment he'd feared had already happened, was happening now. The first time he'd uttered her name aloud, and it was going to be the last. She was leaving. Without him. He was losing her.

He couldn't lose her. The thoughts of pushing that damned button on the phone vanished like dry paper in a fire. He didn't care what she was, didn't care if she was a monster or an alien or a demon. He *needed* her. He could *not* lose her now. "Please!" He hated Big Dark more than he hated Ma, so fully he would have given both eyes to have his hands around the man's throat. Christ, he'd gut him like a hog.

He grabbed her by the tattered, tie-dyed shirt. It tore as she pulled away. She squirmed out of it, shedding it like old skin.

"Stop!" He caught her by the arm.

She hit him. Hard. One moment he was yanking her from the door, the next he was flat on his back, seeing stars and tasting blood.

When his vision cleared she was standing over him like an assassin, hands doubled into fists. No longer was she a porcelain doll, so delicate you'd think she'd melt in the rain. She was no longer Angeline. She was all hard angles and sharp teeth. And the way she looked at him now tore a hole in his soul and filled him with more pain than he thought any human could hold.

He lay back, closed his eyes, and hoped she would finish the job the monsters started days ago. He had no desire to keep breathing without her, with nothing but the misery of his own company.

She didn't kill him. Nor did she leave. She stood in perfect silence while seconds crawled by.

Bare feet slid across the floor and a cool skin brushed his cheek. He opened his eyes to find her kneeling beside him, her face softer, the hatred gone. A shard of hope pierced him deep enough to draw a groan.

"Don't go."

Her brow furrowed as she passed a thumb over his split lip.

"It's fine." He sat up, grabbed her hand. She let him do both.

"I'm sorry."

She took the torn shirt, held it out to him, mouthed a word he had no trouble deciphering. *Mine.*

The silence that followed made her seem less human than before. She cocked her head, asking if he understood, black eyes fastened on him. He didn't care. What mattered was that she wasn't leaving. At least not for good. Not yet.

He took it. "Where are you going?"

Her face darkened. She looked at the open door.

"Why?" He winced, shifted position. He must have bruised his ass real good when he fell.

That fury that had animated her moments before settled back into place. New fear bit down on him.

"Angeline, what are you going to do? Those guys aren't coming back. Just leave them alone."

She put a hand to his mouth and held it there. He waited until the fire in her eyes died. She put a finger to his chest, then pointed at the floor. *You. Stay.*

Sure, Ma. Like a good boy.

She pointed to herself and then to the door.

The matter was closed. All he could do was hope she would keep her word, and that she knew how to keep herself safe. He hated it, but hardly had the stones to argue with her now.

He got to his feet, knees and spine grinding as if he were older than Judd McPherson. "Whatever you're going to do, you be careful, okay? Come back to me."

She turned and ran, naked and shadow-swift, into the fading light. He watched her disappear and remained there long after, cradling that ugly shirt like a child. He held it to his face and breathed deeply of her, remembering the gift she hadn't given him before leaving, feeling the tingle in his lower back. Already feeling her absence, both inside and out, he went back into the barn as a cold rain began to fall.

27

MIDNIGHT CURSE

- Noah -

He was determined to wait up for her, but couldn't. Exhaustion crept up on him and stole away his consciousness. Night was when he usually felt most human and alive. Not without her. Daylight slipped away. The afternoon heat lost its stranglehold on the barn. He fell asleep huddled against the door, to the gentle patter of rain.

Sleep was not restful.

In his half-dreams he heard that thing upstairs scraping the walls with dry fingers and making the bed frame knock against the floor like a muffled fist on the inside of a coffin. It should have brought him right back up again, but waking up was like trying to swim through tar. Every time he was about to break through, someone would pull him back down again, cackling like broken glass.

Why was she still here? Wasn't he doing what she wanted? Wasn't he fixing it?

He ended up in the corner of the loft before he finally got away from her. He couldn't remember what Ma had done to him, but he still felt the pain of it on his back and legs, bands of fire that burned his skin everywhere the ground touched him. When they finally cooled, he curled up and cried himself back to sleep.

The barn was pitch black when Angeline returned. She shook him awake. He sat up and threw his arms around her.

She let him hold her for a while, his face pressed into bare skin, breathing in her scent, until she pushed him back, held his face in her hands and crawled on top of him, peeling him from his clothes. When it was over, he didn't resist as she turned him onto his side and coaxed him over the edge of sleep again, knowing this time at least he'd sleep dreamlessly.

~

For two days the Glen remained quiet and undisturbed. But Angeline was restless. She paced the barn like a caged animal. Sometimes she would climb through the hatch on the roof and sit up there for hours, not moving. She went through the supplies too, over and over again, sniffing, touching, shaking the boxes and cans as if she were searching for something.

She never found the phone, thank God. She would have smashed the thing to crumbs. He'd hidden it in the corner of the tack room under a loose floorboard, weighing it down by a beefy toolbox. Though Noah would rather lock himself in that upstairs bedroom and curl up in Ma's bed than see Tan Man a second time, something told him to hang onto the phone and keep it safe. It was probably the sanest thing he'd done in weeks.

She never let up on him in that one way. Despite everything, her frantic watching, his fading energy, she took what she needed from him. If he happened to be asleep, she'd wake him. If he'd managed to leave the barn to do some halfhearted chore – he no longer had the chops to attempt house repairs, especially since Ma had made it clear she wasn't buying it – Angeline would come and find him. It never mattered that Noah was sometimes so exhausted he could barely stand. His body didn't seem to need him there to do it anyway. The right functions took over and his body did what she needed it to. He figured he could probably make some sex doctor a hell of a lot of money if he let them study all this. Make Viagra look like Valium.

Now he thought he understood how a man could get a girl pregnant even if he was so drunk he couldn't remember who he'd slept with, though the idea of getting *her* pregnant seemed unlikely. Once he'd mentioned it to her, and she'd looked at him like he'd just offered to take her on a vacation to Mars. She never worried about that, but of course, why would she?

And why should he? She wasn't human. It wasn't like there was anything he could do to stop it anyway.

"Why are you so upset?" he asked her on the evening she disappeared for the last time.

She wiped the sweat from his brow with her tattered shirt, stared at him like she was trying to memorize his face, the way she had when they'd first met. He kept the question on his face until her expression darkened. She looked at the south wall, then back at him.

"Listen." He pushed her hand away and managed to pull himself up. "They won't touch you. Do you hear me? I won't let them."

He rested against the wall, breath labored. She gave him a look.

"Then we'll leave. If you're that worried, let's get the hell out of here. I know a place."

She went back to staring at the door, going dark again.

She was right, of course. What could he do in his present state? The energy he'd enjoyed a few days ago, when the idea of getting rid of the ghost upstairs seemed possible, had withered and died. Noah was astonished how much he'd deteriorated in three days. If those fake FEMA people came now, what would he do? How much longer would it be before they ruined everything?

28

PERIMETER BREACH

- T. Allen Curtze -

Curtze slipped into his quarters and locked the door behind him. He fitted an earpiece into place as he strode down the narrow, dimly-lit aisle to his desk. He sat, plucked the cigarette from his lips, stubbed it out in an overflowing ashtray, and pushed aside the disordered piles of paper to find the keyboard and mouse. Two screens flickered to life.

The hum of generators and engines outside filtered through the thin aluminum walls, mixing with the rattle of cheap air conditioning. He touched the earpiece and spoke in a clear voice. "Call Gene Morgan."

As the headset buzzed, he clicked the mouse and dragged a checkerboard display of aerial maps and satellite images onto one screen, and a blinking set of security camera displays on the other.

"Yeah, Chief." A groan. A voice heavy with sleep and laced with irritation. "What is it?"

"Sorry to wake you, Gene." Curtze double-clicked one of the camera feeds. The image filled the monitor, revealing the colorless greys of a forest cast in night optics. The asymmetrical swirl and sweep of trees was punctuated by a back-slash of a truck and trailer beyond a pale road gouged into a hillside. The angle of the image suggested the camera was mounted on a tower or a tall tree.

"You didn't, actually. Jameson did." The rustle of clothing, labored breathing. The sound of a large, ungainly body struggling into clothing in tight quarters.

"Bit early for a shift change, isn't it?"

Curtze leaned in to study the screen. Nothing moved save the time stamp on lower left, which said 02:06:32 and counting. Then a trapezoid angle of a window in the trailer's flank lit up.

"Team Two hasn't checked in," Morgan said. "Jameson's been trying to reach them for the last two hours and they're not answering. I'm on my way to find out what the hell's going on."

"Emergency procedure, yes?"

"Yes. Don't get your dander up. I wouldn't dream of violating sacred protocol. It's probably another goddamned equipment malfunction and they're all out there holding each other's dicks, trying to figure out what to do."

"Another? What do you mean?"

With a turn of the mouse wheel, the camera zoomed out, taking in more forest and road. Then the blocky shapes of vehicles appeared, along with the fiery haloes of bodies in infrared moving between them. More trailers. More forest. A river.

Curtze settled back with a sigh of relief. He lit a cigarette.

"I mean for the last six hours this whole overwatch has been a complete, goddamned cluster." Morgan's heavy boots resounded through the headset. A grunt of effort. A door slamming.

"One minute we've got false readings popping up at random across the grid, the next minute the generator's sputtering and the whole grid is on the blink. I just got back two hours ago from helping Masters swap out a generator with a bad fuel line."

Curtze shifted in his chair, watching the blazing white silhouette of a man emerge from the trailer onscreen, shouldering into a coat and making its way across the road toward the cabal of vehicles. His voice was soon accompanied by the rumble of engines.

"Now the power's out completely and the whole grid's down. Say, can you see the camera feeds from up there?"

Curtze unlocked a desk drawer and pulled out a rugged-looking laptop, which he placed on his lap and switched on. "I'm afraid I'm not at a place where I can see. I'll have Kovalevsky check it out. Though I certainly haven't heard of anything that would indicate a problem."

"Yeah, well, Twelve could waltz right through our little net right now and dance on the hood and we wouldn't know. I don't know why we can't just take care of the host and finish this whole thing clean and simple. At the very least set up across the river where we could actually monitor the situation with standard equipment."

The laptop screen glowed dark green, revealing the murky outlines of manmade structures from the vantage point of Low Earth Orbit, a house and a circle-drive surrounded by several outbuildings. He pulled up a menu superimposed on the map and typed in the word trace, and hit enter. The screen blinked. A soft red line extended from the largest outbuilding and wound its way offscreen. The image shifted, following this wobbly line until it terminated in a flashing red dot.

"I told you. You're not going to catch this one with the usual methods. You got to wait for her to come to you."

Gene barked an order at someone. "Look, I never said I wasn't going to follow through with it," he said into the phone. "I just don't like feeling like a worm on a hook out here. With my men as bait. You put a tracker on that phone, right? Any movement from Weismann?"

"No, he's still there. That's a good sign."

"If the son of a bitch doesn't drop the phone down a well."

"He could. But I don't think that's likely."

"Your optimism is charming. Now did you call just to let me get my bitch on, or did you actually want something?"

Curtze closed the laptop and shifted his attention back to the desk monitors. He pulled up a view from a different security camera. An image very much like the previous appeared, except that the heat signatures scattered among the vehicles were faint and ominously still. A pulsing light flickered and undulated from the rear of one of the trailers as if something were on fire.

"I called to reassign you, actually."

Gene went silent, heavy breathing stilled. "Sorry, what did you say, Chief? I must have heard that wrong."

"I want you to meet me back here at the lab in twenty minutes."

A bark of indignant laughter. "You got to be goddamned kidding me. You just told me how much this exercise matters and now you're pulling me off the job? Allen, I got an emergency to attend to and a man's head to kick up his own ass for breaking protocol."

"Let Jameson handle it. I need you here."

"I'm not leaving the team to do my dirty work. Can you give me an hour?"

"No."

Gene muttered curses, shouted at an unfortunate bystander to get Jameson and to tell him to get his ass moving.

"What's so damned important?"

"We found another morph five clicks north of Benton. Down in Whitman's Pass. Maybe a nest, maybe not."

"So, let the extermination team take care of it. That's their job."

"We haven't found it yet. Matthews spotted the host a couple of hours ago, so all we have is a possible perimeter. Unfortunately, Benton is right at its edge, so this is officially a public hazard. I want to handle this quick so I need your command and control up here."

"And you're willing to risk letting your Supermorph slip through our fingers just to catch up with one more number."

"Get moving, Gene. That's an order."

"Fine," he growled. "I'll head your way as soon as I give these men their marching orders." His heavy steps hastened. "And I wish to Christ you'd make up your mind." He ended the call.

Allen Curtze slipped the laptop it into a desk drawer and locked it. He grabbed a shoulder holster from the desk, pulled out the gun, and checked the magazine before slipping the holster strap over his head. He threw on his blazer and left.

29

LOST

- Noah -

He knew something was wrong the moment he opened his eyes. The first thing that tipped him off was how he felt. It was like waking up and realizing you've missed your alarm and you're late for work because you're too rested. The second thing was that sun was up, high enough to warm his face through the hole in the roof.

He sat up, which was a mistake because his head almost spun off his shoulders. He had to brace himself on the cot until the barn stopped moving.

He called out. She didn't answer.

Slowly he got to his feet and made his way down the ladder. The barn was empty. All there was of her to be found was the ratty shirt lying on the floor beneath the loft.

"No."

He picked it up, unfurled it. The left sleeve was torn to hell. It was stained and half the letters were missing. It said MA LOV. He held it to his face and cried like he hadn't done since they'd told him Jessie was gone.

He waited all that day for her to return, knowing she wouldn't. And through the following night, unable to sleep, unwilling to sleep, until he passed out sometime just before dawn.

He woke up well after sunrise and ate canned peaches like a madman. They were pure heaven, light years better than cupcakes and Twinkies. By late that afternoon he had enough strength to start feeling really sorry for himself.

He kept the shirt with him constantly, wringing it in his hands, trying to decide what to do. That evening, he sat outside to watch the sun turn pink and set the forest on fire, the machete lying across his lap.

What if she was gone, not because it was her time, but because Big Dark and his cop friends had caught her? What would they do to her, knowing she wasn't human? Would they put her in a lab and stick her full of electrodes? Or would they kill her outright? The hours crept by, helpless rage eating at him like a maggot in a wound until all he could think about was that fat, dark-faced man putting his filthy hands on her.

He was stronger now, able to move again since she wasn't draining him twice a day. Instead of going to bed, he packed a bag with food, bottled water, a flashlight, a knife, a change of clothes, and a blanket. At first light, he left.

He had no idea where to find her, or how, but she had been fixated on south, toward Benton. Perhaps he would find an infestation of these crypto-cops there. Or perhaps stumble upon an outpost or a stray vehicle. Maybe he could force somebody to talk at the edge of the machete, tell him where to find her. Maybe he'd just find Big Dark and shave off a few pounds for him. More likely he would end up in a cell or a padded room, or dead of a broken neck at the bottom of a cliff.

He received his first shock at the bridge. The old brain still wasn't working right because it took several minutes to parse out what the hell was wrong with the whole scene. The water was long gone, the river back to a picturesque riffle down in the rocks where it belonged.

But there were big concrete barricades, like giant's teeth, on the other side of the trusses. His truck was gone.

Lying bastards. They weren't here to help anybody. They'd never intended for Noah to leave this place alive. *And they stole my goddamned truck.*

He slipped past the barricade and went on.

The road had been bladed, mud and debris pushed to the ditches like dark snow, and the shoulder was scored by huge tire tracks. Angeline had been right. These people had been very busy. The rest of the landscape was a wasteland, trees with ruined trunks and foliage buried in silt. The ground was at least hard enough to walk on.

The next shock came when he reached the Galloway farm a couple of miles later. The place was a wreck. The house was mud-stained up to the kitchen window, the property stripped bare, the car shed gone as if actual current had taken it. Tin siding from sheds that no longer existed were wrapped around trees like windblown chaff around a fence post. Even the house looked twisted and ready to fall, though Frank's old Fairlane was still sitting there, by God. It hadn't even shifted on its blocks.

He felt a stab of sympathy for the Galloways and hoped to God that they were okay, that they'd gotten out of here before the aliens had come. Looking at the house, he had reason to hope they had.

There were more tire tracks in the drive, the same heavy tread he'd seen on the road, and there was a big red X spray-painted on the front wall of the house. The door stood half open, and even from a distance Noah could see the thick layer of dried silt that cemented the door in place. He scanned the ground for tracks as he stepped onto the front porch, though obviously Big Dark and his posse had already been here and gone.

Inside was bad, like the river had taken a shit in the house. The floor was a bed of mud. The air stank and flies buzzed around the kitchen sink, which was full of muck and an ugly grey lump that must have been what had the flies all excited. It looked like a dead rat.

Most of the cupboards stood open, innards scattered over the floor: canned goods, pots, pans, and plastic containers like body parts all covered in dried slime. The refrigerator was open, half full of mud and other nasty things he wasn't interested in looking at too closely.

He saw something in the hallway that gave him pause. There were the footprints he'd been looking for, but not from Dark Man's people. They tracked across the living room from the broken front window. Whoever made them had been barefoot. He followed them down the hall. Whoever had left them was a big boy. Not one of the Galloways, certainly not Rocky or Frank. Noah could have put a boot into one those prints with room to spare.

He followed them past a television with a cracked tube lying face up, its cord trailing like a rat's tail, until they reached the closet below the stairs. Empty food wrappers were scattered everywhere. A few cans and jars still lined the shelves, but most of them lay on the floor along with a spilled box of Cap'n Crunch. The little orange kernels crackled under his boots. Some had already been smashed to powder, ground into the dried mud. There were silver Pop-Tart wrappers and an empty Snickers carton too. The guy must have known where all this was because the tracks hadn't wandered. They'd made a beeline for this spot.

He followed them back out into the hallway and around the corner to the stairs where they were joined by another set of prints, which stopped Noah cold.

These were small and delicate, making only the faintest mark in the mud, but they were easy to see. He wondered how old they were. Several days at least. Were they *hers*? He hoped they would overlap, one set inside the other, so he could see which set was older. They didn't. Both sets led together into the mud room and out the back door frame. The door itself was nowhere to be seen.

Noah left.

He walked the road for another two hours, passing two more neighbors, finding their houses in the same shape, right down to the big red X. There were more tire tracks and well-worn ruts that said unfriendly traffic was getting heavier. There were new side roads hacked into the forest that went nowhere. By the chewed-up trees, he guessed they'd been cut by bulldozers. He started seeing trash in the road too. An empty cigarette pack here, a crushed Coke can there, enough to tell him his new friends were probably just around the corner. When he caught the tang of fuel in the air, something not quite diesel, he decided it was time to get off the road.

He walked on more slowly, keeping to the fields or ditches under the forest's shadow, stopping every so often to watch and listen. Everything remained quiet. Benton was maybe six miles away now, which meant he'd come about four since leaving the farm. The sun was high. Noon, maybe, which meant he'd made damn good time considering his condition two days ago. The only thing wrong with him now, other than feeling a little winded and hotter than a moth in a bug zapper, was that he needed a cigarette. He would have murdered for one just now and smoked it to the filter even if he puked himself inside out. He hadn't felt a craving like this in years. His head buzzed with it.

A while later he spotted another barricade on the road, this one serious because there was a fence stretched across the gravel and large landscape boulders in the ditches. A red-and-black sign hung on the fence, which turned out to be a gate with wheels at its base and sealed by a massive padlock and chain.

When he was close enough to read the sign, he saw:

QUARANTINE AREA
Restricted Access
Authorized Access Only, Under Secretary of Health and Human Services 42 U.S.C 264(b)

Noah left the road for good, cutting cross-country into the forest. There was supposed to be a hiking trail that ran north out of Benton. He'd never been on it, never had reason to, but figured if he went more or less straight west, he'd eventually stumble across it.

That was the thing about the woods here. If you didn't know your way around, it wasn't hard to get lost. But the river lay a few miles to the west and the blocked road went all the way to Benton. If he kept between the two, he'd get there eventually and maybe without being seen until he wanted to be.

Was that what he was going to do? Noah did not doubt that Dark and his black-clad mercenaries were there somewhere, with their guns and chain-link fences. Was he going to storm Benton with a machete? When he'd left that morning, the end goal hadn't seemed so important. Now that he was clearer, the practicalities of his next move hounded him like a toothache.

Angeline was gone. If Tan Man and Big Dark had taken her, this was his best shot at finding her again. Going or staying wasn't really a choice now.

He clawed through thick underbrush for the next few hours, finding the occasional respite in a forested meadow, but just as often stumbling into a bog. It was late afternoon before he finally tore free of a rat's nest of rhododendron and fell onto the fabled path.

By then he was too tapped out and miserable with heat, limb-lacerated skin, and fly bites to celebrate. There was an old three-sided shelter a few yards on, where he sat down to catch his breath and take a drink of water. When he decided to move on, he discovered that deciding and doing were different enterprises.

He felt real strange. That cigarette buzz had swelled to full-body vibration that went far beyond a craving for nicotine. He scratched at his lower back, thinking he knew what it was.

He made camp there on the shelter platform, hoping to sleep for a few hours despite the heat. As the sun fell and the wind died, the mosquitoes and no-see-ums came out and made sleep impossible. Another gift from above. The little monsters swarmed his head all night. Their one desire seemed to be to end their short, pointless lives smothered in his nose or mouth or eyes. He never stopped slapping at them.

There was a lot of noise coming from Benton too. The distant roar of big trucks and the clatter of diesel engines colored the hiss of wind through the trees. Once or twice he thought he heard shouts.

Darkness revealed the lights. The south horizon lit up in a big white dome where Benton should be.

It was a long night, not just because of the noise and bugs. He was getting sick. An evil, wrong kind of sick that felt like poison. The fever hit some hours after sundown. With it came the fits of shivering that grew more violent as the night dragged on. He wrapped himself in a blanket, which didn't help much. He sipped water to ease his burning throat and finally pulled the shirt out of the bag and buried his face in it, missing her with an almost physical pain.

30

DISCOVERIES

- Noah -

He woke before dawn. A savage cramp in his gut reanimated him, sent him to the edge of the platform where he vomited himself empty.

There hadn't been much in him. Even so, the ordeal lasted long enough to pummel his ribs and scrape his throat raw. His head pulsed with agony. His eyes burned. He would have laid back down if that were possible, but pain and an all-consuming need drove him from the shelter and onto the path.

Dark as it was, the path was easy to follow. The still-distant sun had bleached away the stars and was working on the dome over Benton. His eyes were screwed up again. Whenever his gaze rose above waist-level, the world would shimmer and gyrate. The trees swam in ugly colors like oil on water and the underbrush rippled like snakes dancing on their tails. A noise like rushing water filled his ears, making his nausea worse. He kept his eyes on the ground.

Hours crawled by, but the sky never seemed to get any brighter. The sun never rose and the forest kept swirling in odd colors. His sense of time was gone.

Once he thought he heard screaming, distant and hard to catch, laced with blood and terror. He didn't stop, knowing his senses were lying to him, his rotting brain glitching. More than sick, he was running out of time.

When the hallucinations finally faded, a noon sun blazed on his back and had scorched his ears raw. Time had marched on without him. Or rather had picked him up and dropped him in the middle of nowhere.

He looked around to get his bearings. Nothing was familiar. The path was gone. He had no idea where he was and no idea in which direction Benton might be. He was lost.

"Shit."

He stood at the edge on an overgrown access road overlooking a meadow that was choked with purple loosestrife, sweltering with the humidity and fetid with the stench of a nearby bog. More great news. He didn't have his backpack either. Or the machete. Or water.

"Fucking hell!"

In his psychedelic haze, he'd walked off and left everything at the shelter. His situation had just gone from bad to screwed sideways from both ends.

With nothing else to do, he kept moving, following the access road around the meadow.

He spotted the truck late that afternoon. By then he was in bad shape, dry heaving every few minutes, purging what little liquid he had in him. His tongue was swollen to the size of a football and stuck to the roof of his mouth. He was desperate for water.

The flash of metal stopped him in his tracks. Blurred vision made it hard to focus on the source. He retraced his steps, half-convinced he was seeing things again.

There. The gleam of metal or glass was unmistakable. A vehicle, the window of a house, a rifle-scope of one of Big Dark's mercenaries about to put him down – *God please, do it now*. There was no call for caution. He'd been hours without water and could hardly stand. He may as well walk into the light. He did.

A road materialized first, not much more than a dirt path. A shape resolved itself from the backdrop of the forest and became a black truck. He lost sight of it for a while as the ground sloped steeply downward and the horizon line rose. He groaned as he minced into a draw, knowing the climb back up would be hell.

The grass thickened, rising above his waist, adding to his labor until the ground went soft. He paused, heart leaping at the beautiful sound of trickling water somewhere nearby. He stumbled, nearly fell, making his way forward until a cool rush enveloped both feet. Then he was on hands and knees sucking like a parched horse, not caring about germs or deer piss or any other gut-rotting bacteria he might be swallowing.

He rose, dripping, gasping, giddy and half-giggling with pleasure, no longer at death's door. And vomited.

The spasm wrung him dry before letting go. He got his act together and drank slow. The nausea didn't go away, but he held it down this time, as if his body had finally gotten the message that death was just around the corner. Thirst at last vanquished, he got up and dragged himself up the hill.

The truck turned out to be an SUV. The windshield caught his eyes like a spotlight when he crested the hill. He ducked, shielded his eyes. The same fancy rig that Tan Man and Dark drove. No movement, though. No sign of black uniforms. Everything was still.

He changed course and moved down the draw toward the treeline, staying low, watching, aware of a prickle up his spine. Something was very wrong here, something not explained by his fear of the truck's owners. An instinct older than religion had him watching the underbrush, the thick patches of grass, ears pricked for rustling ferns.

There were two vehicles. No more than twenty yards apart, both apparently abandoned, everything eerily quiet.

A few steps later he found a body.

His gaze was fastened on the second truck, which had a smashed driver's side window, when a fly landed on his upper lip. He slapped it away, then tripped on something soft and pliant under his boot.

He stifled a scream. A human arm lay at his feet. The arm became a torso, which became a body, face down, the skull crushed in a mass of gore.

A flash image of Daddy hit him hard enough to block out the sun. He backpedaled, nausea cresting as he tried to push the picture out of his head. His back hit a tree, his eyes slammed shut. When he could breathe again, he made himself look at it, as much to assure himself that the dead man was a stranger.

Whoever had killed him had taken him from behind. The way the body lay said he'd been running. The upper half of the grey uniform was stained black.

He found more bodies in the road. Four scattered between the two vehicles. There were guns, big ones, and not the kind you used to hunt deer. One rifle lay under the nearest truck. Two others still had hands on them. One of those hands belonged to a body that was face up and still wearing a scream. The road and ditch glittered with brass casings.

Listening hard and hearing only the wind through the leaves, he scanned the forest. Nothing moved. He thought about taking one of the rifles, but considering how little they'd served to protect these men, he didn't bother.

He needed water more, so he searched the nearest truck, the one with the smashed window. The glass bulged like a boil, shattered from inside and stained crimson. A dark object lay against the opaque surface, which proved to be a head. The rear door hung open, the door-ding sounding. Another corpse lay half in and out of the back seat, face down.

There was no smell to these bodies. Blood still leaked from the face of a victim lying on the ground. These kills were fresh.

He took another step toward the body in the truck door. The back of his uniform was torn open, exposing pale flesh, and there was a wound just above his beltline.

The sight stopped Noah dead in his tracks. The wound was the size of his fist, leaking blood and a thin, yellowish fluid. It was ringed red with puncture marks, like tiny teeth, as if a giant lamprey had slithered out of the river and had a go at him.

"Jesus." Noah backed away, bile rising again.

The mystery of what had happened here wasn't difficult to tease apart. The odd vehicles and uniforms, the guns. Big Dark and his goons weren't here for flood relief. They weren't here to rescue anyone. They were on roach patrol. They knew about the aliens, one of which had proven tougher and meaner than they'd expected. At least for this particular crew.

The photograph. Tan Man's asking him if he'd seen her. The fury in the girl's eyes the night she'd come back and found the supplies.

Noah turned and ran.

The sun hung low and red over the trees when Noah stumbled onto a mud flat. The earth was devoid of trees and hazy with flies, the air so thick with heat that it shimmered like smeared glass even as the sun sank. Beyond it lay the river, which churned just out of sight. Tortured with thirst, Noah made his way across the blasted earth toward the sound of rushing water until his feet tangled and he fell face down.

He lay in a heap of exhaustion, longing for his bed, for home, for death just to come and be done with him. With a groan, he rolled over and got up, started forward, then stopped, not understanding what he was seeing. When it finally sank in, it wasn't with much emotion.

He nudged the lip of the hole with the toe of a boot and almost laughed, watching the dislodged clod fall into a black void and disappear. The hole was the size of a basketball, rimmed by marbled clay that had been pushed up wet and dried hard.

Lucky he hadn't fallen into it. That shit was deep. Deep enough he couldn't see the bottom. Wide enough to swallow Tanner Weismann whole.

His gaze drifted across the mud flat. He forgot about the heat, forgot about his thirst, his cracked lips and burning skin. He even forgot about Angeline and the fact that he was never going to find her. In that moment there was only Daddy's old story, its message multiplied, manifest in baked clay, as real as Noah's own heartbeat. They spread out like crop rows, or like the pear trees in the Glen. A field of man-sized holes. Not a few. Not even a score. Dozens of them dotted the mudflat and disappeared under the shade of the forest. He didn't bother counting. He turned and pushed on, making his way to the river.

~

Pure survival instinct drove him on. Or maybe it was some latent chemical she'd put into him that kept his feet moving, forcing his body to march on, zombie-like, until it was either satisfied or dead.

As the sky darkened, Ma's cracked voice began to whisper in his ear. She told him they were coming for him, that *It* was coming. One monster made just for him, hungry only for him, reveling in his helplessness, savoring his fear and taking its time.

No hurry now, no one here to protect you, Noah.

She said it was going to drag him down one of those holes and eat him slow, drain the life out of him and leave him a husk. She said he shouldn't bother to pray because it was too late for that.

But Noah was done wasting breath on prayer.

Your Daddy prayed. Remember? He prayed with all the breath left in him, begged for the pain to stop, begged for a mountain to fall on him, begged to die...

"Shut up!"

But God wouldn't let him die. Wouldn't let him off so easy. His sin-black soul deserved to suffer. Oh, you'll suffer too, Noah. I promise you. You'll beg just like he did...

"Shut up!"

Noah kept walking, eyes swimming, one foot in front of the other. All lies. All of it. Daddy had never begged. He never prayed. Hadn't said a word, not even to ask for cup of water. Because he couldn't. Jessie had been the one to beg, while the rest of them pissed away his life on their knees babbling to a deaf god.

At least out here, lost in the wilderness, Noah was far away from that coffin of a house where that woman was still locked up. All she could do here was whisper. All she could do was...

He stopped.

At the edge of a small meadow, barely visible in the grey twilight, outlined against the forest, stood a figure looking back at him. Another hallucination. Just another ghost from his sick head.

It didn't shimmer or fade. The edges were solid, though it didn't move.

"No."

It's not him. It's not real. Just walk away.

"Daddy?" His own voice, mutinous, treacherous, betrayed him.

Noah slapped a branch aside, tore through a stand of elderberry and made his way toward the ghost of his father, who was standing a few yards away. He stumbled into the meadow and faced a man he hadn't laid eyes on since he was eight years old.

Braden Weismann wore the same tattered overalls and grey plaid work shirt. Same broken spectacles glinting in the half-light. The same stooped posture Noah could have picked out from across the world.

"Daddy?"

His father didn't move, his shirt soaked black, his hair matted to a skull that wasn't shaped right. A single eye stared back at him through a cracked lens, sad and accusing. The other eye turned up in its socket, white and staring at the inside of his crushed head.

His good eye blinked. His left arm jerked spastically, hand opening and closing. His face contorted in a grimace as shoulders hunched in little shrugs before the image began to waver like a mirage.

"No, don't go," he said. "Daddy, I'm sorry. Don't!"

The mirage spoke. "I told you to stay out of the Glen, Noah. Didn't I tell you?"

It was as if the sky had torn open and sent a lightning bolt through him. Noah couldn't speak, couldn't even breathe.

I'm sorry. I'm sorry. I'm so sorry, Daddy.

The words rattled in him like flies trapped in a jar. Daddy lingered a moment longer, then turned and melted into the woods, leaving a wall of branches trembling in his wake.

"Dad!"

He stumbled across the meadow, punched through the gap where his father had gone, and took a whipping to his face. It was false, spasms of a broken mind. Noah chased him anyway.

"Why him?" The words came out in sob. "Why did you have to make it him?"

If things had happened a little differently. If Daddy hadn't been drunk that day, if he'd gone south instead of north, if Noah had gone with him. If. If. If...

Christ, hadn't he been through this enough? Hadn't he spun this same useless circle so many times, the maybes, the should haves? Maybe it wouldn't have happened, maybe Ma would have stayed sane, maybe Jessie wouldn't have left and she'd still be alive.

Now, after all these years, Noah was still spinning in the same old nothing-dance, unable to escape, still uttering the names of demons that now had the power to manifest in the real world. And power enough to tear him to pieces.

Flashes of his father flitted through the underbrush, just enough to drag Noah stupidly forward until he found himself in another clearing.

The sudden shift from blind thickets to open ground made him stumble and fall. The clearing wasn't much bigger than the inside of the barn. There was an ancient rusted gate strung between two posts, the fence to which it once attached long gone. Behind the gate was a cabin. Its moss-furred roof was bowed but intact, the porch roof collapsed over the front door. Daddy stood there like a man showing off a new home.

Welcome, son. Come live with me in Hell.

"Dad?" Noah climbed to his feet. But it wasn't Daddy. Didn't even look like him. How could he have thought it? It was just a kid, a boy, no more than a teenager. Noah recognized him.

"Rocky?"

Rocky Galloway was a mess. Tattered and filthy, shirt nearly rotted off his body. His hair was limp and oily, his eyes sunken and bloodshot, cheekbones sharp as blades like he hadn't eaten in weeks.

Neither of them moved. Rocky obviously didn't recognize Noah. The look on his face was that of a startled wolf trying to decide whether to flee or attack.

"Hey Rocky," Noah said. "It's me. Noah Weismann." He took a step forward. "You're going to be okay."

Rocky peeled back his lips and snarled like an angry dog. "Get away from me!"

Well, at least the kid could talk. Rocky charged, hands curled into claws, screaming like he'd been cut. Noah raised his hands, bracing for impact, but the kid stopped halfway across the clearing. He waved his hands as if shooing a raccoon out of the trash, and retreated to the cabin.

"Stop!" he said. "Rocky, your folks are looking for you."

Rocky didn't stop.

The front door was gone, buried in the collapse. There were no windows, only a depression in the crumbling foundation. This was where the boy fled, falling to his hands and knees and slithering into it like a rat into a drainpipe.

Noah reached the cave as the boy's bare feet slipped into darkness. The edges of the hole were blurry, rimmed with cotton, the earth packed hard and saddle-smooth, like an animal's den.

A smell hit him, pungent and familiar, a knife to the heart.

Noah knelt, recognized the soft mass for what it was, the tiny, silver threads stretched across the mouth glittering in the twilight, merging into a bed of white that lined the hole's throat like goose down.

His insides contracted as he brushed the bed of cotton with a palm. It was soft as angel hair, giving off more scent of flowers and rain. He ignored a distant voice in his head that screamed at him to run.

"Rocky?" He peered into the mouth of the den, fingered a coiled tendril of cobweb, which wasn't so much a thread as a spring. It snapped back into a tight nest when he let go of it. He put his palm to his face and sniffed.

He was suddenly not there, not in front of a dirt hole where he'd just watched a missing child disappear. He was in the barn, wrapped in a blanket, with *her,* under her, inside her, enfolded in her. The agony of his need drew a moan out of him. He wanted to drag Rocky out by his ankles and tear out his throat. Throw his mangy, thieving corpse into the river to rot.

"Rocky!" It sounded like a snarl.

He could hear something down there. Grunting and shuffling, some feet below ground, as if the hole went down as well as in.

"You come out of there. Now."

No answer.

"Listen to me, you little shit!"

More movement. Muttering. A wet, angry hiss, like a steaming pipe. That wasn't Rocky.

Something was coming up the passage. Fast, gliding like a snake.

A stirring in the blackness. The glint of eyes, two bright specks in the darkness, then gone. A shape materialized, white as the cotton walls. A visage that almost stopped his heart, the sweep of forehead, pale cheek.

Oh God.

A perfect oval face cradled in a curtain of hair black enough to make bright the very darkness that bore her.

His breath caught as she emerged into the light. Longing and agony swallowed him whole as he gazed into her huge, dark eyes.

"Angeline."

The wrongness hit him like a punch. The smell. Earth and flowers turned rancid, became filth and sick-sweet decay in his nostrils. The face was all wrong. Details now stood out like sores on a leper. A chin too sharp, lips wide and too thin. Eyes that burned with hate.

Not her.

Relief turned to revulsion. Hope crumbled to dust. He scrambled away, but too slow. The creature slithered from the hole and wrenched itself up on pale limbs.

Even as its lips parted, mouth splitting wide open, he knew what he would hear. A maw too wide to be human drew breath and slowed time. The scream hit him like the dry wind of a locust swarm.

31

DADDY'S FINAL HOURS

- Noah -

"Noah, go out there and check on your father."

Ma didn't have to tell him. He was already moving, eyes locked on the spot where they'd heard the crash, where Daddy's chainsaw had gone quiet.

Daddy had been real drunk when he'd left a half hour ago. Mad, too, tired of Ma's badgering him about all the work that didn't get done while he drank. It didn't matter that it was Saturday. *Those calves can go through that fence any day of the week, Braden Weismann. You'll be chasing them on a workday you can't afford to miss.* He'd finally stormed off with the chainsaw for the timber and wouldn't let Noah go with him.

The crash that had silenced the saw moments ago had been big, like the whole forest falling down. Now the three of them were gathered on the porch, Noah, Ma, and Jessie, listening. They waited for the saw to start back up, for the sound of his cursing a pinched bar, or to see him sidle out of the timber because he'd run out of gas and hadn't taken a can. Time crawled on and nothing happened. No sign of Daddy.

Noah jumped the porch rail and hit the ground at a run. He was only eight, but he was fast, could outrun Ma and Daddy no problem, could even outstrip his big sister if he had enough runway.

He didn't feel fast then.

Noah cut a trail through the Glen like a shark slicing through seawater. He came to the edge of the forest and stopped, shaking all over, not because he was tired, but because he could see the tree limb. It was big. Way too big, and half-cut, clinging to the trunk by a shattered ligament. The chainsaw lay on its side beneath it. Daddy was nowhere to be seen.

Noah stepped into the forest, smelling fresh sawdust and burnt gas. He stooped and righted the saw. Didn't see any blood, not in the saw's teeth or on the ground. That was good. But where was he?

"Daddy?"

Noah waited. Listened.

"Daddy!" The trees soaked up his voice and gave nothing back.

He began to walk. Slowly. Keen for movement, for the slightest noise. A few paces later he saw something bad.

Blood.

Spattered on in the leaf litter. Dark and too thick. Noah made a circle, tracking the way his father had showed him how to track a wounded deer. Small circles became wider circles, taking him farther into the woods, toward the river, his eyes hard on the ground. Ten steps, fifteen, then twenty, then more blood. Bright red drops like rain spots. A puddle as big as a fist.

"Daddy, no."

He weaved through the trees, following a beaver path where the branches were thin and there was more and more blood, smeared on the ferns and saplings. It got on Noah's hands and shirt. There was blood everywhere now and Noah started to cry.

A branch snapped. Noah looked up and saw movement.

Daddy.

His round shoulders were all stooped like always, but something was different.

"Dad?"

Noah shoved past a young spruce and ran to catch up, then froze. Daddy was walking all wrong. Slow and to the side, like one leg was bad. His shirt was all bloody and it was spreading into his overalls. His hat was gone. His hair was greasy and matted thick and wet.

"DADDY!"

Daddy kept walking, like he was done with them all and walking away forever, with his funny-shaped head, but it wasn't funny because heads shouldn't look like that and there shouldn't be so much blood.

"Daddy." It came out as a moan. Noah stood there like a statue, like he was stupid. Because he couldn't think of what to do, couldn't even scream for help because all the air and sense had been knocked out of him.

His father stopped, like he'd heard the voice of God. He cocked his head, turned and looked straight at Noah.

In all the years that would follow, Noah would never forget the flood of relief he felt in that moment. He nearly drowned in it. His father held his son's gaze with his one good eye. Clear and blue and sharp – himself. Teasing Noah with that half-smile.

What's wrong with you, boy? You suck on a lemon?

It was going to be okay. His father was hurt, but not so bad. *It's just a scratch.*

His father's lips parted, like he was about to say it out loud. Then his face emptied, and he wobbled and collapsed like a felled tree.

Noah opened his mouth to scream.

"Braden!" Someone beat him to it. Someone knocked him aside hard enough to send the wind out of him. As he hit the earth, he caught the sweep of a flower-print dress, a flash of calf. The smell of laundry soap and talcum powder.

Ma was faster than Noah thought. She was already standing over the spot where Daddy fell. She went to her knees, let out a noise he'd never heard from his mother.

"Oh...God. Braden. Braden!"

Her hands shook. They hovered at either side of his head, as if she was afraid to touch him. Then she started tearing her dress, pulling off strips and holding it to Daddy's broken skull. The yellow fabric turned ugly brown.

Noah was aware of Jessie somewhere behind him, her breathing quick and shallow, each one ending in a cry. He staggered toward his mother. She looked up at him with eyes that were great dams holding back a flood. They searched Noah's face, confused, begging for help. Not Ma at all. She cradled Daddy's head, which was wrapped in a crown of bloody flowers. A river of red streamed down Ma's bare thigh, cresting over her knee. Daddy wasn't smiling anymore. His head was broken. He was going to die. Noah saw the truth of it in his mother's eyes, even as they hardened to steel and she became Ma again.

"Noah, listen. You go back to the house and get me towels. Wet them down with warm water. Bring them back here."

He couldn't understand. He took a step forward.

"Noah!" Her whip-crack voice made him flinch. "It's going to be all right, understand? Your father's going to be fine. But he needs you. Hurry." Her voice wobbled only a little. She shifted her gaze. "Jessica, come here. Help me."

It was a lie. Noah had already seen. That naked look on Ma's face. She already told him what she believed, what anybody would know looking at him now. She couldn't take that back no matter how much she pretended.

Daddy's head lolled as Ma got under him and tried to lift him. Noah turned and ran.

Ma and Jessie were nearly to the porch by the time he had the towels. Ma had Daddy under the armpits. Jessie had his feet and struggled to keep up. Daddy's whole head and face was covered by more of Ma's dress. Ma's bare legs peddled like mad.

Noah cradled wet towels to his chest, stepped aside as Ma kicked the door open and hauled him into the house.

"Get him to the couch. Nice and easy. Jessica, you stop that crying."

Ma eased him onto the sofa, somehow keeping his head afloat, tossing decorative pillows out from under him. She snatched a towel from Noah, dropping the rest on the coffee table and began wrapping them over the blood-soaked headdress.

"Noah, I told you to get me sheets and a blanket. Now."

Daddy moaned, his good eye fluttered. "Shhhh." Ma stroked his cheek. Jessie's face was all screwed up. She sobbed quietly as she backed away and stood by the television.

"Brady, can you hear me? You listen now, it's going to be fine. We'll get through this."

Ma wasn't crying. Her face was iron. But her eyes bled tears. Daddy's eyes were open too, one blue as the sky and almost as big, fixed on the ceiling. The other was dark crimson. His lips were moving as if he was trying to speak.

Ma bent close to hear. Her hand worked his stubbled face as if to rub it smooth. Veins stood out on her shaking hands.

"No. Braden, don't you talk like that. You hush. It's going to be all right."

Jessie looked at Daddy as if he was a monster. But at least she had done something. She stood there at the head of the couch with a glass of water, holding it out to Ma. Noah just stood there like a statue, useless. Ma stared at the glass, took it, tried to get Daddy to drink, but it went wrong. He choked and went into a fit. Ma held him as if she were keeping him from falling apart.

"We need to call the doctor." Jessie words were faint as a breeze in late summer.

"Addie." The word was watery and thick, but clear. His one good eye fixed now on Ma. His bandaged head shook. "No."

Ma whispered to him, told him to hold on, that it was all going to be fine. "Braden, be quiet. We're going to get you help."

"Take me upstairs," Daddy said.

Jessie fled the room. Ma raised her head, face like melted wax. She began to scream.

It took three days for Daddy to die. Jessie begged Ma to call a doctor, but Ma made them all pray instead. She never left his bedside, sending Noah away to get Daddy more water or fresh towels for his head. She never ate or slept. She just prayed and stroked his cheek. After that first hour Daddy never woke up again, or at least never enough to recognize any of them. When he was awake his one eye stared at the ceiling, mouth opening and closing in a silent prayer of his own. As the hours passed and God failed to bring the healing Ma said He would, promised He would if they just prayed hard enough, Daddy began to twitch and jerk, his left hand flailing until Ma told Noah to hold it down.

"Pray, Noah! You pray and hold your Daddy's hand. Do you hear me?"

He did. He prayed as hard as he knew how, harder than he'd ever prayed in his life, mixing his voice with Ma's in a kind of song for God to raise up Daddy and make him whole again.

Before he died, his moving lips at last made a sound. It started as a hiss and through the hours gained volume and clarity until it became a word. "Please." Nothing else, just that one word over and over again. "Please...please...please..."

If it was death Daddy had been begging for, it was granted to him early on the third morning. It came in the form of a seizure that hit him hard enough to make Ma and Noah scream in what became their last-ever moment of togetherness as mother and son. Daddy's left hand nearly crushed Noah's as his back arched above the bed. A fresh plume of blood swelled from his wrappings and his tongue curled in his throat. Ma tried to wedge something between his teeth, but before she could pry his jaws apart, he let out a scream and collapsed back onto the bed and never drew another breath.

As Noah watched the life pass from his father, an odd memory came to him. The last words Daddy had said to him, pausing in his anger long enough to tousle his hair.

"That woman's going to be the end of us all, son. I swear." At the time it must have been a joke to goad Ma for working everybody so hard. The thought had seemed silly then, something lost in the tide of grief and exhaustion that followed. But as hours stretched into days and then into weeks, Daddy's words set down roots in Noah's brain. He realized that God had had nothing to do with his father's horrible last hours, if God existed at all. And as the weeks turned to months, Noah slowly began to realize that it wasn't God he hated.

32

BURNING MAN

- T. Allen Curtze -

In an isolated grove deep in Whitman's Pass stood a small cabin.

Stood was an overstatement. The structure had been abandoned for over seventy years. The original tenant, a retired commodities trader named Claude Bakersfield, had been vacationing there in the fall of nineteen thirty-six when a massive flood hit the Piscataqua Valley. Bakersfield, along with twenty-one other residents of a narrow, ten-mile corridor north of an unincorporated mill town called Benton – all of them male, all between the ages of fourteen and forty-nine – were never seen again.

In the years since Bakersfield's demise, the once airy meadow in which the cabin now moldered had largely overgrown. The cabin had not so much yielded to the forest as donned it like a garment. Moss-draped, garlanded in necklaces of ferns, the structure slept within a cathedral of towering tulip trees, safely fenced behind thick hedges of American hornbeam and ironwood.

The few human witnesses of this deep forest glade were mostly hikers, strays from the Robert Shackford Memorial trail that stretched north and south between Benton and Pittsburg. Under certain conditions, after a heavy rain, say, or during sustained periods of low barometric pressure concurrent with particular phases of the moon, a person with certain genetic markers might catch the scent of honeysuckle and spring balsam, find himself drawn down one of the overgrown logging roads, fighting his way through thickets of sugar-bush. When he stumbled into the cool hollow that cradled the cabin, he would have noticed the mattress-like feel of the earth beneath feet, heard the babble of a nearby stream and marveled at the fairytale beauty of lacewings dancing through narrow shafts of sunlight.

He would not have understood the nature of his intense and unfixable longing, nor the mounting trepidation that prevented his taking one more step toward the grove's center. The hiker would have briefly considered staying for an early lunch, only to be taken by a sudden bout of homesickness before slipping back the way he'd come.

For nearly a century the cabin, and the life form that slept beneath waited.

Then, near the end of an unusually hot summer, just before the harvest super moon of 2015, Hurricane Angeline dumped volumes of rain upon the valley, such as had not been seen since Bakersfield's last days. Floods softened the soil. A long dormant creature woke.

After the worst of Angeline had passed, a teenage boy named Richard Galloway Jr. had wandered away from his home, followed the swollen river into Whitman's Pass, and found his way to the logging road. An unusual array of airborne chemicals invaded his olfactory system and fired ancient neuropathways in the cingulate gyrus of his brain. He followed the logging road to the grove. Unlike his predecessors for whom the *Troffea* spores had only partial effect, Richard's symptoms had presented fully. He'd made his way to the cabin and found the creature that had called to him, never to leave the grove or see his home again.

~

The sacred grove was spoiled now. The fern beds were flattened, the ironwood hedge had been breached, and the hollow of the cabin was whitewashed by floodlights. The once sweet air was polluted by the stench of fuel and chemicals.

Allen Curtze surveyed the array of trucks with their aggressive tires that formed a vanguard of iron around the clearing, grills leering with weaponized teeth made for tearing vegetation. Their human masters, sheathed in rubber and heavy boots, uncoiled hoses, brandished fire-tipped wands or sprayers that leaked vile fluid. He tossed a cigarette at the underbrush.

"Well done, Mister Morgan." His voice rose over the clamor of diesel engines. "Now comes the fun part." He clapped his large companion on the shoulder and stepped away. "Good luck, soldier."

"Thanks a lot," Gene Morgan muttered to himself before making his way to an orange mesh barricade strung across the meadow. He fixed his gaze on the two figures huddled at the base of the cabin, the epicenter of the spotlights. One shielded his eyes and fussed with a black case with silver clasps spread open on the ground. The other wore earmuffs and a ballcap and probed a shadowy depression with a metal rod. Looming above them both was a lean, hatchet-faced man with a pump-action shotgun.

Morgan struggled over the barricade. "Carter, what's the problem?"

The man with the case glared at him, face red with sweat and indignation. "I just calibrated this fucker last night and now it wouldn't read if I shoved the sensor up a Humvee's asshole. That's the problem."

"You didn't calibrate it before we left?"

Carter stood. "I got tapped five minutes before we shipped out. Hell no, I didn't calibrate it, because nobody bothered to tell me we were working another nest. Mason pulled me out of bed at twenty-one hundred hours!"

"All right, take it easy." Gene raised a hand, then did a double take at the man's partner, who sat on his heels at the mouth of a cotton-lined cavern. His head cocked, mouth ajar, he was focused only on whatever came through of his headset. Gene had never seen this one before. He was young, with long, straight black hair, a receding chin and dark-tinted lips. He looked like Marylin Manson in Orkin gear. *Christ, no wonder this company is going to shit.*

"This isn't the first time we've had equipment failure, Ray. Just tell me what needs to happen so we can get this over with."

Carter shook his head, thumb hooked in a hip pocket. "What I need is an hour to get my equipment working so I can see what the hell's going on down there."

"We don't have an hour. Is this an active nest or no?"

"Yeah, it's a nest all right. But that's all I can tell you. Something's very wrong here."

Gene angled himself away from the floodlights so Carter could meet his eyes. "Wrong how, Raymond?"

"Look at this place." Carter waved a hand at the cabin. "If you had active metamorphosis going on down there, you wouldn't be able to put your hand against that hole without practically being burned. For another thing, look." He tapped his nose and sniffed with an exaggerated huff. "You smell that?"

Gene shook his head.

"Exactly," Carter said. "Nothing. It's dead. It should reek of Troffea spores, telling every lifeform within one hundred meters to fuck the hell off. You should be pissing your pants right now. But here you are."

"What's your point? You want to abort? You want me to tell Mason to put up his toys and we all go home until you get your shit together? I can make that call."

Carter scowled, looked at his partner's back. "Look, just give me ten minutes, will you? Can you do that, at least?"

"Sure."

"Hey! Boss!" Goth Rock clamped a hand to one of his earmuffs, body tense with excitement. "I've got it, people!" He waved them over. "It's here. I've got a heartbeat."

"Is it the organism?" Carter scooted in beside him. "Or just the host?"

"Forty, forty-five beats a minute. Damn, it's hard to read. Systolic stroke's way too long. But no, it's the organism. I'm positive."

Carter sighed, straightened.

"Are you satisfied?" Gene said. "Or is there something else you need?"

"I'd be more comfortable if I could apply a nerve agent to this before you light it up. Just so this doesn't blow up in our faces. I doubt you'll give me that time."

Gene looked back at the barricade where Curtze's compact silhouette lingered, distinct against the wall of light.

"You would be correct." Gene said. "You two go on and get behind the safety line. Good work."

Carter folded up his instruments. Death Metal hefted his gear. They both crawled over the barricade and disappeared into the light. The gunman settled his eyes on Gene expectantly, his weapon trained on the hole.

"Sir?"

Gene suppressed a shudder. "Yeah, let's get out of here." He turned and followed the two men over the barricade, the gunman at his heels.

"Fire teams, take your positions. Let's go!" Gene's voice carried over the rumble of engines and the howl of hydraulic pumps.

As if they had been waiting for the order, four men sheathed in fire-retardant suits, protective gloves, and face shields dragged black hoses toward the barricade. Despite their heavy gear they moved with quick efficiency.

Gene settled in beside Curtze. "You all right?" Curtze asked.

Gene shrugged. "Ask me again when this is over."

The firemen formed a staggered line behind the barricade, their black umbilical cords snaking out behind them, and aimed their nozzles at the sky.

"Safety teams! Move!"

Six more men with short-barreled shotguns slipped out of their hides and stalked the firemen like a pack of wolves, fanning out, raising their weapons to half-mast.

"Fire teams, twenty second burst! On my mark. Ready. *Go!*"

The four firemen braced as jets of thick liquid arced over the meadow and sluiced into the cabin. The onslaught flattened ferns and veiled the ruin in a pale mist. Great gouts of foam boiled from crevices and piled up along the foundation, quickly burying the downy maw. The spray continued, the hiss of the poison shower matching the noise of the pumps, until Gene gave a sharp whistle.

The jets cut out one by one, each leaving a clean tail that fell into the cabin's flank and died. Pump engines wound down, guttering to a hum. The forlorn cabin slumped under a dripping, white gown that quickly soaked into its rotting timbers and filled the air with an acrid reek.

For a moment there was silence save for the growl of idling engines. Then a new sound rose, at first directionless, vaguely like the howl of a hydraulic pump. Gene cocked his head, face contorting in recognition. "Shit!"

"Gene." Curtze's voice was iron-hard. "Tell Mason to move. Now!"

"Mason! Torches! Get in there. Now!"

They were already moving. Two men with gleaming carapaces on their backs trundled past the firemen and over the barrier. They carried flame-tipped wands.

The low howl rose to a scream, ragged and bloody. The cabin writhed, shedding liquid like dead skin. Meanwhile something stirred at the cabin's base, a plant breaking through soil, a hatchling breaking through the shell of an egg.

"Hurry." Curtze stepped forward, eyes locked on the den.

The screams grew louder, cleaner. A hand burst into the light, then fell, groping, dragging a shadowy bulk to the surface. A head and torso emerged, hunched and disfigured, and began to rise.

"Fire! Now! FIRE!"

A pale, naked body. It might once have been a man, but no longer. Eyes milk-white, blind with pain, skin raw and ravaged by chemical burns, it reached out as if in supplication and stumbled forward.

Tongues of fire lashed from the ends of the two wands. The cabin erupted with a great whoosh. For an instant the man-thing was silhouetted in brilliant gold, then the fire embraced him, swallowing him whole, turning him into a phoenix.

A pitched shriek joined the roar of flames. Then the figure was gone and the only sound was the crack of burning timbers.

"Fuck. Fuck me...fuck..." A young man was crumpled over the fender of a truck, head over his knees. He was half peeled out of his rubber suit.

Gene Morgan rested a hand on the young man's shoulder. "You're all right. It's done."

"Just a goddamned kid." The man accepted a wetted towel and pressed his face into it.

"He was no more human than the thing that fed on him. Not anymore."

Morgan glanced at Curtze who stood a few paces away, his expression impossible to read, his face cast in shadow.

"Now get up, James." Morgan stepped back. "We've got work to do. The sooner we finish, the sooner we go home."

The young man found his nerve and shouldered into his suit before slouching after his companions behind the curtain of smoke where an antique cabin had once stood.

Curtze handed Gene a silver flask. Gene accepted it automatically, uncapped it, and took a deep pull before handing it back. "Thanks," he said, lowering himself onto the fender that young James had just vacated. He ran a hand over his face. "That could have gone better."

Curtze sat beside him. "Given the circumstances, I'd say you handled that rather well. Congratulations."

Gene stared at the twisted, sinewy trunks of musclewood that hemmed in the logging road, happy to have something to look at besides smoking. "If I have to see something like that again, you can call the E.D. and tell her where she can stick my contract. I'll take my walking papers straight to the velvet cage." Gene swiped at his brow, then inspected the smear of ash on his palm. Curtze pushed a bottle of water at him. "Thanks, Mom." He drank with more enthusiasm than he had the alcohol.

Curtze propped a leg onto a knee and sat back, sipping from his own bottle. "A month of seeing our own countrymen packed behind chain-link fences like animals. It can diminish one's enthusiasm for the job. It's not always like this, though. You know that. This scene isn't typical."

"Nothing is typical here, Allen. Every mission is like walking blind into a warzone. This one just happens to be within driving distance of a Starbucks. More or less."

The hiss of firehoses began to die. Smoke wafted past them in thick clouds.

"You should ask for a raise," Curtze said. "You could walk into Jaqueline Moreau's office at this point and ask for whatever you want and she'd pay it. I'd back you up."

Gene grunted. "Don't underestimate my avarice."

Curtze lit a cigarette. "You'd be surprised at the compensation packages the Board has approved in times of transition. For people we can't afford to lose."

Gene looked at Curtze. "Transition?"

Curtze shrugged, flicking the match away. "I'm retiring."

"Bullshit. They don't let guys like you retire."

"Jaqueline and I've discussed it. She's known for a while, has already signed the paperwork. The board has approved." He looked at Gene and smiled. "As of next Tuesday, I'm a free man."

"Jesus, you're serious." An incredulous smile touched Gene's face. "You're actually quitting? *The* great and powerful Allen Curtze. What in God's name are you going to do with yourself?"

Curtze shook his head vaguely, eyes distant. "I don't know," he said. "Maybe..." A pause. "I don't know."

Gene laughed. "He who walks to and fro upon the face of the earth, walks no more. Well, congratulations."

"Thank you."

A moment's silence passed. Gene raised the bottle to his lips.

"I have a daughter," Curtze said.

The bottle froze. Gene turned.

"She's going to have a baby soon. A boy, I believe. I would very much like to meet him."

"Holy shit." Gene stared as if his partner had just changed shape before his eyes. "You? Have a family?"

Curtze glanced up as if surprised to find him sitting there. "I wouldn't put it quite that way."

"I've known you for twenty goddamned years, Chief, and you never told me you were married."

"No, no." Curtze gave his head a shake. "I was never married. Just...well, I was involved with someone. For a while. A short interlude. Years ago, now."

"What happened?"

"It's not worth getting into."

"The hell it isn't."

"Life happened. I started a new job. We grew apart." Curtze lifted the bottle and turned it in his hand, suddenly fascinated with the label. "It was quite nice while it lasted. And we did produce a beautiful child." He smiled faintly. "She's all grown up now. About to start a family of her own. I think I'll enjoy spending some time with my grandchild."

For a moment Gene simply stared, mouth slack. Then he began to laugh. "I'll be goddamned. You think you know someone." He took a swallow of water and wiped his mouth. "Here I always thought you were some kind of monk. Or" –he shrugged– "you know."

"Know what?" Curtze gave him a look.

"Well, come on, Chief." Gene studied his own bottle. "I shouldn't have to spell this out? I mean, you never showed the slightest interest in women. And it wasn't exactly the only sign."

Curtze snorted. "Christ. Not the only sign? As if any of us had time for women."

"Speak for yourself."

"Well, I'm not gay. So, you and your rumor-mongering friend Amos Meyen can just lay that one to rest. Christ Jesus." He shook his head, but he was smiling.

Gene said, "Don't you read Glamour Magazine?"

"Vanity Fair, you ignorant troll."

"Is there a difference?"

Curtze laughed. Gene did too. As the smoke mingled with water vapor and ash in the atmosphere, the two men enjoyed their final moment of peace and friendship.

The smile on Curtze's face faded. "Gene, I need you to do something for me."

"Yeah, what now?"

"I need you to take E-Team, head down to Cawlyer Creek. Check on the perimeter team."

Gene looked at him. "Why? What's wrong?"

"They haven't checked in for a while. We've been trying to reach them, but with all the radio problems we've been unable to make contact. I need you to take some bodies down there and see what's going on."

Gene Morgan set his bottle down. "Why didn't you tell me? You didn't send a crew before now?"

"Yes, of course I did. I sent Tessendorf down there a couple of hours ago. I haven't heard from him."

Gene stood. "What?"

Curtze was on his feet now too, braced subtly as if prepared for a stiff wind. "Look, we've got a couple of repeaters down. It's probably just bad reception. Take a team, make sure you're protected, and check it out."

"Goddammit, Curtze." Gene Morgan looked like a cumulous cloud ready to let go. "You don't call me out here to head an extermination team and then cut me off from my own men!"

"I know. You're right, Gene. I shouldn't have done that. I'm sorry."

Gene marched around the truck, stepping into the clearing. "Anders! Get your crew loaded up! Truck two. Now!"

He turned and pointed at Curtze. "We're not finished. Understand?" Then he was gone.

33

THE WALKER

- T. Allen Curtze -

Allen Curtze stood staring at the mouth of the road long after the roar of diesel had faded and the smear of taillights had bled out in the pulverized underbrush.

A black-clad figure with smooth, androgynous features stepped in beside him, removed his cap, and scrutinized the empty road. "Are you all right?"

"Sam," Curtze said. "I want you to take Kovalevsky and Rowland, see that Gene finds his way to Site Two. If he needs backup, be there for him. Okay?"

Sam Mason waited for Curtze to face him before answering. "He's going to be your replacement. Don't you think it's time he knew the truth?"

A match flared in Curtze's hand, casting deep shadows in his face. He shook his head, drew a cigarette to life. "Now's not the time. I'm already on thin ice with him."

"He knows there's more to this particular organism than what you're telling him. He's well on his way to figuring out what you're up to. Suppose you explain everything. Before he draws his own conclusions about your motives."

"You're wasting time, Sam. I need you to take your extermination crew and get going. I'll finish up here."

"I take it this is to be a clandestine operation. If he finds Site Two in working order, then we will pass by without stopping for a chat. Do I have it right?"

Curtze released a smoky breath. "That would be very much appreciated." He turned to leave.

"Chief."

"What?"

"I'm going to leave Rowland here with you. Just in case. I see no wisdom in leaving you with zero protection. Should Twelve prove less predictable than you anticipate."

"Fine." Curtze waved a dismissive hand. "Leave Rowland. Do what you think's best. Just go."

Curtze left Mason at the mouth of the road and strode past a pump truck, where several grey uniforms wound hoses onto their wheels. Others jammed equipment or weapons into vestibules and strongboxes of their vehicles.

Excited voices rang over the noise of engines. Two men locked in heated discourse stood nose-to-nose near the cab of a beat-up Humvee.

"Look, I told you, it's not the goddamned unit, okay? It's the repeater. Everything within fifty meters is loud and clear, but I can't get a thing past these damned trees."

An older man in a black baseball cap stabbed a finger at the ground. "So, why in hell are Mikus and Calhoun out of range? A sweep does not mean a patrol, Anderson! It's your job to keep track of your own men."

"I'm not the one who sent them out there, James. Somebody fucking went over my head."

The younger man saw Curtze coming and went silent. His senior turned.

"Deacon, how quickly can you have us out of here?" Curtze said.

The older man hesitated. "Half an hour. Maybe. I've got men still finishing a sweep. They should be back anytime."

"Let me deal with Mikus and Calhoun. You concentrate on cleaning up and let's shoot for o-three hundred." Curtze stepped past an outpost of glowing timbers that hissed angrily as a firehose threw a jet into its center. Deacon opened his mouth to speak. Curtze ignored him, marching past the caravan. He turned opposite the destroyed cabin to the edge of the forest, where the glare of the spotlights could not reach.

He glanced over his shoulder and stepped into the underbrush, weaving easily through a dense thicket of young ironwood. The noise and light of camp receded.

His steps slowed as he entered a huge oak grove carpeted by ferns and dappled moonlight. The distant rush of the river filtered through the trees.

Curtze stopped, closed his eyes, and took slow, steady breaths, as if he were meditating. Or listening. A gentle breeze lifted his hair.

He opened his eyes and turned west, following the breeze, picking his way over moss-covered rocks and gnarled roots, scanning the shadows, avoiding the shafts of moonlight that penetrated the canopy.

His trek continued for several minutes, occasionally shifting direction, taking him around thick clusters of rhododendron or over deadfalls. He moved slowly, like a hunter.

A branch snapped. Curtze went still.

A low curse. Heavy breathing. The sweep of a light throwing hard shadows.

Curzte stepped back and melted into the trees.

~

Former Second Lieutenant Shelly Mikus wasn't afraid until he saw the blood. Oily black beads lit up on the leaves like spider's eyes in his headlamp. He knew what it was the moment he saw it. Worse, he knew who had shed it.

He leaned close. They became bright red emeralds, flecked with bubbles of air, like arterial blood. He drew a sharp breath.

"Shit." He glanced at his back-trail. The light caught nothing but brush-choked forest, spindly branches trembling in his wake. For the hundredth time, he touched the send switch on his shoulder. "Base, this is Fox One. Copy?"

Nothing.

He swore and kept going, hoping to God someone was on their way out to find him. Hoping the blood was from some minor scrape from a fall, or perhaps some poor animal, and that this had nothing to do with his missing partner. He kept the barrel of his pump-action Mossberg high and ready.

His light struck a hulking shape in his path. He suppressed a scream as a prehistoric skeleton reached up to grab him. By the time he realized what he was looking at, his weapon was to the shoulder, safety off. He stared, trembling, at an ancient horse-drawn rake. Its fine iron tines, several of them broken off, resembled the ribs of a huge fish, curved wheels vine-draped. He let out a breath and lowered the weapon.

Water tapped a staccato rhythm on the metal seat, where a puddle had formed. That struck him as odd. It had not been raining. Under his light, the black pool gleamed, cascading through the circular holes in the seat, thin crimson streams drooling earthward. His breath froze. His gaze rose. He found Calhoun.

"Oh my God!"

He couldn't breathe. He wanted to run, but his legs were carved out of wood. His partner dangled several feet above the rake. One of his boots was missing. Blood tricked down his bare foot and ran from his big toe like a spout.

Mikus's gaze followed a torn and blood-fouled pantleg to the torso and outstretched arms. Jaw gaping in an unhinged leer, eyes wide on a blood-spattered face, Calhoun was fastened to a thick limb by the broken tines of the rake. They ran along his arms like great curved pins in a moth, spread cruciform to the large oak. His head was cocked, neck grotesquely swollen, one of the tines stuck through his throat.

Mikus opened his mouth to scream. The scream never came. A hand clamped over his mouth, jerking his head back. Another seized his wrist. His eyes widened in terror. He couldn't move.

"Quiet." A voice he recognized. Stale cigarette smoke tickled his nostrils. Relief flooded through him as the iron band around his wrist softened, though the hand on his mouth remained firmly in place.

Allen Curtze reached up and switched off his headlamp. Everything went black.

"It's here," Curtze said. "She's watching us."

Mikus jerked, terror coursing through him like current. Iron hands held fast. "Be still. Let your eyes adjust."

The monster they'd been chasing for days, but hadn't been able to pin down. The one that was supposed to be smarter than the others. Had wiped out Shackleton's unit near Mud Pond. Twelve. The one everybody called The Walker.

The hand withdrew. His lips regained circulation but he didn't dare speak, barely willing to breathe. At first, he saw only black and the bright eye of the moon through the canopy. Its pale light glistened on the bloody leaves.

Seconds ticked by. The forest slowly materialized. Shapes appeared, followed by open patches in the forest. The river roared in the distance. Nothing else moved. Curtze's acrid breath mingled with the pungent odor of death. And a sharp, spicy-sweet odor he knew damned well for what it was sent an electric current up his spine.

"Do you see it?"

Mikus shook his head.

"Fifteen meters. Ten o'clock. Look up."

His gaze slid to an open patch of earth below another gnarled oak. He followed the thick trunk to a branch stretched over the forest floor. Then back. He would have missed it had Curtze not told him it was there. Pale white, like the face of the moon, it could have been a trick of light. But it wasn't.

"Isn't she beautiful?" Curtze asked.

Mikus's grip tightened on the shotgun, which rose of its own accord. A hand tightened on his arm.

"Don't do that."

"It killed Darrel." His eyes slid to the suspended corpse. The tap-tap of blood continued. These organisms were dangerous if you cornered them or if you stumbled into a nest or a host. But they didn't do *this*. The man was on display like some psychopath's sick torture fantasy. This was just an animal, no more capable of malevolence than a shark. Yet the sight of Darrel Calhoun's corpse would have made Hannibal Lector swoon.

"Yes." Curtze shifted, hands still on his arm and shoulder. "She wanted us to find him."

Mikus moaned softly, swallowed it down.

"Take it easy." Curtze whispered. "It's all right. She doesn't want you. Right now she's just watching. Seeing what we'll do, I think. Seeing which one of us is the greater threat."

"What does it want?"

"Me." Curtze said. "For trespassing."

The thing in the tree moved, shifted like a passing shadow.

"Give me your gun. Now."

He obeyed, letting go as Curtze took the shotgun's weight. Suddenly he felt naked, helpless, every nerve in his body screaming at him to run.

"Now, I want you to do exactly what I tell you. Do it and you'll live through this. Understand?"

He nodded.

"You're going to walk away, nice and slow. Do not run. You're going to count every step, one thousand one, one thousand two. Got it?"

Nod.

"You count to one hundred and fifty. You'll come to an access road. Turn right and stay on it until you reach our camp. Ready?"

"What about you?"

"Don't you worry about me, soldier. Go. Now. And Shelly?" The grip on his shoulder tightened. "Walk."

Curtze released him. Shelly Mikus began to walk. And count. He made it to fourteen before the air exploded in an ear-shattering scream. He ran.

Curtze remained still as the creature fell from the tree and ripped through the ferns like a torpedo. It made no sound as it cut a smooth arc toward Mikus's shambling form.

Just before the collision, a scream erupted as a white form burst from the undergrowth and hit the man with a meaty crack. Shelly disappeared in a tangle of limbs and snarls. The wet snap of breaking bone preceded a scream of agony, thick with blood and cut short.

Curtze dropped the shotgun and walked away, calmly making his way in the opposite direction as the noise of a feeding predator faded. When the forest was silent again, he shrugged out of his blazer, letting it fall, then pulled a knife from his hip and unfolded the blade. After a moment's hesitation he sank the tip into his forearm and drew it down to the wrist. He held his arm out, making a fist, spattering the leaves with fresh blood. Then he ran.

The scream came moments later, several meters behind him. He did not slow as he dodged low-hanging branches and wove through tightly clustered alder groves. He vaulted over a logjam, plunged over the lip of a small ravine and up the other side.

He paused, held his breath, squeezed a fist, forcing the already clotting wound to leak onto the forest floor. Another shriek sent him on again. Curtze climbed a steep rise, hand-over-hand, tearing a pant leg as he pushed through a thicket of rhododendron.

He crested the rise. The underbrush thinned. The roar of the river grew large and omnipresent. Curtze opened into a sprint, making his way along the tree-line to the river. Moonlight cast his shadow, which stretched across the rocky ground to a ledge where far below, the river crashed over boulders the size of cars.

He stopped, peered into the throat of the canyon, then across to the distant trees. Curtze turned his back to the river, drew his pistol and waited.

It came a moment later. The underbrush trembled, parted. Twelve's white form materialized, low and still as stone, not ten strides from where Curtze stood, bleeding, gun in hand.

Curzte raised the gun. The creature hissed. Instead of firing, Curtze ejected the cartridge from the chamber, sending it whickering through the moonlight. It clinked in the rocks and disappeared. He ejected the magazine, letting it fall. Then tossed the gun at his feet.

"Come on." Curtze said. "Let's get this over with."

The creature hesitated, then came forward.

34

THE WRAITH

- Noah -

When Noah regained consciousness, he lay under the blind white eye of a full moon.

The guttering of a nearby creek, its icy breath over his bare skin, and the bite of sharp rocks in his back and ass told why he was stiff and shivering. It did not tell him why his heart hammered liquid terror through his veins.

He staggered to his feet, pain lancing his joints and head. The chill air was pregnant with the sick-sweet smell of rot, laced with the familiar odor of flowers.

"Oh. Shit." The words hit the air like a puff of smoke.

He scanned the writhing surface of the creek, searched shadows along rock cervices on the opposite shore. Nothing moved.

The residue of bad dreams. Just his misfiring head again. He fed the lie, letting himself believe this was just the latest symptom of a body shutting down. The onset of directionless, irrational fear. He'd watched both parents suffer the same thing at their end.

But Noah wasn't dead yet. He had enough mind left to understand that this was different. He was not alone.

As if to confirm this conviction, a scream shattered a crystalline silence.

Like a thunder crack, it tore across the creek and shook him to the bones. How could he have been so stupid? He hadn't escaped at all. That succubus devil from that cabin had tracked him here to finish the job. It had just taken its time, waited for him to drop his guard. Now it was right across the creek.

Noah didn't wait for a visual. He turned and ran like hell.

Moonlight guided him around boulders, over deadfalls, past the reaching hands of low trees. It also cast shadows that reared up and gave chase, throwing him into panicked dashes off a straight course, frying his already battered nervous system.

Another scream erupted just behind him, tight on his trail. He was done, screwed. He'd seen these things move. Knew how fast they were. This time there was no place to escape. No one to come to his rescue. He was on his own.

Yet there was something familiar about that cracked, dry-rattle voice. He knew this one. They were practically chums. But how? The thing was supposed to be done. Expired. Crawled off somewhere to shrivel up and suffer a long, miserable death. Angeline said it would.

She'd been wrong.

That stubborn bitch was here. Alive and well. It had found him out here in God's-ass nowhere and sounded right stoked to rekindle their friendship.

Starving, she'd said. *Great.*

Another scream. *No one to save you this time. You're mine.*

There was desperation there, too. Weeks of frustration and rage. Those strained and malnourished lungs proclaimed his own death. There would be no slow siphoning of his strength, the way Angeline had done. This thing would drain him dry.

He led it on a chase that could have lasted twenty minutes or twenty years. Drunk on adrenaline and fear, driven beyond human endurance, he had no concept of time. By some miracle he didn't fall, twist an ankle, break his neck, or impale himself on a broken limb. He clawed through walls of rhododendron, squeezed through dense stands of underbrush, plunged through fetid, mosquito-infested bogs that left him filthy, stinking, and minus a boot.

His pursuer clung to him like a leech, always a few paces behind. Tangles didn't slow it. It cut through brambles like air. Yet it never gained ground. Several times it should have had him. A slip on a muddy bank, or a foot snagged by a root – he was sure the thing would be on him. What the hell is it waiting for?

He knew. Had it been stronger, it might have just taken him. Diminished as it was, it had decided to soften him up first. Wild dogs hunted antelope this way, running them to exhaustion until their prey couldn't fight. Then they fell on their victims and tore them apart.

Little coward. He should turn and face it now, while he still had some steam in him.

And what would he see? Flashes of the past came to him. He'd never once seen its face, only glimpses, glowing eyes, a flash of white, angles of misshapen limbs, always too fast to catch. He tried to imagine Angeline as it scrambled across the roof, as it plowed into him, or as it crashed through the living room window, but he couldn't do it. He thought of the thing jumping on his back, hot breath on his neck and that awful fire entering him, poison spreading through his body.

Logic wasn't part of the equation. He couldn't have stopped running if he wanted to. He staggered into a maze of buck brush. Branches snapped behind him. The ground gave way beneath him and he fell.

He tumbled ass over toes down a ravine, body breaking against rocks and roots, until he hit earth with enough force to drive the wind out of him for a year. Pain racked his ribcage. He would have screamed had he the air.

A soft thump, like a pear falling in the orchard on a fall day. He could almost pretend he hadn't heard. The awful smell rolled over him, thick as grease, rich enough to turn his vision yellow. A hiss followed, a snake slithering through dead leaves.

At first he saw only gnarled trees and empty black. Then subtle movement as a pale form materialized from the ground litter. Shadows coalesced, took on hard angles. It rose from the ground, a ball of flesh uncoiling.

He'd been afraid it would look like Angeline, or the monster under the house in the meadow. It did not. It was no bigger than a child, but there was nothing human in it. If Famine had a face, this is what it would look like.

Noah rose to his knees, unarmed and too weak to run. The creature cocked its head and sniffed the air like a dog. It made a thick mewing sound that made his skin prickle. For an instant Noah saw the rabid coyote writhing in the road all those years ago.

Some deep instinct told him to stay very still, that if he didn't move, maybe the wraith might pass him over, stumble away, too confused and sick with starvation to get a fix on him. If he had, perhaps he would have been fine.

But what Noah saw next destroyed any chance of that.

His gaze fell to a sunken belly where an ugly pink scar pulsated and heaved, as if something were trying to push its way out. Noah's guts tightened as the gash split open and a coil of flesh fell out of the creature's body, twisting and writhing like an angry snake. From the tip of the organ slid a long, clear barb that dripped vile liquid.

For a horrible second he could feel the small of his back catch fire again. Then the tentacle blossomed, opening around the spike in layers that exposed rows of tiny, silvery thorns that rippled as the tissue flexed.

Animal panic kept him from vomiting. He didn't feel his body move as he scrambled backward. He felt nothing of the forest and undergrowth that clawed at him as he ran. Nor did he see it coming.

He sure as hell felt it.

The creature slammed into his back. He heard his own ribs crack as the ground came up to meet him. A shriek hammered his skull as he turned to face it. Broken teeth gnashed at him. Cold fingers clamped onto his arms and he was drowned in a smell so rotten he could taste it through his skin.

He threw his body into a roll, ignoring the pain in his ribs, climbing on top of it and pinning it to the ground. It was like holding onto an eel. The wraith slithered out of his grasp and launched itself at his face. Clammy fingers filled his eyes and mouth. He bit down, tasting something foul and metallic. The thing howled and tore away, then drove into his middle, bending him double, wrapping its arms around him.

He beat at it with his fists, battering the bulbous head, neck, back, wherever he could land a punch. His knuckles split, the creature's ravaged flesh gave. Delicate bones in its neck and shoulders cracked. It snarled and lunged. He caught sight of two shark-like eyes before its skull collided with his face and turned the world electric white.

His ass hit the turf. The wraith fell on him with a shriek, latched onto his shirt and tore it away. The fleshy organ slithered over his belly, the barb trailing like a poison needle. He was exposed now, ready to be opened up and eaten guts first.

But instinct told him what would happen next. He pressed his back to the ground, putting everything he had into keeping that stinger away from his spine.

The barb traced a line of fire across his belly as the wraith scrambled to get in behind him. He turned with it, locking his hands onto stick-thin arms. It was weakening, its movements slowing, eyes wide with desperation. Noah felt a stir of hope. Maybe he could outlast it.

Then the wraith changed strategies and locked its hands on his throat. He gagged as hard fingers crushed his windpipe and squeezed off his air. He pried at its hands until his vision darkened and his arms grew slack.

A strangled moan escaped him as the creature let go, long enough to turn him over. This time he didn't fight. He tasted dirt as the thing mounted him and fitted itself against his back.

A fire-bolt tore into him, grated against his spine. Liquid heat spread like a shock wave through his body, burning his insides. He couldn't hear himself scream because he'd gone deaf with agony, as if he was being boiled in his own blood. All he could do was close his eyes and wait to die.

He didn't die. White-hot gave way to charred numbness and then to cold as the thing writhed on top of him. Pressure on the small of his back, the pinch, push and pull like a water pump, hit something deep in him. His body knew this sensation.

He tried not to think about it, the idea of alien flesh latched onto him, sucking the life out of him drop by drop. Instead he closed his eyes, his body rocking gently under the creature's weight, and thought of Angeline. Of all the things he could have wished for at that moment, funny that what he wanted was to have that damn shirt of hers. If only he could bury himself in her smell one last time.

When the creature screamed again he was too far gone to care. He noticed with a detached fascination that the noise seemed to come from everywhere. How could such a ruined thing make a sound that big? Why had it gone so still?

Something had changed. The wraith shifted, a jerky motion that tugged at his spine. His soul-sucking little friend was trembling, he realized.

Another scream shook the forest and this time he was sure. The sound hadn't come from the wasted thing on top of him. Someone else was here. The creature leapt off his back, tearing loose with a wet rip that left warm rivulets trickling down his sides.

A storm of howls followed. Snapping branches and colliding flesh erupted all around him. Noah tried to turn his head and managed only a moan. He tried to lift his hand. The middle finger waggled mockingly and went still.

Well, fuck me. I'm paralyzed.

Were you supposed to feel pain like this when you were paralyzed? Someone had left a live coal the size of an asteroid on his back. Acid coursed through his veins, but his body was made of lead. Somewhere beyond sight, two monsters were tearing each other to pieces, shaking the trees and crushing the underbrush.

He closed his eyes, squeezing back tears of agony. This wasn't just pain. Something was going very wrong inside him, like two spirits fighting for his soul and ripping it to pieces in the process.

A warm spray hit is face. A strangled cry came from somewhere close. The fight had turned. Somebody was about to lose. A loud crack, thick and wet, followed by a final crunch.

Silence followed. Subtle movement caught the corner of his eye. The crumpled body of the wraith lay in a heap a few feet away, its thin limbs twisted and bent, quivering like an animal hit by a car. Its bulbous head wobbled on a stick-thin neck. Eyes that were no longer mad with hunger met his before sliding past him. Its hollow face went slack.

Something stirred the leaves behind him, not hurrying. The wraith did not try to get up. He recognized that look, had seen it many times in animals he'd had to watch die. It was the look of a creature who knew it was finished.

Another shape coalesced in his periphery, a solid object drifting into focus.

Her back was to him, but he had no trouble recognizing her. Angeline's body was full and healthy, her smooth curves and strong muscles tight under her pale skin. She was a stone goddess. The creature looked up at her as she stood over it, did not resist as Angeline reached down and gently took its head in her hands.

The wraith came up easily, neck stretching, thin arms slack at its sides as Angeline held it against her belly like a mother holding a child. Noah didn't need to see what caused the creature to jerk like a struck fish. The little body shuddered and went limp.

She released it. The corpse fell to the ground in a heap and remained still.

When Angeline turned, her face wasn't what he remembered. There was nothing human in her expression. No pity or compassion in her black eyes. Too numb to feel much about it, Noah saw the little pink scar on her belly, the thread-like needle glistening as it licked the air and disappeared. Noah closed his eyes and fell asleep.

35

TRUTH

- Noah -

Noah couldn't move without pain. Just raising his head to sip water was agony in those first hours.

He found himself lying on his cot in the loft. Angeline had somehow managed to haul his dead ass out of the wilderness and up the ladder while he'd slept. He hurt too much to be astonished.

Dust motes drifted through the soft sunlight that streamed through the trap door in the roof. The cool air was gentle on his fevered skin. With an effort he turned his head, found her sitting cross-legged at the edge of the loft, studying something in her cupped hands.

Angeline wore that tie-dyed shirt, of course - what was left of it. To his amazement, the pack he'd left in the woods sat near the foot of the cot, along with his machete. And that fucking lost boot that wouldn't stay on him.

Despite his suffering, despite everything that had happened, he felt a surge of intense happiness. Whatever she was – alien, vampire, demon - it didn't matter. She was his and she was *here*.

He'd been neither surprised nor afraid when, after killing the wraith, she'd shaken him back to consciousness and turned him onto his side to fit up against him. He'd welcomed the pain when it came. It hurt like hell. But it was right. It was clean. It was hers.

He'd been sure he was going to die. As usual, he was wrong. As his body warmed with her venom, death had pulled up stakes and ran. He'd wondered as he slipped into oblivion once more if he wouldn't be real sorry about that when he woke again.

She looked up as if feeling his gaze, abandoned the object, and padded over to him. The mystery item turned out to be the cell phone from Tan Man. Of course she would find that. It now lay in pieces on the floor.

He tried to sit. A bolt of lightning shot through his spine and ended that. She put her hand on his chest, shook her head, then helped him raise his head and pressed a bottle to his lips. Wonderful, cool water ignited his thirst, but she gave only stingy sips. A damp cloth fell over his brow and that felt good too. He let his eyes drift shut as she slid into the cot and pressed her belly against his back. He welcomed it. Sleep came an instant later.

She gave him two more of her injections that day, which he mostly slept through. She'd wake him long enough to make him drink and then sting him. Each time was less painful. As if there was less of the wraith inside him, like she was killing it all over again. By that evening he could sit up and take food.

She brought him a bowl of chicken soup, of all things. It was warm and smelled like heaven.

His mouth watered as she handed him an oversized wooden spoon. When he burnt his mouth and it cascaded down his chin, she snatched the spoon away and gave him a hard look before blowing on it.

Jesus, she could be so human at times. She was getting good at these simple mannerisms and expressions. It was terrifying, really. He knew all too well what she looked like when she wasn't pretending to be a woman.

He sipped carefully. The taste was as wholesome and familiar as white bread. After that crazy cult had driven Ma nuts - or maybe she'd gotten into it because she was already nuts - she would have called it food of the Devil, because anything with a picture or a label on the package was food of the Devil. So was anything you saw too often on TV commercials. Despite that, or probably because of it, he'd pretty much lived on that stuff after she'd gotten too sick to cook, mostly because it was easy, but also because he liked the irony of spoon feeding her shit that cooked her soul while it nourished her body.

Was he being fair? Had Ma really stopped going to the grocery store, making them all eat boiled dandelions and plantain because she was nuts? Or because there was no money? Because Daddy's income had shrunk as his drinking increased and then vanished altogether once he'd stopped breathing? Noah pushed the thought away.

Right then, Devil's food tasted pretty damned good. He couldn't get it in fast enough and Angeline wouldn't let him have the spoon back, or the bowl.

Slow, she mimed.

Something as basic and American as canned soup in a bowl should still be foreign to her. She must have found it in the stack of cans the FEMA crew had brought.

When the bowl was empty she set it down, pointed at him, face a question mark, and made a sign with her thumb and forefinger. *Okay?* she asked.

"Better," he said. "Thanks."

Noah examined his hands while Angeline waited for him to say something else. He plucked at the tattered shirt she wore and laughed. The thing was shorter than it used to be and almost one color.

"Thanks," he said. "For coming back."

Her black eyes were like neutron stars, huge and light-starved. They pulled at him like gravity. Noah tried to decide whether or not to ask the questions she was clearly waiting for. He might not like the answers. Her expression said she didn't care.

"So, I guess you're the one who fought that thing on the access road the other night. When I twisted my ankle."

Though unable to look directly at her, he saw her nod.

"And that night at the river," he said. "It had me, and..." He stopped and cleared his throat. "And you were there too."

He raised his eyes when she didn't answer. He already knew that he hadn't put the question right. She waited for him to say it. He glanced at the cell phone, which lay on the floorboards in a million pieces, all organized in neat little rows. He had no idea how such a small thing could have so many parts or that she could have gotten them all separated without breaking or losing anything. He had no doubt that every single piece was there and in its proper place. He was surprised and disturbed that she'd found it in the first place. He thought he'd hidden it well. Thank God she wasn't angry with him.

"You're the one who stung me."

She hadn't rescued him at all. She'd marked him. Not only had she marked him as hers, but she'd put something inside him that had changed him.

Love potion number nine.

She exhaled, like she was proud of him for figuring it all out. *That's a good, smart boy, Noah.*

He felt no revulsion or fear or anger or any other emotion that might have made sense. If anything scared him, it was the fact that he knew what she was, knew why she was really here, and didn't care.

"It was simple competition, wasn't it? She...it. *She* wanted the same thing you did. You got there first?"

His throat was raw from days of thirst and fever. He wondered if he would have to explain the word *competition.* If she was confused by it, she didn't show it. Or maybe she got the context. She leaned forward and very slowly touched her lips to his forehead, and sat back to watch his face. He didn't know exactly what that meant. But if it was an answer, he supposed it meant yes.

"Was it you that I saw in the Glen that first night? The one who ran away? Or was it her?"

She touched her chest with the tip of a finger. *Me.* She gave a faint smile with her eyes.

"You looked younger. I thought it was a trick of the light or something. But it wasn't, was it? You grew."

Her eyes seemed to catch every twitch of his face, like she was dissecting him.

He looked again at the gutted phone and shuddered. *All just by watching.* Everything from language to machines, from simple things to really complicated ones. Even something like spoon feeding him Campbell's chicken soup from a bowl was something she must have observed somewhere. He thought then that the flavor she'd picked probably wasn't accidental. How many times did one of those commercials come on anyway? The only thing she might not have gotten from a picture of a mom spooning broth into a sick kid would have been the act of heating it on the stove, but she'd figured that out by seeing steam rising from the bowl. He wondered what she could do with all that she was learning, what she'd already done.

"I saw some dead men out there, while I was looking for you," he said, wishing he wasn't asking but unable to stop it himself. "Did you do it?"

She didn't move, her gaze a dark void.

"Did you?"

For several moments neither of them spoke. Noah let his eyes fall to his hands, noticed how thin they were, how brittle and cracked the nails, how transparent the skin. He thought of the wraith. He thought of his mother.

Angeline's eyes were hard not to see even when he wasn't looking at her. At this moment, she was as alien on the outside as she was on the inside. Had he been seeing her for the first time, he would not have mistaken her for human.

She broke the silence with a touch.

She pointed at him and gestured. He frowned, not sure of her meaning. She repeated it and mouthed a single word slowly. *Safe.*

You. Safe, she said.

From you? He left it unsaid. *Did you come out of one of those holes? Which one? How many more like you are out there?*

It didn't matter. That she was no more human than a sea urchin didn't matter either. Why dwell on it? None of it changed a damn thing about what he wanted.

"What's going to happen to us?" he said.

The question snuck out of him even before he knew he was saying it. And it was the question to which he least wanted the answer.

She knelt in front of him and took his face in her hands, making him look at her. He didn't know what she wanted him to see because her face was unreadable. But when she gently kissed him, he accepted it.

He lay awake for hours that night, unable to sleep. She breathed deeply and easily beside him, her back resting against his. Except for the kiss, she hadn't touched him since she'd brought him back, not in that way. Hadn't even hinted at it.

He was surprised to feel as much longing as relief. She was doing him a favor, of course. But with a little stab of horror he realized that, as sick as he was and with everything else he knew about her, all she had to do was initiate and his body would wake up like a smoking coal.

Love potion number nine.

The next day he could get out of bed and walk. The wraith's venom was gone and he felt better than he had in weeks. Stronger. Whatever was different about hers, it had somehow reversed the damage, like an antidote. Somehow hers belonged. His body not only accepted it now, but needed it.

What would've happened if she hadn't come along and the wraith had just had its way? He'd be dead, of course, sucked dry and discarded like an empty soup can.

But wasn't that what had been happening anyway? Just a little slower?

That's enough. Stop it.

The questions kept coming. And as his body got stronger, so did his obsession with them. *Why,* he wondered. *Why everything? What did they want with humans? Why do they look like us, imitate us?*

What happens next?

Over and over again, it always came back to the worst one of all, settling into it like fresh dirt over a grave. He wanted to turn off his brain and just be with her, enjoy her, which he could do now because she never left him, never let him out of her sight.

The questions might have been fueled by a memory that kept returning, one he at first thought had nothing to do with anything, but now seemed ominously relevant.

He remembered finding her watching television a few nights ago, before she'd disappeared. She'd found some nature show on a local station. He hadn't given it much notice at first, until he saw how fascinated she was. TV had gotten a little more common to her by then, so, seeing her so focused made him sit down beside her.

"What is this?" he said.

She'd barely noticed him. A flick of the eye and no more.

Some kind of spider in a rainforest was weaving a web. A fine English accent said what species it was but hell if he could remember. He thought of the mass in Judd's engine several days back as the pale-yellow creature did its thing. He held down a shudder.

The twist of the story was that the spider was not the predator in this tale. The spider had a passenger. A small wasp grub was hitchhiking on its back. And little did the spider know that the thing was slowly drinking its blood, eating it a bit at a time as the spider trapped food and rebuilt its web each morning. The spider carried the grub around for days, without noticing or caring. Then one day everything changed. The poor spider went crazy.

Instead of spinning a perfect web with straight angles, it spun a ball of chaos, apparently forgetting how to do what spiders do. The grub, meanwhile, kept munching away, oblivious or indifferent to the spider's distress. But the whole thing turned out to be the grub's doing. It had injected the spider with a chemical that had rewired its brain. And when the host finally finished spinning and had worn itself out, the grub woke up.

It sucked the spider dry, suddenly ravenous for its life. It drained it to a husk and threw it away before nesting itself in the ball that the spider had made. After some finishing touches with its own silk, the little grub went to sleep. Weeks later it emerged again as a much different creature. It flew away as a full-grown wasp to lay its eggs and start the process all over again.

"Boy, you better read more and daydream less or you'll fancy your way right to perdition," Ma might have said.

Is that why she'd come? Was she a parasite who'd come to fuck him and eat him and leave him a husk?

Now there was a story, a plot so good it had to have been written just for him. His guardian angel turned demon, his savior turned destroyer. Because there had actually never been a demon in the first place, or rather there had never been any angel. They were all demons. He was surrounded by them. One sent to kill his body, the other sent to kill his mind.

Which would go first?

~

He knew he must have been dreaming the moment he opened his eyes. Such an ugly noise couldn't be real. The floor below the loft boiled with a dry hiss. It was everywhere, as if legions of locust had invaded the barn. He reached for the machete, but couldn't move.

His hands and feet were tied. Bedsheets were knotted around his wrists and ankles. His arms were stretched over the cot's metal frame, legs spread-eagle by cords whose ends he couldn't see. He jerked frantically, but the knots held.

The hiss gathered itself and congealed at the base of the ladder, as if all those insects were merging into a single body. Something began to climb.

He heard the scrape of claws against wood as it latched onto the lower rungs and dragged itself upward. He threw himself against the cords, turning his wrists bloody, but the sheets didn't budge. The knots went tighter still. The cords stretched until he felt like he was being pulled apart. The corner of the cot's frame beat against the floorboards.

"Oh, sweet Jesus. Mary mother of God, please."

A noise that sounded horribly like words crackled below the ladder. "Too. Late." The voice sounded like dry paper catching fire. "Too. Late. Noah," she said. "Too late to pray."

The voice rose to a cackle and the thump of hands on the ladder planks came faster.

"Too late!" She shrieked hateful laughter as he watched the head of the ladder shake, wide-eyed for the face he knew was coming.

"Too late for your damned soul!"

The stench of shit and latex filled his nostrils as a skull rose like an inflamed moon over the loft. He tore at the ropes as a ribcage followed the head. The thing clawed over the ladder. Grey skin hung in strips from bones and shrunken flaps of what had once been breasts swung as the demon tottered over the top rung. A knobbed foot hit the floor. The creature stood upright, a horror of wasted flesh and bone that wore his mother's face.

She clutched a pillow in her fists.

He found his voice then. His scream filled the barn. Her swollen belly gaped like a mouth, opening and closing in a line of needle teeth. He looked down at his wrists, wishing he could chew through them. Now he saw that the knots that bound him were not bedsheets. Oh God, no.

As fetid, alcohol breath washed over him, he realized that the cords were ropes of spider's silk. It was the last thing he saw before the pillow fell over his face and the world went black.

36

SPIDER'S WEB

- Noah -

His body recovered quickly. His mind was another matter. The nightmares came for him even when he was conscious; the demon upstairs had become a permanent resident. Sleep was impossible now without Angeline's help, without the drug she gave him. He craved it not just because it felt good but because it kept *her* out of his dreams.

He was restless too. His body needed to move. At first, he blamed it on the recovery from weeks of exhaustion. But that didn't explain why he was doing stupid shit like stacking and re-stacking soup cans or sweeping the floors over and over again. He might have gone back to something useful, like roofing the house, but he wasn't going near that place. At night his mother screamed and beat the floor. During the day she paced behind that curtained window, leering at him from the darkness of the house. He went to the spigot for water and thought he could actually smell the reek of shit and rot wafting from the kitchen door.

He and Angeline ate the canned soup and plastic-wrapped food from their supplies in the barn. *He* ate. She hadn't fed since the night of the wraith. Even when he begged her to, she wouldn't. He studied her carefully. Was her color fading? Did she look thinner, more listless than usual?

"You need to eat too." The thought of her body shriveled to bones, of her face on that horrible, wasted corpse, drove him to near panic.

I'll eat soon, she said in her own combination of hand signs and mouthed words.

"Yeah? Well, you haven't in days." Was she still worried about him? He was fine. He could handle it now. Better now than he could have a week ago. He'd tried to initiate himself, but she'd stopped him.

"You'll die! You'll starve like the other one did."

She stung him unconscious before he could feel sorry about it.

"You stubborn bitch." He stared at the bedroom window.

It was early morning. The woman should have gone back into hiding hours ago. Yet she was up there screaming to raise Hell, so real he could practically see the glass shake in the window frame.

Too bad Angeline couldn't just go up there and put an end to her too. But she couldn't help him with this, not something trapped in his own skull. And that was good. He needed to deal with this on his own, because he'd created this mess. He'd been the one to put her up there in the first place.

The yellowed curtain swayed, as if awoken by a passing body.

"You want to hear me pray? Here's my prayer for you, Ma. Roast in Hell."

Angeline was watching him. Always close now, she left his side only long enough to slip away on one of her secret errands, always while his attention was somewhere else. She would return about the time he noticed her missing.

Now she sat, perched on the tractor tire, studying him as his lips moved.

He stepped outside to get out of her sight.

"She's for you, Noah," the demon whispered. Its cracked voice spoke directly into his head like the voice of God. "She's going to swallow you whole and drag you to Hell."

"You want me to beg?" Noah asked. "You want me to feel sorry, is that it? Guilty? Well, piss on you. I don't." His voice grew, feeding on the anger, pushing away old fear. He started walking. "You did this to me, remember?" he said. "You started it, you hypocritical bitch. I left you to your prayers just like you left Daddy. Just like you wanted. Your god abandoned you."

The shadow lurked behind the curtain, but remained still. And it wasn't true, exactly. He hadn't just let her die in her own way, had he?

"At least Dad had the guts to die before he was shitting his own sheets."

As Noah advanced on the kitchen door, the shadow shrank from the window. The house itself seemed to rear back and cower under the trees. It looked naked and humbled with its bare roof.

"Where's your god now? He was supposed to save you, not me."

The house was silent. The stench was gone. The curtain was still, the window empty and dark. But she was still there, lurking behind the walls like a shifty rat. Maybe she cowered in a corner, or maybe she was tied to the bed. Maybe she waited behind the kitchen door, ready to fall on him the moment he entered.

"You're going to go away, do you hear me? I'm going to make you go away."

It wasn't God who had sent her here any more than it was God who had taken her. Her prayers had gone unanswered because there was no one to hear them but Noah. God hadn't withheld mercy, because there was no god to grant it. In the end, it was Noah who'd had to answer her prayers.

Well, he would kill her all over again. Since Noah was the one who'd raised her from the dead, so he must exorcise her.

"I will bury you."

The idea budded and flowered even as the words left his mouth. It was so simple. He could feel the rightness of it.

The cellar. Everything in that rat-infested room up there, he'd bury it all right where she'd horded her little treasures all those years, where she'd hidden her little sin she thought no one knew about, where she'd sneak off to, out from under the eyes of Jessie and Noah and God himself to wash away her own guilt in the months after Daddy's death.

He'd found it of course. And he'd emptied the bottle into the river just because she couldn't say anything, because it was supposed to be secret. Wherever she'd hidden the next bottle was anyone's guess. But what a perfect place to bury the rest of her. Let her soul have all that was hers and they could rot together.

He looked at the earthen mound under the forest's shoulder and smiled. *This would work.* As he turned back to the barn to prepare, his body rejoiced in the anticipation of the work that awaited.

"I have something I need to do," he said as Angeline followed him back inside. He didn't look at her, didn't want to see anything in her face that might put doubt in his head. "But she won't all fit until I make some room."

He found tools; sledgehammer, crowbar, a pick ax and shovel, a burlap sack. He grabbed two galvanized buckets from the tack room and made his way to the cellar, carrying everything in a wheelbarrow.

He threw open the doors and stepped into musty darkness with the sack, hammer, and crowbar. Angeline stood at the top of the staircase as he filled the sack with the old Mason jars from the shelves. Some of them lay shattered on the floor from his night spent in the cellar, days ago, months ago, years ago. He filled the sack, then emptied it into the wheelbarrow. When that was full he rolled it to the back of the property and overturned it at the dump, watching glass tumble and shatter at the bottom of the pit. When the shelves were empty he tore them out, hauling the lumber to the same place.

He made several trips, filling, hauling, emptying. Whether she followed him each time he didn't know. He knew only that she never tried to stop him.

An hour later, the cellar was clean and the cement floor was bare. He hefted the sledgehammer and broke the floor into pieces, which he carried out and stacked in the wheelbarrow. He thought about starting the tractor and hauling it off with the trailer, but all that noise and clatter would ruin the sanctity of the enterprise. Instinct told him that he must do this himself, with his own hands. And his body *wanted* it, needed it like Angeline's drug.

He worked all that day, barely noticing the sun brighten and fade. Not until the cellar was too dark to see what he was swinging at did he notice how late it had gotten. Even then he didn't stop, but found the little box of matches from Tan Man in the barn and lit a lantern. Then he went back to work.

Angeline huddled on the cold steps, looking small and fragile in the lantern light.

What the hell are you doing? A still, small voice. He realized he hadn't eaten or drank since that morning. His muscles were cramping. He didn't care. He attacked the dirt like he was digging for his life. Though his shoulders knotted and his back ached, his body begged to go on, rejoiced in every stab of the shovel and in every swing of the pick. He could feel the demon breathing down his neck, watching its grave get deeper, losing strength with each load he carried away. Every bit of dirt he tore loose took a little piece of her from his mind.

What do you think you are going to bury here?

He was three feet below the cellar floor now, enough room for Ma's old cedar chest maybe, but not much else.

You going to haul the whole room down here, stuff it all right here? You going to bury her? What the hell is there to bury, Noah?

He traded the shovel for the pick ax and chopped into the back wall under the foundation.

It didn't matter, really. What if he buried himself here? That was it, wasn't it? Wasn't he digging his own grave?

It had all happened. It was done. He was crazy and those hole-creatures had put their poison in him and driven him mad. He threw the pick and shoveled clumps of dirt into the buckets. Soil had turned to clay, sticky and heavy, clinging to the shovel, making the work twice as hard. When both buckets were full, he lifted them to the jagged lip of concrete, pulled himself up and hauled them up the stairs. Angeline slipped aside to let him pass. He heaved each bucket into the wheelbarrow. They gave up their loads grudgingly, with a wet squelch. He was careful not to let a single clod fall to the grass, for reasons he didn't understand, but accepted as vital.

As he grabbed the wheelbarrow poles, a hand touched his shoulder. He turned. Her pale face was hard to make out in the thickening darkness, but he didn't need to see her worry to know it was there. He could feel it in her touch.

"I've got to finish this." He tried to shrug her off. "I'll be done soon."

She shook her head and gathered his hands in hers. He squeezed and pulled away.

"I'm all right." He noticed suddenly how tall she was. God, she was taller than he was now. He had to look up to meet her eyes.

"Why don't you go on inside? I'll be in in a minute." He *had* to do this. If he ever wanted to have any peace. He was going to finish this. Tonight. But he had to hurry.

Hurry, he thought. Time was short. He didn't have much time. Somehow, if he didn't finish soon, it would be too late.

He picked up the wheelbarrow and stumbled on, careful to avoid the paths he'd followed earlier. *Don't want to leave a trail. Can't have someone following.*

He made the trip quick and quiet. His legs ached and a new cramp bit into his calf, but he kept going, breathing in wheezy gasps. *Why the hell am I so tired?*

You don't have much time.

Her voice? No, this one was his. Not harsh and accusing, just simple fact.

He shook the load over the cliff, watched the heavy clods break over the rock and old scrap metal. He could picture it all down there; old bicycles, rotted car parts, mattress springs, and probably enough soup cans to buy the whole state if somebody would gather them up. A hundred years and three generations of Weismanns down there, and God knew who else.

Noah had gone treasure hunting down there a few times when he was a kid until Ma caught him and told him she'd beat him black and blue if he ever went down there again. She told him it was because he'd get lockjaw, but Daddy said it was because some things just needed to stay buried.

Twenty paces from the cellar, the cramp got serious and locked him up from calf to ass. He spilled over the wheelbarrow, lay in the dirt squeezing his hamstring in both fists, eyes leaking tears, trying in vain to massage the agony away.

Angeline's hand was on him. He tried to push her away, but she wouldn't go. When the cramp let off, she handed him a bottle. The water fell over his tongue, waking a thirst he hadn't known was there. He drained the bottle in breathless swallows.

When the bottle was empty, he stood up, accepting her help. His mutinous calf gave a warning flutter but stayed quiet. He expected her to try to stop him again, but she must have decided there was no reasoning with a madman.

Back in the cellar, he got in one good swing before his body shut down. The spasm hit his hamstring hard enough to fold him in half. Angeline had to drag him out of the pit.

He lay face down at the greasy edge of the concrete floor, trying not to scream as she worked her hands into his muscles, just as he had done moments ago. When he tried to get up she held him down, eyes hard, not fucking around now. She made him drink.

"I need to finish this," he said. She ignored him, helped him lean against the wall and stretch out his leg. He emptied another bottle and set it down, made one last attempt to get up, but he was finished. He sat back and cursed himself for his frailty.

"You must think I've gone crazy," he said, settling against the cool stones. He gazed at his mud-streaked body and threadbare jeans. The sunken hollow of his belly.

Jesus. He'd never exactly been fleshy, but the sharp angles of his hips and skin thin enough to read a newspaper through made him wonder how he'd had the gumption to do any of this. Maybe it made sense that she wasn't feeding on him. There wasn't much left to feed on.

He looked at the pit, at where the foundation stones hung like teeth above a hollow that reminded him of the den at the cabin. Why had he dug that? Why was he digging a cave into the wall of the cellar?

He shook his head. "What the hell am I doing here?" Why hadn't he just sat down and thought this through before tearing the place apart? "I'm sorry," he said. "Sorry you had to watch this. Sorry I put you through it." He gazed at the black maw of the cellar's opening beyond the stairs and sighed. "What do you say we get out of here, huh?"

She just sat, watching him in the lantern light. The smallest hint of that eerie glow in her eyes flashed as she turned her head toward the entrance, toward the silent house and then back at him, her eyes questioning.

He frowned. "Can you hear her too?"

She shook her head. *I see you,* she said.

"Yeah." He sighed and nodded.

Why afraid? she pressed.

"It's hard to explain." He swallowed, cleared his throat. "I've been...a little distracted the last few days."

That was an understatement. Even without Ma hounding him from the hinterlands of Hell, he'd been through enough to make anybody crazy.

"I'm not going the way *she* did," he said. "No goddamned way. I won't let that happen." He looked up at her and scowled. He was doing it again, and she had no idea what he was talking about. He stared at his feet.

"Sorry," he said. "This is the last thing you need to be listening to. It's not even worth saying. I just need to get my head out of my ass."

He meant to get up then, to walk out of that hole and do just what he'd said – clean up and go to bed – but he just sat there.

"Not like it's something the whole valley doesn't know about anyway," he said. "Goddamned vultures." He picked up a handful of clay and flung it. "You don't keep secrets around here, you know? Not from these people. But I guess, how would you keep shit like that down?"

There was a tear in his pants near the knee where the pale flesh and a long, purplish gash showed through. The edge of the tear was bloodstained. He couldn't remember it happening. The vision reminded him of Judd McPherson.

"My whole family's made itself kind of a sideshow circus for everybody over the last few years. Hometown entertainment at its best. Better than Jerry fucking Springer. Everybody keeps waiting to see when young Noah will sail out to sea like everybody else. Fucking assholes. They're all so goddamned sneaky about it too, pointing and whispering like I don't know what they're saying."

Noah wished he could shut up because nobody wanted to hear this, particularly not himself.

"Oh, everybody's real kind and sorrowful to my face. When Jessie died, they all brought their little gifts and spoke their little sermons. 'Hang in there, Noah.' 'She's in a better place.' I still can't go to the grocery store without some well-wishing fuck giving me a look or saying some bullshit like that. Then they turn around and ask each other if I'm acting a little - you know." He twirled his finger around his temple and laughed.

"I guess they've got a point, right?" He scratched a mud scab on his arm, watching the orange paste disintegrate and fall like ash to the floor. His arms and chest were covered with it. His skin cracked every time he moved. He felt like someone who'd been buried alive and had dug himself out.

37

GRAVE DIGGER

- Noah -

Angeline shook him awake. The shock of being dragged from oblivion to a scraped-raw consciousness didn't set well.

"What?" He sat up, heart thudding, adrenaline like acid in his throat. "Are they here? Where are they?"

How could he have been so stupid? So complacent? Tan Man and his Yeti friend had come before he could finish the job, and now they would burn them both alive and it was his fault.

Hands gripped his shoulders, gave him a fierce shake. He searched her face and found no fear, no reflection of the second coming. Only calm expectation.

He sighed. "What is it? What's the matter?"

She shook her head, pulled him up. He was still in the cellar. Morning light streamed in through the open doors, casting her in a halo. He stared.

Jesus, why is this happening to me? Why her?

He had less time than he thought. His sick mind was making

things up everywhere, mocking him with the truth that he was getting worse every day.

Angeline was changing before his eyes. Her skin had drained of color and looked like smoked glass. He could see the little blue veins in her face that ran up her forehead and disappeared into her hairline. Little prismatic flashes that reminded him of mayfly wings caught when she turned in the sunlight.

Worst of all were her eyes. They didn't disappear when she blinked because her lids were translucent. They were so black he couldn't tell where she was looking.

He turned away, hoping she hadn't seen his horror, knowing it wasn't real. She gave a gentle push. Toward was the pit. The tools. He must finish this. Before it was too late.

He worked steady and hard, the night's pain and exhaustion forgotten. Angeline kept him watered and fed, though he was barely conscious of eating or drinking. He took whatever she offered and never stopped long enough to sit.

He felt Ma wake as he dug, felt her writhe as he burrowed beneath the floor of the cellar. He felt her pain and terror as if each stab of the shovel went into her body rather than into the dirt.

The work slowed. There were tree roots now, as he dug further from the foundation. He chopped at them with a spade or cut them away with a handsaw. There were rocks too, which he would dig around until he could pry them out with a rock bar. And the shaft was small and tight, forcing him to work on hands and knees and crawl out backward like a crab once his buckets were full.

The upside of it all was that he didn't have to carry the dirt to the dump anymore. That time had passed. This dirt he would keep because he would need it soon. He piled it up on either side of the cellar stairwell, leaving room to work and move.

He started to tire early that afternoon, sleep deprivation finally catching up with him despite Angeline's attention to his needs. He sat down as the muscles in his thighs and lower back cramped. His lungs and heart were working double time. Pain set in on him the moment he relaxed and an incredible desire to lie down and sleep pressed upon him.

She wouldn't let him. She shook him, her face urgent, firm.

"I'm tired."

She nodded but kept pushing.

"Just a few minutes. I just need a few minutes." She took his hands and pulled him to his feet.

I have to finish this.

He knew that. The thing in his head, the thing in that bedroom up there. Tan Man's army. They were all coming. He couldn't rest until it was finished. Until it was all closed up with the two of them safely sealed inside.

Stop this.

The thought was an irritant, a temptation that he couldn't listen to even for a moment. He had to keep going because there was no other choice. He grabbed the shovel and crawled back into the hole.

The cellar was filling up. Soil and rocks and root chunks, some as big around as his waist, were heaped up along the walls from end to end so that the walkway to the staircase was no more than a couple feet across. But he was almost finished. A little more and he would be done. The soil was root-bound now. He thought it would be stable as long as he was careful and didn't take out too much.

They slept in the cellar again that night. Noah more or less drug himself back out of the shaft and collapsed on the earth floor in the vault shaped chamber he'd dug the first day. It was well past dark. She lay down beside him, and whether she stung him or not he had no idea. He fell into a sleep too deep for nightmares.

"Tomorrow I'll be finished," he told her. He didn't know whether she'd heard or not, but the feel of her squeezing his shoulder as he slipped away made him think she had. He slept untroubled until Angeline shook him awake again.

38

THE NEST

- Noah -

Early the next morning he ate two granola bars, drained a can of condensed milk, and got started without any prodding from Angeline. The difference between how he'd felt last night and the strength he had this morning was incredible. Ma was silent too, no more than a shadow in a black corner of his skull. But he felt her pacing the little prison up there, the one he and Angeline were building for her, scared and desperate. With every stab of the shovel that prison got smaller and tighter. Soon she'd be crushed to death and would haunt them no more. He and Angeline would be alone and in peace.

He tired quickly, and by late morning she was pushing him again. His hands were raw with open blisters and the roots were getting harder, thicker, the air heavier and hotter. He ached to lie down, to listen to the tiny voice telling him to stop. But whenever his pace slowed, Ma would stir and scratch at the walls. As the day wore on and his energy faded, the demon began to thrash and scream in her dry, dead voice. Soon the bed frame hammered the floorboard in the bedroom upstairs.

Christ, it was so real. So true, surely Angeline heard it. Every time he looked at her now, he wanted to cry. She was so different. Alien. Transforming by the hour. She looked like a jellyfish squeezed into the shape of a girl, translucent, her legs and arms streaked with little bands of indigo.

She would shake him, push him, drag him back to that hole, her face getting more urgent as the day waned. She too knew that they were running out of time.

She never lifted a finger to help, though. Not once did she take the shovel or pick up a bucket. It was as if touching the work itself was taboo or forbidden. Her hands were only for him, bringing him food or water or getting him up.

Sometimes she would disappear for a while, usually when he was deep in the hole. He'd sometimes crawl out to find her climbing back down the cellar stairs and breathing like she'd just ran a fast four hundred. Once he'd come up out of the cellar wondering where she was to see her slip around the corner of the house from the kitchen. He wondered if she'd actually gone in there but she didn't give him a chance to ask before she chased him back into the hole again.

He worked until his body was ready to shut down and his mind was about to collapse from the effort of holding Ma in her cell and pretending Angeline was still Angeline.

A little more. Almost done. Almost right.

It was finished. At last! He had widened the end of the canal into a kind of cell, a rounded room just big enough turn around in. He could crawl out of the canal forward instead of backward. He needed another bucketful or two to smooth it out and the job would be done.

When he was finished, he was so tired and elated he couldn't stop laughing. He was barely aware of Angeline joining him in the darkness. This time, instead of pulling him out and back up to the cellar floor, she tugged him to the middle of their little cell and curled around him.

He was asleep instantly.

39

NOAH IS A WHORE

- Noah -

No simple matter doing this job, with that woman jerking on the straps and shrieking like she was being tortured.

Jesus, the woman was in fine form tonight, the bedpost doing one hundred-eighty beats per minute if it was one. Her shrill voice grated at his ears, like rats chewing through the walls.

"Yeah, I'm working on it, for fuck's sake." He said it under his breath, because swearing only made her worse. The pills were stubborn, refusing to break under his trembling hands. The bowl was full of jagged little knives in a skiff of white powder and would probably kill her if he gave it to her like this.

"She's a whore, Noah. A dirty, flighty little whore, do you hear me?"

A coffee grinder would make this all so much easier.

"Yeah, I hear you."

The Magic Dust was the most recent addition to Ma's special recipe: One cup applesauce, a half-cup of chicken broth, half-cup of whipping cream, and an extra high-octane additive of Jack D. It probably tasted like shit, but since he put it down her through a feeding tube the flavor was the least of her worries. And the mix hadn't included the Alcoholic Angel of Mercy when she'd fed Daddy during his last agonized days, so drink up, bitch.

"Where the hell is the spoon, Ma? What'd you do with it, huh?" Noah sifted through the junk on the nightstand: feeding tube, funnel, steel shears, spent pill bottles and wet wipes. He kicked aside a bale of adult diapers and peered under the cot.

"She's a whore, Noah. Your sister. I saw her. I saw her with him."

"Shut up."

Only thing under there was a pair of old boots and that cell phone from that freaky FEMA guy with the pale eyes. That, and a picture of Daddy and Jessie.

Why the hell was he doing this in the loft? He should have done this in the kitchen where he wouldn't have to listen to her prattle.

He couldn't tell what was real anymore. It was all so fucked up he couldn't figure out why he was sweating and shaking all over. The smell of shit puree was about to make him vomit.

He picked up the feeding tube and funnel. There was dried blood on the transparent tubing, which meant he hadn't remembered to clean it last time. Shit, he should have done this in the house instead of the barn where he had light enough to see.

"Goddamn it, Ma, will you shut up?"

Lightheaded. Legs rubbery. Where was Angeline? He could really use her help with this. Jessie should be here. Why the hell did she have to go and die on him?

"I saw them. Your sister and..."

"I said shut up!"

The thrashing and banging had stopped and Noah wished it would start up and she'd go back to screaming, because she was leering at him. Sometimes the woman would lapse into these cruel moments of clarity when she could actually use the powers of speech to get under his skin, which he hated more than her shitting the bed.

"She would wait for him, Noah. Wait until he was drunk and weak."

He poured the puree into the jug, pulled the tube through the lid and tightened it down. The quicker he got it down her, the quicker she would be silent.

"Your father was weak. He was a weak, weak little man."

Noah turned to the bed, gaze falling on those skeletal legs, their swollen knees under tight, purple-veined skin, blistered and red and suppurated from the ropes that bound her.

"She's a whore. A whore, a little whore who ruined everything, do you hear me?"

When had he traded the tube for the pillow? And why? He wasn't sure, but he had it now. And when he looked at her face, her mouth stretched in a grin like she knew some lewd joke about him, her black eyes the size of fists, mocking.

"Fuck you, you lying bitch."

He covered her face so he wouldn't have to look at her. God, the woman was strong. She kicked and fought like she actually wanted to keep breathing. At least she was quiet. Almost. He held her down until she stopped thrashing, stopped screaming and at last fell asleep. He kept holding, to make sure she would stay asleep. No more pills, no more booze, no more diapers. No more lies.

40

FUNERAL PYRE

- Noah -

He woke to darkness. The darkness was right. But her absence was not. They should both be here. Together. Why was she not here?

Panic rising, he dragged himself from the cell that he'd made for them, through the canal, to the lip of the concrete floor. He could already hear the wailing from the dead house.

He called for Angeline. She didn't answer.

He stumbled outside, blind. He ignored the house, the shaking walls, staggering in the direction of the barn, his eyes refusing to work. He screamed for her over and over again, but she didn't come.

The smell from the house was overwhelming. He clamped a hand over his mouth as he passed the porch. Holy God, the stench of shit and rot and death was real.

"Will you shut the hell up?" What would he have to do to get rid of her? How many times would he have to kill her? Get her out of his head?

He shouted and screamed. God, if she would just answer him, even with that awful insect cry of hers.

"Where are you? Please!"

He stood like a sailor on the bow of a ship, holding onto to the porch rails against the wrath of a blinding storm.

"I'll cut my own throat if I have to, but you'll be dead when I'm done. Do you hear me?"

He turned to the front door, knocked it aside, and made his way to the kitchen, stumbling over rubble from the collapsed ceiling. The smell was omnipresent and all-powerful, hot enough to turn his stomach to liquid. He groped the countertop until he found the knife block and pulled a blade free. His eyes were waking up now. The dim outline of the carving knife was solid against the kitchen window. He turned to the staircase.

"Let's finish this!"

Broken plaster crunched underfoot. The ceiling rained dust and loose bits of gypsum. There were no words in the screaming anymore. No curses. No begging. Just pure animal terror, deep and guttural. The chandelier over the stairs rattled in harmony with the drumbeats of the bedpost on the floor.

"Don't you have anything to say to me?" he said. "Scream, then!"

But it wouldn't do her any good. Not this time.

Are you afraid of me now? The thought made him laugh.

He stared into the staircase and could almost see it. For a moment he had a vision of himself at the top of those stairs, closing that door for the last time. He actually heard the latch click. The Noah of two years ago turned and stared down at him, showing no surprise to see himself staring back. The man's eyes were empty, without emotion, full of a soul-deep weariness that no sleep could cure. He still had the pillow in his fist.

The staircase held its breath, encasing them in silence, as if waiting for something to happen.

"It's finished," the other Noah said. "Now let her go."

Then he was gone. The staircase was empty but for the reek of death. The pounding on the floorboard resumed at full tempo, as though it had never stopped. A bloody scream tore through the staircase. This time, it did not come from the bedroom but from his own lips. The knife clattered to the floor as he stumbled backward. Hot, desperate tears blinded him.

He fell. Someone caught him. A warm body fitted against his. Her scent filled his nostrils. Something broke loose in him. The dam behind the tears collapsed. Misery poured out of him. Years of it.

He turned to face her. His Angeline. To convince himself that she was really there, that she wasn't just another vision, he touched her face, feeling the warm reality of her skin, breathing in the familiar comfort that enfolded him even through the toxic air. She no longer looked like Angeline, but she was real.

He opened his mouth. What came out of him was not what he expected. His voice was foreign to him.

"I can't get her out of my head."

Angeline nodded.

"Help me. Please!"

She took his hand and led him away from the staircase, away from the stench and into the kitchen.

He saw the gasoline cans. Two of them sitting side by side on the floor, giving off a sharp perfume. She tapped his shoulder, looked at him as if asking him if he understood, then nodded at the living room.

She was so strange, so tall, lit from within. Beautiful. He'd never seen anything so beautiful.

He smiled. She'd always been smart. *You don't have to die, Noah. Not yet.* Her eyes told him so. *You can end this.*

"Yes," he said. It was so simple. Why hadn't he thought of this?

He picked up a gas can and uncapped it. The wonderful, clean odor surrounded him in a protective shell. She took the other and did the same. Together they plunged into the house and emptied the cans onto the walls, the floors and the furniture. Noah sang as he anointed Ma's home.

"It's over," he told himself. "It's over," he told her.

He splashed liquid in blessed arches on Ma's old shrine in the corner of the living room, where the King James Bible sat, rotted and water-stained, its pages sealed by corruption. Finally he turned to the staircase and emptied the can, dousing the walls and pitching the can at the second story landing where it landed with a hollow thump.

He joined Angeline at the kitchen door, reveling in the pungency of a pyre ready to ignite in purifying flame. He took Daddy's lighter from his pocket. It glinted eagerly in the faint light. He held it up high so Ma could see it, then struck flame.

"This belongs to you, Dad," he said. "It's time you had your say."

He pitched the lighter into the maw of the house, where it erupted into a river of fire. Noah and the girl watched it flow across the floor like blood, pushing toward the heart of the house.

"May we all rest in peace."

The halls and living room began to glow and then became a nova as the old, dry wood exploded.

They turned and ran, shielding their eyes and holding each other as the house disappeared in a halo of white. The speed at which the house went up was astonishing. Like a trapped soul waiting for release. It left its body with glorious violence, with a phosphorene light that followed the heart of the flame toward Heaven.

The screams turned to a pitched shriek, rising above the roar, high-pitched and sharp. As if Ma really did feel the flames in which she was burning. For a horrible, raw moment Noah was certain that she was really up there after all and that God had been holding her all this time for this punishing flame.

Glass shattered. The shriek rose and burned away into frequencies beyond human hearing. And then there was only the roar of fire.

She was gone at last. *Gone for good. Gone all the way*. It was over.

They kept backing away, driven further by the rising heat.

Something inside exploded with a boom, sending a shower of flaming debris clapping at their feet. The hot water heater, maybe. Noah thought of the stove, glanced at the propane tank, which now caught the expanding glow of the inferno. It wouldn't be long before that went too. They didn't want to be here when it did.

He was about to say something when a new sound reached his ears. Like the rush of a fire or a distant wind, escalating to a heavy, deep-in-the chest rumble. East.

She was already looking, her face set and expectant, as if she knew what was coming.

A beam of white light punched through the trees, blinding him. The noise became a roar that challenged the fire. A gust of hot wind stole his breath.

Angeline spun him around and shoved him toward the root cellar. She ran, dragging him by the hand, and Noah struggling to keep up.

Wind howled and whipped the trees, filling the air with the stink of river and acrid jet fuel. He turned to look, but she dragged him down, pressing him into the gooseberry bushes as the beam slashed past them. Noah screamed through an angry shower of heat and red embers, shielding his face. She hauled him up, then ran ahead to the cellar.

At first he thought she was going inside, that they would take shelter there from whatever it was that had invaded the sky. It had passed out of hearing though he could still see the roving eye of a spotlight stabbing the edge of the property. She didn't go in. She slammed the doors shut and fell on them, as if she had collapsed. Belly-down, she pressed her mouth to the seam where the doors met, as if in a lingering kiss.

He ran to catch up, watching transfixed as she slid down the door, face to the boards.

She rose and wiped her mouth with the back of her hand.

He stared at the cellar door, now frosted with glittering white fibers as if the cellar had become a freezer and leaked cold air. But it was not frost.

Angeline jarred him awake, thrusting a pack at him. He took it automatically. Her eyes were hard with impatience, as if saying, *You know what I am. Don't act surprised.*

He didn't have time to dwell on it. The air exploded again as the hard light broke over the trees and strafed the yard. He nearly dropped the bag. She shoved him at the forest and they were running again.

This time she didn't let go, but dragged him into the trees as a deep thudding hammered his eardrums. Wind beat them as the beam raked the edges of the forest and swept over the cellar where they'd just stood. He fell once. She hoisted him up and they reached the cover of the path as the thunder of a huge black beast passed overhead. They knelt in the underbrush as it circled and cast its light over Mother Maple, over the raging house, then the barn, which glowed red under the fountain of flames.

As if struck by a final blow, the house cracked and collapsed, folding in on itself with a crash that sounded like Judgment Day. Flaming chunks of debris fell onto the yard and Noah felt a sudden, irrational pang of fear for the barn, wondering if it too would catch fire.

The flying beast circled the farm like a bird of prey over a wounded animal, dragging its beam from one end of the property to the other.

He watched the rest of his childhood crumble. A throb of despair overtook him even with the relief of seeing the end of so many years of misery. What perished in the cataclysm was more than just evil spirits and a long history of suffering. His father's barn, which had offered safe haven from the madness with which that damnable house had long been infected, and ultimately something of himself, was being finished here. A final death, the collapse of the vessel into which his soul and sanity had been siphoned and bottled up like an extract. It was all happening before his eyes.

Whatever escaped this place tonight, whatever Angeline took with her, would be a shadow of what she'd first found. A hollow man, nothing of what he could have been or would have been. He was nothing more than a wraith. But whatever her intentions, they didn't require a whole man, did they?

They huddled a moment longer, watching the circling eye widen until it caught the tops of the trees and ran far out into the Glen. Then she squeezed his hand.

Time to go, Noah.

He cast one last look at his old life and fled.

She drove him hard, but he never stumbled, nor did the branches do more than brush his skin. It was like she could see everything, guided by the light emanating from her own body. Every tangle and root that should have caught up his feet and hindered his path missed him. They floated over gullies, around brambles, and under low branches as if they weren't there. Had Noah been blindfolded, he would have hardly known he was in a forest.

The eye of the monster brushed uselessly over the canopy without once casting their shadows and fell farther and farther behind. Hand in hand, they threaded through the forest like ghosts, Noah seeing only her glowing form as she pulled him deeper into wilderness.

She was like a forest spirit bearing him away from the wrath of God, an angel rapturing him from the ruin he deserved. Behind them, the fire screamed as if it knew something had been stolen, snatched away just as it had finally decided to claim it.

They climbed, making their way up the spine of the mountain. The lights stopped chasing them and the silence of the forest thickened. Up, they continued, without stopping until Noah snagged a foot and went down, jerking Angeline to a stop.

She knelt, pulled a bottle of water from the pack. He drank greedily, not realizing he was so thirsty. She let him sit and gulp air just as needfully.

"Where are we going?" he gasped.

She took this to mean he'd gotten his wind back and pulled him up, dragging him onward, slower this time but steadily, on a pace that he could barely keep up. Where they were going didn't matter. She was taking him with her. That was what mattered. It was all he wanted in the end, wasn't it? Of course it was. What happened to him now didn't matter.

Soon they were high over the valley. He could see the red bowl of the farm as the fire waned, its fuel source dwindling. The angry eye of the monster was still; the air beast no longer circled. Perhaps it had gone down to feed.

They watched for a while from a rocky overlook, from which they might have seen the peaked roof of the house had it still been standing. Noah thought he could just make out the outline of the barn and felt a stir of pointless relief, glad it might still be standing after he was gone.

He could see signs of movement down there too. Other lights, smaller lights, flitted around the Glen. Some moved in pairs in lateral arches like the eyes of vehicles. Some went in jagged zigzags like searchlights. The glow of orange gave way by the minute to a harsh, artificial white, until a fountain burst from the bowl, followed a few seconds later by a thunderous boom that echoed across the valley.

They watched the fire billow, then fall.

"Propane tank," Noah said, watching the lights grow frantic. Amazing it hadn't gone sooner. He wondered if anyone had been hurt in the blast or if they'd anticipated it and stayed away.

He looked at the girl who watched with grim satisfaction on her face, her eyes hard and frightening.

"I guess you're running from demons of your own, aren't you?" he asked.

He was tired. How he'd made it this far without collapsing was beyond him. How he would take another step he had no idea. His mind swam, flicking in and out of clarity like a lost radio station, the world rolling by like a muddy current.

Not demons of the mind though. Real demons. *Humans.*

"Why do they want you?" he heard himself say.

She didn't answer in words, didn't answer at all at first. She took his hand and held it for a moment. Then pressed his palm to her belly, just above the scar, all the more visible in her strange, glass like skin. She'd left the shirt behind and he could see all of her. It was the same from head to toe, all of her a crystal statue that glowed from the inside. She met his eyes, pressed him more firmly into her body, and he understood.

"Pregnant."

The world slid out of him like a curl of smoke and the world spun deeper into absurdity. How could she be pregnant? She wasn't human. She was no more human than the fire down there that had devoured his home. She was no more human than the thing that had masqueraded as his mother. She saw these thoughts on his face and released his hand, turning back to the flames. But he couldn't stop staring.

Why do you want me?

The question came, but wouldn't form into words. She wouldn't have answered him anyway. And whatever she might have said, had she been able to, it wouldn't have changed anything.

Soon she reached out without turning, took his hand, and pulled him back into the forest.

They continued their flight north, deeper and higher into the mountains. After their rest at the overlook, Angeline never stopped. The march seemed to go on for hours. All he could do was concentrate on staying on his feet, putting one in front of the other. He walked asleep, body operating off its last reserves, driven by a will that was not his own, like a salmon brute-forcing its way upstream for one final, biological imperative.

He wasn't sure when he first noticed the deep thrum of falling water, but by the time he was conscious of the chill, mist-flecked air and moss-carpeted earth, he knew. "Pikes Falls," he said, astonished. There was no other place it could be. But how? The place was twelve miles from home. They must have walked most of the night.

They topped a rise and the roar hit him like a blast. Droplets of perpetual rain swirled around them, gathered on his face and arms. The air sweetened with the smell of earth.

They must have been high, because he couldn't hear the boom of the pool at its base. He was sorry he couldn't see because it was so beautiful from the valley. The waterfall came out of a huge cliff that Daddy used to call the Face of God. It fell hundreds of feet straight down to an oasis where the river was still just a stream and chocked full of fat brook trout that would strike a bare hook. Daddy used to bring him up here as a kid and they would catch them by the score, after which they would roast them over a fire and Noah would eat until he was ready to burst.

When he'd grown tired of fishing, Noah used to lie on his back and look up at the Falls. His gaze would follow the silver ribbon of the water up the rock face until it disappeared in a white haze, then he'd get lost in the grey crags set against the impossibly blue sky. He'd asked Daddy once if they could go up there sometime and see where the water came out but he'd just laughed. *Only way up there is by whirlwind or a chariot of fire.*

She led him to a narrow lip where the rock jutted out of the cliff and formed a small path across the face. Ferns and moss and a few willowy trees grew along this slip of earth bordered by earth and sky. He pulled back when he realized what she was doing.

"I don't think I can do this," he said, not knowing if she heard over the roar.

He did do it, though. She pushed him forward, hand on his shoulder, and guided him across. He was too numb to feel the terror he should have. They moved slowly, a step at a time, until the ledge widened and then gave way to an odd formation in the rock that made walking easier.

She turned him to the rock face, which rose and disappeared into darkness, nudged him forward until he saw the cave, a small black mouth that he would never have seen had Angeline not pointed him toward it. It was wider than it was tall and low enough that he had to get down on his belly to get into it. She urged him inside and he crawled, watching the faint light close off behind him and the roar of the Falls grow quiet as she slipped in after him. He dragged himself army-style as the tunnel narrowed.

He should have been afraid. But the cave was full of her scent – familiar, like the cellar. Rather than feeling closed in he felt cradled, comfortable even in the darkness. The floor of the tunnel was soft as goose down and he could feel rather than see the ceiling, hugging him close, coaxing him deeper. The floor dropped into a kind of bowl and grew softer, a feather mattress into which his hands and knees sank. Here Angeline brushed against him, pulling herself alongside him where they lay down, settling into each other's arms.

They were cocooned in the soft, pale glow of her body. He studied her face, felt her soft breath mingle with his, felt her kiss on his forehead, his cheek, and then his mouth. She squeezed him hard and he could feel her praise in it. For a while she lay curled against him, letting him breathe, letting their hearts slow.

He was never so happy to be off his feet and lying in such a comfortable place. He closed his eyes and let his mind go still, feeling two years of hell and more lose its hold and drift away.

When she at last rolled him onto his stomach and crawled on top of him, he wasn't afraid, even though he knew that this time it would be different. He knew in his very bones that whatever was to happen here and now, it would be final, and that he would never leave this cave.

He was glad.

He felt her belly open, the little scar parting and a tongue, moist and warm on his bare skin fasten to his back, as it had a thousand times before. The pain was sharp and to the bone. He bucked from an electric charge more intense than he'd felt before. She tightened around him as his body struggled, then relaxed limb by limb, muscle by muscle, the poison sinking deep into him. A wonderful heaviness covered him like a warm blanket and he sank into the deepest peace he'd ever known.

It was a good way to die, better by far than the slow flood of insanity that God had fated for him. He would never lose her now. As he faded, he felt a smile cross his face, knowing he had escaped.

Had it been like this for Tanner? Had he gone so softly? Noah hoped so.

Oblivion took him.

FINAL DEATH

- Noah -

But God wasn't done with him. Fate was a cruel, hungry thing with a long reach. It was not the end for Noah Weismann. And when he opened his eyes again, his dark, comfortable world had changed.

The gentle light of her body was gone. There was only darkness. He knew instantly that it was all was wrong because he was still alive. The space around him was no longer kind.

It was hot. Hot like an engine room. Sweat streamed out of him, plastered the hair to his face. He would have wiped it off, but he couldn't move. His arms and legs were fastened to the floor by what felt like hooks through the skin.

He jerked at his arms but nothing happened, just the bite of his restraints. He kicked and thrashed, but to no good. He was pinned hair to heels like a bug to flypaper, couldn't even turn his head.

I'm in Hell.

He'd been wrong about everything. There was no peace beyond death. There was no escape. Not for someone like him. Only torment.

He was a sacrifice bound and suspended over a pit that smelled of sulfur and blood. Was that his heart beating? Were you supposed to feel your body once you were separated from it? And why was he still breathing?

Impossible. This was not *his* heart. It was too deep and slow and omnipresent. The sound surrounded him, as if he were trapped inside of a pair of lungs, hearing each breath from the inside. That was where he was. That was his Hell. To be stuck inside himself, trapped in the stale, dank misery of his own self-abuse.

Furnace bellows. The space around him expanded and contracted, a great stomach digesting him.

He twisted his wrists, arched his back, wrenched against threads of pain that tore gashes in his ribs and thighs. In the backwater of his mind, in an echo of fading dreams, he heard laughter, brittle and sharp as broken glass.

Angeline was gone, but he wasn't alone. The demon from the bedroom was here with him, gloating, feeding off his suffering, rejoicing at his fear. She had followed him into his own grave.

No. If he could still breathe, he could still fight.

He tried to lever his arm off the floor, using the elbow as a fulcrum, straining against the floor, which crackled in protest, grudgingly letting go inch by inch. His forearm broke loose. He kept pulling, ignoring the pain, until he had his whole arm.

Something hissed above him. Close and liquid. Hot wind brushed his cheek. The rasp of movement, a large body shifting mere feet above his head.

Frantically he twisted, gritting his teeth as a thousand tiny fibers let go, one by one, breaking loose like stitches in a suture.

He remembered. He'd fallen asleep in a cave. Perhaps he wasn't in Hell after all but still in that cave, wrapped up in a cocoon like Judd's truck engine. And there was something in here with him. Something not Angeline.

With his free hand, he grabbed a fistful of the fibrous mass that covered the floor and pulled with all his might, ripping until everything but his hips and legs were free. He clawed at the thick, viscous glue that held his ass to the ground.

As his legs began to move, the steady in-and-out thrum of the bellows caught. The cave held its breath, then exhaled a deep, heavy sigh of waking. He moved faster, flexed his legs until both thighs were loose. Then his backside. He was free!

Stray cords clung to him like hair and little rivers of sweat or blood flowed down his arms and legs. He groped forward with no sense of direction and no way of knowing whether he was headed toward escape or deeper into the cave.

His outstretched fingers touched hard stone, which became a convex wall. He felt along the mercifully cool, solid surface. But the breathing thing was inescapable. He felt eyes follow him like a dark search light.

What is it waiting for?

He dragged himself along an endless loop. The confines of this prison held him under the watching eye like a planet orbiting a sun. His nails broke as he clawed at the rock, pulling himself along, inch by agonizing inch until he was ready to scream and then...

Air.

He tasted the tiniest, sweet draft, lapped it up like cold water, grasping at it like life. He grew frantic with hope, pressed his face against a seam in the wall.

Something not quite solid, a barrier stretched across his path like a drum skin. He pushed against it. Then beat on it, clawed at it, but it was tough as oilcloth. His trembling fingers explored the edges until he found rock again. He was trapped in a corked bottle.

There was a soft crackle, like dry leaves, as the whole ceiling shifted. He turned, groping for something, anything – a rock, a stick, a fucking chainsaw – to either chop his way out, or fight. There was only the ubiquitous spongy mass.

Numb fingers brushed something new, something not stone or web.

Cloth.

The pack!

God, he really was in the cave.

He jerked it to him, fumbled with the zipper and shoved his hand inside. Bottled water, cellophane, coarse denim and soft cotton.

Give me something! Come on!

Nothing. No light, no knife, no chainsaw. Nothing to help him get his ass out.

Matches! The little box rattled against his fingertips. *Now there's something, by God.* Clumsy hands fumbled to get it open. He swore as the contents spilled and bounced off his bare legs.

Fighting for calm, he shook one last match into the palm of his hand. *Don't fuck it up, Noah!*

The sound of a heavy body dragging itself toward him. On the ceiling.

He swiped the match across the strike paper. A spark flared, but no flame. Once, twice. It caught.

The match flared white, then faded to a dull orange. The room swam into view. Every surface sparkled like a field of ice crystals. It might have been beautiful if it wasn't so terrifying. He scanned the shimmering ceiling, seeing only a nightmare spiderweb as his vision adjusted.

Then the ceiling separated into something much worse.

A huge sphere, like a crystal ball, bulged from the ceiling. Once seen, it was impossible to miss. The orb was alive and pulsating, clear as glass save for a dark line running down the center like a sealed mouth. He cringed as it rippled and began to open. He hoped like hell it was just a trick of the light and that he was still just crazy.

Crazy didn't seem so bad anymore.

But that hope was shattered as other horrors took shape. There were legs, or what looked like legs. They sprouted from the belly like spokes on a wheel, long and jointed, clear as glass. They angled from the ceiling like bridge girders and bent back into the web. Some were as large as telephone poles and spanned the room. Others were small and delicate, tipped with tiny black hooks. They were all moving, churning like the legs of a stalking spider. The whole damn room was moving. The web crackled and hissed. The orb lurched across the ceiling like the moon across the night sky.

Had he known what he was seeing, had he put all the pieces together in time, he might have closed his eyes right then, spared himself the horror of what came next. Just let it happen. That would have been better. But there was no kindness left in that room.

Something else drew his eye. God, something human!

A small ribcage, pale as smoke, fused obscenely to the orb. From there came a pair of arms stretched crucifix style, clinging to the feathery ceiling with invisible fingers. Between the arms were a woman's breasts, a delicate neck and a face.

"No." Dry words from cracked lips. "God, no."

A glass heart beating silently behind clear bones. Veins and arteries churned liquid silver from her chest to her chin. Everything else was a perfect copy of her. Angeline's face turned to him, her lips parted as if pleading, eyes black pools.

She flickered as the match shook in his fingers.

"God, please!"

"Shhhhh," the face said. It was her face but the insect's voice. And it made the fusion between human and animal all the more real, too real to be nightmare. Behind her, the spider's legs pushed the girl-body toward him even as her arms, the arms that had held him so many times before, let go of the ceiling and reached out for him. He pressed himself against the cavern wall, shrinking away, watching the little flame die as her fingers stretched.

They were almost touching him. Her lips moved in a voiceless prayer for him to come forward.

"Noooaaaah," she hissed.

The light in the room went from orange to blood-red and her shadow lengthened and swallowed the cave. The flame shrank to a button and everything but her arms and face faded into darkness. The orb and the spider's legs were gone.

It was a mercy, because just before the light left, the belly split open along the dark line. He let it leave his mind and focused only on her, pretending it was as it had been, that she was whole and his and human.

Terror faded with the light, giving way instead to a soft resignation as her hands brushed his cheeks and her familiar breath enveloped him. The expression of awful tenderness vanished as the tiny flame died and everything went black.

The dead match fell from his fingers. He gave himself over to her warm hands that first caressed, then encircled, then pulled. They lifted him from the floor. As soft arms embraced him, thin wire fingers closed around his ankles and wrists and steel limbs wrapped around his legs and back. She pressed him into her body, the softness of her breasts and mouth joining with him. The rest of his fear vanished.

He gave back her kiss and clung to her, not minding the alien heat of the belly pressing against his thighs. She whispered in his ear, soft words he'd never heard her say, words of comfort that mingled with the pleasant warmth already spreading through him. She had stung him and he hadn't even felt it.

He felt his body curl involuntarily as an irresistible urge to fold himself up came over him. His feet and knees slid along the great belly as they rose to his chest. The spidery grip loosened to allow it. Then a stronger warmth like bathwater fell over his legs.

It tickled, tongue-like over his toes, and then his knees and then hips. The strange legs started to push, working him slowly down and away from her but that was okay, because with every inch he fell, he only got that much closer to her.

He curled tighter and sank deeper, sliding from her hands even as he was swallowed up. He felt her body roll to catch him, bearing his weight and taking him in. Her fingers traced his cheeks as bathwater came over his shoulders, chest and neck. But he didn't feel himself go under because the heat that was spreading inside him reached his head first. He closed his eyes and fell asleep for the last time, plunging at last beneath the waters of the patient and relentless slow flood.

THE REVELATION

- T. Allen Curtze -

The roar of the excavator wound down. Steel teeth sank into the scored earth and the valley was once again enveloped in silence.

Gene Morgan and Allen Curtze stood side by side, surveying the remains of an old root cellar. Behind them was a vast, sun-soaked meadow. Above them stood a confederation of elderly hardwoods in a solemn half-circle around the freshly dug grave.

Gene, stone-faced and arms crossed, ignored the sweat that trickled down his cheek. His partner smoked, posture at ease, as four men wrapped in blue plastic suits converged on the mound of earth, shovels and white plastic bags in hand.

A portly, red-faced man in faded overalls climbed off the backhoe and stumbled away as if drunk, handkerchief pressed to his face. He spat an angry curse at the cellar before fleeing to a fleet of vehicles clustered in the yard.

A radio at Gene's belt crackled. "Sector eight is clear, sir."

He didn't respond at once, but stared at the broken ground as if he might have burned the hole there himself. The four men in plastic shrouds descended single-file into the pit, like damned souls into hell.

Gene lifted the radio. "What's left, Mason?"

Dirt flew, a shovelful at a time, to join a grey mound of clay that dwarfed the root cellar.

The radio said, "We should be done with sectors seven and nine in three hours."

"Make it two," Gene said. "We're getting the hell out of here as soon as this place is clean."

He returned the radio to his hip and went back to scowling. A breeze played at his sweat-matted hair and enlivened the nearby beech trees.

"Sweet Jesus." His face lost shades of color. He pressed a hand to his mouth, turned on his heel and put his back to the cellar.

The shovel blades slowed. There was a rustle of plastic and the static of amplified chatter. "Sir!" The electrical voice rose from the pit, followed by a masked face peering above the mound. A black rubber hand gave a thumbs-up. "We've got it."

"About fucking time," Gene muttered.

Curtze squeezed his shoulder. "After this, we can all take our pensions and run. You'll never have to look at any of this again."

Gene Morgan swallowed and with an effort, straightened his face, following his partner toward ground zero.

"I hope your E.D. has her checkbook ready, because she's got a shitstorm to clean up here. And I hope to hell you're right about this."

The crew emerged from the pit with a white body bag stretched between them, each man grasping a corner.

"Everything's going to be fine." Curtze pitched the cigarette. "Trust me."

Their load wasn't heavy, but they treated it like a bag of poisonous snakes, keeping it as far from their bodies as possible. When they reached level ground they eased it down and stepped away.

Curtze glanced at the hole, which descended in a cone to a depth of about ten feet, before turning his attention to the body bag.

He kneeled, peeled back the plastic to reveal the wasted, ash-grey body, and waved at the already gathering flies.

Morgan stood over him, but remained on his feet, hand to his mouth. Curtze reached into his pocket and produced a tube of salve which he applied to his upper lip before handing it to Gene.

"That's not Twelve, Chief," Gene said after anointing his own lip. "No way."

Curtze removed his jacket, maneuvering it carefully over his bandaged arm. Gene took it from him and handed him a pair of plastic gloves. With some difficulty and the use of his teeth, Curtze pulled his good hand into one.

The corpse looked like a small child, something seen in Time Magazine from the '80s of all those dead babies taken by famine. No more than four feet from heel to crown, the body hadn't a strand of hair on it. The bulbous head was naked, arms and legs stick thin, joints swollen, fingers dried and curled to claws.

But it was not human.

An ugly coil of dark red tissue poured out of a gash in its bloated belly. It looked vaguely like spilled intestine. But an odd, lotus-like bulb at its end destroyed that impression. The bulb hung agape, its parted lips lined with rows of tiny barbs.

With his good hand, Curtze examined each limb, starting at the heel and moving to the hip. "Broken left femur." He glanced at Gene. "See all the bruising?"

His quick fingers probed the upper body, gingerly laying the strange organ aside. "Crushed ribs. Broken left clavicle. Sternum too." He squeezed the sinewy neck, the jaw, and the crown of the overly large head. "Fractured skull."

Curtze withdrew and sat back on his heels. "What do you think, Gene?"

Morgan shook his head. "Chief, look at it. There's no way. This thing doesn't have the kind of development to start a nest, let alone defend a territory. This isn't the one."

"Morphology varies from organism to organism. You know that." Curtze gave his head a shake to dislodge a fly from his cheek. "Some of them just don't grow rapidly. Especially if they spend a lot of energy fighting for territory. Or protecting a host. Or following our camps."

Gene said nothing.

"Look, we never found a body." Curtze gestured at the corpse. Flies dotted the raw opening in its belly, the red flesh of the organ. "This creature's injuries are consistent with the fall it took when it attacked me at Whitman's Gorge. Besides, the resin samples from the cellar match. What other theory can you offer me here?"

Gene looked away, stared across the meadow where the chopper gleamed under the bright, afternoon sun. Curtze waited, resting his bandaged hand on a knee.

"It just doesn't make sense." Gene faced his partner. "The fire, the body in the house." He scanned the ash pit where several more blue-suited men still sifted through debris. "Why the hell would Twelve just leave its host in there and then seal itself in the nest alone? And what started the fire, Allen? Sheriff Rawls had a point. This wasn't some random accident that caused this place to go up like a torch the moment we decide to call the cavalry down on this place."

"So, what are you suggesting?" Curtze shifted, pulled the plastic over the corpse. "Do you think Twelve found itself another morph, killed it, and brought it here before sealing it in and burning the place down around Weismann?"

Morgan sighed. "Look, I don't know. Either way there are a lot of unanswered questions, and every alarm in my head's going off right now. Seeing this body's only making it worse." He waved a hand. "It killed sixteen of our men, Chief. This thing couldn't have killed a housefly."

"What do you want to do? Do you want me to cut it open?"

No answer.

"There's one more thing we can try here. If I cut this thing open and it has viable eggs, then it's injected a host. Parthenogenesis can't happen without a consistent food source." His gloved hand hovered over the coil of flesh. Gene grimaced and looked away.

"We can check its esophagus for teeth and venom sacks, which would indicate it's been actively feeding. If you're right, we won't find any of those things." Curtze gazed steadily at Gene. The fingers of his wrapped hand twitched. "It'll take five minutes. I'll go get my kit."

The breeze played again at Gene's thinning pate. The leaves in the scorched maple rattled drily. Ash twisted in a cyclone of grey haze that drifted across the motley vehicles scattered about the remnants of the farm. The only structure on the place that wasn't stricken by heat or time was the barn. It stood unmoved and indifferent to the beetle-black forms that crawled in and out of it, hauling away its insides.

Something shifted in Gene's posture, a settling of the shoulders, a subtle bow in the back. "Forget it." He shook his head.

"You sure? I want you to be solid here."

"Let's get the hell out of here." He turned to his partner. "I want to go home."

For a moment Curtze watched the bigger man's face, saying nothing, as if not trusting that the debate was over.

"I do too." Curtze used the thumb of his wounded arm to strip off the glove, dropping it on the body bag. He stood. "I think we've earned a vacation." He squared with his partner and said, "You did your job here, soldier. With excellence. Jacqueline knows that. There's nothing you could have done for them. You know that. Sometimes we lose men. It's ugly, but it's the way it is."

Gene's expression rippled and for an instant his eyes fell. Only for an instant. His face hardened to steel again. He nodded. "Yeah. So what's the plan here? What do you need me to do?"

Curtze did a quick sweep of the ash pile. He seemed to avoid looking at the barn. "We're going to pack this shit up, get our men, and get the hell out of here." His slate grey eyes fastened on Gene. "Then I'm going to a place where not even God can find me. What do you think about that?"

"I think that sounds like a fine idea."

Curtze turned to one of the blue figures who stood by. "Torch this. Weismann too. I want it all burned and buried within the hour."

The man nodded, turned to his companions who wrapped up the

corpse, along with Curtze's plastic glove, and bore it to the pit from which it had been taken.

Curtze lifted his own radio. "Pete, this is Allen Curtze. I need you to find Michaels and send him back out here to fill in this hole. Over." He turned to Gene. "Why don't you go back to my office, pour us a drink? I'll get these boys started and be there in fifteen."

Gene Morgan looked back at the trailer as if considering. "Actually, if you don't mind, Chief, I think I'll grab an ATV and meet Mason, help finish up the last sector. Speed things up a little."

"Go call in your troops," Curtze gave a tight smile. "As soon as you get back we'll be out of here."

Five minutes after watching his partner disappear down an access road, Allen Curtze stepped across the threshold of his mobile office. He drew a breath through his nose as if smelling the air and settled his gaze on the disordered desk.

"Gene." He let the air out of his lungs and made his way forward, resignation in his steps, as if his feet were encased in concrete. A laptop sat open and blank on his desk.

He kneeled, examined the ruined lock of his desk drawer, lifted the screwdriver from the floor, turned it over in his hand as if it were some arcane artifact from an archeological dig. The damaged drawer squealed when he pushed it closed.

After moment's hesitation he tapped the screen, which glowed to life. In the center of a map screen pulsed a vivid red dot, like a glowing coal. Curtze closed the laptop with both hands, with an air of grim finality, then turned on his heels and hurried from the trailer.

~

Gene Morgan cut the engine of his ATV. He lifted his gaze through the treetops, shielding his eyes against a towering cliff that burned pale white in the afternoon sun. He tapped his cellphone, checked a map display of Google Earth, then studied his immediate future. The jagged rock spur looked steep and narrow.

With a sigh he heaved himself off the machine, checked his weapon, and began to climb. Silently, grimly, he made his way up, hand-over-hand. Minutes later, chest heaving, a tear in his knee, he crested a saddle where the trees broke to give him a stunning view of the cliff face, the gleaming silver river pouring from its peak, and the muscular valley spreading out beneath it. Had he been in a different frame of mind, he might have paused to stare in awe at the breathtaking beauty.

Instead he made his way doggedly up a twisting game trail that followed a steepening ridge, hands on his knees, occasionally looking over his shoulder as more and more fell away below him.

At last, the trail ended at a thin land bridge created by a seismic shift that had split the rock eons ago. An outsized lip stretched across the rock face and disappeared around a ledge. The roar of the waterfall mingled with the soft scent of mist and earth. The air temperature had dropped ten degrees.

Morgan studied the trail, face slackening at the moss-covered bridge that narrowed in places to mere inches. He checked his phone again.

"Well, fuck me." Gene sucked in his gut and stepped onto the ledge, flattened himself against the cliff as much as his heavy frame would allow, and sidestepped over hundreds of feet of open air.

He clung to the rock with clawed fingers and forceful curses. Once he nearly went over when the ground gave under his feet. A chunk of earth fell silently away, leaving the toe of his scuffed wingtip suspended over nothing. Despite the chill atmosphere, his face streamed sweat. He kept going.

Even as his eyes fell upon on the end of the land bridge where the rock absorbed what little of the path remained, he kept sidling forward, seemingly determined to complete his mission or die trying.

But before he ran out of path, the rock face abruptly cut inward, the narrow lip widening as it neared the thunderous water. He spotted the cave at once.

It was small, feathered into the shadow of the rock, and would have been difficult to see had it not been for the silvery skein across its mouth. His face betrayed neither pleasure at having found it nor relief for having been delivered from the brink.

Gene Morgan kneeled beside the nexus of white and fingered the fine, gossamer tendrils that lined outer edges of the seal. He was pushing on the membrane with a palm when his expression changed and his hand went for his holster.

"Welcome to the Face of God, Gene."

Gene Morgan sighed, more irritated than surprised, and thumbed the clasp off his weapon.

"It's what we used to call this place," Curtze said as he stepped onto the ledge and looked out over the valley. "When I was a boy. Christ, it's as beautiful as I remember."

Gene rose, drew his weapon with a grace and ease that defied his size, and put his sight pin on Curtze's center mass.

Curtze smiled, held open his jacket to show he was unarmed. "Relax, partner. You won't need that."

Gene said nothing. Nor did he lower the gun. He studied his former colleague as if looking for a trick or a lie. "That's close enough."

Curtze stopped. Hands open and visible. "I just want to talk."

"There's nothing to talk about. Not with you. Now turn around." He gestured with his head, not daring to move the barrel. "Put your hands behind your head and lace your fingers."

"Gene, for God's sake."

"Now."

Curtze obeyed, not resisting when Gene patted him down and shoved him toward the waterfall and the cave, putting himself between Curtze and the exit.

"Let's not do this," Curtze said. "Please hear me out."

Gene glanced over his shoulder, checking his position. "There's nothing you can possibly say to explain this." He reached into his jacket and pulled out his cell phone, holding out the map display where Curtze could see it. "Why I found these coordinates on your computer. The fact that you're here already doesn't help your case."

He put the phone away. Pain and disgust spread across his face. "I can't begin to imagine why," Gene said. "Your own goddamned men. You are responsible for the deaths of sixteen innocent people, Curtze. People we've known for over twenty years are dead because of you." He jerked the gun at the cave. "I trusted you. *We* trusted you, Curtze!" He took a step closer, rage pouring off him in waves. Curtze held very still.

"Every man who lost his life out here, who isn't going home to his wife and his kids, is dead because you lied to us. Lewinski. Mikus. Argenbright. Calhoun. Stephens. You knew these men!" He stabbed the gun at his former partner. "Why? You tell me why."

Curtze didn't answer.

"Talk." Another step. "You tell me why the fuck your killed you own people to protect this thing."

Curtze's grey eyes flicked to the gun. "I need you to calm down there, soldier."

"I am three seconds from blowing your fucking head off your shoulders. I advise you not waste words."

"I did it because it's my job, Gerald. It's what I'm paid to do."

Gene's face was a mask, as if he hadn't heard. Then the words hit. He blinked. The muzzle of the gun tipped a fraction of an inch. A tiny moment, then gone. Control back in place.

"Your *job* is to destroy these things."

"My job is to preserve and protect a niche species." Curtze rounded, facing Gene. "One too important to humanity's own future to allow its extinction."

Gene's finger tightened on the trigger. His hands shook. "You've lost it," Gene said. "That's what's happened. You've been in this game so goddamned long you've finally fried your brains. I should have seen it coming. Maybe if I'd stayed on these last eight years, I would have.

"The world's foremost morph expert has gone all 'save the whales'. Is that it? Have you gone native or something? Did you finally forget what you've been drilling into everybody's heads all these years and let them get to you? Forgot that this species evolves so fast it could replace us as the dominant species within a few generations?"

Curzte shook his head, gaze drifting. "It's what I've always done. What I was doing long before I recruited you. It's what *we* have always done."

"I don't know whether the Executive Director will have you locked away in a rubber room or just have you dispatched outright."

"That's what I'm trying to tell you." Curtze held Gene's gaze. "Jacqueline knows exactly what I do. You really think I do this alone?" He gave a harsh laugh. "It's what this whole organization is about, Gene."

Morgan raised the gun. "Keep those hands where I can see them."

"If you understood the nature of this species, you'd accept this. Let's go down to my office. Let's talk this through. I'll call the E.D. You can talk to her yourself. We can salvage this."

Gene cocked the hammer. "Hands!"

"For God's sake," Curtze said, raising his hands again. "I'm unarmed. You outweigh me by eighty pounds. What could I possibly do to you?"

"You're insane, Curtze. Not stupid." He motioned with the gun. "Why don't you turn around and face the wall."

"Please." Curtze dropped his hands, looked pleadingly at a man he might once have considered his protégé. "I am still your friend. How can I make you believe that? If you would just sit down and talk with me, you'll see that this is all so much more complicated than you realize. We have only the best interest of our species in mind. And I of you, Gene. Please believe me."

"You shut up now." Gene seemed to deflate, the emotion draining from his face. Decades settled on him in seconds and weighed down on him.

"I want you to turn around." He spoke in a dead voice, his eyes as empty of emotion as the gun in his hand. "Get down on your knees and put your hands over your head."

He made his way forward, grabbed Curtze by the jacket, and roughly shoved him to his knees. The smaller man did not resist as Gene pulled a set of plastic cuffs from his pocket and slid a loop over his hand.

"How did you figure it out?" Curtze asked.

Gene peeled back the bandage of his left arm, exposing the wrist.

"You had too many holes in your stories. There were too many things I knew you weren't telling me, and what you did tell me didn't add up."

He pulled both wrists together and pulled the second band tight with a dry hiss. Then he removed the man's shoes and, after a second's deliberation, flung them over the edge of the cliff.

"I started checking things out after we destroyed nest eighteen. I retraced our steps, started talking to the boys and found out that you'd told Mason exactly where to go before I'd even triangulated it. When we found you after Twelve killed Mikus and Calhoun, you said you had run it off a cliff. But your only injury was a cut on your arm. Stephens told me you'd shot it, and that's why it fell.

"I went back to where you said the attack took place and found everything you described, but something just didn't smell right. Maybe because it was just too perfect, like it was set up that way. Or maybe it was because I already had doubts. Point is, I kept looking.

"I found a bloody shirt sleeve in the woods a few hundred meters downstream of the nest we destroyed."

He stood and came around to face Curtze, but didn't look at him. He looked out over cliff. "I searched the area and found this." He pulled a brass cartridge from his pocket and held it up without seeing it, then put it away.

Curtze nodded.

"I didn't know what the hell went on down there in that pass, but I knew it was you. And I knew that whatever happened had been something you didn't want me to know about."

His gaze settled on Curtze. "I got to thinking about the transmitter you planted on Weismann, wondering if it had actually gone out like you said. While Sheriff Rawls had you occupied, I broke into your office and found your computer. The one you hadn't even bothered to password protect." He shook his head. "You always were an arrogant son of a bitch. Anyway, I found the transmitter signal."

For a moment he said nothing else. He looked like he was having trouble forming words.

"My men found the cell phone in the barn. What was left of it. And for a while I wondered if maybe I was just seeing things all wrong. I mean, until a few days ago, there wasn't another person on the planet who I would have entrusted my life to like this. I guess I was hoping you'd come straight with me once we'd dug up that morph, that you were just playing things close to the chest because you were still trying to work it out. Or maybe because of all that Walker worship bullshit.

"Then you looked me straight in the eye and lied to me. I knew the whole thing was bullshit. I went back to your office, I took down the coordinates on the computer and came here."

He glanced at the nest.

"Where did you hide the transmitter, anyway? The real one?"

Curtze looked up as if he hadn't expected a question. He half-smiled. "A box of matches, actually. In the supply package we sent Weismann. I knew Twelve would find the cell phone, but a single box of matches?" He shrugged. "I knew Weismann would probably keep them."

Gene put a hand on the back of his neck, rolled his shoulder. "That our repeaters would pick it up at this range is a damned miracle. I don't see why you bothered. I'd have never found this place otherwise. Your secret might have been safe."

"It was a gamble. I lost this one."

He nodded. "Thankfully for the rest of us, it's your last."

"So, what now?" Curzte said. "What are you going to do?"

Gene glanced at the cave.

"First, I'm going to grab a few magnesium flares and torch this place like we always do. After that, I'm going back down the hill to blow the lid off your little enterprise."

"And me? You going to burn me with it, or haul me back to base?"

Gene made his way to the land bridge. "I'm going to leave you here." he said.

He nodded at the precipice, the spiked pines far below, "Consider it a last gesture of kindness from an old friend. You're resourceful enough to get yourself out of those. I'll leave it up to you to decide whether you want to face the agency's idea of disciplinary action or if you would prefer to disappear on your own terms."

Curtze smiled. "That's generous of you."

Gene holstered his weapon and stepped onto the ledge. He paused. "One more thing."

Curtze looked up.

"The body in the house. Who was it? Do you know?"

Curtze gave Gene an appraising look. "You might be able to guess that one."

He thought. "McPherson. The old man whose place you burned down. You never found him."

Curtze shifted as if trying to find a comfortable position. "We tracked him for two miles down Akerman's Pass before I called off the search. My theory is that he went off to find his closest neighbor and found Twelve instead.

"I'm not sure why she kept him alive. I expect perhaps she used him as a secondary food source, which is what allowed her to range so far. It's probably why Noah was still strong enough to greet us during our visit." Curtze smiled to himself. "You were right, of course. If Kovalevsky or Sheriff Rawls had taken a close look at that skull, they'd have seen instantly that it wasn't that of a young man."

Gene laughed. "Good thing you had it burned."

"Yes, good thing. Who knows? Maybe it'll make your accusations harder to prove. Maybe the E.D. will find me incompetent instead of guilty. Maybe I'll get leniency."

Gene shrugged. "We'll see." He raised a hand in mock salute and said, "Good luck to you, Curtze." Then he slipped down the path and was gone.

Curtze released a long breath. Pain and discomfort seemed to melt from his shoulders as he settled into his bonds. His gaze drifted across the vast expanse of forest where the sun sat low, casting the river in burnished bronze.

Several minutes passed before his face hardened in concentration, his shoulders shifted unnaturally, retracting beyond the limits of human capacity. Bones and joints popped as his neck stretched. His arms and wrists lengthened and thinned as if made of wax. His skin went paler still, taking on the translucent cast of smoked glass.

In a smooth motion he stood, sliding out of the cuffs and standing a foot taller than he had moments ago. As his body pulled itself back into shape and took on color again, he tossed the cuffs aside and made his way to the land bridge, stepping onto the ledge.

"See you soon, Noah." Then he went in pursuit of his lieutenant.

~

Gene Morgan moved with slow, ponderous steps as he approached the ATV. His shoulders bowed as if they bore a great weight. Falling heavily into the seat, he closed his eyes and took several deep breaths before reaching for the ignition key. His fingers found nothing.

"You tricky son of a bitch." Gene began to laugh.

He heaved himself up, made his way to the rear vestibule. There was no key there, but there was a radio and short, muscular handgun with several bulky rounds that were either grenades or flares. An instinct drew him short, hand hesitating over the weapon. He straightened and turned.

Gene's expression held more resignation than surprise when he met his former mentor's gaze. Curtze's eyes were still black, his skin much whiter than it should have been. With a sigh of something like boredom, Gene reached for his gun.

His hand never touched the grip. Curtze grabbed the bigger man's arm, jerked him off balance, and slid an arm around his throat.

A look of annoyance crossed Gene's face, followed by astonishment as his struggling failed to dislodge his attacker. His face reddened, eyes widening in shock as he struggled for breath that wouldn't come.

"I'm so sorry, Gene." Curtze closed his eyes, tucked his head into Gene's shoulder as the man thrashed uselessly. "It's not your fault."

Gene clawed at the vice around his neck. His lips moved, but no sound escaped. As his brain lost oxygen, his movements slowed.

"I'm the one who failed. Not you." Curtze said. His partner went slack in his arms. Still Curtze held on. He held the man until he ceased to breathe, until his heart stopped beating. He held him until his eyes went glassy and void.

"I'm sorry." Curtze lowered Gene's body gently to the ground.

~

"Mason, are you home? Over." The access road widened onto the blasted border of the Weismann farm, ushering Curtze from the shadow of the forest into a pitiless heat. The radio answered.

"We're all finished here, sir. What are your orders, over?"

"There's smoke to the east. Maybe a mile from the river. Do you see it?"

A pause. "Affirmative. You want me to check it out?"

"Make sure it doesn't belong to one of us, will you? I'm sure it's nothing, but let's be sure before we take off. Curtze out."

The rattle of engines and human voices faded as Curtze stepped into his office, then disappeared as he locked the door. He peeled off his visor, fell into the chair behind the desk, and put his head in his hands. When he sat up minutes later, there were no tears, no sign of human emotion, but his hand shook as he reached for the cellphone on his desk.

"Hello?" a female voice answered.

"Ma'am, the mission is over. We're on our way out."

"Is everyone safe?" Her voice was softly cautious, as if reading Curtze's mood.

He swallowed, cleared his throat. "Almost. Seven of the eight pairs are accounted for, including number one-thousand, one-hundred-twelve."

An exhalation of breath. "But you've suffered a loss." It wasn't a question.

"Yes. Gene Morgan. I lost Gene."

A silence followed, muddied only by the distant throb of a chopper firing up outside.

"Tanner, I am so sorry."

"I'm done," Curtze said. "For good. You know that."

"Yes, I know."

"I'll help with the extraction of the newborns in six months. After that, I'm out."

"I appreciate your years of service. We all do. I know the sacrifices you've made. I know I speak for everyone when I say that this organization would not be what it is today if not for you. Thank you, my friend. Is there anything you need?"

Curtze's posture tightened. He rose as if he were being filled with air. "Yeah. I want my estate to go to Gene's family, to Karen and Aliyah. All of it. See that it's added to his death package with no questions asked. Can you do that?"

"Tanner..." The voice hesitated. "Are you sure about this?"

"And I want them to know he died serving his country. Will you do it?"

"Of course," the voice said. "I'll see to it personally."

Curtze nodded as if she could see him.

"Listen." The voice picked up again. "I know this mission hasn't been easy for you, but I'd like to ask something, If that's okay."

"Go ahead."

"What does it feel like to see your home again, after all these years?"

Curtze took a breath. "This isn't home anymore, Ma'am. It hasn't been for a very long time."

Thirty minutes later, Curtze sat back in the contoured seat of the chopper as it prepared to lift off. He gazed at the Glen through the tinted window, settling on an old pear orchard in its center. After a moment, he turned his head and closed his eyes.

As the cabin tilted and the chopper took to air, he did not look at the farm, at the rust-colored barn whose main doors stood open. Nor did he look at the pit that was once a house in which three generations of Weismann boys grew to manhood. Or nearly three. The erstwhile Tanner Weismann had been only fifteen when he'd disappeared, having allegedly drowned in the Piscataqua River.

Before the farm fell away forever, he risked once last glance at the large meadow lately known as Tanner's Glen. He frowned and leaned into the window as something moved at the edge of the Glen. The last thing T. Allen Curtze saw of his childhood home was a tiny life form.

A small black cat slipped out of the grass and darted across the yard. It paused at the edge of the driveway long enough to look up. The prick of its feline ears suggested that it tracked the strange bird's progress across the sky. Just before the cabin window angled away, Curtze watched the little creature lower its head and disappear into the barn.

THE END

ABOUT THE AUTHOR

Dan Cheuvront lives on a small farm in eastern Kansas with his wife, mother-in-law, and two children. His incompetence at animal husbandry and equipment repair have relegated him to simple tasks that afford him space to brood and make up stories. He doesn't set out to write about dark, gritty, and awful things, but that's usually what happens. Tanner's Glen is his first novel.

Made in the USA
Las Vegas, NV
06 July 2022

51173012R00194